Dublin ink

A DUBLIN INK NOVEL

SIENNA BLAKE

Dublin Ink: a novel / by Sienna Blake. – 1st Ed.
First Edition: May 2022
Published by SB Publishing
Copyright 2022 Sienna Blake
Cover art copyright 2022 Cosmic Letterz. All Rights Reserved Sienna Blake.
Stock images: shutterstock
Editing services by Proof Positive: http://proofpositivepro.com.

✽ Created with Vellum

CONTENTS

To found families.
To those who need them.
And those who take us in.

1

AURNIA

The red and blue lights flashed wildly on the narrow brick walls of the alley, exploding against the thick layer of clouds that hung heavy above me, threatening, as always, rain. If I had been a typical seventeen-year-old—Christmases split between Ma's and Da's, homework copied from a friend against a locker before class, college brochures piling up in the perfectly suburban mailbox—the red and blue lights might very well have been fireworks. A family reunion with frozen hamburger patties and screaming toddlers. Some public holiday, a three-day weekend spent at the shores of Rossbeigh Strand in County Kerry with only slightly pervy uncles. A Saturday night with friends pretending to be drunker than we were off weak beers stolen from our fathers' garages.

But I wasn't a typical seventeen-year-old.

The flashing red and blue lights weren't fireworks. They were the lights from a cop car, a cop car I was handcuffed in the back of.

I knew enough of the law, them being more consistent visitors to my father's house than dear old Saint Nicholas, to know that they needed very little excuse to turn things from bad to worse. I'd dropped out of high school a year earlier, but I honestly don't think that would have made much of a difference: it's not like my Algebra teacher (a big-bellied man whose "one-on-one guidance" involved explaining a problem with his sweaty hand on the side of your neck, his hot breath against your cheek, and his eyes down your shirt) was going to go over the negative impact of resisting arrest between the quadradic equation and solving for "y". Besides, it was pretty much common knowledge, right? If you get arrested, ask for an attorney, keep quiet, don't make things any worse.

Just a few problems: one, I didn't have enough money for food most nights, let alone an attorney. Two, I didn't exactly *do* quiet. And three—and this one's the kicker—I *wanted* to make thing worse.

A radio cracked and popped in the front seat, but whatever message was related about jewellery missing or searched side streets or incoming backup was inaudible over the slamming of my heels against the hard plastic divider.

The metal of the cuffs cut painfully into my wrists. It was only made worse when I slid down on the bench to lift my legs, but my rage served as a kind of shot of adrenaline: all I could really feel was the pounding of my heart, fast and erratic and showing no signs of slowing down.

I couldn't feel the strain of my shoulders from my arms being wrenched behind my back. I couldn't feel the scrape on my cheek where I'd been slammed by the officer roughly against the brick wall. I couldn't feel the bruises from being tossed, with nothing to catch my fall, into the backseat, riveted plastic as hard as concrete.

I thought my rage might beat right out of my chest. It probably hurt worse than everything else combined, but at least it erased the lingering touch of the officer who had searched me: his fingers between my black jeans, dipping inside the waist, yanking up my hoodie, sliding a little too slowly between my tits.

"I'm going to give you one chance to stop," the officer said as I drove my heels again against the dark grey plastic, leaving black scuffs.

The officer's eyes found mine in the rearview mirror. They were bored, uninterested. What was it to him that a teenager wore herself out in a state-owned car? He probably had a car of his own at home. A wife to sit in the passenger seat, clutching her purse in her lap. Two kids, one boy, one girl, to quarrel in the backseat, Cheerios littering the carpeted floor.

My feet momentarily stalled, sank to the edge of the seat, toes balanced over the edge. The officer drummed his fingers against the steering wheel.

"I mean, think about it, kid," he said. "You're already busted. I think we both know that the security video at the jewellery store will show you there. You're going to have to face some consequences. But, and you really should think about this, I can help you."

The officer twisted around in his seat to look at me through the thick wire mesh.

"You want me to be good?" I asked, sweetly I think, though sweetness was rather foreign to me so I couldn't be sure.

The officer's eyes narrowed briefly in suspicion, but then he nodded and said, "That's right. Be good."

The officer was about to turn back around to his crackling radio, to the red and blue lights flashing on the icy hood, to the thought of his wife asleep in bed, or the woman he wished was asleep in bed, when I asked, "What kind of good?"

His eyes again found mine in the rearview mirror.

"Part my legs 'good'?" I asked. "Lean forward a little so you can catch a glimpse down my hoodie 'good'? Open my mouth real good, like?"

I watched the officer's eyes flicker over my body. Even with it crammed up against itself, I knew he was seeing exactly what he wanted to see. I'd hid enough times under a pile of threadbare sheets in my bed as the door creaked open, yellow light spilling across me along with the pounding of bass and the reek of pot, to know that men didn't need a naked woman in front of them to see a naked woman.

"I can make your life hell, girl," the officer finally said through clenched teeth, tearing his eyes from me like ripping a Band-Aid from an open wound.

I laughed and the officer's gaze on me was more wary than if I had been a six-foot-ten, three-hundred-pound man than a waif of a girl who could barely reach the top shelf of the convenience store to steal a loaf of stale bread.

"Make my life hell?" I laughed. "*You?*"

Confusion painted the man's face in the front seat. Of course it did. What did he know of truly mean men? What did he know of cruel smiles that struck more fear in me than a thousand of his raised batons? What did he know of sneaking in through bedroom windows to avoid tiptoeing over druggies passed out across the living room floor? What did he know of the consequences of waking one?

He had his kids' prep school tuitions to keep him awake at night; I had a hungry stomach. He had a wife's credit card debt (too many shoes, too big a closet) to worry about; I had a father with a needle and a bottle of pills. He feared the long stretch of boredom before inevitable death; I often feared I wouldn't make it through the night.

Without warning, I began kicking again at the back of the plastic divider. When the officer shouted once more for me to stop it, I just kicked harder, faster. I knew he couldn't do anything *to* me.

My life was already hell. And I was more than used to it.

It felt good to drive my anger like a piston through the heels of my black combat boots. It felt good to lose control, because then I didn't have to pretend that I had any in the first place. It felt good to send pain radiating up my legs, to feel like my ice-cold toes were going to snap off with each bone-rattling thrust. It felt good to blow up my life.

Because I was mad at myself. That felt a whole lot better than being mad at the world, at my father, at the fates that robbed me of a mother, a stable childhood, a chance at happiness, mad at my teachers, mad at the system, mad at Dublin, cruel, cruel Dublin, mad at the way men looked at me, mad at the way they possessed me but didn't protect me, mad at my friends, Jack and Lee and Mia, mad at them for leaving me, mad at everyone for leaving me, mad at everyone for always, always, always leaving me.

I was vaguely aware of the officer finally shoving open his door, vaguely aware of him throwing open mine, vaguely aware of his fist wrapping around the front of my hoodie, shaking me like a bad dog. But I kept kicking and thrashing and maybe laughing or screaming, I'm not sure, because it felt good. It felt damn good.

I was mad at myself, and I liked it.

My elbow painfully caught the side the doorframe as the officer hauled me out, and I thought I felt something crack in my cheek when he slammed me to the concrete which smelled of grease and shit. There was shouting. More officers came. I felt their boots on the backs of my legs, trying to hold me down as I fought them. I was making things worse, far worse, but I couldn't stop myself.

I didn't want to.

There, forced and held in my field of vision with no way for me to look away from it, was the reason I was so mad at myself. Everything had gone according to Jack's plan at the jewellery store. I spray-painted the security cameras in the alley with the cans I always kept with me—robbery or not. Mia, with her twitchy fingers and red-rimmed eyes, had picked the lock. Lee opened the glass cases with a key he'd snatched the day before from an older woman who leaned in a little too close toward his boyish curls and flashing smile while showing him a pair of earrings intended for his "dear, *dear* mother".

The diamond necklaces and emerald rings and gold hoops were safe in Jack's tattered backpack as he walked right out the back door. Mia went next, biting at her nails with a gleeful laugh. Lee followed, grinning at the camera in his ski mask. I was last into the alley.

Maybe it was the sense that we were in no danger that made me linger. No alarms. No bells. No alerted shouts. No distant wailing of sirens. Or maybe a part of me didn't want to go with Jack and Mia and Lee. Because once we divided the loot they'd leave, one by one. Perhaps not till dawn, but eventually. Then I'd be alone once more. If I stayed there in the alley, at least I would be the one to do the leaving. Or maybe, if you believe in that sort of thing, the inspiration hit me so hard that there was no resisting it.

Jack had been nothing more than a shadow at the end of the alley when he yelled back that it wasn't smart to linger, that police would probably be on their way. I'd shouted at him, spray of paint sweeping in a wide arc in the dark, that it would just take a second or two longer, that I would be right behind them.

"You're on your own then, Aurnia."

As if I fucking didn't already know.

I'm not sure how long it took me to finish the piece. I never really know when I'm drawn in like that, transfixed. Time has a way of losing all meaning. All I know is that suddenly there was those damned red and blue lights and just a stroke or two left. I thought I could finish it and still run. I had been wrong.

So it was my fault. All my fault that I was being arrested, that there was a knee at the small of my back and vice-like grips on my arms, scrapes on my cheeks and mars on my record, and a new blackness to my already dark horizon.

The paint wasn't even dry, I noticed, as the red and blue illuminated my artwork in alternating pulses. The dripping paint made it look like the girl on the abandoned, dirty, lonesome alley wall was crying, crying purple and green and blue. She looked down at me with eyes that I hadn't meant to be so sad as I kicked and resisted and laughed. She watched and there was nothing she could do for me and nothing I could do for her.

We were on our own.

I was on my own.

In fucking hell.

2

CONOR

*O*utside Dublin Ink the dead leaves whipped up on a fierce wind, brittle pieces bound for dust. Inside, I followed their path, whipping forward before turning on my heel, marching back, and starting the process all over again.

"Would you sit down?" Rian complained from an old tufted leather chair, his long pale fingers gripped over the worn armrests. "You're making me nervous."

I eyed him before turning away. "What makes you think you shouldn't be nervous?"

Mason was leaning against the window, checking out a woman passing by who was struggling to keep her skirt down in the whipping wind. He spoke without looking away, "Now that's the winning spirit, Conor."

My nails dug into the sensitive skin on the inner part of my wrist as I gripped my hands behind my back. Did they think this was what I wanted? Did they think this was what I dreamed of, all those years ago before that fateful night? A failing tattoo shop. An apartment decorated with eviction notices. A future as bright as the neon light on the faded floral wallpaper that announced to the rare customer "ub nk".

"It's not about 'winning spirit'," I said.

Mason craned his neck to catch the woman (and perhaps her ass) before she rounded the corner. Rian's gaze went blank, drifting as usual to some other world, maybe one where we weren't broke as fuck.

"It's about facing reality," I continued, though I wasn't entirely sure I was being listened to, I was never entirely sure I was being listened to. "Staring down the cold, hard truth with cold, hard eyes. Accepting that this is the way things are for us."

For me, I thought bitterly.

Mason would one day snag some rich old lady and hide his Americana tattoos under British silk. Rian needed the parlour like he needed a paint-by-numbers box set; he had more talent in his watercolour-tattooed pinkie than half the artists in the city. One day he'd realise that he had better things to do than twiddle his thumbs in a hand-me-down leather chair and stare at a pink fringed lamp blinking against the lengthening shadows as the front door remained unopened.

It was me who was stuck. My chance had come years before. I'd fucked it up. And now it was gone.

This was my purgatory.

"How about some sort of refer-a-friend incentive?" Mason suggested as a homeless man stumbled by on the beer bottle-littered sidewalk out front.

I ignored him. It was debatable whether Rian, wherever the hell he was at the moment, even heard him. I felt Mason's eyes on me as I turned again to march the opposite direction, the length of the townhouse's living room we'd semi-converted for the parlour hardly long enough for my restless purposes. No, in fact, pacing just seemed to make me feel even more like I was in a cage. I knew what he saw as my feet landed heavy on the shag carpet: broad shoulders stooped like some weather-faded gargoyle, fingers blackened with ink, tattoo and pen residue blending together till one was impossible to tell from the other, the hair in my bun a little unwashed, a little unkept.

. Mason wanted me to say it was a good idea. He wanted me to smile (I didn't smile), to tell him everything was okay (I didn't lie), to hold his hand and tuck him into bed and bring him a warm glass of milk (I didn't fucking coddle anyone). But we'd played this game one too many times before. The fact was we were fucked.

We set up shop in the *wrong* part of Dublin. Dolphin's Barn was known for needles, but not the kind that came with ink. Nobody knew about us and the ones who did certainly weren't willing to risk getting their tires slashed when they could throw a stone from their bedroom window and hit some hipster douchebag with an "it'll do" portfolio. We'd been open for a year and in that time the bank had gone through more ink sending us late notices than we'd gone through for customer tattoos. We could tattoo each other, Rian, Mason, and I, with art that would blow your mind, but that didn't exactly pay the bills, now did it?

The phone, an old rose-coloured antique rotary that had belonged to Mason's mother and her mother before her, that had been passed down along with the rest of the crumbling, granny wallpaper-plastered townhouse, rang suddenly, a rare occurrence I assure you at Dublin Ink. Neither Mason nor Rian gave the impression of going to answer it, Mason with his pierced nose smushed against the glass and Rian with his eyes closed and his finger shifting through the air like a young trash polka tattooed Mozart.

I stalked over to the phone with a humph of irritation that neither of them noticed and snatched it up in a fist.

"*What?*"

"Ah, lucky me," a familiar voice said cheerfully, which just irritated me further. "I played Dublin Ink roulette and I got the bullet."

"I'm kind of busy, Diarmuid," I said brusquely.

"Pleasant as always, my friend."

Diarmuid Brennan could call me his friend all he wanted. I supposed that to anyone else that's exactly how our relationship would appear: friends, that is. We met as teenagers through our mutual Juvenile Liaison Officer, Brian. He figured the best way for delinquent boys to get out their frustrations was through guided, structured, rule-enforced violence, aka boxing. That first day at O'Malley's boxing gym the rules of the sport meant nothing to us as our fists introduced each other again...and again...and again... After that we fought a thousand more times, though most times it ended at the insistent ringing of the bell. I guess that's as close as my definition of friendship got: caring enough not to take someone's head off.

Even with Rian and Mason I felt like they were closer to me than I was, or ever wanted to be, with them. Sometimes I thought they knew it. Sometimes I thought it was only so long that they would accept it before...well.

"I won't take much of your time," Diarmuid said before I could hang up as I was prone to do.

"Unless you want to schedule a tattoo or take down the address to send a check for a tattoo, I don't have any time," I said. "Not 'much' or otherwise."

The phone was already moving toward the rusted receiver when Diarmuid shouted, "C! C! Wait, it does involve money!"

This earned him a thirty-second reprieve. I raised the phone back to my ear. This raised the attention of Mason from the window, Rian from his ethereal tattoo composing.

"Is that the bank?" Rian whispered.

"Is it Samantha?" Mason asked, already sneaking toward the door.

Samantha, I had to assume, had been the girl in her underwear and nothing more drinking orange juice from the mini fridge that morning. It wasn't like I ever bothered to learn the names of Mason's many...*friends*. Why would I?

"It's Diarmuid," I told them and then to Diarmuid, "And he was just getting to the goddamn point."

"Is that Mason?" Diarmuid asked, hope (what a stupid thing) in his voice. "Rian? Maybe put one of them on."

This made me immediately suspicious, or more suspicious, I should say. I was always, as a well-earned habit, suspicious. Of everything. Of *everyone*.

"What do you want, Diarmuid? Like I told you, we're busy."

Fuck, you could practically hear the crickets in the silence of the parlour, practically hear the mould growing in the walls. I told you I didn't lie, but as it turns out, that was a lie. Fucking deal with it.

"Right, right," Diarmuid said. I heard him shuffling some papers on his desk. He had followed in Brian's footsteps and had become a JLO himself. Why? I hadn't a clue. "So, listen, I don't want you to shoot the idea down right away, okay?"

"You're not making a great case for whatever it is you're talking about," I told him, patience already waning.

Mason, curious not just about what was under a lady's skirt (any lady's skirt), came over to move his ear in close to mine. I shoved him away. He pouted. I gave him the middle finger.

"Look, Conor, the point is that there's *money* involved," Diarmuid said. "Remember that. Hold onto that. Money."

"I'm not putting anything in my butt," I grumbled as I held Mason's nosey-ass self back with a stiff arm.

"I might," Rian said with a contemplative shrug. He grinned and then said, "Mason definitely would."

Mason's tanned fingers were wriggling in my face as I tried to keep the phone away.

"Let me talk to him," Mason whined. "Diarmuid! Diarmuid, what butt stuff? What's the girl look like? How much is she paying me?"

I swatted at Mason. Diarmuid sighed and mumbled something I couldn't quite make out.

"What's that?" I asked before glaring at Rian. "Would you *do* something, please?"

Rian's face was dreamlike as he said softly, "I'm thinking of a tattoo of a peach. A soft, fuzzy, *peach.*"

"Diarmuid," I said through gritted teeth. "You have three seconds to say, and say clearly, what exactly it is you're offering before I hang up."

At that moment, Mason got distracted by a woman out front, so it was just me who got to hear Diarmuid's proposal. Just me who got to respond.

I slammed the phone down so hard in the receiver that I thought for a moment that I had broken it. Mason jumped from the window and Rian shook his head like I'd startled him from a deep slumber.

"You hung up?" Rian asked.

"We don't need his money," I told them, flopping down into one of the leather tattooing chairs that had cost a fortune and hadn't even come close to paying for themselves. "Believe me."

Rian and Mason both started to protest, but I ignored them. Diarmuid had proposed something so wretched, so horrible, so terrible, that the two of them had no idea what good I'd done for them, what heartache I'd spared them. Diarmuid had wanted...shit, I could barely allow the thought to cross my mind without squirming in discomfort.

"Guys, guys," I shouted, holding up my hands to calm Mason and Rian. "Relax. We don't need that money. Not that bad at least."

Diarmuid had suggested taking on a mentee in the Young

Offenders Program in exchange for a government grant. He said
he had a particular mentee in mind, but I hadn't given him
more time to go on. I'd heard all I needed to hear.

I knew what those juvie kids were like. Hell, I'd been one of
them. No thank you. No *fucking* thank you.

Rian was standing now, his clear green-grey eyes on mine.

"Why don't you at least let us have a say in deciding?" he
said. "Deciding whatever it is."

"Yeah," Mason agreed, rather petulantly I thought. A pouty
lip didn't exactly go with his curly black mohawk. "We're a team.
A family."

What was I supposed to tell them? That I didn't really think
we were a team, let alone a family? That in the deepest part of
my chest I knew that this parlour meant more to me than to
them? That I feared one day they'd leave for better things and
I'd have nowhere to go?

Yes, they were co-owners of Dublin Ink, but in my view it
was only my ass on the line, my soul on the line.

I was bailed out by the ringing of the little brass bell above
the front door.

"See?" I said, doing that thing people do where they force up
the corners of their mouths. "Nothing to worry about, just like I
said. Here's a brand-new customer right here."

Before I could put my arm around the man's trench coat-
covered shoulders, he raised an envelope sharply between us.

"From the bank," he announced curtly. "Final notice."

I stood frozen with the envelope held limply as the little
man turned on his heel and slammed the door behind him.

Slowly I turned toward Rian and Mason. Rian had his arms
crossed. Mason was already holding the phone out for me.

"Fine," I grumbled. "I'll call him back."

Not that I believed a few pennies from the government was

going to make a difference. Not now that we were welcoming a devil into our little hell.

3

AURNIA

*W*hen my JLO gave me the address for the stupid mentee program, I thought at first that he was trying to kill me. What better way for the government to deal with dead-end children, dangerous, drugged up, depressed children? Who was ever going to notice if a few never returned from "a chance to better themselves"? What was another missing file folder in a stack of thousands?

Mr Brennan had apparently seen the confusion (and dread) on my face because he laughed and assured me it was safe. "The guys", whoever the hell they were, were safe.

As I stepped down from the 27 bus, I was starting to not believe him. This part of town wasn't so different from mine, but at least in mine I knew where to run if I was being chased.

The bus left with a cough of black exhaust. It didn't so much dissipate as blend in with the tendrils of grey smog that twisted overhead. I checked the address once more: I was only a block or two away. The streets weren't going to sprout rose bushes and clean white picket fences, that was for sure.

In my black jean jacket pocket (the one without a hole in it), I gripped my fingers tightly over the mace. In close quarters my knife was better. But I wasn't going to allow anyone into close quarters. The knife was only required in one place and one place only: my own fucking house.

The short walk to the address I was supposed to report to ended up being pleasant enough. I could handle a little fresh vomit, a broken needle or two, and a junkie passed out between two rat-torn bags of trash.

I found the door to the tattoo parlour, though I wasn't quite sure they wanted me to. There wasn't any sign out front. The door was covered in newspaper, the glass probably gone from a recent break-in. And if you were to press your face against the big front window and cup your hands to spy inside, you'd jump back and hurry on for fear that you just snooped on a poor little granny who was quilting or baking cookies or doing whatever in the hell grannies do. I wouldn't know.

A little bell announced my entrance, echoed up the old faded wood stairs. I stuck my head inside and glanced around. It was dim, the only light coming from a mostly broken neon on the far wall and a few frilly lamps casting soft, hazy glows. It was light enough to see, though, that the place was empty. Maybe even abandoned.

I stepped inside with a soft, "Hello?"

The door clicked shut behind me, but I didn't release the maze canister still gripped in my pocket. If this place shut down recently, say, in the two weeks it took for me to be assigned and processed after the robbery, then who knew how many squatters had already claimed their warm night's sleep.

"Hello?" I tried a little louder when I heard nothing from upstairs, nothing from the dim back rooms.

I wandered curiously through a mix of antique furniture and new equipment: highly polished leather tattooing chairs; metal trays laden with tools that shined like they were straight out of the box; tall, sleek mirrors that kept making me jump stupidly at my own reflection. The two styles clashed violently, mixed as well as water and oil, and yet there was a strange, undeniable charm to the place. A misfit, it seemed, like me.

"Honey," I cupped my hands to call out, "I'm home!"

I stood in the centre of the room, my shadow long and thin across the antique rug woven with dusty pale flowers. I stood and I waited.

The only sound was the brittle scrape of dead leaves against the big window half concealed by thick marigold-velvet drapes. I drummed my fingers against my black jeans, rocked back and forth on my heels. At least there were no squatters. Or, at least, no conscious ones.

What now? The bus wasn't returning for at least another thirty minutes; trips to this part of town weren't exactly in high demand, especially this close to nightfall. It was cold outside, the wind biting, the sky ominous, and it was warm inside with the heat of the old furnace, its pipe stretching up to the tin-panelled ceiling. The bus stop was nothing more than a plywood board nailed down to four metal posts. There were more chances to be snuck up on standing out there in the open than, say, by the big black metal cash register, a relic of the past, perhaps holding cash of the day.

My fingers walked along the back of the couch, brass rivet by brass rivet. I moved slowly toward the silver-lined, turquoise Formica counter and checked over my shoulder once more. The front door remained closed. The stairs, half hidden in a murky dusk, remained empty. No moans came from the floorboards upstairs. No sound of opening doors. Of chairs rolled back. Of bathroom sinks turned off.

I was, I was certain, alone.

There shouldn't have been anything stopping me from dashing to the cash register, pounding whatever button sent the tray springing out with a victorious *ding!*, swooping up whatever lay hidden within, and sprinting for the door with it all stashed away in the inner pockets of my jacket. In a dog-eat-dog world you do whatever is necessary for your survival. Why didn't I seize upon the opportunity right then and there to provide for myself at literally no cost? For all I knew there was a week's worth of food in that cash register, a month's even. I shouldn't have hesitated at all. I shouldn't have let anything slow me down. I shouldn't have lingered, not even for a second.

Maybe if I hadn't, things would have turned out differently. Maybe everything would have turned out differently.

An open sketchbook caught my eye. I recognised it as the same stirring in my soul that made me stop outside the jewellery store, the same foolish pursuit of beauty in an ugly world. The moment I recognised it, I should have pushed aside the feeling; it was, after all, the reason I was in this legal mess.

And yet, I found my determined footsteps slowing. My fingers stretching as if the thick pulped page of soft ivory was a fraying rope. My eyes drawn in like there was more gold in there than the cash register.

The rough sketch, drawn as if in a hurry, or, I thought with a shiver, a rage, was hauntingly beautiful. A flower, lovely and tender, but dead.

The rustling of paper as I turned the page sounded as loud to me as if I had been hammering at the uncooperative cash register. And yet I didn't stop. I didn't pause to check for noise, for signs of life in the parlour that was darkening with the dusk. I skimmed my finger over a sketch of a butterfly trapped in amber, the black of the pencil somehow catching light. I turned past a frozen waterfall, all jagged knives and sharp icicles. I lost myself in an eye that reflected in its blackened pupil a wide chasm. They all stabbed at my heart, but it wasn't until I flipped to the very last page that I felt a real sort of pain.

The drawing was of a woman. Her beauty made me feel like

a child. She was all heavily hooded, seductive eyes, deeply painted lips with a cupid's bow that could cut, and intelligently arched eyebrows.

I was quite the opposite: large eyes, the more to fill with fear it seemed, pale lips more likely to be coloured with blood from chewing on them too often than lipstick, eyebrows hidden beneath a sweep of dark hair that I let fall where it may, a silly freedom in a world of ugly walls.

I knew at once that this woman, whoever she was, was real. Real to someone. To whom, I had no idea, but to someone, I was sure. What I mean is that she was not the figment of an imagination; she was not brought to life by the charcoal of the pencil alone. She lived and breathed and gazed with those cat-like eyes at the person who drew her, touched their cheek, ran her finger down their chest, broke, I saw, their heart.

For across the woman's face, drawn realistically as if the paper were actually torn although it wasn't, were five long slashes. And it was in those slashes that I felt the artist's pain. I could feel the building of anger and hurt and disappointment, building and building, till it burst. The artist had wanted to destroy her, but they couldn't, couldn't bring themselves to it. So they destroyed her on the page, in the art, the only way they knew how. I understood turning to art for that kind of anger, for that kind of outlet.

It was embarrassment that finally sent me fleeing from the sketchbook to the comfort of the cash register, cold and hard and reassuring beneath my slightly shaking fingers. My cheeks reddened as if I had been caught, though I was still dreadfully alone. I felt certain I had peeked at someone's secret, at someone's heart. I had taken what wasn't mine to take, what I hoped no one would ever take from me.

It was a relief to grab ahold of the cash, small stacks of small bills, but still. Cash. Something safe.

Maybe it was my pounding heart that prevented me from hearing the door open. Maybe I hadn't yet escaped from the siren song of the mysterious woman and her scarred face. Maybe I was still preoccupied searching for the artist's face in her lovely eyes.

Whatever the reason, I was completely and utterly helpless. I didn't stand a chance. With my back to the front of the tattoo parlour, I had no idea anyone else was in the room with me, let alone looming like a monster's shadow across my back.

A tattooed hand was locked in an iron grip around my wrist before I could even let loose a shriek. I twisted around, pain blossoming like the flower before it withered in that damned sketchbook. The man, whoever he was, blocked out the light from the windows. His face was in shadow, high above me. He said not a word, as if he was made of stone. I yanked my wrist with a whimper, but he only tightened his grip.

I cursed whoever drew those sketches. I cursed whoever left it open for me to fall into like a well-laid trap. I cursed whatever it was inside me that insisted on seeing beauty where there was none.

Because I was caught once more. There was nothing left to do but fight and curse my own bleedin' self.

4

CONOR

I'd gone for fucking aspirin. I'd wanted something stronger than aspirin, a shot of whiskey, to be more precise. But if I allowed myself something stronger every time the weather threatened rain in goddamn Dublin, I'd be there on the sidewalk outside the unmarked curtained rehab centre along with all the other shivering, muttering, shaking addicts.

Slate-grey clouds had slid in early that afternoon to swallow the shifty white haze. I hadn't needed to even glance up from my sketchbook (another dead flower as it turned out, another one not quite right as it always was) to know it was threatening rain: the familiar dull ache in my leg had warned me as it always did.

It hadn't been a surprise to find the pharmacy bottle in the kitchen at the back of the shop empty. I'd left Dublin Ink to get my painkillers before it grew worse (it always grew worse) with Rian lying upside down on the couch, his fingers drumming his temples, and Mason flipping through tattoo options with a busty blonde, his chin on her shoulder, his eyes down her ample tits.

I'd returned with four capsules on my tongue and a grey blur at the edges of my vision to find no one there at all. Except a little figure, that damned juvie, robbing the cash register.

When my hand gripped a narrow bone, a stretch of pale skin, I'd barely even registered in my mind that it was a girl. All I could think was my leg fucking hurt and Diarmuid was fucking dead. I knew it was a terrible idea to welcome in with outstretched arms a little fiend who wouldn't think twice about stabbing someone—*anyone*—in the back. I knew this would happen eventually, though I'd didn't expect it to be within thirty seconds of the little brat arriving on our front steps. Juvie teens were juvie teens for a fucking reason: they were no good, they couldn't *be* good. The best they could be was restrained, their worst attributes dulled and mitigated, a rabid dog on a good, solid chain.

"Mason!" I shouted as the little thief thrashed in my iron grip. "Mason! Rian!"

When I'd caught the brat by surprise, cash had gone spilling everywhere. It was under my feet as the tiny thing tried to backpedal, to squirm away. It wadded up beneath my boots, got smeared with mud. I yanked the little thief back toward me and bellowed into the parlour, "Rian! Mason!"

"Let me go," the little thing growled at me, indignant for a thief.

Of course, what was I to expect. Those kids thought the world was theirs for taking. Who gave a damn who it belonged to or how hard they'd worked for it?

"Let me go," the thief shouted again as a tiny fist came to land with the violence of a canary on my chest. "Let me go, let me *go*!"

My cell phone was in my hand, my thumb dialling the numbers as I strengthened my grip on the thief's wrist. It felt as if my fingers had to wrap around it not twice, but three times. The waif kept trying to yank her wrist away, kept thrashing, kept kicking, kept shouting at me as the phone rang and rang.

In quick succession, I shouted once more for Mason and Rian without response, I received Diarmuid's irritatingly chipper voicemail informing me to leave a message or call the police for an emergency, and the little thief placed a well-aimed swing of her military boot right to the jagged scar above my left knee. If I was seeing grey before, it was red that now flooded my vision. It took all the self-control I'd built like a house of cards over the long, painful years to not snap the wrist in my hand right then and there. I squeezed my eyes shut and exhaled through my nose.

The thief stilled slightly, sensing either a reprieve or a chink in my armour, but her efforts renewed doubly when I opened my eyes, trained them fixedly on the front door, and began to drag her along beside me.

"What are you doing?" she shouted, clawing ineffectually at the leather of my jacket, a gift from Brian. I would have been upset about the long scratch marks if it hadn't already been to hell and back with the scorch marks and tears and frayed edges to prove it. "Let me fucking go!"

The little bell above the door nearly snapped off as I kicked the door open and shoved the girl ahead of me. It was my bruising grip on her wrist alone that kept her from falling onto the sidewalk which was now dotted with large black drops of rain, a promise of more to come. A few people hurried on their way past us, some with hoods drawn tight, others with bent and broken umbrellas, most with nothing at all atop their glistening, feverish foreheads. I ignored them, because they ignored me: it was the code of the neighbourhood. Keep your head down. Don't hear anything. Don't see anything.

My motorcycle was parked on the street just outside the

shop and yet even that short distance made my leg warm with prickled tongues of fire; it was going to be a bad one, I knew. I bit back a groan as I slung my leg over the seat of the motorcycle. The thief looked like a skittish black colt as I drew her, resisting each step tooth and nail, toward me. She was all thrashing hair and long, skinny legs. If I'd bothered to look at her face, I was certain I'd see little more than the whites of her frightened eyes.

"Let me go!" she shouted. "What are you doing? Let me go!"

I didn't care that she was scared. She could cry on Diarmuid's shoulder; he could offer her tear-stained cheeks a tissue. I was taking her to his office and I was telling him exactly where he could shove his government money. And then I was leaving: back to the peace of the tattoo shop, back to the bottle of whiskey in the bottom drawer of my desk, back to the tattoo chair where if I stretched out completely and stayed perfectly still the pain was not bad enough to make me pass out.

As I started the ignition on the motorcycle, I was at least able to admire if not the strength of the thief's body, at least the strength of her stupidity. It was obvious, and I was sure, obvious to her as well that there was no way she was escaping. I easily had a foot on her and I wouldn't be much surprised to find that I was double her weight. Where my muscles from the boxing gym filled my leather jacket, hers might as well have been flung over the low-hanging branch of a bleached white aspen in the dead of winter. It was in all ways an unfair fight, and yet someone hadn't told her or she didn't care, because she just continued to fight harder and, as I was quickly to take notice of, shout louder.

In the time it had taken to mount my motorcycle, to fight back the wave of nausea from the pain in my leg, and to reaffix my grip on the little thief after starting the bike, a small crowd had gathered around us, in the pothole-littered street and even on the opposite sidewalk. Crowds only gathered in this part of town for two reasons: a serious crime had just been committed that didn't involve them or a serious crime was just about to be committed that didn't involve them. With raindrops beginning to fall and dark eyes fixed all around me, I suddenly saw the situation more clearly.

I was a giant of a man, thirty-one going on fifty, tattooed and muscled from head to toe, who was forcing a young girl, nothing more than whisper of a thing, obviously against her will, to get on his motorcycle. I stared around me at the shocked eyes of people who from years of violence and cruelty had long ago lost the ability to be shocked. I looked at my grip on the one handle of the motorcycle, at my knuckles white between my black tattoos. I followed my shaking arm, muscles twitching with strain, all the way to the pale wrist that trembled even as it fought to escape me. It was only then that I paused to finally take in the sight of the little thief.

A pain worse than anything my leg had ever punished me with stabbed at my heart at the sight of the girl, at the sight of the *child*. From my conversation with Diarmuid, I knew to expect someone young, but I never could have imagined she should be *so* young. In my mind, in the blindness of my rage, I had thought I was holding onto a hardened face, a set jaw, a pair of eyes etched with a compromised self, old age come early as it does for those who have to fight for life.

But the little thief had innocence in her eyes even as she narrowed them at me in anger, in a pathetic attempt at intimidation. Her eyelashes tangled with the dark hair that fluttered in the wind, tangled like sheets of a napping child, sweetly and messily and warmly. She was shouting at me—obscenities, I was sure, by that time—but all I could see was the plumpness of her cheeks, strawberries at the end of the season, red to the point of positively bursting. Contrary to everything I had imagined, the girl, the little girl, was full of youth, full of life.

I released her with a suddenness as if I had been burned. She, too, reeled, surprised at her abrupt freedom. Her bright eyes widened, but only for a moment. She was smart, I saw. You didn't survive a tough upbringing without learning never to question a scrap of bread; you just take it and run.

After that brief hesitation, that startled inquiry where her eyes met mine and neither she nor I blinked, the girl darted away like a rabbit released from a snare. Her boots smacked the concrete as the raindrops splattered around her. She weaved through the small crowd who followed her escape with turned heads as they dropped their cell phones back into their deep rain jacket pockets.

I sagged against the handlebars of my motorcycle with a weariness that went straight to the bone, burrowed in deep within the marrow. A cold came over me, the kind of cold that hours before a stone-blackening fire cannot vanquish. I squeezed my trembling fingers against my throbbing leg and let my head fall to my chest for an exhale that rattled like I was dying of pneumonia.

It was just by chance that I glanced back up, looking through the strands of hair the cruel wind had tugged loose from my bun. At that very moment, the girl, the little thief, in a run as if for her life looked back over her shoulder at me.

It was only for the blink of an eye that we connected before her hair fell back over her face like the wing of a raven. She turned her head and disappeared around the trash-littered corner.

But the look stayed with me like the distortions in your vision when you stare too closely at the sun.   ʼ

I tried to blink her away, to squeeze my eyes shut and make

her go away. But there she was, present before me. Accusatory. Alluring. All-consuming.

The rain was turning my leather jacket from brown to black, save the white claw marks she'd left on my arm, and my leg was burning anew, but I did not turn off the ignition. I revved the ignition, said fuck it to the tattoo parlour and drove headlong into the pain.

5

AURNIA

*E*very ring at the front door the next day sent me scrambling over my bed, slinging my backpack (packed and at the ready on the only post of the four-post bed that hadn't been snapped off) onto my shoulder, and hoisting myself up to crouch on the deteriorating frame of the open window. The beds of my fingernails would turn bright red as I pressed them tighter and tighter against the splintering wood and strained to listen down the dark, narrow hallway to the front door.

It was always with a painful release of tension that I sagged back down and collapsed in exhaustion onto my bed when I failed to hear footsteps approaching my closed (and locked) bedroom door.

On the one hand, it was a relief to know that it wasn't the police, that it was just a quick drug deal, a "friend" of my father's come over for a smoke, or one of the several dealers that lived out of the basement coming back from God knows where. On the other hand, it was no relief at all.

Because I knew. Because I *knew*, eventually, the police were coming, the police *were* coming for me.

At least when you're robbing a store or vandalizing a side street, you're on the move. There's constant action, there's plenty of movement to burn off the adrenaline that makes your chest tight. But the day after I tried to rob Dublin Ink there was nothing to do but wait.

Waiting sucked. I had been waiting all morning, all early afternoon. And all that the rest of the day promised was more waiting and then...juvie.

There was nothing to be done. They were absolutely coming, the police. I wasn't an expert on the terms of my parole, I'd tuned most of it out to be honest, too busy watching a girl get finger-wagged at by her father for stealing a pair of earrings from the mall. Ha! My father would have berated me for stopping at the earrings. I could hear his slurred voice: *what, you couldn't fit the necklace in your backpack? The bracelet was too heavy for those little hands of yours you never even lift a pinkie to help your dear old dad?*

Anyway, I knew enough to guess that trying to rob the place where you were supposed to be working off your parole (for robbery, no less) was *probably* in violation.

The doorbell rang again, a quick succession of rings that implied urgency. A part of me hoped this was finally it as I went through the whole drill that had become rote: scramble, grab, climb, wait. A part of me hoped it was the police and that they'd been smart enough to post someone at the chain link fence in the back. A part of me hoped the officer who caught me would pat me, not unkindly, on the back, and guide me to the car, saying, "Now, *you*." A part of me thought that juvie couldn't possibly be worse than what I had at home.

And when I heard *his* voice slither down the hallway toward my bedroom, that part of me grew. Instead of hopping down from the window's ledge in relief, I lowered one toe and then the other as slowly as possible. I inched carefully across the dirty carpet, careful not to step on the places that I knew creaked. I didn't dare climb back onto the bed for fear of the old springs moaning. I just stood in place, holding my breath, as footsteps, slow and meandering, moved down the hallway. A whistle was on his lips as usual. I covered my mouth with my hand when his shoes came to a stop outside my bedroom door, two black voids in the strip of yellow. The whistling stopped and this terrified me most of all.

I imagined a hand pulled from a ratty army-green jacket. I imagined it moving toward the doorknob of my bedroom door. I imagined it turning, slowly. The quick jerk when it caught on the lock. I knew how easy it was to open, how feeble the lock I placed so much of my sense of security really was. To keep out all the other goons in the house out of my bedroom, I wedged a chair beneath the knob. But I didn't with *him*; I knew it would only prove to him that I was in there.

I so hated the way he called to me through the closed door, the way he drew out my name, the way he drew out a whistle: *Auuuuuuurnia.*

"Nick!" my father called from the living room. I turned my eyes to the ceiling in thanks. "Nick, you bastard, we're missing some of the shite! Where are ye?"

The shoes hesitated for just a moment before disappearing, footsteps growing distant as I exhaled. This time when I fell back onto my bed, fingers drawing shakily through my hair, it was a different kind of impatience that swept over me, a new kind of frustration. I suddenly became indignant.

What in the hell was taking the police so long? I thought with a wildly beating heart. They should have been here by now. Why wasn't someone, anyone here to take me away? To take me, I thought with a pained longing that constricted my chest, far, far, *far* away?

I became angry at the man from the tattoo parlour, that

giant covered in striking art who took my beating upon his chest like he somehow deserved it, whose fingers were still wrapped around my wrist like a bracelet of amethyst and sapphire. What was taking him so goddamn long? What was he waiting for before calling Diarmuid? Was he trying to torture me? Was that his plan all along?

Staring up at the prickled ceiling in the dying light, I remembered back to the prior evening. There, on his motorcycle, muscles shaking, knuckles straining, he had looked at me with such vehemence in his pale green eyes. I could only imagine where he would have taken me had he managed to get me onto his motorcycle. He looked like he had wanted to yank my body against his and drive the two of us straight off a cliff. I could almost feel how his heart would have beat against my back. I could almost feel his heat, almost feel the press of his thighs against mine, almost feel the place where he would hold me tight: right between my breasts, right against the ridges of my ribcage, right where he could feel my own heart most strongly, feel it most rewardingly when it stopped beating beneath his searing-hot touch.

He had hated me, I was sure of that. He had felt nothing toward me but pure rage. I had ignited something in him with deep, dark roots. So why, I thought with a sense of hopelessness that I hadn't experienced before, hadn't he turned me in? Why, I thought, hadn't he called the authorities to tell them what I'd done?

As I heard Nick's voice in the living room, I twisted into the sheets and drew up my knees to my chest. Why hadn't he saved me?

6

CONOR

*I*t seemed to me that if I was already in inescapable pain, I might as well add some more pain on top. And if anything was as painful as my leg in the rain, it was trying to draw up the perfect tattoo for the one remaining spot on my chest and failing again and again and again...

The rest of my tattoos were years old. I had drawn them all, drawn them all in a flurry of inspiration, a few minutes of a furiously scratching pencil and they had been done. I had never doubted a single one of them. The shavings had still been there on the page, fresh as the morning dew, when I'd turned them over to Mason or Rian or a few (a rare few) other artists I trusted. It wasn't long before there had been only one spot left, the spot just above my most favoured tattoo: a rising phoenix. Just one more tattoo to complete.

And yet the spot, or the hole, the gaping hole as it often seemed, had remained unfilled for years and years.

I'd wasted hours upon hours attempting to draw up the perfect tattoo. The hole in my chest only seemed to grow larger, only became harder to fill. I'd gone through dozens of sketchbooks, rejected page after page, filled wastebasket after wastebasket, snapped off the tips of hundreds of pencils, stabbed so hard onto the sketchbook when it wasn't working that it tore through at least five pages beneath. Sometimes I would fly into such a fury that I'd work till morning rearranging everything in the shop so that when Mason came downstairs with whatever woman on his arm and Rian returned bleary-eyed from whatever late-night drug-infused "artistic journey" he'd come from, the only proof of me completely and utterly losing it was a dent or two in the wall half hidden by Mason's grandmother's dying ficus.

I didn't know what was wrong with me. I drew perfectly fine things for our clients (which, admittedly, were few and far between, but still). If Mason or Rian asked for something, I never failed to produce artwork they were happy to have forever on their bodies. But nothing I drew for that hole in me, that fucking hole in me, ever seemed to be...*enough*.

And so it was again that night.

The wastebasket beside my drawing table was rising like foamy flood waters and the pencils were going down like a forest of downed trees. The familiar anger, anger at *myself*, was growing painfully in my chest. I was halfway through a lotus, a symbol for self-regeneration, and I already knew it was wrong. Wrong. It was perfectly lovely, of course. I knew the extent of my artistic talent. I knew it was beautiful, some of my finest work in a while even. But was beautiful and it was *wrong*.

I was in the process of tearing it from the sketchbook when the bell at the front door interrupted my tormented thoughts.

It might have been Mason, though it was early still. When he went hunting, he liked the chase just as much as the final success, just as much as the mutual feasting of warm flesh. Just past eleven would hardly give him time to tease the lucky lady's inner thigh beneath the bar.

It might have been Rian. He wandered into the shop whenever he and his "inspiration" damn well pleased; his time sheet read like a bingo card of times of the day and night. It might even have been a client. Dublin Ink's hours were technically noon to nine, but if one of us was here, we usually kept the lights on and the door unlocked. Partly because why the hell not? Partly because we weren't exactly in a position to be imposing on whoever happened, by luck or stupidity, to want to give us money.

But when I looked up from my half-torn page, there, standing in a widening puddle of dirty rainwater just inside the shop, was my little thief.

The pale pink neon of the broken Dublin Ink sign caught the side of the girl's face, cupped her supple cheek like a hand would. The other half of her face was hidden behind her dark hair, wet from the rain. In the lamplight through the rain-dotted front window it looked like glass, or black ice: deadly. Her lips were tinged blue, as were her fingertips just visible beneath the long sleeves of her black jean jacket, the same one she'd been wearing the day before. Her dripping clothes hung on her small frame. Their size only made her look smaller. Everything about her looked fragile, looked on the verge of breaking. Everything except the one eye with which she stared at me. In the dark, her steady gaze was like a lighted arrow arching high, well-aimed for my heart.

The girl stared at me and I stared at her.

The rain pounded on the roof, on the windows, on the slick stretch of black asphalt outside the shop. I'd never in a million years expected to see the little thief again. I'd driven her, literally, out of my head. The ride I took after letting her go, after watching her run away, had been a long one. It took miles to get the pulse of her inner wrist from the tips of my fingers. It took many more after that to feel that my heart was beating on its own accord and not because her little fist was pounding against it. It took goddamn near all night to feel like I was alone on that long, lonely stretch of road—because she had been there. Her thighs against mine. Her cheek against my back. Her arms around my waist. She had been there, her body tight, leaning with me, moving with me. I had *wanted* her to be there. And I had to drive till I no longer wanted that. Because I couldn't. I couldn't want that.

Within seconds of my little thief standing there, staring defiantly at me, it was once more what I wanted.

Before I could open my mouth to tell her to leave, the girl took a step forward and demanded, with an indignant jerk of her little chin, "Why haven't you called the cops already?"

Her question caught me off guard. Not that I had been particularly on guard, with her there, once more before me, once more within reach.

I shook my head and managed with a tight throat to say, "Look, we're closed."

The girl didn't even bother pointing to the illuminated sign in the window that read, clear as day, Open, as she took another worrying step toward me. She didn't give one damn whether we were open or not. I was sure that I could have been dead asleep in bed, feverish with pain, bare chest covered in a glisten of sweat, and she would be there, with her ridiculous questions, by my bedside. She was a child, after all. And she was acting like one.

"Did you hear me?" I said, pointing toward the door. "We're *closed*."

I lowered my head, like that was the end of things. I focused on tearing the rest of the page from the sketchbook. It was something to do right: metal prong by metal prong, tear the page free. I needed to do something right. Before I did something wrong.

"I'd like to know when you plan on calling them," the girl said, her voice sounding dangerously closer. "If you don't mind."

"I do mind," I said as I balled the page in my fist.

The most important thing was to get the girl to leave. It was crucial that she got no closer. As long as she didn't get any closer, I could send her away. But if she got any closer...

I looked up and drew a sharp inhale, because the little thief was already past the couch. Her fingertips were behind her, brushing the edge of the faded floral pattern, keeping contact with it like it was the only thing keeping her from a deadly fall. I knew, with certainty, that *I* was the deadly fall.

"Get out," I growled, rising to my full six-foot-three height to physically intimidate the little thing, a bear rising onto its hind legs before a rabbit.

The girl fell back on her heel at the sight of me, but she did not retreat. She stared at me curiously, raised a dark, arched eyebrow.

"I'm not here to steal from you again," she said, her words probing.

She didn't understand my anger, didn't understand the fear I was hiding with anger. I spit out a laugh; something I rarely did. With me between her and the cash register, the thought of her managing a dime was funny. The girl, incredibly, seemed to take this as a personal affront. Her fingertips left the safety of the couch, something I hadn't intended, as she crossed her arms over her chest as if to say, "Shall I show you?"

"Get lost, girl," I said. "I'm not calling the cops on you."

This was a mistake, telling her this. Because in her surprise she took another step forward. There was little more than my drawing desk and a few fateful steps between her and me. I gripped the edges of the desk, felt the soft wood splinter between my shaking fingers, wondered just how long it would hold me back.

"Why not?" the girl asked, all accusation, all suspicion.

"What does it matter?" I said quickly, biceps beginning to shake. "Just take your reprieve and go."

The stupid thing didn't leave. No, she just came closer still.

"I want to know why," she demanded.

For such a small thing, she had quite the mouth. Or really, quite the nerve to use it.

"I'm working," I tried, almost desperately. "You know, the thing you do to *earn* money."

The girl's lips curled into a mischievous smile and I was apparently damned to say all the wrong things.

"You need to go."

"Tell me why you aren't going to bust me," she insisted.

I jerked back when the little thief's fingertips came to the top of my drawing desk. When had she gotten so close? How had I *allowed* her to get so close? She looked up at me through long dark eyelashes that had caught the rain like blades of wild grass. She tucked her hair behind her ear. I was doomed to stare down into both her wide, wickedly innocent eyes.

How was I supposed to tell her the truth without multiplying the questions on the tip of her tongue, a little wild raspberry perfect for plucking, for holding between my teeth? How was I supposed to provide an answer behind which were a dozen more answers, a dozen more reasons to step closer, a dozen more reasons to *stay*? How was I supposed to explain something that would take longer than my resolve to have nothing, absolutely nothing with my little thief could possibly last?

If I told her that I knew the hells of juvie and wouldn't, even for the life of me and certainly not for trying to snatch a few crumpled old bills from the cash register, doom her to that fate, I knew, I knew with a certainty that I could not explain, that she would ask me how? *How* did I know? She would move around the side of my drawing desk. Her fingers would come to rest on my forearm. And it would be all over just like that. I would take her. I knew I would.

If I told her that I'd been like her before, that in the darkest moment of my life I could have used a grace, a kindness like the one I was offering to her if she would just fucking *take it already*, then she would ask me what I meant. She would sink down onto the edge of the couch. She would lean back. She would draw her legs up, crisscross applesauce, but only for as long as it took to stalk over to her, to throw her over my shoulder.

And if I told her the truth, the rotten truth that a dark part of me wanted her and couldn't resist her if she stayed even a fucking second longer, then...well, I was terrified that *she* would say something stupid with a seductive quirk of her head, like, "Well, what are you waiting for?"

So I did what I thought I must do. For the second time in as many days, I grabbed ahold of the girl's wrist and dragged her toward the front door.

"Hey!" she shouted. "What the hell?"

"Listen," I said through gritted teeth, lifting her almost high enough that her toes barely scraped the old shag carpet. "Is that something you can do? *Listen?*"

"We were having a civilised discussion, you brute," the girl growled back.

I suddenly hit resistance and looked back to find the girl holding onto a tattoo chair. The devil of a thing was grinning at me victoriously.

"Now," she huffed, blowing her hair out of her eyes, "let's just sit down and—hey! Hey!"

It was like knocking over a domino, tipping her over into the chair. Then it was as simple as lifting the chair itself, the little thief positioned nicely atop it. I carried the chair toward the door as she scrambled to look at me over the top.

"What's your problem?" she complained.

"My problem is you," I said as I set the chair down by the door with a grunt. "So, listen—"

I quickly boxed her in before she could escape.

"*Listen*," I repeated in a growl as I yanked open the door, a gust of bitter wind and biting rain sweeping inside against us, "I don't want you around here, alright? Dublin Ink, I'm afraid, no longer requires the assistance of a thief, and a stupid one I might add, returning to the scene of the crime."

I managed to push the girl from the chair. She fell onto the sidewalk and glared up at me, fire in her eyes. A fire I hated to admit that I liked. I filled the doorway with my bulky frame to cut off any ideas of her regaining entrance.

I pointed a finger at her and said, "Now, I'll cover for you with Diarmuid, with all that Young Offenders bullshite. But you're not to come round here anymore. Do you hear me?" I gestured to the night and added with a sarcastic flourish, "I'm setting you free, little thief."

Before she could say anything to make me change my mind, I slammed the door shut, locked it, switched off the "Open" sign, pulled shut the velvet drapes over the window, and turned on the speakers to full blast, Talos' "This Is Us Colliding" drowning out any shouting or pounding the girl might be foolish enough to try. I left the tattoo chair where it was; Mason or Rian could deal with it whenever they came in. They had some making up to do after leaving the shop wide open to robbery.

I returned to my work at the drawing desk after another shot of whiskey and two more aspirin. My leg hurt worse than ever after all that. But I found as my pencil moved in quick, violent bursts across the page that I was drawing the very thing I'd just kicked out, my little thief.

I tore the page, then tore it again, and again.

I'd really meant what I'd said about setting her free. I knew first-hand the damage someone like me could do to her life. If she thought it was screwed up now...

And to truly set her free, I couldn't draw her, couldn't dream of her, couldn't allow her into a single thought.

Or I'd be tearing that door open and pulling her back into my hell with me.

7

AURNIA

I dreamed I awoke with a hand on my cheek.

The hand was warm. I could trace the calluses of the hand like constellations behind my closed eyelids. The hand rose and fell with my gentle, even breathing.

In my dream, I knew who it was who had laid his hand on my cheek. I didn't even know his name, but I knew the size of his hand, the softness of his touch, the closeness of his breath.

He had come after me in the rain. He had run, puddles in the street lamps splashing against his dark jeans. He had run for me. His fingers had wrapped once more around my wrist, like that first time we met. He had squeezed me tight. He had twisted me around. He had dragged me to him, to his body.

In my dream, he was there beside me in bed, because that's where he had taken me, out of the rain, out of the cold. In the warm glow of the neon, in the narrow stairs, he had stripped my soaking wet clothes from my body first, then his from his. He had laid me atop the mattress like a rose upon a grave. He had slipped in beside me. He had raised the sheets, thick and plush and warm, atop us, buried us together beneath them.

In my dream, he was cupping my cheek with his hand,

because I'd fallen asleep in his arms, pressed tight like we would have been if I'd let him drag me onto his motorcycle. The dawn was breaking and there in the first of the morning light, he'd had his first chance to look at me, to truly see me.

In my dream, when I opened my eyes, slowly, a butterfly's wings unfolding for the first time, he would kiss me. He would kiss me and his hands would touch more than just my cheek. He would touch all of me. And he would press his body, large and imposing and impossibly strong, onto mine and the ink from his tattoos would transfer to my skin like a stamp.

It was a nice dream, the one with the man's hand on my cheek.

If only it were just that...a dream.

A wash of ice-cold terror flooded my veins at the sudden realisation that I was awake, fully awake, and that there was a hand on my cheek. I choked back a little moan that had been rising in my throat and jerked back as my eyes flew open to see Nick at the edge of my bed.

I instinctively drew the sheets up toward my neck before remembering with a deep-boned shiver that I had fallen asleep in my wet clothes from the night before. I was deadly cold, but the heartless laugh that fell like a diseased bird from Nick's lips made me certain that seconds before I had been suffering from the heat of a life-threatening fever.

"Didn't mean to scare you," Nick said, holding up his hands as if he wasn't in my room, uninvited, unwanted, *alone.*

I drew a hand that I hoped he couldn't see was shaking over my face.

"But it's not really my fault that you scare so damned easy, baby Aurnia!" Nick added, his fingertips finding my neck beneath the sheets as he laughed again.

I needed to get away from the feeling of Nick's fingers on my skin, but squirming away from him would only make things worse. It was the game of cat and mouse that he truly wanted to play. So I disguised my backwards motion with a wide yawn. Nick's hand fell to my pillow, the tattoos he tattooed himself jerky and uneven across his scarred fingers.

I pushed back my hair and with another start found Nick staring at me, a grin on his chapped lips. Nick had eyes so black that it was a whispered debate whether it was his pupils blown wide from near constant drug use or whether his irises were truly that colour; though I never said anything for fear of it getting back to Nick, I always thought it was the second: it was just like Nick to suck in for himself all the colour, all the life around him.

I tried not to squirm beneath Nick's steady gaze, his hands now folded primly over the leg he'd propped up on my bed. The key wasn't playing dead, necessarily, the key was play uninteresting. Prey that didn't play along was just no fun at all.

"Is my dad not home?" I asked, getting out of bed under the guise of getting ready.

I caught Nick's eyes, already on mine, sharp and attentive, in the broken mirror above my dresser as I reached for a brush.

"No, he's here," Nick said.

I nodded like this didn't upset me.

"And..." I said, drawing the brush through my still damp hair, "and he knows you're..."

"In your bedroom, baby Aurnia?" Nick completed the thought for me, his grin widening. "What is it that he's always saying when he's high? 'What's mine is yours'?"

I tried my best to ignore this. It wasn't like it was particularly surprising anyway. No matter how many times I stupidly kept expecting my father to do just the bare minimum for a father—like keeping his daughter safe, like making sure dangerous men didn't wander into her bedroom while she was asleep—he always had a way of making me feel even more like a fucking fool. I lived in my father's house, slept under his roof, ate his food, but I was an orphan in every other sense of the word. I was, in every way, abandoned.

I hadn't sensed Nick moving, hadn't heard him get up from the bed despite the noisiness of the springs. He was there behind me, looming with his black eyes in the mirror, before I even had time to think about escaping.

"Give that to me," he said, and with a creeping sensation I knew it was the same voice I'd heard him use with my father.

It was a casual voice, an easy voice, a friendly voice even. It was a voice that was intended to make the person feel like they had a choice in the matter, that they could easily say no if they wanted. But just beneath the surface was a very real threat.

Nick's voice was a sparkling river whose current you didn't realise the force of till it had dragged you under. Nick was going to take over my father's drug business whether he knew it or not. And he was going to card his fingers through my hair whether it was with me standing before the mirror or pinned on the floor beneath his knee.

I handed Nick the old brush.

I don't know which would have been worse: him being rough, yanking the brush through till it caught on a tangle and yanked my head back, or him being sweetly tender, him being *slow*? It wasn't long before I knew. The brush moved like molasses and Nick's eyes never left my face the whole time.

When his fingers reached forward to skim searchingly over the top of my dresser, over the things I kept trying to feel like a normal teenager—cheap makeup pallets, teen fashion magazines and bejewelled pictures frames with the stock photos still inside—it was like a spider crawling out from one of the many cracks in the wall. I wanted to scream. But I couldn't.

When he plucked up a sparkly pink hair band (a stupid thing I stole because I saw another girl pick it out with her mother and liked the way they went back and forth about it like it wasn't just a cheap piece of fabric wrapped around an even cheaper piece of rubber), I could see the grime beneath his too long nails, I could see the way the ink of his tattoos bled, spread. I would need a shower after he was done.

Nick parted my hair, torturing me by making it more precise than I'd ever bothered doing for myself, and then drew half my hair into the band. He was giving me fucking pigtails. And there was no one I could shout to for help. No one who could hear me. No one who would do anything if they could. The strangers out on the couch, down in the basement, crouched in the attic were either passed out or working for Nick, under the guise of working for my father, who himself was probably passed out. I was on my own. I was helpless.

"Ready?" Nick asked when he'd finished the second pigtail.

I met his eyes in the mirror.

"Ready?"

"For the job," he said, hands on my narrow shoulders.

I stared at him in confusion.

"You're the distraction," he said. "You're the innocent little girl, the pretty little thing, the poor little lost soul who will need assistance from the big, strong security guard with the gun."

His grin curled up at the edges when I continued to just stare at him mutely. He spun me around to face him. I twisted round like those dummies seamstresses use. Nick's finger lifted my chin.

"Why else do you think I did all of this?" he asked, twisting a finger round one strand of hair, following it with his eyes till it fell just above the top of my black tank top across my chest.

His eyes flashed when they darted back to mine.

"You don't think I did it just for the *fun* of it, do you, baby Aurnia?" he asked in a low whisper. "You don't think I did it just because I *could*?"

I managed to force a smile well enough. I laughed and twisted the other pigtail the way he had done and said, as casually as I could, "Of course not."

I slipped past him to grab a shoe. I looked at him over my shoulder. "I mean, you're not psychotic," I said, laughing.

He laughed, too. It was the start of the game, after all. I dragged on my boot at the bottom of my bed, eyed Nick as I yanked at the damp laces until I thought they might snap.

"Little problem, though," I said. "I can't do a job today."

"No?" Nick asked with an amused arch of his eyebrow.

"Probation stuff," I said, tightening one hair band.

Nick nodded slowly. "From the jewellery store?"

"If I don't show up, the police will be knocking on that door just down the hallway there within the hour."

Nick was silent, watching. I hopped up with a grin and shrugged my shoulders.

"I mean, we can't be having that, can we," I said, patting Nick's chest. "What with all the drugs and stuff just lying around."

I flicked the little bag of cocaine I knew was in the front pocket of his army-style jacket. I winked. I went to leave.

Nick blocked my passage. He filled the door frame as if he had been poured in like concrete. There was only one man I knew who was bigger, stronger. And I was determined to get to him, whether he wanted me with him or not.

He had told me that he was setting me free, but exchanging one prison for another was not setting someone free. I would show him that I could help him, help Dublin Ink. I would make myself useful. I would make it so that he couldn't get rid of me, couldn't send me back here.

With Nick and his black eyes and dirty fingers there before me, I wanted nothing more than to step back and collide with *his* chest. I wanted his big arm to come around me, to guide me behind him. I wanted to hide in his shadow like an enveloping blanket. I wanted to close my eyes till he told me to open them, till he put *his* hand on my cheek. I wanted to open my eyes and have his hand on my cheek and it not be a dream.

"Should I have my JLO call you or...?" I asked Nick.

His long fingernails dug into the peeling paint of the door frame, but then he grinned and stepped aside, sweeping his hand for me to pass.

"Next time then," he called after me as I tried to keep my footsteps even down the hallway. "Baby, Aurnia."

I stepped over druggies slumped against the wall in the living room and with a shudder realised that amongst the blank, nameless faces was my father. He'd always had a problem, but he hadn't always had a megalomaniac to exploit it. Things were worsening at home faster than I thought possible.

Because I was certain that Nick was watching through bent and broken blinds, I waited till I was around the block, dogs snarling at chain-link fences, to yank my hair free of the pigtails. I winced in pain, but I just tugged harder. Because it was *my* pain.

If I was going to remember pain from my childhood, it was going to be my own.

8

CONOR

The next morning I was more than happy to exchange the old pain in my leg for a fresh new hangover. I even managed something nearing a smile at the hammers that pounded my temples, the nails that drove through the top of my skull, and the ice picks that stabbed into my eyes every time I squinted against the sun.

There was to be no rain that day. There was to be no little thief that day. There was to be a return to normalcy.

That alone somehow made the mounting business debt, the late rent notices piling up on my counter, and the general sense of doom regarding my future feel rather manageable.

I was positively beaming as I strolled into Dublin Ink; only one little old lady had flinched away from me on the sidewalk.

But Fate was a tricky bitch. I should have expected she'd have something up her sleeve for me.

I stepped inside the parlour and was greeted with the sight of the little thief manhandling an expensive tattoo gun and laughing like the money she'd pawn it for was already in her grubby little pocket.

Fuck. I'd rather have the rain.

Even worse? She was not alone. There beside her was Mason (predictable) and Rian (predictable too, I suppose, given his absolute unpredictability). Their merry little chatter masked the sound of the bell. With their backs turned to me, hunched over together like they were plotting how to once and for all drive the business into the ground, I leaned unnoticed against the closed door, arms folded against my chest, and simply watched.

Mason was explaining how the equipment worked. The girl nodded enthusiastically, as his hand creeped lower and lower down her back. He thought he was getting lucky, but I knew better. I knew the little thief.

Mason was an easy mark, after all. All she'd have to do was keep batting those dark eyes, rimmed in a smoky charcoal that made her bewitching even though it was probably makeup she hadn't bothered to take off in days; Mason would go on telling her how loading the ink worked, how unlocking the storeroom in the back worked, how selling off all the parlour's valuables in the middle of the night and getting away with it before anyone even had a clue worked. He thought he was going to bed with her, the poor fella; little did he know that she was going to the bank with him.

Rian would be a little more difficult for the little thief to crack, but as I watched her study him out of the corner of her eye, tucking a strand of dark hair innocently enough behind her ear, I was certain that she was more than capable. She was more of a pro than I gave her credit for. Smart. Clever. Well-aware of her...*gifts*. She was a child and yet I was certain she hadn't been a child for a very long time. I knew first-hand how that paradox felt, how it looked.

She would need a minute or two to figure out how to use Rian to get what she wanted, but probably not more. She would see his eyes on her fresh young skin, just like Mason's eyes were on her skin. But she would also see that it wasn't just flesh for him. She would see that it was more like a pale, smooth canvas. I'd seen Rian giving the goddamn moon that same dreamy, distant look.

"You know," the little thief said to Rian when Mason began rifling through the bottom drawer of the stand to show her another thing to steal later (and maybe to look between her legs), "you know, I've always wanted a tattoo."

I rolled my eyes when Rian's got wide.

"I have a few ideas and stuff," the girl said, trailing her fingers up and down her forearm. "I really just haven't had the money yet."

Bing-fucking-go.

I could see it as clear as day: Rian would offer to do her first for free, because money was nothing more than an abstract concept that I occasionally (and more frequently) yelled at him about. The girl would ask him to draw up a few ideas, something "he thought would look good on her". Maybe she'd lift the side of her shirt, draw her finger down her waistline. A bigger canvas meant a bigger piece of art. A bigger piece of art meant more time. Rian would disappear into his sketchbook, into that world he escaped to. His eyes would be open, but he wouldn't see as the little thief piled up our things high into her arms. He wouldn't as she whistled her way straight out the door.

"You know," Rian was saying, drumming his fingers against the girl's arm, "we're really more about the art here than anything else and, well, I don't see any reason why I couldn't do your first tattoo for—"

"Morning, boys!" I announced, reaching up to smack the little bell atop the door so it jangled like an alarm. The three of them whipped around in surprise.

I had only eyes for the girl. "Morning, *thief.*"

I kicked open the door with my heel, held it open behind me with my palm. I gestured rather politely, I thought, through it.

"Time to go," I said to her.

Mason and Rian both stood and came toward me.

"This is Aurnia," Mason said.

"She's the kid Diarmuid said he was sending," added Rian.

I eyed the girl from between their shoulders. She was twirling the tattoo gun on her pinkie, grinning at me. Through my immense irritation, I managed to notice briefly that she was in the same clothes from the night before. I remembered days like that, and, more darkly, the reason for days like that.

Still, I said to her more than anyone else, with no warmth at all in my voice, "I know who she is."

Mason said, "She was saying that she got caught up the other day and couldn't make it when she was supposed to."

I raised an amused eyebrow and said, still looking at the grinning girl, "She got 'caught up', did she?"

The girl, her eyes fixed on me, said, "Impossible to escape, really."

Rian's eyes darted between the girl and me. To cut off any chance of suspicion, I thumbed over my shoulder toward the sidewalk.

"Listen, Aurnia," her name on my lips for the first time caught me off guard and I quickly cleared my throat, "sorry for making you trek all the way out here, but we don't need your help, I'm afraid. I've cleared everything up with Diarmuid. So…"

I gestured again toward the door, but Aurnia just crossed her arms over her chest, that damned grin still there on her little petite mouth.

"Funny," she said, tilting her head slightly to the side, "because Diarmuid called me this morning and said you were all really looking forward to meeting me. You especially, Conor."

She said my name so casually that I almost believed she'd

known it the whole time, that she'd held this power over me without me ever knowing it. By the look on her face, hair falling childishly over one eye, I expected she thought she now had a secret weapon against me, having my name, a secret weapon in this game of chicken.

She'd have to wield it more than once for it to take me to my knees. She'd have to say it over and over and over again, bottom lip between her teeth, chin tilted up toward me, eyes consumed by blackened pupils, for me to fall.

But in this little war of ours, I made one mistake. I assumed that I had allies, Mason and Rian. This, however, was wrong. The two jackasses had gone turncoat.

"I mean, we really could use the help," Mason supplied before I could send my volley at the girl, at Aurnia. "There's lots of stuff she could do. And she's eager to learn."

"Very eager," Aurnia said behind his back.

"And she's free," Mason added before twisting around and blabbering, "I mean, your labour is free. And not that kind of labour, you know? Physical labour. But not that kind of physical labour. You'll work for us for free. Not, like, on us or anything like that. Not that that's what you were thinking. Or what I was thinking. I mean, I always buy dinner. Appetizers at least. I mean, I'm always good for a beer first. At least, you know?"

I rubbed my fingers with a tired sigh against my temples. Aurnia, to her credit, just nodded along good-naturedly. Mason, for perhaps the first time in his life, was red in the face with shame (foreign to him, I assure you) when he turned around. Maybe it was because she was a fucking *child*.

"What Mason here was so eloquently trying to say," Rian interjected, giving Mason the side-eye, "is that Aurnia is looking forward to participating in the Young Offenders Program in a location that can help foster her own love of art."

"Right," Mason said, nodding back at Aurnia with a sheepish smile. "That."

I'd lost the troops, that was clear. Aurnia was beaming behind them with an obvious air of victory. Her chin was jutted up. Her grin had grown. Her eyes sparkled at me.

"Alright," I said, matching her grin with one of my own, though I'm sure it looked slightly maniacal from disuse. "I know right where you can start."

Mason and Rian parted for me when I walked past them, suspicion on their faces. Aurnia did not scramble away as I rested my arm across her thin, narrow shoulders.

"Right this way, dear," I said in my best imitation of a sweet voice, guiding her toward the back of the parlour.

"See, he wasn't all that hard to convince," Mason called out to Aurnia, who was glancing nervously back at the two of them over her shoulder.

"He's not as scary as he looks," Rian added, though he didn't sound entirely convincing as I led Aurnia farther away.

She looked up at me after glancing at my hand around the base of her neck and said, "You're letting me stay?"

"Why, of course," I answered, snatching up a broom as we passed and jabbing it toward her. "You managed to convince me that you were definitely not going to steal anything. I totally believe that your intentions truly are just to take an opportunity to learn a new trade. There is no doubt in my mind that the other day you were just sorting the cash in the register."

Aurnia began to squirm when I threaded a mop bucket on her thin arm, shoved a broom in her hand, slapped a dirty rag over her shoulder, and tucked a bottle of some sort of bathroom solution beneath her armpit.

"Conor?" Mason shouted back at me.

"Just doing a little new employee orientation," I called back as I kicked open the back door which led to the alleyway.

I managed to cup my hand over Aurnia's mouth just as she was about to holler at Mason and Rian. Her eyes were enraged above my fingers which consumed half her face as I walked her and her armful of cleaning supplies outside. I kept going till her back collided with the brick wall of the opposite building. She tried to press back against me, but it was, of course, futile; she was never going to win that battle against me, no matter how hard she tried.

Hunched over to meet her eyes, my face was close to hers, closer than it should have been. From there I could see too much.

The light freckles across her nose. The striations in her eyes, golds and ambers amongst the deep brown. The bags that coloured her undereye in varying shades of purple, blooming against the paper-like skin. It clashed with the youth of her eyes, the vibrancy of her stare, the fire of her anger. Someone so young, so alive, shouldn't have that kind of weariness, that kind of weight.

It was almost enough for me to hang my head, to sigh, to take back all the things I'd burdened her with from her arms. She could have come inside where it was warm. She could have sat beside Mason or Rian as they worked. She could have slept on the couch if she wanted. But then there would be the temptation to put a blanket round her shoulders. To turn up the heater for her sake. To slip an extra pillow beneath her head. And I feared if I did those simple things, it would be like a tipping point: there would be nothing in the world that I would not do for her, give for her, sacrifice for her.

My aid would ultimately be a curse. Just as *hers* had been all those years ago.

So I pressed my hand tighter over Aurnia's mouth as she tried to shout.

"You wanted to make yourself useful. So make yourself useful."

I released my hand and she glared up at me. Her face petulant, childish, beautiful. I crossed back to the door and tossed her backpack out with her. It was heavier than I expected. I glanced once more over my shoulder and found that Aurnia had not moved from where I left her. She held the broom like a spear, the bucket like it was filled with ammo, the cleaning solution like a fucking grenade.

"I thank you for the opportunity," she said through gritted teeth. "I hope not to disappoint."

I snorted in amusement and slammed the door.

"Mason!" I called. "Rian! We need to talk!"

She thought it'd be that easy, infiltrating her way into Dublin Ink. But I had a few tricks up my sleeve, too. And I had more on the line than she could ever know.

9

AURNIA

His name was Conor. Conor. I knew his name and it was Conor!

Even though I had just been essentially kicked out onto the curb with nothing more than a thin jacket, a muddy backpack, and a broom, I couldn't help but smile. The alleyway was lined with dumpsters teeming with rats, but I was smiling. Those moments were rare and so I wasn't going to spoil a good thing.

With an almost childlike glee, I rushed back at the door after Conor slammed it shut. I didn't hope to pry it back open; I knew he'd locked it the second the hinges had stopped rattling enough to allow him. But heart beating and eyes wide, I wanted to hear what was being said inside. I pressed my ear to the grey metal door covered in gang tags and closed my eyes, fingers next to my head like I was dreaming.

Was this what it felt like to have siblings? To have older brothers who shoved you out of their room and didn't want you around their "cool" friends? With my eyes closed I could almost imagine I was in a carpeted hallway with those streaks you get when your mom vacuums. Could almost feel the crappy band poster on the door I was snooping at. That it wasn't piss and stale beer I was smelling, but instead Dad's famous meatloaf cooking downstairs and my brothers' horrible body spray, applied heavily in lieu of a shower.

I laughed a little because the fantasy was all a little ridiculous. I mean, Mason wanted to fuck me (that wasn't happening). Rian probably wouldn't remember my name the next day. And Conor? Well...Conor had literally thrown me out onto the street three times now. They were also all almost twice my age.

I guess what made me feel the way that I felt was because *they* were a family. An odd, created family, but a family, nonetheless. I'd known it the second I saw the three of them together, how they seemed to communicate with one another without speaking, without me knowing what was going on. I'd just wanted to be a part of that, to insert myself into that. It wasn't their fault that I was fucked up.

It didn't take long for the three of them to raise their voices loud enough for me to hear them.

"None of that matters," I heard Conor growl, "all that matters is that *I* don't want her here."

This didn't hurt as much as one would think. I mean, it wasn't exactly hot-off-the-press news at that point.

"But why?" Rian asked. "You still haven't said *why*."

"And I don't fucking have to," Conor replied.

I covered my mouth to conceal a burst of laughter. They sounded like old hens bickering at one another. With the granny decorum of the parlour, all the three of them needed was a set of hand-woven shawls to complete the image.

"Is it because I want to bang her?" Mason asked.

That wasn't exactly news either. I wasn't sure Mason even knew the word "finesse". His game was a full-frontal attack. I preferred a bit of a slow burn. A chase. Tension building and building till...

"Wait," Mason said, interrupting my thought, "wait, is it because *you* want to bang her?"

"No one is banging her," Conor snapped. "She is seventeen years old. The reason she is not working here is because I said so."

I pressed my ear tighter to the door.

"That's not a very good reason, Conor."

"No?" Conor said. "Well, I don't care."

"You're such a dick sometimes," Mason said.

"At least I don't think with mine all the time," Conor shot back.

I heard something break against the wall and then laughing.

"How fucking old are you?" Conor said with humour in his voice before asking, "Is Miss Last Night still asleep upstairs?"

"I like the ones that come down and make us pancakes," Rian said. "Is this one going to make us pancakes?"

"How am I supposed to know?" Mason laughed. "It's a miracle if I even remember their names."

"One of them made a smile in the pancake," Rian said. I could hear that there was a smile on his lips. "That was nice."

"Susan," Mason said.

"Sally," Conor said.

"I wonder what else you could draw on a pancake," Rian said. "Do we have flour?"

"Ask Susan," Mason laughed.

"Sally," Conor corrected.

"Oh, hey, I almost forgot," Mason said. "Someone called earlier about coming in this afternoon. Wanted something small, but still."

I could just make out Conor's huff of irritation. "How many times have I asked you to put all the messages on the board? It can't be that hard."

"Look," Mason said. "Susan can really do wonders for that stick up your ass, Conor. I can give her a call right now."

"Sally," was all Conor said before Rian shouted, "Hey, how do you make pancakes?"

A realisation hit me at that exact moment. My smile, which I had held the entire time I'd been eavesdropping on the conversation, fell. My fingertips slipped from the door as I stepped back from it. The warmth disappeared from my body and the harsh wind suddenly found every weak spot: at the frayed collar of my jacket, beneath the oversized waistline, between the gap of my threadbare sweater and the top of my jeans. I shivered, arms coming to wrap around myself. I glanced around me and the sky seemed greyer, the trash bins fuller, the ground dirtier.

How quickly they had moved on from me. How quickly I had been dropped from the conversation, forgotten out in the cold alleyway. I knew for certain that I would not be brought up again that day. Conor had won and Mason and Rian had accepted that. They'd chosen him over me, because of course they would.

They were a family.

I was not a part of it.

I think that's why the cold felt colder now. I had felt, if only for a little while, true warmth. It had been so nice inside Dublin Ink. The old worn-in furniture. The soft lampshades. The buzz of the broken neon sign. Mason and Rian on either side of me. The tools laid out. All their promises to teach me this, teach me that. Who knew, maybe I'd even make something out of it. I could be a tattoo artist. In those little warm moments, I was sure I could have been anything.

I decided that it was worse to grab onto something that would be taken away than to never have held it in the first place. Better, really, to not grab ahold in the first place.

I thought that Conor was keeping it secret that I had robbed

Dublin Ink to protect me. But I was wrong. He hadn't told them because it hadn't mattered. In his mind, he had already moved on. Conor was done with me. And now so were Mason and Rian.

I knelt beside my backpack with a mixture of anger and hurt in my heart. Anger at Conor, because he was cruel and judgmental and cold. Anger at myself for not seeing it from the start. Anger at myself for letting myself be hurt by it. Why, why did I keep making the same mistake over and over again? Why did I always stop to find beauty where there was none? Why did I stop every time when I should have run?

It happened like it always happened. I was conscious of the cans in my hands, the cold of the metal biting my skin. I was conscious of the wall as I brushed my fingertips against it, feeling, it seemed, for its heartbeat. I was conscious of the tightness in my chest: tight with emotions that thrashed and tore. But then I was conscious of nothing more. Something inside of me took over. Something I didn't have control over.

The last thing I remembered thinking before I thought no more was this: Conor had called me a little thief. But he was the one who had stolen something from me.

And worse.

I had let him.

10

CONOR

I never got distracted while working on a tattoo. It was like a sort of trance I entered. The methodical rise and fall of the tattoo gun. The art coming to life beneath my fingertips. Wiping a rag across skin and revealing something new, a literal transformation before my eyes. It was some of the rare times when I didn't have to be Conor Mac Haol, when I didn't have to feel like I was living the wrong life; I could just disappear into the work. I could become no one, absolutely no one.

But then again, never had the sidewalk just outside the parlour's big front window ever been quite so busy.

For not the first time that afternoon, Declan had to jab his finger at my chest to shake me back to the task at hand, me realising stupidly that the low drone in my ears was coming from the gun running in my suspended hand.

"Sorry," I said again, bending back over his ribs on his left side. "What were you saying?"

It was a bad time to be distracted from my work. It wasn't like we got enough clients into the shop to screw up a little bit one here or there. Besides, Declan was another one of those what someone on the outside of our relationship would call a "friend". Add onto that the fact that this "friend", despite falling about a head shy of me, somehow had packed on about twenty more pounds of muscle. I supposed it was common sense to keep the world's number one MMA fighter as contented as possible. Even as I tried to focus once more on the scrawling cursive "G" design, I found my eyes trailing up toward the windows as a pair of college-aged girls passed by with Starbucks coffees and Gucci backpacks. How was I supposed to focus when suddenly the suburbs were invading?

Curious, I was leaning my head to try and spy more of them when a pain burst in my arm. I hissed in pain and rubbed at the spot where Declan had punched me. I gave him an incredulous look through watering eyes.

"You still weren't listening," he said with a disinterested shrug.

"I heard you," I grumbled. "But I'm still not taking your money."

This earned me somehow another punch to the arm. In exactly the same spot so it hurt even more than the first. Declan wasn't the best for no reason.

"I said I heard you!"

I raised a threatening fist of my own. I didn't have anywhere near the talent or the strength of Declan, but I trained with him at his own gym and I could get a hit or two in before he took me down. Or at least, I thought I stood a chance to.

"I know," Declan said, grinning at me. "That was for being an asshole. I'm rolling in more money than I know what to do with. You might as well take some before my wife does."

He laughed, but I saw that there was something lingering behind his eyes.

"Should I stop?" I asked, glancing down at the half finished initial of his new wife, Giselle, the international supermodel.

"I'm only kidding, you dickwad," Declan said. "Things are great."

I couldn't claim to be particularly attuned to others' emotions, but even I noticed how Declan avoided my eye as he said this, how he picked at the stitching at the edge of the leather tattoo chair, how he changed the subject the first chance he got.

"At least let me pay you for the cost of the tattoo," he said. "I can't take no for an answer on that."

I tugged my attention away from a cab that had pulled up outside the shop, though it was more than difficult as four people piled out, checking their phones and pointing down the street. At this rate, Declan's tattoo was going to take all fucking afternoon.

"Declan," I said, "you know I can't take your money. We're friends."

"Yeah, and as your friend, I want to help," Declan said. "I mean, you clearly need it. Goddammit!"

"Sorry," I mumbled, wiping away a bead of blood from his side. "Did that hurt?"

"You did that on purpose!" Declan shouted.

I gave him a level gaze.

"It's a tattoo," I said, waving the gun for him to see.

Declan narrowed his eyes at me in suspicion, but then settled back into position, shaking his head.

"You fucker," he muttered and after a few quiet moments as I worked added, "Alright, how about this? How about you let me promote the shop? Eh? Perfect solution between friends!"

Despite sensing even more movement on the curb outside Dublin Ink, I remained focused on the tattoo. Declan, who had clearly expected a quick approval from me, flicked my forehead.

"Hey!" he said loudly.

I pushed back slightly on my stool and drew a hand over my hair.

"Really," I said, "you don't have to worry about it. It's on me. A wedding gift or whatever. I'm not going to use you like that. You've got enough bloodsuckers around you as it is."

"What's that supposed to mean?" Declan shot back, his rather infamous temper flaring up.

I held up my hands.

"If that meant something to you, it's got nothing to do with what I said," I told him.

He covered his outburst with more loud laughter.

"What does it matter?" he said. "I'm on top of the fucking world right now. Hot wife. Number one title. Big fucking mansion. What more could I want?"

I didn't respond. I felt Declan's eyes on me. But I was too preoccupied again with the window.

"You know," he said at last, wagging a finger at me. "For a man who wants to save his business, you sure do a lot not to save your business."

But I barely heard him.

"Hey, give me a second, would you?" I asked, though I was already off the stool on my feet.

"Well, sure, Conor ol' boy," Declan replied, craning his neck to watch me as I stalked past his chair. "What more do I have to do with my day than lie here in agony waiting for you to go and satisfy a whim for God knows how long?"

I waved my hand back at him distractedly and mumbled "thanks" before slipping out the door.

I heard Declan call out, "Have I told you you're a jackass yet?" before the door closed behind me.

On the sidewalk, a girl nearly collided with me because she was so preoccupied checking her lipstick in a little compact mirror she held directly in front of her face.

"Watch it," I growled.

"Are you going to let him talk to me that way, Bobby?" the girl whined to the guy trailing behind her, who I could only assume was her boyfriend.

Bobby took one look at me, his chin rising, rising, rising, and quickly grabbed ahold of his lady friend's arm to drag her away. I walked with my hands stuffed irritably into my pockets, collar turned up against the wind and whatever further bullshite was coming for me farther down the street.

I heard the crowd around the side of the building before I saw them. Normally the only thing you heard from the alley on the side of Dublin Ink was the occasional breaking of glass, a drunken shout or two from the times of noon to 6 a.m., and every so often the thud of a rookie police officer's chasing foot-steps, always wearing out his bright-eyed optimism for how he was going to "clean up the neighbourhood".

I was certainly not accustomed to hearing anything resem-bling giggles, the click of heels (even the hookers around these parts didn't bother given their clientele), and such ridiculous things as "okay, and now a portrait", "did you get the good side of my face?", and "can you see my highlighter?"

I practically recoiled in disgust when I finally rounded the corner behind Bobby the Bitch and his lovely lady and found a crowd of phone-raising, scarf-wearing, mascara-applying, hip-popping, bright-white-teeth-smiling, fake-laughing, Instagram-posing hipsters. They were everywhere, truly this decade's most indestructible cockroach.

And now Dublin Ink had an infestation.

I barrelled through the lot of them, not giving a damn about their "hey, there's a line", their "um, I was next" and their "dude, not cool" complaints. My elbows flew and if it knocked some-one's lip filler loose, then they could get in the long line of people that wanted to collect money from me.

Pushing to the front, I found myself standing before some-thing that didn't exist for miles in any given direction: street art. This neighbourhood had plenty of gang tags, plenty of hasty scribbles from bored teenagers, plenty of bodily fluids splashed indiscreetly against brick walls.

It did not have anything that could even generously be awarded the title of "art". And yet, like a yellow dandelion between the cracks in the concrete, there was art. There was something truly beautiful.

It was a big, ominous-looking safe of deep blacks and harsh greys and inside was a red heart. It was the red heart that was most incredible. Somehow it seemed to pulse. Somehow it seemed alive. You could see the outline of the bricks through the paint and yet you were somehow convinced that it needed freeing, the bright, little red heart. Written atop the piece in a looping cursive were two words: Little Thief.

The style was raw, distinctive, but untrained, unrestrained even. It was clearly the work of an amateur, but an amateur with obvious talent. I really had no doubt who the artist was, but those two words, bold and daring and seemingly calling out to me specifically in the crowd, sealed the answer in my mind.

A girl had just finished having her picture taken and another one immediately took her place, posing as if she were trying to pry open the safe, as if she were trying to reach in for the special heart behind those bars. I watched her twist her head this way and that at the command of whoever was behind her phone. Behind me two girls were chatting in low, excited voices.

"You know, there's the tattoo place right next door," one said. "I bet they could do this as a tattoo."

"A tattoo! Your mom would kill you."

"Yeah, but she doesn't have to know."

I whipped around and they both shrank back from the intensity of my glare.

"They're not taking on new clients," I said.

"Okay," they both stammered, practically clutching at each other in fear. And people said I wasn't charming.

Without another word, I shouldered my way back through the crowd, all thronging forward, pushing and shoving for their turn. The safe and the heart and the two words "Little Thief" would be put on social media and shared and tagged and more people would show up.

The brats would knock on the door of Dublin Ink, stick their pimply faces inside, ask meekly if they could get "what's outside" on their hip, on their thigh, on their ankle. But the art didn't mean anything to them. It was just a pretty, trendy thing to shock their parents with, arouse their horny boyfriends with. The art would flare up in popularity and burn out as it always did and no one would care about it the way I did. It would never mean to them what it meant to me. And I couldn't stand it. I couldn't fucking stand it.

A little line of young people followed me timidly like they were ducklings and I was their fucking mother.

Inside Dublin Ink, Mason and Rian were both talking with girls who were raising their sweaters or tugging down the collars of their button-down shirts, pointing excitedly.

"Out!" I said, holding open the door. "Out, out, out."

Mason and Rian began to protest, but I spoke over them.

"Sorry, loves, we're closed."

Mason jotted down his number for one of the girls, but I snatched it from her fingerless gloves on the way out. I slammed the door and switched off the "Open" sign and drew the drapes.

Declan was grinning at me from the tattoo chair when I turned around.

"A private session," he said. "Lucky me."

11

AURNIA

I returned to Dublin Ink the next day because the social media account that I set up for them was blowing up. Because the art that I graffitied in the side alley was clearly drawing people to the parlour, despite the wretched location. I thought I had done enough to prove that I could earn my spot amongst the boys, that I was worthy of being a part of what they were doing.

The second I stepped inside the parlour with a smug grin on my face and a skip in my step, I should have known that I was wrong. Terribly, terribly wrong.

The little bell above the door clanged. Conor, who had been pacing back and forth with stooped shoulders and a tight jaw, whipped around to face me. His nostrils widened and constricted as he breathed noisily. His eyes were dark, his brows low and knitted together.

I tried to keep my smile on my face as I walked slowly past Conor's rapidly rising and falling chest and took a seat on the couch. I forced myself to try to look relaxed, though every muscle in my body was held tense.

"So I'm guessing you saw the art," I said as he glared down at me. "Aaaand I'm guessing that you really, really loved it."

Conor said nothing still.

I tugged up the corners of my lips a little further and gave a little modest bow of my head. "You're welcome."

Out of the corner of my eye, I spotted Rian entering the room with a sketchpad under his arm. When he saw Conor—more importantly, when he saw *me*—he quickly retreated. I heard doors closing upstairs. Mason and Miss Last Night probably.

Well, the cavalry is not fucking coming this time, Aurnia.

"Look," I said as Conor continued to seethe with silent rage, "you don't have to pay me for anything, okay? Not for the art. Not for the social media expertise. I'm not even asking for a percentage off the top from what you make from all the new clients. We can call it even from the whole hand-in-the-cookie-jar incident, if you know what I mean. I'm not asking for a dime. But I think it would be fair if you taught me how to tattoo."

Conor loomed high above me, his broad shoulders outlined by the flickering pink neon, his eyes hidden in shadows as the afternoon grew dark.

"So should we shake on it?" I asked, extending my hand.

"Do you know what you've done?" Conor asked at last, his voice shaking.

I shrugged my shoulders. "I helped."

"Helped?" Conor spit out with a bitter laugh. "You vandalised my property!"

His voice boomed around us, a harsh contrast with the dollies beneath the fringed lamps and the floral pattern couch that I sat on.

"Vandalised?" I repeated, unable to believe my ears. "Did you say vandalised?"

Conor leaned his head down toward me. "I don't believe I whispered, Aurnia."

I gripped the edge of the couch cushion. I wasn't sure which emotion was winning out: fear or anger. Maybe it was the combination of the two that was making my fingers shake as my nails dug into the old fabric.

"That's my art," I said.

"And that's my wall."

I glared up at him as I laughed. "It's in a fucking alleyway. If there was anything else on it before I got there, it was piss."

"You had no right," Conor said.

"To paint over piss?"

"That's not the point."

I rose to my feet. To my surprise Conor retreated. I studied him curiously for a moment before taking a step closer. When I did, he took a step back. I licked my lips, narrowed my eyes.

"Clearly," I said in a soft voice.

As strange as it sounds, I almost felt that Conor was afraid of me in that moment. He seemed ready to leap back should I lunge forward, even though neither of us had any doubt that he could have his hand around my throat in the blink of an eye. His eyes darted between mine and my feet, as if he didn't want to miss the exact moment that I advanced on him.

"What is that supposed to mean?" Conor asked. "'Clearly'."

"It means," I said, crossing my arms studiously over my chest, "that I don't think this is really about the wall or stupid 'vandalism' or whatever you call it."

"What else would it be about?" Conor growled.

"You tell me." I took a step forward.

Clearly, I read something wrong. I'd pushed things too far. I'd missed some crucial sign along the way. I'd gotten too cocky. Conor, instead of taking a step back to match the one I'd taken forward, closed the distance between us so that when we both took ragged breaths, glaring at one another, our chests brushed one another's. I didn't think he would hurt me. But I was no longer entirely sure.

Instead of attacking each other with words, we seemed ready to attack each other with our bodies. I wondered if he saw what I was thinking about as our angry breaths filled the tattoo parlour.

Him flipping me over in bed. Me slipping free, trying to pin his arms above his head. Him grabbing my waist. I wondered what he would do to me if he did...

Uncomfortable heat bloomed in my cheeks and my lower belly.

"Let me tell you," Conor said, moving his face closer to mine, his hair falling out of his bun, "since you asked. It's about me wanting you gone and you not being gone. It's about me telling you not to come back and you coming back. It's about me not wanting to see you, think about you, be reminded of you and you painting a goddamn giant fucking reminder on the side of my fucking business."

"What did I do to you?" I asked.

"You robbed my—"

"Bullshite," I said, clearly taking Conor by surprise.

"Children shouldn't speak like that."

"I'm not a child," I spat out. Hadn't been for a long time. "What did I do to you that was so terrible?"

His eyes searched mine before inflaming with even more anger. "You vandal—"

"*Bullshite.*"

I jerked my chin up at Conor defiantly. I could see in the tension of his shoulders that he wanted to grab me, to pin me against the wall again. What did I say to make him hate me?

"What?" I prodded. "What could I possibly have done? What horrible, unforgivable sin have I committed that has doomed me in your holier-than-thou eyes, Conor? What? Tell me what!"

"You came back!" Conor roared.

I shook like he had wrenched me back and forth like a child's ragdoll. Conor whipped around and punched a tattoo chair. It teetered, fell. The crash shook the floor beneath my feet.

"That was it," he said, not turning back around to face me. His shoulders were slumped, his hands hanging loosely, defeatedly. "That was all you had to do, Aurnia."

He was silent for a moment. I continued to quiver in his long dark shadow that swallowed me whole.

"But that was more than enough," he said softly. "Believe me."

"I..." Emotion was thick in my throat as I forced the words. "I don't understand."

"It's not for you to understand." He knelt and slowly returned the chair to its standing position. "You're far too young to understand."

Conor gripped the armrest of the chair, gripped it like he would fall otherwise. I stepped toward him. I wasn't sure whether he heard my footsteps or not. I wasn't sure he would have allowed me to get so close if he had.

"Why can't I be here?" I asked, standing just behind him.

He was so tall, so big. I wasn't sure I could reach all the way around him. Not even if he took me into his arms.

"Why can't I be here with you?" I asked, brushing my fingers against his.

Conor jerked back his hand and he had me by the collar of my jacket before I knew it.

"Because you're a thief," he said, and I knew I'd lost him yet again. "Because you have no respect for my property. No respect for authority."

I swatted at his arm, dug my heels in, tried to yank back, but it was like trying to stop a roaring wave. I was never going to win on physical strength alone. Conor would forcibly drag me out again and again until my ass was black and blue and the door was falling off its hinges. We were halfway across the tattoo shop and I knew I was losing my chance with every step.

I wasn't even sure I was fully aware of what I was doing. All I knew was that I didn't want to leave. All I knew was that I wanted to be let in. *Needed* to be let in.

I grabbed the back of Conor's neck with both hands and crashed my lips against his. They were warm and oh so much softer than I imagined they would be. He tasted of whiskey, sharp and fiery, intoxicating my tongue. Intoxicating my blood. I wanted more.

I tugged myself closer, only vaguely aware that his hand had fallen off the back of my collar. He stilled against me. But he didn't push me away. He *didn't* push me away. In fact, I swear his lips parted ever so slightly. He leaned into me a touch.

For some reason, in my kiss-drunk brain this was permission. Acceptance. I pressed my breasts against his chest, my hard nipples aching at the pressure. I couldn't help the moan that escaped me as I suckled his thick bottom lip.

Perhaps it was the noise I made, deep, throaty and womanly. Perhaps it was the desperate way I clawed at him, trying to get closer, trying to dig myself into him so that he could never get me out. Or perhaps my pleading tongue that I swiped against his mouth like a plea.

Whatever it was, it unfroze him. He grabbed my shoulders. For a second, I thought it was to pull me closer, or to push me up against a wall. To have his way with me.

Instead he pushed me away. Away from him.

"What..." he stuttered. "What the hell, Aurnia?"

I said nothing. My turn to freeze as the consequences of my

actions washed over me like ice water. Had I imagined his reaction? Mistaken the lust-laced tension between us?

Conor shook his head, snorted in unamused laughter. But his eyes were fixed on mine. No, he wanted me. There was hunger in his eyes that he couldn't hide. But in them was also...fear.

His hands snatched off my shoulders as if I'd burned him. "Don't do that again," he growled.

"But you kiss—"

"*Don't.*"

"Why not?" I dared to ask.

The tense moments passed, one shaky breath after another. When Conor stepped up to me my breath hitched. When he moved his face toward mine, I stopped breathing.

He was going to kiss me again. He'd realised there was no reason *why not.* Or perhaps decided he didn't care.

My eyes fluttered closed but shot open when his lips brushed my cheek on their way to my ear.

"You just don't get it, do you?"

Without warning, he was dragging me back toward the door, this time he held me at arm's length, as far as he could hold me away from him. I cursed at him as I had done before. I swatted at him as I had done before. I kicked and thrashed and fought back as I had all done before.

One thing was certain: something had to give. We couldn't keep doing this, trapped in this damned cycle. Neither of us getting what we wanted. Neither of us satisfied. He could deny the chemistry between us all he wanted, but it didn't stop the air from crackling whenever we were in the same room. We were going to drive ourselves insane otherwise.

Something had to give.

One more thing was certain: it wasn't going to be me.

12

CONOR

*H*er soft lips on mine had taken me by surprise. Her insistent hands at the back of my neck. But even more so was how my body had reacted. A savage need, a roaring hunger flared to life in me like the devil's firepit. The moan that'd come out of her, the siren's call she had breathed into my mouth had almost been my undoing. It sounded like a woman's moan and for a split second I had forgotten I was about to take advantage of a girl.

My hands were grabbing her shoulders to pull her closer before I knew what I was doing. It was only the feel of her tiny shoulders in my large hands, those fragile bird-like bones, that had reminded me that this innocent child was not mine to ruin. That if I gave in, it'd be a sin I could never wash off.

It had taken every single ounce of willpower to push her away. To break the spell. Even then when she asked *why not?*, I couldn't answer. I was afraid she'd tear holes in whatever defence I spun as if they were mere spider webs. Afraid she'd find a crack in my armour.

It was only a matter of time until she'd weaken me beyond salvation, till I crumbled beneath her relentlessness. She was like a wave that broke and broke and broke against a stone wall; it was only a matter of time before it gave way. I was not sure I'd survive another kiss.

I dragged her across the parlour, determined to send her fleeing from Dublin Ink for a final time.

I should have known that something was going to stop me. Luck had never been on my side.

My fingertips stretched toward the door, brushing against the well-worn brass handle. I was so close to wrapping my hand around it.

The door swung open on its own accord and I had only a half second to jump back, to release Aurnia, to push her away and smile, smile, smile! when I saw who it was.

"Diarmuid!" I stepped even farther away from Aurnia. "Hey there, you. How's it going? It's been a while."

Diarmuid halted inside the shop, his eyes narrowed in suspicion as he glanced between Aurnia and me.

"You don't smile," he said warily as he walked between the two of us.

With his back turned, I glared at Aurnia and jabbed my fingers at my lips. Her victorious little grin made me want to wring her neck. I was about to hiss a threat when Diarmuid suddenly glanced back over his shoulder halfway toward the kitchen in the back.

"You *definitely* don't smile."

Aurnia stepped forward, hands politely linked behind her back as she rocked back and forth on her heels like goddamn Dorothy. Only I could see the middle finger she raised as she said, "He's just really happy about all that I've done for the shop so far."

Diarmuid raised a surprised eyebrow. "Is that so?" he asked. "So things are going well?"

He disappeared into the kitchen and I shook Aurnia by the arm.

"No funny business," I hissed as water ran in the kitchen.

Aurnia blinked innocently up at me and whispered, "I have no idea what you're talking about, Mr Mac Haol."

"Well?" Diarmuid asked as he returned to the living room with a glass of water. He glanced over some of Mason's work at his desk before looking up at me. "Aurnia's been behaving herself?"

I was in a shite position and I knew it. Worse, Aurnia knew it. I could feel her smile on me as I scrambled for a way out of this. If I told Diarmuid the truth, that Aurnia had not only tried to rob me, but had then gone on to vandalise my property, she would be taken out of my life. That would certainly solve one problem: the one being that she was far too young and I was far too drawn to her.

Shite. If he knew that she'd kissed me not two minutes ago...that I had been close to kissing her back...that I had *wanted* to kiss her back. That I wanted more. He'd definitely remove her. I'd never see her again. I might never see *him* again.

It would also send her further into the system, certainly to juvie at the very least.

I couldn't do that. Not even to her. Especially not to her.

My only option was to lie. This is what Aurnia was expecting, exactly what she was hoping for. I knew I was walking into a trap, but it seemed that there was no alternative.

"Things have been...alright," I tried.

Aurnia sat on the edge of the couch, one leg crossed primly over the other. She drummed her fingertips against her knee as she watched me, clearly enjoying herself.

"No major complaints," I added in a grumble.

"Well, that at least sounds more like you," Diarmuid

laughed. "When I came in and saw you grinning like an idiot, I thought surely something must be terribly wrong."

"Nothing's wrong," I quickly said before just as quickly adding, "Not that anything is terribly right either. Things are just..."

"Alright?" Diarmuid supplied.

I shrugged my shoulders.

Diarmuid drew up a stool and lowered himself onto it as he pulled a legal pad from his leather satchel. He chewed the lid from a pen. "Well, since we're still working out the kinks of the Young Offenders Program, I like to drop by at the beginning to get a sense of how things are going."

"I just said they're fine," I said, my irritability rising.

I could feel myself getting drawn into something I didn't want to get drawn into. Aurnia herself was already a vortex. I didn't need the state throwing me deeper into her depths.

Diarmuid gave me a pointed stare and said, "I kind of like to bring more to my supervisors than 'fine'."

"Really fine," I grumbled.

Diarmuid ignored me and tapped his pen against the pad of paper.

"Now, Aurnia was saying that she's already helped out," he said, "can you tell me how?"

"I painted some art on the side alley," Aurnia jumped in. "And just before you came in, Conor was telling me how much he loved it."

"That's fantastic," Diarmuid said, jotting down notes.

Aurnia fixed her mischievous eyes on me. "He said that he loved the initiative that I took in making something beautiful out of such an ugly space. He said that I showed a lot of promise as an artist. He said vandals used to come and tag the wall, but that mine was nothing at all like that. Vandalism, I mean."

Diarmuid looked up at me. "You didn't ask her to do that?"

"No."

"Well, wonderful job, Aurnia," Diarmuid said, returning to his notes. I shot Aurnia a glare when he wasn't looking. "That does show initiative. Conor was right."

Aurnia beamed.

I repressed a growl.

"Conor *was* right," she said.

Hidden inside my pockets, my fingernails dug into my palms. "Though we also discussed, just before you came in, Diarmuid, that I am Aurnia's supervisor. And in future, she needs to run these things by me. Because my word is final regarding the shop."

Aurnia narrowed her eyes at me.

It was my turn to grin when Diarmuid nodded along. "Yes, yes, very good," he said. "You *do* need proper boundaries, Aurnia."

"Oh, I agree completely," my little thief said through clenched teeth, lying not coming as easily as I might have expected from her.

Then again, maybe it was all a bluff for my sake.

A second later she turned toward Diarmuid. "That's why I made sure to ask Conor about the social media account for Dublin Ink."

I was about to blurt out "Like fuck you did", but I refused to be a child just because Aurnia was one.

Diarmuid looked at me, clearly waiting for my response.

I grumbled, "Everyone has been saying that we needed a social media presence."

"See!" Diarmuid said, excitedly slapping the legal pad against his knee. "See, this is exactly the kind of benefits I'm trying to sell people on for the Young Offenders Program. Mutual gain for the community. Symbiotic growth. This is great to hear, absolutely great to hear."

"And Conor promised to teach me how to tattoo," Aurnia said, the little opportunist.

"Conor, how generous of you," Diarmuid said, writing this down as well.

Aurnia was practically squirming on the couch, clearly pleased that she'd won. I would have found it endearing had I not been so pissed.

"Now, now, Aurnia," I said, fully intending to rain on her fucking parade, "remember what we said you had to do first."

Diarmuid glanced up as Aurnia's smile fell. I pulled my hand out of my pocket as I began to list things.

"You'll need to sweep up the floor every night," I said, moving a few steps closer to her. "You'll need to clean the bathrooms, of course. There's the trash bins to be emptied, the storeroom that needs organising, the kitchen that needs restocking. You'll need to make teas and coffees for our customers. And for us, of course."

Aurnia couldn't flinch away as I squeezed her shoulder, a friendly pat.

Just like I couldn't say that she robbed me, vandalised my place, and drove me fucking crazy with sinful lust.

"Of course," she said. "You said if I did all those things that you would teach me to tattoo."

I tsked her and squeezed her shoulder a little harder. "I think you're forgetting a little something."

Aurnia faked trying to remember, her finger tapping on her chin. She was probably used to people eating up whatever she served, but I was a more discerning customer. As Diarmuid watched her, she slowly shook her head.

"No," she said, smiling sweetly (an act!), "no, I think that's all we agreed to."

"You don't remember anything about not talking during working hours?"

"Nope," she said.

"Are you *sure*?"

She hid a wince as I dug my thumb against her collarbone.

"Positive," she said.

I patted her, hard, on the back and she coughed.

Her eyes were on me as I wandered toward the cash register. I drummed my fingers on it, a bluff to reveal her indiscretion unless she played along. She glared at me before smiling at Diarmuid who had been watching the two of us with rising suspicion. I would have to be more careful.

"Ah, yes," Aurnia said, with obvious resentment in her voice. "Something is coming back to me about keeping quiet while you guys are working."

"I believe it was 'total silence'."

Her glare and mine battled each other over Diarmuid's head, which swivelled back and forth.

"But boss," Aurnia said, her pink lips perfectly pursed, "how am I supposed to ask what menial, demeaning task I'm to do next if I can't talk?"

I matched her plastic smile and gestured toward the desks. "There's pen and paper at your service, my dear. You *can* write?"

Diarmuid stood, his legal pad held at his side. "Is everything really alright here? Because I'm getting the sense that there's some...*tension*."

I laughed and Aurnia laughed.

I held out my arm and she bounded to my side like a little doe. I'd had her in my grasp more than a few times at that point, but I'd never held her close like that, her ribs expanding and constricting against mine, the heat of her body at my side, her head leaning against my chest. My fingers came to rest on her elbow, as sharp as a knife point, as fragile as a bird's bones. I squeezed her firmly, though gently.

How easily I could break her. I had been so worried about

ruining her life that I hadn't considered how with one wrong violent outburst I could end it.

"We're buddies," Aurnia lied.

"Bestest buddies," I confirmed, signing my one-way ticket to hell.

"I mean," Aurnia continued, "I couldn't have landed in a better pair of hands, really. I mean, I really feel like Mr Mac Haol has got a good, firm grasp on *me*; on who I could be."

Diarmuid eyed the two of us.

Why did I feel so fucking guilty? I hadn't done anything. I mean, I had *stopped* myself from doing anything. Weren't my actions enough? Regardless of what I wanted? Needed. Craved.

It was really *his* fault that I was standing there with Aurnia's hair gathering static electricity from my leather jacket, her scent rising to my nose like a fragrant rose. If he hadn't decided to show up unannounced like this, Aurnia would be kicked out once more, this time for good.

"Damn it," Diarmuid said, dropping his chin. "Damn it."

He knew. He figured it out. A part of me was relieved. He'd sensed that there was something inappropriate going on and he was going to take Aurnia away. The city couldn't have that kind of scandal on its hands. Juveniles going for a chance to get their lives straightened out and instead getting taken advantage of by some monstrous older man.

It was for the best. My self-control could only hold out that much longer anyway. Maybe I would have gotten rid of Aurnia on my own. Or maybe she would have come back as she'd done again and again.

This was for the best. Aurnia could live the life she was meant to without me throwing it on its head. I could move on from her in peace. Once I removed that goddamn graffiti, of course.

"I knew I should have brought my camera," Diarmuid said,

snapping his fingers. "The board would love to see stuff like this."

No, I thought, pushing the dirty thoughts from my mind of crumpled sheets, of Aurnia's naked body upon them. No, the board most certainly would *not* love to see *that*.

"Warms the heart," Diarmuid said.

It warms something...certainly not my heart.

I shook my head, horrified at my thoughts.

"Here," Diarmuid said, tucking his legal pad beneath his arm and pulling out his phone. "The camera's not great, but it'll do."

"Jaysus..." I muttered through clenched teeth as I forced a smile.

Diarmuid lowered his phone. "What's that?"

"Nothing," I said quickly, tugging in Aurnia so it would end sooner. "Just do what you need to do already."

Diarmuid laughed and fiddled with the phone.

"Come on already," I mumbled.

It was too much. Too much of Aurnia. Too much of her too close. Too much of her scent. Too much of the shape of her body. Too much of *her*. The point was to get farther away from her.

Now I had committed to heart every curve.

"Say, 'Dublin Ink!'" Diarmuid said.

Aurnia shouted it merrily and squeezed me tight.

"We're going to have so much fun together, aren't we?" she asked, smirking up at me.

I was going to murder her.

13

AURNIA

*R*ian flipped a page in my portfolio and said something I didn't hear.

I really should have been more grateful for his help with my art. He was the one who mentioned looking over my portfolio in the first place.

I'd frowned and asked, "Portfolio?"

He had been kind enough not to burst out laughing.

Art for me had always been a way to escape, a way to process my emotion, a way to selfishly make someone else feel what I was feeling, to unload some of my burden, as ridiculous as it sounded. I'd never considered art as a future or a career (a poor paying one at that). Hell, I hardly even thought of it as a hobby. It was just...part of me.

But Rian explained that a portfolio was crucial in high-lighting my work for the right people. He said, "If someone has fifteen seconds to give you, what would you want to show him?"

I'd took his advice one night when the house was quiet and taped some photos of my street art onto an old school notebook after tearing out three half-hearted pages about King Lear (mostly just doodles). It was embarrassing next to Rian's, which was professional printed and bound, all glossy photos and stylish font.

Still, he took my portfolio into his hands without a trace of mockery. He lowered himself onto the stool beside where I sat perched on the edge of his desk and opened the first page with a studious eye, all business, taking me more seriously than I ever took myself.

I should have appreciated that more. I should have given him my attention as he tapped this photo or that. I should have at least *tried* to listen to what he had to say—the invaluable advice and critique he was offering up for free.

But I had to devote my eyes, my ears, my anger and my lust and my frustration and my desire on the asshole.

Conor was across the parlour, just about as far away as he could get. I'd never caught him in the act, but I swore day by day he was inching his tattoo station farther and farther into the corner of the living room. It was the most isolated part of the shop and the place where I had the least reason to go to except for emptying his wastebasket and sweeping the pencil shavings and eraser bits from his drawing desk at the end of the night, a time where he made absolutely sure to be anywhere else.

His back was to me as he bent over a client—a client, I might add, who was brought in to Dublin Ink because of *me* and *my* art and *my* social media posting (not that I'd ever in a million years get a thanks from him). This, I guessed, was also a strategic move to avoid me even further.

When I first arrived at the shop, his stool was on the opposite side of the tattoo chair, presumably so he could see the rest of the work area, greet (if a scowl and a grumbled "what?" can be considered a greeting) anyone coming through the front door, and keep an eye on Mason if there was a lady present and Rian if there was a kettle on the hotplate. But now whenever the others worked or someone entered or Mason groped or Rian, in one of his distant places, didn't pay attention, all they saw was Conor's wide shoulders, the ripple of his muscles beneath his thin charcoal-grey t-shirt, the little hairs at the base of his neck that wouldn't be drawn into his daily bun, little hairs I imagined sometimes brushing my pinkie along.

Conor would deny consciously turning his back, I was sure, but I was also sure that this pointed move was absolutely because of me.

Rian was gesturing all over the page of the picture I took of my work outside the damned jewellery store and his lips were moving a mile a minute, but it was like he was on mute. I forced my attention away from Conor, dragged it away like a misbehaving child, and focused as best I could on Rian's mouth. I even inclined my ear for a moment or two as if that was the problem. But like some sort of voodoo I blinked and found my face was turned in Conor's direction.

I chewed at my fingernails as I watched him work. I squinted at him like I could somehow force him through the intensity of my gaze to turn around. I squirmed impatiently. I used every ounce of willpower inside of me not to get up and start pacing back and forth as he continued with a laudable effort and unwavering consistency to completely and utterly ignore me.

To put it plainly: he was driving me fucking nuts.

In the rare moments where he did give me an iota of attention it was always and without fail pure disdain. One morning I came in and found him waiting on the middle rung of a ladder. The second I walked in the door he climbed to the top and began, with his muscular arms stretched high above him, shirt riding up his tattooed back, to install a security camera.

"Subtle," I grumbled as I snatched up the broom angrily.

Conor's only reply was, "Crime's gone up in the neighbourhood recently."

If I lingered too close to his drawing desk while he was

sketching out tattoos, he would raise his eyes angrily. If I didn't back up in what he considered an appropriate amount of time, he would stalk toward me with his pencil held at his side like a spear.

A few times, after completing his Wicked Stepmother-worthy list of menial, demeaning tasks, I dared to ask him if he might have time to start teaching me to tattoo like he promised in front of Diarmuid. To these requests, Conor would get up, snatch my jacket and my bag from the hooks on the wallpapered entry, open the door, and smile unkindly as he said, "Definitely tomorrow."

Needless to say, tomorrow never came. If anything, the violence with which he shoved my things at me by the door only increased.

I knew Conor hated me. I hadn't thought that his hatred could actually *increase* with time.

He wouldn't accept tea that I made, he wouldn't sit on the couch if I was there, even perched on the edge with my arms around my knees as I listened to Mason's daily conquest story, he wouldn't even give me a nod hello in the morning unless both the other guys were there in the living room at their desks.

He wanted nothing to do with me at best. He wanted me gone, at worst. And if I'd learned anything in life it was to bet on the worst.

And yet in that moment as I watched him work, I wanted nothing more than for Conor to turn around. To glare at me. To roll his eyes at me. To give an irritated sigh in my direction. But the drone of the tattoo gun continued and his back remained solidly turned away from me. It was then that I picked up something that Rian said.

"What's that?" I asked, turning my face a little too quickly down toward him.

He glanced up at me, just about as startled that I was there listening as I was that he'd been talking this whole time. I supposed that was some sort of consolation for my rudeness: Rian disappeared places, too. I just disappeared into people. Not people. Person. *Him.*

"What? Oh. Um. What did you say?" Rian muttered.

"I was asking what you said," I told him, smiling a little at his slightly unfocused eyes, like he'd just awoken from a dream. "What did you say just then?"

Rian shook his head. I realised I was asking quite a lot of him. I wasn't sure Rian often remembered the day before. He lived from psychedelic moment to psychedelic moment. Usually in his head.

I blushed slightly as I cleared my throat and whispered with a tucked chin, "Um, you said something about Conor."

"Right!" Rian said, snapping his fingers. "Right, Conor. Right. Conor. Conor. Conor."

I almost shushed him. I would have died of embarrassment if Conor knew that I was asking one of his friends about him. I mean, I wanted to know everything about him, but I couldn't just pry around for information. I had to be sneakier than that. My cheeks grew hotter and I whispered, "Yeah, what was it you said?"

Rian drummed his fingers against my photo. Conor thankfully didn't turn around. Not to say he hadn't heard. But at least he was pretending that he hadn't.

"Ah," Rian said at last, "I said this reminds me of Conor's earlier work."

I glanced again toward Conor, toward his broad back, strong and well-defined. For the first time in days, I hoped it would stay facing me, that he wouldn't turn with his angry, fuming eyes. I did my best to keep my voice low so he couldn't hear me, but casual, non-committal if he somehow could.

"Like when he was just starting out?" I asked.

Rian was studying the crying girl, his head tilting this way and that. Almost distractedly, he said, "Yeah. Well, I mean. I guess I don't really know when exactly Conor started working on his art. Or who got him started or whatever. But this reminds me of his style when we were in school together."

As Rian shifted my notebook, turning it at different angles, his focus completely consumed by my art, I realised that he probably wasn't all too aware of what he was saying.

After shooting a look toward Conor's back, I said, "I didn't know that you two went to school together."

Rian was somewhere else and said dreamily, almost as if he was sleepwalking, "Limerick Art School. I needed a cheap place when I enrolled and I kind of got distracted with some things and waited till the very first day of school and I just lucked out that I found Conor who was renting out his one-bedroom. He must have been more strapped for cash than I was because he took the couch in the living room."

"For a whole semester?"

Rian flipped the page of my portfolio and gave a little shrug.

"It wasn't like he was the most dedicated student in the world," he said. "He didn't have this perfect record that was in jeopardy from a few sleepless nights. The guy ditched class all the time. We didn't have many classes together, but I don't remember a time when I saw him there."

I didn't put too much weight into this part of story given that Rian would often come into the parlour, work for several hours, and then ask where I had been all day like I hadn't been literally scooting aside his foot to get to his wastebasket five minutes earlier.

"But he was gone from the apartment all the time," Rian continued, "so he must have been doing something at the school. He showed up to classes at some point, because I would find his art in the dumpster out back when I snooped around for old sneakers or such a time or two. You know, the whole starving artist schtick."

I looked toward Conor for a moment, frowning slightly. "He tossed his classwork?"

"Wouldn't really surprise me all that much if he never even turned it in," Rian said, drumming his chin as he looked at one of my first piece of street art, a messy, hastily done sun. "I like this one."

I don't know why I put that one in at all. I flipped the page for him and pointed at a lady's face morphing into the wind. "This one's better," I said. "Why wouldn't it have surprised you?"

Rian tried to go back to the sun and I stopped him. It was easy enough in the distracted, distant state he was in.

"I don't know," he said. "Because Conor was like that. It was like he was there, but he wasn't there. He never made any friends besides me and honestly, I don't think even that would have happened if we hadn't been roommates. He never socialised with the other art students. Never met up at the coffee shops or the bars after class. He never talked about his professors or his assignments. He'd stay up painting or drawing, but in the morning he'd be gone and the finished work would just be sitting there on the easel or on his desk. Like he'd gone to class and just...I don't know, forgotten it. I mean, the alternative is that he left it behind on purpose. But that doesn't really make sense to me."

Without me realising it Rian had gone back to the sun drawing I hated. I regretted putting it in. I promised to rip it out the moment I got my portfolio back.

Rian was studying it as he said, "Like this. Conor could have done something like this back then."

"And then thrown it away?" I asked.

Rian nodded. "Kind of beautiful if you ask me," he muttered.

I stared at Conor's back. I felt that something was missing

from Rian's story. Pieces that didn't add up. To someone like Rian that was how life was; I don't think he particularly liked when things just "fit". But I could sense something more...something darker...

I was trying to figure it out as Rian continued with his critique of my portfolio when Mason came down, obviously ready for a night on the town. He glanced over Rian's shoulder and gave an approving nod before saying to me, "Hey, you can get out of here, you know? Just because these two losers don't have a life on a Friday night doesn't mean you shouldn't."

I glanced at Rian, but he was absorbed in my art. A glance in Conor's direction revealed no change at all.

"Oh, um, yeah," I said, forcing a smile. "Right. Cool."

I gathered up my jacket and my backpack, checking the whole time whether Conor would look over at me, whether he would invite me to stay where it was warm and safe, whether he would fake the excuse of organising a stupid spice rack or wiping down the tools for the second time that day. But when I said a hesitant goodnight at the door no one answered.

Maybe I was wrong. Maybe Conor didn't hate me. Maybe Conor just didn't care.

14

CONOR

$\mathcal{I}$t was only after Aurnia had gone, I could finally exhale, unwanted desire like fetid air in my lungs.

After Dublin Ink closed, I sank down onto the couch with a glass of whiskey, my nerves near their snapping point.

My eyes burned like I hadn't slept in days—I hadn't, not properly. Not with a certain thief stealing into my dreams. She'd walk right up to me while I was frozen in place, dripping wet in her torn black jeans and oversized jacket, hair fallen over one eye, and stare down at me before straddling me with one leg and then the next.

I was unravelling and I could feel each thread coming undone as the pressure built squarely between my eyebrows.

I had barely a second to catch my breath, when I thought I heard a sound in the back.

I listened for any noise without breathing. My muscles, held tensed all day, were shaking.

There. A light footfall. The rustling of clothing. Someone was moving in the back. Moving in the soft way someone moved when they didn't want to be heard.

I set down the glass of whiskey onto the old floral rug. As

quietly I could, I pushed myself up from the couch. There was a weariness in my body like I'd been back training consistently at Gallagher's Gym. It was the ache of constantly punching, of constantly being punched: pain given, pain taken. And yet in my bloodstream adrenaline coursed as if I'd just taken an injection of it straight to the heart.

I don't know whether it was the dimness of the shop, only a single lamp left illuminated, or whether it was my mental state that sent my thoughts spiralling to such a dark place as I wrapped my fingers around the baseball bat resting in the corner. But I was suddenly certain that it was past coming to get me.

My breathing was ragged in my ear, loud and imposing, but I could hear with almost crystal clarity his laughing words that terrible night, blood between his teeth, blood under his nose, blood pooling in his eyes, *"I'll get you one day, old friend. One day I'll come for you, pal of mine."*

The pain in my leg flared but it was not the kind of pain the rain brought. It was a pain I hadn't felt since that night: fresh pain.

Why not now? I thought as I moved quietly past the darkness of the kitchen, eyes adjusting too slowly. Why not when I was at my weakest because of the girl? What if she was a part of it? What if he had sent her to torment me before he took his revenge? I was bigger now, after all. Stronger now. He'd have to find a way to assert an advantage.

I felt feverish as I inched toward the storeroom, a damp, dark space beneath the stairs we'd converted with shelves and boxes. I felt more mad than scared. I was imagining old enemies. I was getting the past and the present confused. Was I after him, like I'd been that night? Or was he after me? The hallway, narrow and confined, was so dark that I had nothing to tether me to the here and now. Was I still in Mason's grandmother's townhouse? Still in Dublin? Or was I in Limerick? In that godforsaken apartment? With the weak thread of light alone coming from beneath his door as the old springs creaked and moaned?

I gripped the baseball bat tighter as if by holding on a little more firmly, I could keep my grasp of reality. But the truth was Aurnia had unmoored me.

My hand wouldn't stop shaking even when I squeezed it tightly around the handle of the little door beneath the stairs. I tried taking a deep breath, but how could I when there was no air in my lungs? I reminded myself that it might not be him at all. But when I closed my eyes to keep my vision from swaying it was his eyes that I saw, somehow blacker than the darkness around him.

I yanked open the door. Something scurried back against the stack of the day's deliveries. I fumbled for the light with my bat raised.

"You fucker!" I shouted as I tugged on the chain, light flooding the small space.

I was blinded momentarily from the light and if the grey dots in my vision would have remained just a second longer, I would have done something I never would have been able to forgive myself for.

With every ounce of strength in my body, I stopped the bat mere inches from Aurnia's cheek. Her wide, fearful eyes stared at the end of the bat till it dropped from my exhausted hands. It clattered to the floor. I sagged against the doorframe, dragging a hand over my tired face. She and I stared at one another.

She was cowered on her knees, hands still up by her face, fingertips shaking as she looked up at me. She seemed more like a lost child than I'd ever seen her before.

Maybe things would have been different if I'd been able to pull myself together faster. Maybe things would have been different if I'd been able to utter even a single word. Maybe things would have all been alright if I would have just reached out my hand for her, drawn her in close, and held her as we both shivered.

But I was still seeing *him*. Every time I blinked, he was still lunging for me.

I didn't notice until it was too late the dawning of panic in Aurnia's eyes as she recovered first from the ordeal. She lowered her hands. Breathing heavily, she rifled through her backpack before drawing out a small stack of limp, filthy bills from her wallet. She pushed herself up and shoved them against my chest as she passed by me.

"Happy now?" she said angrily. "You've finally caught your little thief."

Her eyes met mine once more, but only for a moment. It wasn't anger that screamed at me from within; it was fear.

The bills fell to the floor and I stood there, still leaning against the doorframe, motionless as I heard her stomping toward the front door. It slammed with a rattle behind her. I still didn't move.

It was then that I noticed the folded-up hoodie in the back, a mock-up of merch Mason had made for Dublin Ink that I'd shot down without even glancing at it. I noticed the little Tesco bag of groceries. A quilt and pillow I'd sworn I'd seen in a guest bedroom upstairs.

I gathered the bills into my hand. Following a hunch, I went to the cash register after switching off the little light, comparing the contents with the receipts. I frowned in confusion.

Aurnia had not stolen a single dime.

So then why had she claimed that she had?

15

AURNIA

I hated Conor. I hated him, I hated him, I hated him. I hated him more than I hated Nick. I hated him more than I hated my father. I hated him more than I'd ever hated anyone else in the whole entire world.

I'd never had a home. I'd never had a place that was safe and warm, a place where I didn't have to check around corners, a place where I didn't have to worry about whether to lock the door.

And I was *fine*. I was totally and perfectly *fine*.

I was surviving. I knew how to handle the druggies that wandered into my bedroom during the middle of the night. I knew how to placate Nick, how to check my father's tongue when he passed out, how to hide food in the kitchen so it wasn't snatched by someone so high they couldn't even read: Not yours, asshole! I had it all figured out. If I needed to get away, the public library was open till six, the McDonald's till eleven, and if it still wasn't safe to return to my father's place, then there was a hotel just up the street that charged by the hour. The school opened their doors at 5 a.m. for the swim team and the guard never checked whether I was still enrolled, at least not when I gave him a toothy smile.

Life was rough, but I was strong. I knew I was strong.

But I wasn't strong anymore and that was why I hated Conor most of all.

After I ran out of Dublin Ink, I huddled in the back of the bus I'd had to sneak onto. I couldn't remember feeling so cold. One Christmas Eve, I'd wandered the streets of Dublin till dawn and hadn't felt nearly as cold. It was only November. I wrapped my arms around myself more tightly, but the shivering only seemed to get worse. The lights on the bus were low, half of them burned out, and I feared every bundled-up mass that stirred near me.

Before, I would have been assured that I could outrun someone who tried to attack me. But my toes had gone numb a long time ago. If someone had cornered me before, I knew just which pocket my mace was in. But I couldn't remember where I'd even last seen my mace. Was it at home? Was it at Dublin Ink? Had I lost it somewhere along the way and hadn't even noticed the familiar weight was gone? Even as a last resort, there had always been the option of going on the attack myself: go for the dick, go for the eyes, go for the dick again. But that fire had dwindled inside me, snuffed out by Conor's big, strong hands.

I didn't want to have to fight. I wanted to be protected. I wanted to be safe. I wanted someone to finally have my back.

I was *weak*.

When the bus dropped me off at the corner just down the street from my father's place, I stood there for a long time. I wanted to think there was another option, but there wasn't. I'd thrown the last of the cash in Conor's face. That had been the price of my pride.

The first time I'd snuck back inside Dublin Ink after leaving,

I told myself it was just that once. And only because I knew Nick had been looking for me.

But then it happened again.

Dublin Ink was warm. It was quiet. No one would come for me. So of course it kept happening. And kept happening. I hadn't been home all week. I was actually sleeping.

But it was only a matter of time before someone came for me, before someone found me out.

It was all my worst fears realised when Conor threw open the door with a bellowing voice, flipped on the lights, and attacked me before I had a chance to get away. It might have been a different location, but it was all the same. It was everything I'd ever feared.

I'd dared to think that I could have a home at Dublin Ink. That the boys, in some twisted way, could be a family for me. At last.

This was my punishment for daring. For *hoping*.

I'd tested fate and fate threw me right back on my ass. The only problem this time was I'd lost the ability to get back up.

I forced my steps toward the house. I considered the neighbour's yard for a moment; there was a shed, half collapsed and fully stuffed with rusted tools, but probably dry enough, should it rain.

But there were the dogs and their gnashing teeth at the chain-link fence. Whatever evils lurked in the shadowy corners of my father's house couldn't be worse than that, could they? Nick couldn't be worse than that, could he?

As I neared the house it was a relief to see that at least a small part of the survivor in me remained after Dublin Ink, after the toxic allure of Conor Mac Haol: I remembered at the last moment not to go to the front door.

The front door meant shoving aside someone passed out against it. The front door meant tiptoeing over tripping strangers in rags. The front door meant noise and visibility and being outnumbered. Most of all, it meant a long, dangerous path to my bedroom.

Better to go through my bedroom window.

You would think that having a perpetually broken window that anyone at all wandering the trash-lined streets at night could get through would lead to sleepless nights. That would be the case if the thing you feared the most wasn't already inside the house. If he didn't already have a perfectly functioning key.

It was easy enough climbing up to the window. There were more than enough empty beer bottle crates to craft tidy little steps. Sure, that made it easier for an intruder, too, but more importantly, if I needed to escape in the middle of the night, I didn't have to worry about a broken ankle slowing me down when I ran. Priorities, am I right?

The latch on the window had never worked as long as I could remember. Lifting the window normally wasn't any difficulty. But that night my muscles seemed to fail me. I was more aware than ever that I was a small, young girl. Before Dublin Ink hung the seductive mirage of safety before my eyes, I could see something more than the frail little thing in the mirror each morning. I saw the clever eyes instead of the prominence of my collarbones. I saw the deftness of my fingers instead of the thinness of my wrists. I saw a heart that wanted more, that was going to get more, instead of a chest that flinched at every noise down the hallway.

Reality faced me like a mirror in the dirty pane of glass. I struggled with gritted teeth to get my arms above my head.

As I raised the window, I heard noise from inside the house. There was the steady drone of thudding music from the basement. Sometimes it shook my bed at night; sometimes it was low enough that I thought it was just me who was shivering. There were voices from the living room, too. Loud and laughing:

not a good sign. It was better when my father's "guests" were too out of it to do more than slump over and drool on themselves. They were dangerous when they thought they were capable of making conscious decisions.

On nights like these it was most important not to make a sound, not alert a single soul to my presence in the house. It said everything in the world about the state I was in that for the first time in my life I knocked over my lamp from the bedside table when climbing down into my room.

I felt the very moment my toe connected with the battered shade. I felt it and I knew. I whipped around when I landed, already too loud, on the carpet and lunged for the wobbling lamp, still not sure whether it wanted to betray me or not. I lunged and my fingertips stretched, but I was too late. I was always going to be too fucking late.

It didn't shatter or anything like that. It just fell with a dull thud on the carpet. But it was enough. I knew it.

I crouched low behind my bed, out of sight from the door, as if it made a difference. I strained my ear like I didn't know with one hundred percent certainty that someone was coming. And someone was coming.

I held my breath like there was still a chance that if I didn't make another sound, things could be different.

When I finally heard the footsteps, loud and lumbering, I shouldn't have been surprised. The old me wouldn't have been surprised. One, because she wouldn't be in this position in the first place. And two, because she would have been out that window the second that lamp fell over, which it wouldn't have.

But I had nowhere else to go.

I had nothing to do but wait.

Whoever was coming toward me wasn't sober. I knew that at least. Big thuds against the walls echoed toward me as I shrank in tighter to myself. The chair wasn't beneath the doorknob because I hadn't been here for so long. I could have hurried toward it. I could have shoved it in place before it was too late.

Instead I made myself tinier. I tugged my knees in closer. I buried my face against my chest. I wanted to cry like a little girl, like a child.

The only noise I made was to whisper, again and again, with the words catching in my constricted throat, "I hate him, I hate him, I hate him."

And I didn't mean Nick.

The door opened wildly, loudly, and I knew from that alone that it wasn't Nick after all. Nick didn't lose control. No, no. Control was the single most important thing in the world to Nick. Control of himself. More important, control of others. Druggies were easy enough to control. So were little girls.

It wasn't Nick who nearly fell as he stumbled into my room, holding onto the shifting door handle to keep his feet beneath him. I thought maybe he was drunk or high enough not to see me. Maybe I would get lucky and he would lumber away, the big brute who had more marks in his inner arms than probably years on earth? Then again maybe my mother would show up and say it was all a mistake, her leaving me, and whisk me away to the suburbs?

"Yer kinda small, aren't ye?" the guy said, his words slurring.

He saw me. Surprise, surprise. I stood, my knees shaking.

"You're in my bedroom," I said. "The bathroom's down the hallway. Near the front door." I pointed.

The man wobbled slightly on his feet but did not leave. "I thought ye'd have bigger tits."

I tugged the strings of my hoodie tighter and wrapped my jacket closer as the intruder squinted at me.

"Yeah," he said, moving forward but not far enough that he had to leave the door, which was apparently the only thing keeping him upright. "I thought bigger tits. And definitely a bigger arse."

I shook my head, stepped farther into the shadows of the corner. "What?" I asked.

The hulking man hiccupped and shrugged. "The way Nick goes on and on about ye. Checking in here every day and all. Buying t'ings for ye. Asking yer pops about ye when he ain't passed out... I thought ye'd have bigger tits is all."

I stared at him, paralysed with a sudden fear. The phrase ignorance is bliss never felt so true. Nick searching after me was one thing. But *knowing* it? I wasn't going to be sleeping that night. Nor any night any time soon.

He raised an unsteady finger. "And definitely a bigger arse."

"I'd like you to leave," I said, more softly than I'd intended. The Aurnia of before wouldn't have been so meek. *I hate you, Conor. I hate you, I hate you, I hate you.*

"After ye, luv," the guy said.

He swept his hand toward the door and nearly fell over.

"I'm not going anywhere," I told him. "Didn't you hear me? This is my bedroom."

I retreated when the ogre moved farther into my room, his big paw knocking everything off my dresser as he caught himself from falling.

"Didn't ye hear me?" he slurred. "Nick wants to see ye."

My stomach dropped. "He's here?"

"In the basement," he answered. "So...I don't really get it 'cause yer tits don't look nearly as big as the girls at the strip club, but Nick gets what he wants so...let's go."

"No."

The word was out of my mouth before I really considered the ramifications. The stupid oaf took several seconds to process what I'd blurted out. When he did, he moved fast. He rounded the corner of my bed as I crawled atop it to get away. There was nowhere to go except the corner. He'd beat me to the door should I run for it.

"Nick's top dog around 'ere," the man grunted as he clamoured toward me across the bed. "And I'm gonna get on his good list by bringing him a little treat and yer not—"

His hands reached toward me. I pressed myself in closer to the corner of my room, praying I disappeared into the peeling wallpaper. I could smell the liquor on his breath, practically taste the sweat on his fingertips. I braced myself.

The doorbell rang as the tip of his finger brushed my neck, making me recoil.

He pointed a beefy finger at me, jabbed it between my tits.

"Yer not goin' anywhere. D'ye hear me?"

16

CONOR

I told myself I followed Aurnia out of curiosity. Surely this was all a ploy, a tiny piece of a bigger con. It made no sense otherwise. She was manipulating me. Tugging on heartstrings she stupidly thought I had. Setting me up to feel bad for her. Playing the long game to catch me completely unaware when there was more money than a few crumbled bills on the line.

I didn't allow myself to question where exactly Dublin Ink or I was getting this money that was worth investing a lot of time and effort and trickery into stealing. If I did, then I'd have to consider that maybe I wasn't following Aurnia purely out of curiosity.

And I didn't want to go there.

I'd run out of Dublin Ink just in time to catch Aurnia grabbing a local bus. My keys were already in my pocket, my helmet hanging from the handlebars of my motorcycle. It didn't even cross my mind that I was leaving Dublin Ink unattended. Some curiosity...

It was bitterly cold on the bike with just my leather jacket on. I trailed behind the bus as it blew out black smoke at red lights, lingered as it pulled over for the rare person to hop off, the even rarer person to hop on.

The distance between the street lamps grew more distant as we wove through the city streets. The number of bulbs blown out and forgotten became more frequent. Dogs barked. There was the occasional shattering of glass down some seedy alley-way. Other than that, the streets were quiet. No, not quiet—abandoned. Anyone who happened to be pacing on a corner turned to give me his back as I passed.

I felt wary eyes on my back as I drove slowly past, engine sputtering too nosily. A few blocks later the bus pulled to a stop where a sign was toppled over on a patch of dead brown grass. Aurnia alone got off. The lights on the bus switched off after pulling away.

We were at the end of the line.

I remained far enough back that Aurnia did not notice me as she started off in the opposite direction, her hands stuffed deep into her pockets, her shoulders shivering slightly. I knew enough about neighbourhoods like this to know that you didn't walk through them the way Aurnia was walking through them. You kept your head up. You checked behind you more often than you think you need to. You held something sharp or hard or something that goes bang in clear sight. You didn't stop.

Aurnia should have known this. She should have known she wasn't being safe as she stopped at a dark corner. An attacker had plenty of places to appear from to catch her completely off guard.

I was surprised to find my fingers tightening on the handle-bars. It was somewhat startling to realise that I was mad. Really fucking *mad*. Mad at Aurnia. Mad that she was putting herself in this situation. Mad that she wasn't being smarter.

Was this how she was when I wasn't around? Was she this

reckless? This stupid? Did she taunt fate often when I wasn't there to even the scales?

I tried to remain calm, to remind myself that I was there for Dublin Ink, for the security of my business. But I found myself wanting to yell across the street at her: "Get! Get out of here, you stupid little eejit! Go somewhere safe! Get!"

It was a struggle to keep the front tire of my motorcycle straight when Aurnia began to walk again. Her quickened step was all that kept me from throwing down my bike, stalking toward her, and grabbing her by the nape of the neck.

I rolled along the empty street after her and stopped in the shadow of a dilapidated warehouse when she slipped into the side yard of a trailer house.

I knew immediately what it was when I saw it. Any police officer would too, if they bothered coming down these godforsaken streets. All the most obvious signs were there: boarded front windows with light between the cracks, an old faded door with brand-new bars across it, and, most obvious of all, a wretched smell.

It was a drug den. A crack house, if you insisted on using the word "house". I didn't.

I leaned over my handlebars and forced my frozen fingertips to uncurl from my shaking fists. Aurnia was climbing up to a window on the side of the place and it made me want to punch a brick wall. I watched her with fury in my eyes as she pushed the glass up and then slipped one skinny leg and then the other inside. The last I saw of her was a sweep of glossy dark hair.

She was the closest this place would ever get to a shooting star. Just like any shooting star, I blinked and she was gone. Gone into that place. Into smoky rooms. Into needle-littered hallways. Gone into that house of horrors.

I could not see her. I could not protect her.

Any illusions I had that I was there out of curiosity were

gone. I had one focus and one alone: get Aurnia the fuck out of there.

I would curse her for being stupid later. I would yell at her for putting herself in harm's way like that later. I would shake her, if needed, to scare her into never, ever going back. That would have to wait till later. Because I still needed to figure out the now.

Think, Conor. I tried to come up with a solution that didn't end up with me squaring off with a room of drug dealers. Fuck. I didn't have time for this shite. Every second she remained in there was like a noose tightening around her neck.

The window Aurnia had crawled in through remained dark. *Come on, turn the light on. Let me see you moving around. Let me see your silhouette. Let me see you're okay...for now.*

Nothing. Just blackness.

Goddamn her.

I pulled up outside the house. I still had no plan. Had no clue what the hell I was going to do as I stalked angrily across the weed-infested sidewalk. I just had to get to Aurnia.

I raised my fist to the barred door and rammed against it. Knocking on the front door of a drug den. Great plan, Conor. I had no clue what I was even going to say when someone opened the door; I wasn't even sure I *could* say anything in the state I was in.

The shitty music and drunken laughter fell to silence. I heard hushed voices, then footsteps toward the door.

I was ready. Ready to throw a punch at the first person I saw and fight my way in to wherever Aurnia was, doing God knew what, the stupid girl. A part of me didn't care what happened to me as long as I got her out, got her *away*.

The door inched open a crack and a wary eye blinked out at me.

I hardly recognised the voice that came from me. "Evening.

I'm Aurnia Murphy's Juvenile Liaison Officer. I believe she is here."

The eye, bloodshot with a dilated pupil, looked me up and down. I tried to stand like Diarmuid stood. Less like a convict, stooped over and imposing. More like an officer of the law, upstanding, calm, secure behind my badge. It felt uncomfortable. Intimidation was easier.

My old leather jacket wasn't exactly the suit jacket that Diarmuid wore over his jeans, but the eye was either too drunk or too high or too stupid to realise. The person opened the door a little further.

"That's my daughter," he said. "But she's not here. She hasn't been here for a while. Don't know where she is. So if you don't mind—"

The man tried to close the door. I wedged my toe in to stop him. I grabbed at the door to tug it a little further open.

"You're Aurnia's da?" I asked, incredulous.

I saw no resemblance in the face that was aged far past its natural years. There was none of the brightness of Aurnia's wide eyes. None of the colour of her cheeks. His hair was grey and if it looked darker, it was only because it was dirty. Everything sagged. There were spots on his skin. He didn't have the heart-shaped face or the lightning-coloured eyes or the lips with the perfect little Cupid's bow. Most different of all was his hardened gaze.

I didn't think someone so soft could be born from someone so sharp.

I had almost a solid foot on the little man. It wasn't difficult to see over him into the squalor of the living room. What little furniture there was was stained and sagging, spotted with cigarette butts and torn in strange, vicious ways. It wreaked of weed and worse. None of the lamps had shades. The bare bulbs cast distorted shadows of the gathered group onto the peeling wall.

"Aurnia *lives* here?" I asked.

The little man had the audacity to raise his chest up at me. "She's my daughter, ain't she?" he said, his voice slurred.

No. No father who was actually a father would allow his daughter to live in such a place, to force her to call it home. No father would invite the type of people who shifted impatiently behind him anywhere near his daughter. No father would lose track of his daughter so completely that she was no more than twenty feet away from him and he swore she hadn't been there in a week.

The only reason why I did not say all of this and more to the asshole's face was because I knew it would not help Aurnia. I was supposed to be her JLO. JLOs don't exactly make a habit of bashing in citizens' faces. Or at least not on their first day.

"I was told that she was here," I said as diplomatically as my clenched jaw would allow me. My fingernails dug into the cheap wood of the door. "Would you mind calling her for me? Check in her room...if she has one."

The little man screwed up his eyes at me, suspicion entering them. The longer I stood there, the more questions he might have. If he asked for a badge or any paperwork, I was screwed.

"Or I can come inside and look for her myself," I said, forcing myself into the threshold, obviously against the little man's will.

"I told you," he snapped, "she ain't here."

I shoved one foot onto the dingy linoleum of the entryway.

"If you go get Aurnia," I said, lowering my face to the piece of shite's so he could hear me real fucking good, "all I'll see is her. All I'll *report* is her. But if you make me take one step more inside this godforsaken dump, then there's no telling what I'll see, what I'll report. Do you understand?"

Aurnia's father had the nerve to jut his chin up at me. Even up that close his eyes couldn't focus on mine.

"She," he spit into my face one word at a time, "ain't. here."

I was about to raise my fist when a small voice hidden behind the door said, "I'm here."

I kicked the door fully open before her father could stop me. The crowd from the living room all leapt to their feet (at least those who could). Baggies shoved under dirty cushions. Needles kicked under stained rugs. Hands disappearing into jacket pockets for God knows what.

There was Aurnia. I could only see half of her, her little fingertips were clutching the corner of a side hallway. Even from just that half I could see that she did not belong there.

The men in front of me were swaying like zombies, but she was still as stone. Their eyes darted here and there, unable to focus, but her eyes did not waver: they were fixed on me.

These bodies in front of me were incapable of feeling anything. The drugs they took had ensured total numbness. Aurnia was all emotion. I saw in her pain and fear and anger and, as she looked at me, something like hope. She was the only thing alive in that dead place.

"You need to come with me," I said authoritatively.

Her eyes widened before darting to her side. It was then I noticed the hand on her shoulder.

Aurnia and I were on a tipping point, a knife's edge. A big man was holding her in place. Between him and me were more than enough people to take me down. I'd go down swinging, but I'd go down.

I addressed the man behind her. "Aurnia has broken the terms of her probation. She needs to come with me. Now."

He didn't move. He didn't let her go.

Out of the corner of my eye the figures in the living room seemed to move toward me like one giant beast.

I gritted my teeth. I had one more card up my sleeve.

"Perhaps I need to make a call to *your* probation officer."

The man flinched. The fingers came away from her one by one. I turned my attention back to Aurnia as my heart beat louder in my chest.

"Aurnia," I said, nodding encouragingly, fighting the urge to run in there and grab her.

The way she looked at me made me think that I'd asked her to tightrope across the Grand Canyon. Her first step was so uncertain that I feared she was already high on something. Her frightened eyes went momentarily to the men lining the hallway on either side.

"Aurnia."

Her eyes returned to mine. I held her gaze, trying to keep her steady when she was not. When she was finally within reach, I wanted to grab ahold of her, to snatch her into my arms, to bury my face in her hair. I wanted to take her away, far away. I wanted to never let her go.

I kept my arms, muscles twitching from restraint, firmly at my sides. I let her walk stiffly past me through the opened door out into the night and kept my attention hyper focused on the throng of dangerous men that were shifting slowly toward me.

"Goodnight, gentlemen," I forced myself to say as I closed the door.

When I turned around on the front steps and found Aurnia just a few feet away, staring up at me, my heart broke. I wasn't quite sure if it broke for her.

Or whether it broke for me.

17

AURNIA

*T*wo opposite things were true: I wanted Conor to let me go. And I never, ever, ever wanted Conor to let me go.

His fingers were far more biting than the cop's handcuffs as he dragged me across the dead lawn outside my father's house. As I stumbled after him across the pitted street, I could feel his bones against mine. I waited till we were near his motorcycle, hidden by shadow, far enough away to not be heard, to dare to speak.

"You can let me go now," I said.

When I tugged at my arm, Conor did not release me.

I repeated myself a little louder, "Thanks for whatever the hell that was and all, but you can let me go."

Conor grabbed my waist and hoisted me into the air. Before I knew it, I was on his motorcycle. Before he knew it, I clambered off it.

"What do you think you're doing?" I hissed. I backed up till my shoulder blades hit against the rough bark of the neighbourhood's single living tree.

Conor advanced on me, faster than I expected for a man so

big. His thumbs dug deep into my shoulder joints as he grabbed me. I twisted around and out of his reach when he tried to steer me forcibly toward the bike once more.

"I am *not* going with you."

"Yeah?" Conor snarled. "Where are you going?"

The contrast between the voice he had used standing in front of my father, calm and professional, compared to what I heard now was frightening. He was a completely different man. A beast. The viciousness of his question startled me far more than the strength of his grip.

"That's none of your concern," I said, jutting my chin. "I get along just fine without you."

Conor laughed mockingly.

"What? In there?" he asked, pointing down the street toward my father's house. "What? In this little park? On that little bench? Spoonsies with the homeless man?"

My jaw tensed as I glared up at him. How dare he question how I live. How dare he act like he gave a single fuck about me. How dare he show up right when I needed him the most.

How cruel was he to pretend that he was going to be there for me? To make me feel looked after and protected and safe.

How dare he give me everything when he was certain to take it all away.

Without a word, I turned to leave. It didn't matter that I didn't know where. All that mattered was not falling into the trap of his big arms around me, of his sharp eyes on me, of his fingers curling into a deadly fist for me.

"Aurnia, get on the goddamn bike."

I slipped into the night. Even in the dark he found me. I was over his shoulder before I could even yelp.

I didn't dare scream, to attract the attention of the vultures in that house. I just pounded at his back as his long, steady strides took us back to the curb. Apparently my fist felt like mere flies.

He threw me roughly onto the bike. I struggled to climb off again. He caught one wrist and then the other and held them above my head as he threw a long leg over the seat. I squirmed as best I could, but Conor managed to force my arms around his waist. He gripped both my wrists in one hand at the centre of his chest as he started the bike.

"I don't need you," I yelled at him as the massive engine roared through my bones. "I don't fucking need you. Let me go!"

Conor pulled the motorcycle out into the deserted street and still I did not stop fighting. I'd force us to crash before I let him take me away somewhere warm, somewhere safe, somewhere *with him.*

I'd never been on a motorcycle before, but I knew enough to know that when two people were riding they had to work together, not against one another. They had to lean together, left or right, right or left. They had to move as one. They had to keep close, to become as much like one single body as they could.

Well, I fucking refused.

Gone suddenly were the feelings of weakness that had made me shiver in the cold, cower in the dark. Gone was feeling small and timid and helpless. Gone was the hopelessness of losing the fighter in me, of losing *me.*

Because who was I, if not a fighter?

Who was I if I had nothing to fight *for*?

I felt a sudden surge of strength as I threw myself as far as possible in the opposite direction when Conor turned left at an empty intersection. The flashing yellow lights danced over us as he swept in a wide arc. The smooth leather of his jacket felt like ice against my chest as I brushed against it. I wondered for a moment if that was what Conor's fingers would feel like against my nipples: ice against my skin. I leaned further and further as we turned. My hair fell like a curtain. I could feel my thighs quiver as they strained to stay atop the bike as I dared to tilt even more toward the asphalt that was drifting away beneath me.

I almost felt like a child on the swings. When you get going so high. When you stretch your toes toward the sun and your hair brushes the wood chips beneath you. But the sun was nowhere to be found. The motorcycle beneath me was infinitely more dangerous than a playground swing set. And I was not a child. I was *not* a fucking child.

The bike wobbled slightly as it picked up speed and a thrill went through me: I was going to do it. I was going to force us to crash. We would be thrown. Our bodies would sail through the misty air. We would either fall into one another. Or we would fall apart.

"What the hell do you think you're doing?" Conor shouted back at me over the whipping of the wind past our ears.

He yanked me back up by my wrists, jerked them forward so I was pressed impossibly tight against him. I screamed curses into the night flying by. With nothing between us but our thundering hearts, I couldn't just throw myself to the side; I had to throw *us*. I couldn't hurl my body over the edge; I had to hurl *ours*. I couldn't let myself fall; I had to drag us both down with me.

I was up for the challenge.

My teeth were gritted except for when I was screaming. I struggled and thrashed and strained every muscle in my body. My feet tried to find something to press against but there was nothing beneath me but road getting dragged under faster and faster and silver pipes that scolded and seared.

Any time I tried to yank my wrists, Conor tightened his grip. I could bite him. I could bash my forehead against the back of his head. I could shove him forward so he went over his handlebars and lost control.

"Goddamn you!" Conor shouted, fury in his voice.

Maybe this was why Conor went faster down those desolate, dark streets. Maybe he sensed that I might. Maybe he knew how much I hated him.

Before I knew it, we were hurtling through the night. Whereas before I imagined rolling across pavement and ending up against a dirty curb with a few scrapes and a bruised elbow, with the speed that Conor was going there was nothing in my mind but certain death.

The engine whined, higher and higher pitched in my ear. The seat vibrated beneath me. Even with Conor's hands gripping me tight around him, it felt like it was only a matter of time before we were torn apart. Maybe that was why he went faster: so that I had no choice but to hold on.

I squeezed my eyes shut. The street lamps in that part of town were few and far between, but they came so fast at that speed that they seemed like a string of Christmas lights I'd never had in my own house. The wind was brutal against my cheeks so I buried my face against Conor's back.

This time when I fought for control of my hands back from Conor's grip it wasn't to push myself away, but to pull myself closer. I wanted to grab handfuls of his leather jacket that was flapping violently in the wind. To pierce my fingernails through the thin, dark grey t-shirt he always wore. To hold onto his ribs themselves if I could.

This time, when I tugged back against him, he released me. Maybe that was why he went faster. He wanted to get rid of me. A few scrapes and bruises wouldn't suffice. He needed me obliterated from his life. I needed to be roadkill.

Conor released me and the wind was cruel on my exposed skin. I hadn't realised how warm his hand had been until it was gone. For a terrified moment, that split second where he wasn't holding me and I wasn't holding him, I thought I might get swept away. The wind would catch my jacket like a parachute. I would go flying off the back of the motorcycle. From high, high up, the last thing I would see would be Conor driving away before I crashed back to earth and everything went black.

I clawed at Conor's chest. I wrapped my arms around him and dug in my fingers to whatever I could grab ahold of and squeezed as tight as I could.

Maybe that was why Conor sped so dangerously. Maybe that was why he pushed the engine to its limits. Why he blew through red lights, accelerating further, and dared the motorcycle to rattle and break apart right beneath our thighs.

Maybe he wanted me to feel like *this*.

I was no longer afraid. I could feel the strength of his thighs next to mine. I imagined them like that around me instead of around the seat. Would they be held so tense? Would they quiver with such power? The vibration of the machine swept up through my body, brought a heat between my legs. Could his tongue feel like this? Could he send shocks up through me all the way to my fingertips like this?

The wind yanked at my hair. I imagined Conor's fingers twisted at the nape of my neck. My heart pounded like a jack-hammer in my chest. Would he stop thrusting into me if he knew my heart was about to explode like this? Would he stop? Or would he fuck me faster? Harder?

We were completely out of control and I liked it.

I wanted more of it. My arms felt strong as I held onto Conor. I felt powerful as we claimed the night as our own.

Maybe that was why Conor accelerated into the dark. Maybe he wanted me to feel strong.

Or maybe he was just a maniac and I needed to run away from him the first chance I got.

How was I supposed to know?

How was I supposed to even think clearly when my body felt so good? When I felt so *alive*?

I screamed once more into the night. To my surprise, Conor screamed, too.

18

AURNIA

I wiped a little circle clean on the fogged-up bathroom mirror and caught sight of Conor in the small kitchen through the cracked door.

A twenty-minute stream of hot water had made my skin bright red, but bright red meant clean, so it was worth the pain. I had a towel against my chest as I twisted the water from my hair and I watched him for a moment, moving about to make tea. He was too big for the kitchenette. The old kettle looked like a toy in his big hand. I was surprised he was able to even manoeuvre the little tea bags and their tiny strings.

He moved with a quiet devotion much like he did when I caught him sketching at Dublin Ink. His permanent scowl softened. His lips relaxed from the tight line he held them in otherwise. His eyes weren't constantly looking away, weren't constantly finding the floor.

Conor glanced up. Through the crack in the door, in the little circle on the foggy mirror that was quickly being reclaimed, his eyes met mine. I blushed and shifted to the side, out of sight. I'd never know if he looked away too. Embarrassed, ashamed. Or whether he'd kept his eyes on me. On the silhouette my naked body made. On the subtle curve of my hip. On the side of breast half hidden behind the fluffy towel. On the line of my spine trailing down, down, down...

Perhaps I was afraid to know. To know that he looked away. Because I was seventeen. Because I was too young. Because I was a child.

I tugged on a torn but buttery soft old sweatshirt he'd lent me. It smelled like pencil shavings and whiskey. It fell in a cascade of too much fabric all the way to my knees.

He'd offered me a pair of joggers, his eyes averted as he stretched his arm toward me. When I'd told him that I didn't think they would fit, he said that was all he had. I'd told him that was alright.

I slipped on a pair of his old socks and even though they flopped over my toes they were warm.

The living area was a small space with nothing more than a sink and stove along one wall, a small table with only one chair where usually there would be a couch. Conor had turned up the radiator which popped and buzzed in the corner.

"Um, I made some tea," Conor said, which crushed me a little.

It meant that he had looked away when he saw me through the crack in the door. He wanted to pretend he hadn't. Because we both knew I had been looking at him. We both knew that I already knew he'd made tea.

"Thanks," I said softly as I balled my hands in the too long sleeves.

"Take the chair," he told me, putting the two cups on the flimsy table.

"What about—"

Conor disappeared into the bedroom before I could even finish my sentence. He returned with a crate, the kind you use for milk cartons or bottles of beer. He plopped it down opposite me without comment. I wrapped my fingers around the cup as the steam drifted up toward my face.

Conor's toe, still in his thick boots, was tapping uncomfortably on the linoleum. He hadn't even taken off his jacket. I could almost still smell the fog on him. The engine fuel. The night itself.

Was he still out there? Did he ever get off that bike? Did he ever stop running in his mind?

The crate scraped nosily on the floor as Conor scooted back from the table, pushed himself up, and threw open a cabinet above the tiny sink. He returned with a bottle of Bushmills that he poured first into his cup, and then into mine.

"I'm not eighteen," I said, though it was hardly to be my first drink.

"I'm not the police," Conor grumbled, adding a second shot to his teacup.

The humming radiator and Conor's tapping toe were the only sounds as we sipped at our tea.

Conor kept his gaze down. The wind had messed his hair and strands from his bun hung over his shadowed face. How long he would let me just stare across the table at him? I kept waiting for him to down his cup, burning hot or not, and storm away. Or for him to lift his angry eyes up to me and growl, "What are you looking at, girl?" Or for him to upturn the table and stalk to the door and hold it open, saying not a word, but shaking as he pointed to the dingy back staircase.

The minutes ticked by. The tea cooled in the cup even as the whiskey warmed in my belly and I was allowed to just simply look.

How would I draw him?

I wouldn't draw him like that. I would want him to look at me. To see me. That's what I would want to capture most of all: Conor *seeing* me.

Conor was the first to speak, surprisingly. "Are you hungry?"

I almost laughed. There I was, at a kitchen table. The kitchen table in my house was either covered with lines of drugs or illegal weapons or bottles of beer from a party the night before. I couldn't recall a time I'd ever sat at it.

There I was, at a kitchen table with a cup of tea. Did we even have tea in my house? There I was, at a kitchen table with a cup of tea with someone asking me if I was hungry. It was the most familial moment of my life. Touching, in the strangest of ways. A stupid little dream come true in others.

Of all the people in the world it was Conor Mac Haol sitting across from me, Conor Mac Haol asking me if I was hungry.

I don't really know if I was or if I wasn't. I'd grown more than accustomed to conquering a grumbling appetite. I knew how to go longer than a seventeen-year-old should without a good meal.

I said "sort of", because I didn't really want the moment to end. Because I wanted to stay there a little longer, with Conor slouched across from me on an upturned milk crate. Because if you don't have a family, anyone can be family. You don't know any fucking different, after all.

Conor still didn't meet my eye as he got up from the table. He hid his face behind a kitchen cabinet door and grumbled, "Cereal all right?"

"I guess, yeah." I grinned. Cereal sounded perfect. I couldn't tell you how many times I'd imagined something as simple as someone pouring me a bowl of cereal in the morning. Sure the morning in my daydreams had been closer to 9 a.m. than 2 a.m., and there had been sunlight and maybe even some laughter, which I certainly didn't expect to get in the current scenario, but still. It was all there otherwise: the sound of the cereal crinkling in the plastic, the uncapping of the milk, the glug, glug, glug as it went into the bowl, the rifling through the drawer for a suitable spoon. I nearly cried when Conor slid the bowl toward me, careful, it seemed, not to get too close, and I saw that it was Lucky Charms. Wasn't it every child's dream to get Lucky Charms in the morning?

"Thanks," I mumbled, either too embarrassed or too emotional to say anything else.

I stared down at the bowl for long enough to almost forget Conor there across from me, pouring more whiskey (and no more tea) into his cup. I'd heard about the ways kids at school had eaten their Lucky Charms. Eat all the marshmallows first, they're the best part! No, you have to save them till the end! If you get a few marshmallows in each bite, each bite will be good!

I scooped up a single rainbow on the tip of my spoon and raised it carefully to my tongue. It was sweet. From there I lost any patience for any particular method. I just ate. And ate. And enjoyed.

At some point I noticed Conor was now looking at me. How long had he been doing that? What had he been thinking? Had he too been wondering about how he would draw me? Did the temptation to draw me as he saw me through the crack in the bathroom door ever creep into his mind?

When I met his gaze, he did not turn away as usual. On his face was a cocktail of emotion. I saw the lingering coals of anger, burning low, but burning nonetheless. There was something in the fine lines around his eyes that I interpreted as distant pain, like he'd been anguished for such a long period that his muscles remembered the position. I saw little flickers of irritation, of frustration, of impatience, sparks from the fire. I saw confusion. I saw, or maybe I just thought I saw, *wished* I saw, a trace of lust as he wet his bottom lip with his tongue. There was the kind of self-loathing I knew from looking in the mirror. Was that what I was to Conor? A mirror? But I saw, most of all, the tenseness of fear.

Conor took another shot of whiskey, this time straight from the bottle, not bothering any longer with the cup that he had set hastily aside. When he spoke his voice was strangled.

"You...you...in that...that *place*..."

If he hadn't pushed aside the whiskey bottle as well it would have rattled against the table in his quivering hands. I watched as Conor hid them beneath the table, wiping his palms once, twice, three times against his thighs.

I saw that it was a strain on him to not look away. I didn't understand why I pained him so. Why the very sight of me seemed to grip his body like a violent fever.

"Aurnia," he said, trying to gain more control of his voice and only half succeeding, "you live there? In that place? With those...with those animals?"

I don't know why exactly this made me indignant. I owed no loyalty to the man I called father. I had no happy memories from those four walls that made up the trailer. I myself hated the place, loathed it, feared going home to it every night. It made me shiver just thinking about it.

I guess to admit how horrible it was would be to admit that I needed saving from it. To admit that I needed saving from it would be to admit that no one had saved me from it. And to not be saved when you needed saving...well, what else was there to believe other than that you weren't worth saving?

"It's not that bad," I said, raising my chin defiantly.

I was suddenly aware of the wet chill of my hair. Suddenly aware of the draft Conor's billowing sweatshirt allowed. Suddenly aware that this was the apartment of a man who I hardly knew, who, up until that point, would not remain alone with me for more than absolutely necessary. Suddenly aware that this was not home.

How had I so easily forgotten that I had no home? How had *he* made it so easy to forget?

"Answer the question," was all that Conor said, ignoring entirely my bravado.

"I do just fine there."

Conor fixed his gaze even more intensely on me as he repeated his words through clenched teeth, "Answer me."

His insistence only made me dig in my heels further.

"Nothing has ever happened," I said.

I jumped when Conor pounded his fists on the table. It made the bottle topple over and spill whiskey over the edge, the teacup clattered in its porcelain saucer, and the empty bowl slid off and shattered on the floor. After the burst of noise it was silent once more. Except now, added to the hiss of the radiator was the drip, drop of whiskey and Conor's panting breaths.

With poison in my voice, I glared at Conor and said, "*Yes.*"

Conor stood and began to pace.

"Is that what you want to hear?" I said to him. "You want me to tell you that I live there, alone, unprotected, in that horrible place?"

"No, you don't."

I blinked. "I'm sorry?"

His fists clenched as he paced. "I said, 'No. You don't'."

Asshole. Did he think I *wanted* to be there? Did he think I *chose* to live in a home about as safe as an alleyway after dark? Did he think that my dreams every night were for a mother to run off, a father who dealt drugs like they were candy on Halloween, and a dozen dangerous druggies as my doting "brothers"?

I leapt to my feet, ready to yell back at him, ready to attack—

"Watch the floor!"

My foot stopped just an inch above the sharp porcelain

shards of the bowl. The fact that I had almost cut myself enraged Conor even further.

"Goddammit," he muttered as his fists shook. "Goddammit, goddammit!"

He was mad enough to punch a brick wall. Hell, if he hadn't been so worried about me cutting my foot just seconds earlier, I would have thought he was mad enough to punch *me*. I stared at him in shocked silence as he continued to pace erratically.

Finally, he said, his voice shaking, "Extra blankets are in the hall closet."

I stared at him. "What?"

"There must be a spare toothbrush in the medicine cabinet."

"What are you—"

"I'll work on getting you a key tomorrow."

"A key?" I repeated dumbly.

It hadn't yet sunk in what Conor was saying.

The rage in his voice had been replaced with his fierce determination. "You do *not* live there anymore. Do you hear me, Aurnia?"

Before I could even manage a numb nod, Conor stormed out of the kitchen. I flinched when the front door of the small apartment slammed shut. I stood there for a few confused, stunned moments before I began to pick up the mess.

I found a rag to wipe up the spilled whiskey, the splatters of milk. I tossed the big shards into the trash and found a dustpan for the littler pieces. I cleaned the teacup in sink along with a few other dishes that had been left over there. I dried them. I put them away. I glanced around the cleaned kitchen.

What else did people do before they went to bed?

Before they went to bed in their own normal homes?

19

CONOR

I didn't go riding. I just sat out on the curb, head buried between my legs, toes tapping incessantly against the pavement. What the fuck was I doing? What the fuck had I done?

When I returned to the apartment, she wasn't in the living room. I checked in the room. My chest clenched at the sight of the empty bedsheets. I went a hundred different places in my head: she returned to that damned place. Those men followed her into her room in that damned place. They were doing things to her, to her all alone in that cursed place.

If I had ever known fear, it was what I felt in that moment before I noticed a tiny foot in a sock far too big poking out from the far side of the bed.

I leaned in farther into the room. It was, of course, my room. I shouldn't have felt any apprehension about entering. With Aurnia inside, it made me tense, nervous. It was irrational.

I was scared to get close to her. Scared not of what she might do to me, my tiny little thief, but scared of what I would to do her.

I leaned in farther into the room, but didn't dare to risk a single step inside. I craned my neck to see Aurnia lying on the floor just beside the bed. She had taken a single blanket, the one that had been thrown along the end of my bed, and had arranged it on the floor. The frayed edges she had drawn up as best she could over herself. I could see from the way she shivered that they weren't enough.

I hesitated.

The radiator was turned up as high as it would go. There was no solution there. The only answer was to walk inside and pull the big duvet onto her.

I dragged a hand over my face. Even from the threshold of the door I could see the way my sweatshirt had ridden up on her bare legs. The moonlight was cast upon them, upon their smooth flesh. I could make out the underside of her ass, the worn hem of her panties. I looked away quickly. My gaze had already lingered too long. Just like it had when I had happened to glance up from the kitchen counter to see through the tiniest of slits in the bathroom door, the sight of Aurnia just out of the shower.

She had looked away immediately, as I should have. It wasn't, after all, right that I should gaze upon someone of her age. She had caught me by surprise. Just like she had from the very start.

The steam from her long shower had lingered around her body, twisting about her like swatches of silk. Her wet hair fell down her shoulders, catching the light like the feathers of a raven. God, how small she was.

And yet I saw, too, that there was a shape hidden beneath those baggy jackets and torn jeans. She was forbidden fruit. I had already failed once the test of temptation.

If I couldn't turn away my gaze when I was a room away with a door between her and me, how was I to expect myself to get close enough to cover her with a blanket?

It remained: she was cold. I could do something about it. This alone was the truth that I had to hold onto.

With a swiftness that scared me because it showed how little I trusted myself still, I hurried into the room, dragged the blanket off the bed, and tossed it onto Aurnia's sleeping form. I didn't even bother to see if it landed on her entirely. Or whether it had fallen over her head. In her dreams she would push the cloud that had brushed against her cheek aside. Maybe with a bit of her sweet little laughter.

I closed the door behind me. Was it because I wanted to keep the room as quiet as possible for her to sleep? Or was it because I saw it as another barrier for my growing lust?

$\sim$

MY DUSTY GARAGE WAS DIM, the only light coming from a low naked bulb. I didn't bother with gloves. I didn't bother even with a few quick wraps of tape. I wanted to feel the splitting of my knuckles. I wanted to see a smear or two of red in the yellow of the street lamp light.

As I circled the bag, focusing on my form, focusing on the strength of my attack, I considered the situation. On the one hand, I felt enough for Aurnia to want her to have a better life than I was dealt. I knew the struggles of her childhood, because they had been the struggles of mine.

I understood being in a shite situation. I even understood the indignation when someone tried to point it out. The helplessness. Because what else were you to do? I knew fear. I knew searching for a way out, any way out.

Aurnia at seventeen was me at seventeen. That could not be changed. But I could ensure that Aurnia at eighteen was not me at eighteen. I could not give her family Christmases at five or birthdays at the roller rink at eleven or pictures on the staircase before the big dance at sixteen. It was the great cruelty of life that no one could.

I could make sure that she did not fall into the trap that I fell into.

I had been vulnerable like she was. Stupid as she was stupid. Desperate, too, like her. If I didn't do something, she would make the exact same mistake as I did: falling for someone older. Falling for someone who was going to ruin her life. Giving up everything for nothing at all in return.

To save Aurnia I had to stay away from her.

The situation seemed as impossible as warming her with the blanket without getting near her. I was salvation. I was her curse. I was a warm bed. I was the storm that always came. I was a brush against the cheek. I was a goddamn black eye.

I circled the bag and my fists flew with less and less control. A sweat broke out across my forehead, beads dripping into my eyes. The windows began to fog from my ragged pants for air.

I was going to have to deny myself.

I wanted Aurnia.

I could not have her. I was going to have to be strong, stronger than I had ever been. I was going to have to push her away with all I had.

I punched the bag so hard that the old leather ripped.

I was going to have to avoid her at all costs.

I was going to have to be mean to her.

I charged the bag with a muted cry, teeth scraping against the rough fabric.

I was going to have to be *cruel* to her.

I hugged the bag close as my fists railed against it on either side, faster, harder, faster, harder.

She couldn't see me as the answer.

When my muscles were shaking and I could no longer punch with any strength, I clawed at the bag like an animal.

She couldn't see in me any kindness.

Soon I was clawing at the bag just to remain upright. My feet were scuffling on the dusty concrete floor and I slipped. My knees hit hard. The jolt made the old wound in my thigh flare up with a searing hot pain. As if I needed a fucking reminder.

She couldn't be with me.

I rested my slick forehead against the punching bag and tried to breathe evenly. I had to get my head straight if I was going to be able to do this. If I was going to be able to resist.

Aurnia couldn't be with me.

I also knew that I couldn't be without her.

20

AURNIA

*C*onor was not home when I awoke, stiff but smiling.

The floor beneath me was cold, the old worn floorboards frozen stiff by the draughty night, but the comforter against my cheek was warm. I breathed into it and watched it rise and fall with the excitement of a little kid inside her first living room blanket fort.

Pale light sneaked under the top of the comforter. I stretched my fingertips to dip into it like it was a still pool, or paint. Paint for a tattoo maybe. A tattoo of a sun.

I felt a strange tinge in my stomach at the seemingly untouched mattress beside me. I stood at the edge of the bed longer than I probably would want to admit wondering whether Conor was the type to make his bed in the morning. Would he take the time to stretch out the wrinkles to the point where no trace of him was left? Or was the reason for the lack of signs of life in the bed the more obvious one: he hadn't slept there? He hadn't slept there beside me.

I fixed myself another bowl of Lucky Charms, though the rainbow marshmallow I selected first with the tip of my spoon didn't taste quite as incredible alone at the little flimsy table. I cleaned up after myself, found the toothbrush Conor told me about. I dragged my fingers through my hair in lieu of a comb.

It was strange, moving about the apartment at ease. I didn't have to check corners. I didn't have to wait at the end of hall-ways and strain my ear for movement. I didn't have to sprint into the kitchen, scoop what I needed (which was never enough) into my arms, and sprint back out. It was strange, but it was peaceful. It was safe.

I searched for little hints about Conor, about who he was. I knew rather little. I had what Mason and Rian had told me, but that information always came with the eventual reddening of cheeks and clearing of throats like they hadn't meant to tell me, like they weren't *supposed* to tell me.

I peered inside dresser drawers, carded through a small, scarcely filled closet. I rifled around a medicine cabinet.

I found almost nothing of note: a brand of deodorant, a single clip-on tie, an old art school sweatshirt that was only interesting for the fact that it looked practically unworn in a sea of faded, torn, and ink-stained clothes, a crumbled Post-it that read: buy oranges.

After circling the apartment and finding nothing but slightly dusty corners, I gave up. As I stood in the centre of the empty, rather (very) lifeless living room, it seemed to me that Conor didn't allow himself places to put pieces of himself. There were no counters for displaying pictures of family, of friends. There were no junk drawers for ticket stubs and bar coasters and receipts for his favourite takeout place. The walls were brick, almost as if on purpose to make tacking personal things up even more difficult.

If Conor had things of himself to hide, he hid them within himself. It was him that I had to search. Him that I had to find the key for.

I expected Conor to be at Dublin Ink, because, well, where

else would he be, if not at one of his two homes? But I was the first in. I considered that I was just early; it was the first good sleep I'd had in...well, I couldn't remember how long. I wasn't used to not dragging myself from the tiniest semblance of sleep I'd managed to grab ahold of just before the ringing of my alarm.

I set about making things extra nice for when Conor arrived. Maybe he'd even be ready to teach me something about tattooing at long last. We'd turned a leaf after all, if perhaps a shaky one. I mean, he was letting me stay at his place, even if he informed me of this kindness at the very top of his lungs...

My list of daily tasks went quickly and soon both Mason and Rian had arrived, but no Conor. I didn't want to ask them if they knew where Conor was. I didn't want to seem overeager, overexcited. Besides, I pretty much knew the answers I'd get: "He should be getting laid, is what he *should* be off doing," from Mason and "What? Conor...oh, right. Umm, no idea, I'm afraid," from Rian.

The day passed slowly as it does when you're constantly checking the minute hand of the clock. But it was the front door that I was checking.

Conor's absence was made even more torturous by the fact that ever since my street art and its social media success, Dublin Ink had seen a steady little trickle of customers willing to risk the seedy location. So whereas before I could sweep and resweep the floor in peace, now I had to look up with a thudding heart at every little ring of the bell.

It was never Conor.

"Hello," this person or that would say, "um, I was wondering if I could talk to someone about a tattoo."

Mason or Rian (depending mostly on whether the person was a woman) would greet them, guide them inside past me, and I would be left watching the little bell come once more to stand still. Wondering what was wrong. Wondering what *I'd* done wrong.

It wasn't until ten minutes before closing that Conor finally came into the shop. The collar of his leather jacket was upturned, his head bent low, his shoulders stooped forward. He went straight to his workstation and without a word began looking through invoices, receipts, bank notices. My smile fell at his abrupt and unpleasant entrance. Maybe it was just the stress of the shop. *We* were better. *We* were good.

After chewing on my lip for a moment in contemplation, I snatched up a tattoo gun and a canister of ink and approached Conor.

"Hey," I said, warmly, brightly, "I was thinking maybe tonight you could show me how to load this."

Mason had already taught me and Rian (who had been there, but not *really* been there when Mason taught me) taught me two afternoons later. But it was one of the simplest things I could think of to ask for.

Maybe I should have seen that I was still walking on eggshells around Conor. I guess anyone else would have seen that as a warning sign, taking three steps back and calling it baby steps. But I was blinded by a good night's sleep, a place to call home, and the memory of Conor asking, in his gruff voice, "Are you hungry?"

Too blinded, it would seem, because it took me by surprise when Conor snatched the tattoo gun from my hands and, without even looking at it, snapped, "You call this clean?"

He was out of his chair, looming high above me, before I could even stumble backwards.

"You can go," he said as he stormed out of the parlour. "I'll do it my fucking self."

Things were to only get worse. Worse, even, than they had been before the night that Conor had come to save me. A key to his apartment was thrown on the kitchen table. A few dirty bills were scattered around it like I was a whore he'd paid to play neglected little girl. I supposed they were meant for groceries, but he never said. He was never around to say.

The bed sheets on the mattress beside where I slept on the floor with the comforter remained as they had been that first morning I woke up: untouched.

If Conor did return to his apartment, he never left any trail of it. The shower tiles were always dry. No steam clung to the corners of the little chipped mirror. Of the few bowls and plates, forks and spoons that Conor owned, they were always in the exact same position as I made note to leave them. I don't know how he was getting fresh clothes. Was he sneaking over me, asleep on the floor, during the night? Was he coming in during the hours when he knew I was at Dublin Ink? Was he taking care to keep every piece hanging as it was in the closet? Because each night I fell asleep looking at the shadows on the folds like craters in the moon, the frayed edges hanging like moss. Each night I committed them to memory and each morning I awoke hoping they were different. Each night I returned to an empty apartment and it was the first thing I checked. They were always the same.

Conor was not coming home at all. What reason could I possibly see but *me*?

On the rarer and rarer occasions that I did see Conor at Dublin Ink, he was increasingly in a bad, volatile mood. He sent me off on long, arduous errands that felt more like goose chases than serious tasks. He snapped at me for not doing work that I'd completed hours earlier.

He not only refused to teach me even the basics of tattooing, but he forbid me from touching the equipment after claiming I carelessly handled one of the guns and broke something. When

I dared to ask him what had I broken, he sent me to clean the bathrooms. Again.

I could hear Mason and Rian talking with him about me, but this always led to them fighting about me. Eventually I told Mason and Rian not to worry about it. As much as I was confused and hurt, I didn't want to take from Conor what I myself would hope to hold onto for dear life should I ever have it: family.

"We're worried about him," Mason told me.

He'd even stopped bringing by his Miss Last Nights because Conor had grown so unpredictable. He showed up when he wanted, did work if he wanted, and was rude to anyone who tried to say anything about it.

"He's never had the sunniest disposition," Rian added in a lowered voice.

We were in the kitchen and even though the parlour was empty, Conor God knows where, no one seemed willing to talk any louder. "But this is different. This is..."

"Bad," Mason said.

Rian glanced through into the living room which glowed neon pink in the dim. "I was going to say frightening."

Conor's irritability quickly extended to the customers. If someone peeked their head in timidly, he would shout, "In or out, asshole. This ain't a peep show." But the moment the person did walk in, he'd grumble, "Booked."

"What?" came the inevitable response.

"Booked," was all Conor would ever say. "All fucking booked."

"How about—"

"Today, tomorrow, forever and ever, goddamn amen. Booked."

If the person left, that was the end of it. If the person, however, dared to let his eye linger over the empty tattoo chairs, over Mason with his face buried in his hands or Rian staring blankly ahead or, worst of all, Conor, sharpening a pencil with a knife, then, well, it was far from the end of it. Conor would stand. Conor would yell. Conor would follow the poor guy out onto the sidewalk, gesture wildly with his arms before slamming the door on the way back inside.

"What the *fuck* has gotten into you?" Mason would sometimes growl. A fight would begin. Fists would even occasionally be raised. I don't know if it was a good thing that things never came to blows; it felt like a gathering cloud that never relinquished its rain. It just grew and grew and grew.

Sometimes, though, Mason wouldn't say anything at all. Those times, somehow, scared me the most.

Soon Dublin Ink hadn't seen a customer in days. They were more than likely scared off by reviews that warned of a giant brooding asshole who turned away everyone. There was a recent crime spree in the neighbourhood and I don't think Mason or Rian or I even once considered that this was the reason for the empty shop. We all knew the problem.

Nobody seemed to know what to do about it.

That morning the rain began early. A heavy mist at dawn at turned into a light drizzle by the time the tattoo parlour opened. By noon it was falling in sheets. It made the inside of the town house noisy. It made it feel claustrophobic as the tense silence seemed to only grow to compete with the rain. It also made us feel trapped. Trapped with a monster. There was nowhere to go and no one coming to save us. I was certain not even the mailman was dropping by in that weather.

Conor snapped at anyone who said anything. He upturned a tea kettle because I brushed too closely to him as he drew. Rian received his wrath for "looking in his direction". Mason had to sneak a girl out while Conor went to the bathroom. His irritability was turned up to eleven along with impatience, his meanness, his pettiness.

I was nearing the end of my rope with him. I wasn't going to take it much longer. Mason and Rian might have been afraid of confronting him, but I wasn't. At least, not anymore now my anger had boiled over.

What's more, Conor looked wretched. Absolutely wretched. He was pale. His skin was clammy. His fingers shook and his eyes were red-rimmed and unfocused. I caught him guzzling down shots of whiskey with a handful of pills in the kitchen.

Was I so fecking horrible that he had to medicate himself just to be around me for a few hours? What had I done that he had to turn to drugs?

"I'm going to talk to him," I said in the kitchen to Mason and Rian.

I had no fear of Conor in the living room hearing me. The sound of the rain on the windows was so loud that I practically had to shout for the two guys in front of me to hear me. Mason threw a big arm over my shoulder.

"No," he said with a sad smile, "you're not."

"Unless you want to make things worse," Rian added. He was studying his tea leaves, turning the cup this way and that. He had been doing that for over an hour.

"But this has to stop," I told them, earnestly looking from one to the other. "What do you normally do when he's like this?"

The noise of the rain fell over us like a wool blanket.

"Well?" I demanded, resisting the urge to slam my palms against the table.

Rian lifted his distant blue eyes to me from the lip of his teacup.

Mason pinched at the bridge of his nose. "We haven't seen him like this before."

I blinked. *Never?*

"And you're not going to do anything?" I asked. "What if something's wrong?"

Rian glanced at Mason, then he said, "Look, Aurnia. We might not know what to do. But we do know what *not* to do."

The rain was deafening as I stared at the two of them in disbelief. I thought Conor was their best friend. I thought they were a *family*. It was like seeing a beloved vase, up close, was riddled with cracks.

"Really, Aurnia," Mason said at last with a sad sigh. "This will all pass if you just let it. You know, dive beneath the wave until it passes over you or whatever."

"Yeah," I said flatly, staring moodily down into my own empty teacup.

Mason patted my shoulder. It didn't make me feel any better. Later Rian left for the night and Conor took another pill, another swig. Later Mason left and then again: a pill, a swig. I was last to go.

Mason and Rian said I would make things worse, confronting Conor. They were probably right. I should probably go. Probably just hope tomorrow was better.

As I gathered my things and moved toward the door while the rain continued in whooshing torrents, I knew in my heart of hearts that I wasn't going anywhere. I knew I wasn't going to listen; I rarely did. Even if no one else would, I would face him.

Mason said the key was swimming beneath the wave. But it was Conor, not me, who needed to dive under.

21

CONOR

Of course she picked that exact moment. Of fucking course.

I had seen it coming. How could I not have seen it coming, like a goddamn freight train down the line? I had seen the way Aurnia eyed me from across the parlour. A confrontation was building. I knew it. Every time I raised my voice at her I was adding fuel to the fire. I knew this, too.

What else could I do? How else was there to push her away? To keep her at arm's length, didn't I have to extend my arm? Didn't I have to raise my fist?

After the night I'd taken her to my apartment, I had avoided her all day. I had waited till I expected her to be gone to come into the shop. I had cursed that she was still there. But I did what I had to do: I yelled at her. Scared her, probably. Scared her a little. She had been expecting a change between us, I supposed. A new kindness from me. A gentleness. A tenderness...

For the first week or so it was that kind of shocked, confused look that she gave me when she thought I couldn't see her. Eyes wide, even more childlike than usual. Her head tilted slightly.

Hair falling over her eye, even after she tucked it behind her ear.

Aurnia must have known that I was an unhappy man, an irritable, moody, slightly violent man. I don't think she quite understood the depths of my unhappiness. It was frightening to her that I wasn't just irritable, but erratic. Not just moody, but hateful. Not, as it turned out, a *slightly* violent man. If I threw something in anger and frustration across the room, it was, during those days, fear with which she looked up at me from her place on the floor, kneeling beside a dustpan amongst shards of broken glass.

I should have known that fear would not last long in my little thief. She was too stubborn for fear. Too clever. Too thick-headed as well. She'd spent her whole childhood learning to chase it off. A girl like her in a house like hers never had the luxury of fear. If she'd given into fear, the world would have swallowed her whole. I knew this, because it was the same for me.

I watched the fear burning off in her eyes like a frost in the sun, the paralysing crystals melting as her gaze grew brighter, bolder. I saw this and I knew what was coming. It was inevitable.

My little thief was going to pick a fight with me. She was going to make her demands. She was going to stomp her little foot and huff hot air from her little chest and cross her little arms in a little sign of defiance. Any other day I would have been ready for it.

Aurnia didn't pick any other day. Aurnia picked *that* day.

I could see it the second she hesitated at the front door. The night was black and rain rattled noisily on the windows.

The street outside was empty. I'd been staring at it for hours while my nails dug deeper into the woodgrain of my drawing desk. A car hadn't come by in exactly one hour and nineteen minutes. I knew because the ticking of the clock was pulsing in my fiery veins as I waited for everyone to leave. Rian wandered out with his notepad and no umbrella thirty-six minutes ago. Mason got into a cab twenty-two minutes ago. And Aurnia had walked to the door nineteen seconds ago.

She had no reason to hesitate at the door. Her bus, as I knew all too well, was pulling up to the stop down the street in less than a minute, just enough time to run through the rain to make it as the doors hissed closed.

Her umbrella, a gift from Mason from the lost and found bin, was in her hand. Her rain jacket was on over her black jean jacket. There was no reason to hesitate. And yet she did and I knew. Through a haze of pain and a fog of pain medication, I knew.

I watched her little hand fall away from where she had reached for the doorknob. It came to rest at her side. I watched her back rise and fall and I prayed—*prayed*—that she was just trying to remember whether she forgot her key. I willed her to lift her hand back up, to dash into the pouring rain, to make her bus. I would have dragged her there myself if it was taking everything in me to stay upright as the pain in my leg made my knees shake behind the desk.

Go, I silently urged her with clenched teeth. *Go, go. Aurnia, please. If I've ever been deserving of a kindness, please, please for the love of God, go!*

Of course she didn't. Of course she didn't because I was at my weakest. My absolute weakest. And she chose *now*.

Maybe the drugs made my eyes sluggish, but Aurnia seemed to move with a superhuman speed after turning away from the door. The umbrella went rattling away into the corner by the front door. The Open sign blinked off as she yanked the cord from the outlet. She slipped out of her raincoat and it went soaring across the room to land on the back of the old couch. I tried to follow her movements as she gathered up an armful of instruments from Mason and Rian's workstations.

It was all happening too quickly. I couldn't think. The pain was making me dull. The painkillers duller. Panic grew in my chest. Tightened and constricted my breathing. What was I going to do? What was I going to do?

It felt like it wasn't the woodgrain of the desk that was splintering anymore, but my nails themselves. I dug them in even deeper, even harder. I was hoping that focusing on a different kind of pain would focus me. It didn't.

Aurnia came to stand in front of me and her eyes flashed like the light off the silver tools she held in her arms. I was helpless before her. I was sure of it.

"I think that's been quite enough," she said.

I could do nothing but force air in through my nose, force air out through my nose.

"You promised to teach me to tattoo and you're going to do just that. And you're going to do it now."

I let my chin fall to my chest. The only reason my arms could support me against the desk was because I'd locked them out completely. There was no strength left in me. Only pain.

A drop of sweat from my forehead plopped onto my sketchbook. I watched it spread over the empty page. I hadn't been able to draw a single thing. I hadn't even managed to put pencil to page.

"Aurnia," I said in a low voice that I struggled to keep even, "can we please do this another time?"

Perhaps if I hadn't pushed her so far, she could have seen that I was in no state to fight. But she was pissed. It rolled off her in waves, like arrows in her glare, in her biting tone. I knew more than most how blinding anger could be.

If she saw me quiver, she must have assumed it was in frustration. If she saw at all the sweat on my brow, she must have taken it for some drunkard's sweat, the aftereffects of some bender. And if she saw me look away from her, she never would think it was because I couldn't see straight; it would have to be that I was disdainful of her. How was I really to argue otherwise?

"Please," I uttered, more an exhale than a properly formed word.

Aurnia was having none of it. Of course not.

"You're either going to teach me how to tattoo right here and right now or you're going to tell me what the hell is going on. Why you won't teach me. Why you won't be kind to me. Why you won't look at me. Why you won't go back to your apartment now that I'm there."

She dumped the contents of her arms onto the drafting desk. I didn't make a move to catch anything as it skidded off the edge and onto the floor around me. I could feel her glaring at me, my silence only serving to make her madder.

"Well?" she shouted. "What will it be?"

I squeezed my eyes shut, but that only made Aurnia's voice louder in my ears.

"I'm tired of you holding me hostage. You won't teach me to tattoo, but that's the reason why I'm here. Why do you keep me here if you hate me so much? If you can't stand the very sight of me, just get rid of me."

Maybe if I could just hold on for a little while. Let her shout. Let her scream. Let her get it out of her system. If she tuckered herself out, she would leave. I'd seen her waiting beneath the rickety old bus stop in the rain before. She would tire. She would leave. Then I could breathe. Then I could scream.

If Aurnia was a freight train she was only gaining steam.

"Because it seems to me, Conor," she said, the volume of her voice rising, "that you brought me in closer to you only so that you can show me the full extent of your cruelty."

This was no longer about tattooing. She was talking about me and her. She was talking about *us*.

There was no us.

There could be no us.

Maybe she could smell the sweat on me. Maybe she would smell it like blood on a wounded animal. Maybe she would see I was sick, that I couldn't do this right now. Maybe she would step back.

Of fucking course she didn't step back. She only got closer.

A sudden gust of wind brought a sheet of rain so violently against the window that even if Aurnia had shouted something at me at the top of her lungs I wasn't sure either of us would have heard it.

I wasn't going to last long. Aurnia seemed like she was just getting started.

"Why won't you say something?" she shouted. "Why won't you say fucking *anything*? You drive me to this, you push me, you prod me, you dare me to say something and when I finally do you just stand there like a statue? What do you *want*, Conor? What do you fucking want?"

Couldn't we go back to talking about shop duties? About the bathroom cleaning schedule? How it wasn't fair that she had to show up on time when all the rest of us wandered in whenever we damned well pleased?

Those were safe subjects. I could handle that. I could grit my teeth and swallow back a wave of nausea and nod. "You're right," I could say. "Anything you want. You've got it." There, I said it. I gave in. Now she could leave.

"I think I know why you don't teach me to tattoo," Aurnia said, "because you don't want me to leave."

Don't say it. Dear fucking God, don't say it.

Aurnia got closer. The pain in my leg was a hot iron.

"The *last thing* in the world that you want is for me to leave."

Don't say it. Don't say it. Don't. I wasn't sure she could get any closer. I wasn't sure the pain in my leg could get any worse. At least not with me still conscious.

"Because it's the only thing you can think of to keep me around short of tying me up by my ankles and wrists in the storeroom."

I was begging whatever god was out there and listening: please don't let her say it, please, please, don't let her say it.

Aurnia's little fingers were on my arm. Couldn't she feel the heat of my fever? Wasn't it burning her? Didn't it give her even the tiniest bit of mercy?

No.

"Because you *want* me," she said, her eyes on fire. "Because you've wanted me from the second you saw me. You've wanted nothing else. And you get off on denying yourself me."

My little thief, with an unknown strength from her or an unknown weakness from me, turned me to face her. I nearly stumbled over before catching myself with a slick palm on the wall behind her. With my arm quivering above her head, she was caged beneath me and yet I was the one who was trapped.

She stretched up onto tiptoes, lifting her face up to me, her features softening as her gaze dropped to my lips.

"Why would it be so bad?" she whispered.

I let out a groan. Unable to form words. Unable to explain. To her. To myself.

"Why..." She leaned closer, so close, her breath against my mouth, a soft cloud of spearmint and the hint of strawberry jellies. "Why can't we..."

Her lips touched mine. It was just a brush but the sensation cascaded down my body. I made a noise in my throat. I hadn't meant to, I swear. But she coaxed it out of me, like she coaxed so many wicked things unbidden from me.

Somehow our mouths were fused, our lips moving against

each other, her fingers tangling into my shirt. Later I'd swear it was her tongue that pressed into my mouth but I couldn't be sure it hadn't been me who had opened up and demanded entrance first.

The heat that washed through my body numbed the pain of my knee. Until I felt nothing but her. The voice in my head that was screaming this was wrong, silenced as I lost myself in her kiss. I let her hands slide down my stomach. I barely registered what she was doing until her hand slid down the front of my pants. I almost buckled at the knees as her small fingers brushed the head of my cock. My hand against the wall fisted, my nails scratching at the wall.

"Fuck, you're so hard," she whispered into my mouth. Her dirty words jarring with her innocent features. "I know you want me. Why don't you just...fuck me." Her eyes bore into mine. "I want this. I want *you*. Haven't I made that clear?"

I was going straight to hell.

"Please," I gasped, still frozen. Still unable to move. Fearing that if I reached out to push her away, my traitorous hands would instead wrap around her throat, push her panties aside, to slide myself in. To corrupt her fully. "We...can't."

"Why not? I could make it so good for you. You could teach me." Her finger swirled my precum all around the tip of me. I had to squeeze my eyes shut against the dizziness that threatened to take me under. She needed no teaching. She was already a deadly siren calling me into her wild waves. My undoing.

"Stop," I begged.

She didn't. She wrapped her fingers around me and pressed closer, her eyes ablaze with triumph. Like she knew I was on the verge of giving in.

My fist was through the wall above her head before even I realised it. Her eyes widened, her intake of breath audible.

"Get. Your. Hands. Off. Me."

She snatched her hand out of my pants and pressed back into the wall; her eyes were wide with fear.

I almost laughed. How had she not seen what she was doing? How had she not seen that it was all coming to this? That this was always how this was going to end?

With me scaring her. With me, yet again, driving her away. I just had to do a better job this time.

"Do not fool yourself," I growled. I would have pushed myself away from her, but I would have fallen back. I was sure of it. "Do not flatter yourself. Tell yourself all the little fantasies you want, touch yourself however you want at night, but do not drag me into it, *little girl*."

I was collapsing down into her because I was having a hard time keeping myself upright, but she mistook it for a threat and cowered beneath me. If I had been thinking straight, I might have stopped. Maybe not. Maybe I was cruel, just like she said.

My voice rivalled the roar of the rain as I snarled down at her, "You are a child that arrived on my doorstep unwanted. You are a brat I need to babysit. A little thief I need to keep an eye on."

"But you...you want..." She waved at my pants, a bulge still giving away my sinful desires.

I snorted. "You obviously don't know much about men. We'd get hard in a stiff wind."

Pain flashed clear in her eyes. Even that wasn't enough to stop my tirade.

My shadow darkened Aurnia's bright cheeks. I put my face right up against hers.

"If I look at you, it's to make sure you're not stealing. If I talk to you, it's to keep you busy so you don't start destroying things. If I don't teach you to tattoo, it's because you're still young enough to colour inside the lines. And if I come drag you out of some godforsaken home, it's because of some fucked up sense of right and wrong in me that I never asked for, because you're a *child*. A *child*, Aurnia. A fucking *child*!"

Aurnia ducked beneath my quivering arm and ran from me. I stayed there as the door slammed shut. I couldn't move. Even if I could, where was I to go?

22

AURNIA

*S*ome kids get backyard treehouses with tire swings and a string of fairy lights. Some kids get a plastic playset out front. Other kids get the gutted trunk of an Oldsmobile Cutlass from the '80s in a junkyard along the freeway.

I'll give you three guesses which kind of kid I was and the first two don't count.

Cars whizzed by just past the rusted chain-link fence, nothing more than noisy blurs in my periphery. You could only see a little bit of the freeway, but that was only because the rest of it was blocked by large stacks of crushed cars. Old, battered-up parts littered the muddy ground around our hangout.

Jack sat on an engine, groping around the back of his mouth for something or other stuck in his teeth. Lee was across the way stacking back up the empty beer bottles along the top of what used to be the back seat of a car.

Had little kids sat on that back seat when it had been a working car? Had they been scolded by a mother for being too loud? Had they dripped ice cream on it during a Sunday ride?

The smack of Mia's bubblegum beside me snapped me out of my thoughts. She was in the trunk beside me, long legs draped over the bumper as she tossed a stone up into the air. A devilish grin curled up her full lips just before she hurled her stone at Lee. It hit him right in the back as he was putting up the final bottle and he howled in pain.

"Feck orff, Mia," he shouted, swatting at the bottles in retaliation. "*You* can put dem up now. How about dat?" He leapt out the back and stormed toward us.

Mia responded by throwing another stone at Lee. He tried to avoid it, but it still glanced off his shoulder. He picked up an old sawed-off pipe from the ground and hurled it without hesitation at her.

I shielded my face with my arms. Mia just laughed as it clanged noisily on the trunk beside her and fell harmlessly into a large puddle by the long dead tire.

"Yeh couldn't hit your Momma's arse if it was wigglin' right there in front te ye," she taunted Lee, her dangerous eyes fixed on him. "But ye don't have to worry about that, do ye?"

Lee shoved Mia over and flopped with an irritated sigh into the trunk as well.

"Right," he grumbled, "like yer mam is on her way with orange slices and wet wipes as we speak, gobshite."

Mia stuck her tongue out at Lee, who flipped her off.

On the engine, Jack flicked a piece of stringy meat from the tip of his dirty finger and rolled his eyes. "Would you two just get a room already?"

Mia sent her sharp eyes toward Jack. "Sure t'ing," she said, "you payin', Daddy?"

I wriggled myself farther away on the trunk. Things just felt...*off*. I don't know if Dublin Ink had changed me or being on parole or he-who-would-not-be-fucking-named, but I was no longer at home in the junkyard where I'd practically grown up with Jack and Lee and Mia.

I felt the dampness of the old carpet in the trunk, smelled its mould. The exposed bolts jabbed at me when they hadn't before. I was more cautious than ever before of cutting myself on the sharp, jagged edges and needing a shot. I felt like a stranger in a place I used to know like the back of my hand. I felt like a stranger amongst people who I thought I knew better than anyone.

I had to change that. I just needed to warm back up to them. This was, after all, who I was. Where I belonged. This was, after all, my "family".

"What about the money from the jewellery store?" I asked, glancing between them.

"You really have been gone a long time, ain't ye?" Mia said with a snort. "Nick took it all."

"What?" I asked.

"Every last fockin' cent," Jack grumbled. His hands were back in his mouth so it must not have been just that one stuck piece of meat.

Lee, ever restless, pushed himself from the trunk and began to pace in the mud in front of the Cutlass. "Said it was his 'territory'." Lee kicked at a rusted piece of metal. "Said that it just wasn't how things 'worked'. Just going out and taking 'whatever we wanted'."

The last time I saw the three of them they were eager to be accepted into Nick's gang. That's practically the whole reason why they (and me along for the ride) decided to rob the jewellery store. For Nick's approval. For Nick's praise. For Nick's acceptance. The attitude had certainly shifted.

"You know," I said, careful over every word, "we could just, you know, do something different for once?"

Lee stopped pacing. The fingers fell from Jack's chapped lips. Mia turned her head and assessed me with a sharp look.

"What d'ye mean?" she asked.

I shrugged, trying to act casual. Why did it feel so difficult?

So forced? These were my friends, weren't they? I shouldn't have to be cautious about what I said, how I said it. Should feel I was amongst family and not like I was in enemy territory negotiating some sort of tenuous peace.

"I don't know," I said, "I just mean that it seems things are only going to get worse with Nick. With the whole..." I waved vaguely, "scene."

My hand fell limp at my side. Shite, the way the three of them were looking at me...was I blushing?

Mia smacked her gum again and moved so that she was facing me. She draped her legs heavily across mine.

"'Scene?'" she asked, the scorn clear in her tone. "'*Scene?*' Aurnia, dis is our life. This is *yer* life."

"I told youse she'd want nuthin' to do with us after they got to her," Jack mumbled. There was no warmth in his eyes as he stared across at me.

"Little Miss Better Than," Lee said before going to set up the beer bottles on the back of the old leather seat again.

It hadn't been much, that leather seat. It hadn't been like the leather seat in an actual car that other kids got. But it had been ours, the four of us. It had been ours together.

I couldn't lose that. I couldn't. I don't know if it was worth saving. Or whether it was because it was once again all I had.

"No," I protested, "it's not like that, I swear it. It's just I know how dangerous Nick is and—"

"He must not be that dangerous," Mia hissed. "Given how many times ye've crawl into his bed."

I stared at her in shock. "I've never—"

"That's not what we hear. Izza right, boys?"

I shook my head. What was happening?

I was being torn in half. And in half once more.

There was the Aurnia of Dublin Ink, doing her job dutifully, chatting easily with Mason and Rian. There was the Aurnia who slept with Nick, the new terror of the neighbourhood. There was the Aurnia who was "different", who was "snobby", who was trying to leave this wretched life before. There was the Aurnia who paced an empty apartment at night. There was the Aurnia who wanted these three people over anyone else. There was the Aurnia who was safe and protected by the strong, tattooed arms of a grumpy giant.

There was the Aurnia who ran from him.

There was the Aurnia who ran to him.

"All I'm saying is that with Nick in charge now we're under his thumb in the neighbourhood. Like you said, he's not going to let us rob a place without him getting his cut and his cut is one hundred percent. So, I mean, I care for you guys and I want you to have the chance that I've had at this tattoo parlour. I just mean that maybe there are other lives out there for us...if we want."

What the hell did I just say? Why the hell did I just say it? It wasn't like I'd changed my fate or anything. In many ways my life wasn't all that different. I was sleeping on the floor now instead of a bed.

But I had some peace in the quiet of Conor's apartment. I felt useful to Dublin Ink and not just in the social media I did behind Conor's back, but even in the menial tasks: sweeping, taking out the trash, making the tea. I was contributing to something. I was a part of something.

I had Mason and Rian who encouraged my work, praised my efforts around the place, joked and teased me like big brothers. I could see myself one day as a tattoo artist despite Conor's stubborn refusal to teach me. Shite...did I actually believe all this?

I did?

I did.

"This old junker will be drivin' down that freeway over dere before you get out of dis life, Aurnia." Mia's words stung like a lash. Her laugh of disdain came in like a bruise. "That's not how it works, eejit."

"But—"

"You are who ye are. You come from what you come from."

I stared into Mia's hateful eyes. I could see it, the resentment. Was it true, what she said? Was I just playing house with Conor and the boys at Dublin Ink? Was I dressing them up as my family? Propping them up in corners like the parlour was my playhouse? Making their hands move the way I thought the hands of someone who cares move?

Conor yelled at me then pushed me away and avoided me. I kept believing that there was something between us. How blinded could I be?

"I..." I trailed off, my confidence gone.

I shrank against the sharp edges of the trunk as a small drizzle began in the junkyard. Mia and Lee and Jack all turned up their hoods, but I had none. They knew they might need one, being out in the elements.

I'd forgotten to because I had moved past the junkyard, past the exposure to the rain and sleet and biting winds.

But there I was. The only difference between us was that I was the only one who was shivering.

"Dis tattoo parlour," Mia said, her grin growing, "where d'ye say it was?"

I hadn't. She knew I hadn't. That wasn't the point. I was trapped. I hadn't mentioned the name Dublin Ink to my friends. As stupid as it was, that place was something I wanted to protect, to keep safe. I guess that said all there needed to be said about my "friends".

Mia had asked *where* it was, but I knew what she really wanted to know: was it outside of Nick's territory.

"It's not worth it," I said. I saw on Mia's face it was answer enough. "Really, Mia, it's not. There's just some crumpled bills in the register. They're practically bankrupt. The bank is going to come take all the equipment and anything of real value any day now, I'm sure of it."

"Not unless we take it first," Mia said with an arched eyebrow.

"What's the story?" Lee asked as he came from setting up the bottles which tinkled almost like wind chimes in the spattering of raindrops.

"We got a new target," Jack answered. "Courtesy of Aurnia here. Eager as she is to prove that she's still one of us."

"It's perfect," Mia said, speaking to Lee, but staring fixedly at me. "Little Aurnia here even has an in. It'll be like taking candy from a baby."

"I don't think it's a good idea," I said, though the three of them were already circling like buzzards on the idea. To them it was already a done deal. "I really don't."

Mia's head quirked to the side. "You feel loyalty toward dem," she said with a pitying laugh. "How long have ye known dese people? A few weeks? You've known us yer whole life."

"It's not that," I said, fingers tucking a wet strand behind my ear.

"What? Are they 'nice' people?" Mia said in a mocking tone as Lee and Jack chuckled. "You t'ink they'll be dere for you? You t'ink dey *care* about you?"

"They don't give a feck about me," I spat out, remembering that rainy night with Conor. "I'm nothing to them. Just a little brat off the street."

Mia smiled victoriously.

"We're de ones who'll stick around," she said. "We're de ones who've got yer back, Aurnia."

I looked across the steady rain at them. They'd left me at the jewellery store. I'd taken the fall for them and they hadn't even tried to see if I was okay. Mia was lying through her teeth.

But could I trust anyone at Dublin Ink any more than her? Or was the only difference that they lied to me beneath a dry roof instead of out in the rain?

"What'll it be, Aurnia?" Mia asked, Jack and Lee standing behind her in the mud. "Come on home or what?"

Home. It was all I wanted. All I'd ever wanted.

"Alright," I said with a sigh as I extended my hand. "Give me your phone. I'll type in the address."

How much exactly did tattoo guns go for on the black market?

23

CONOR

The grey walls of the bank loan officer's dingy office suited me. I liked the uncomfortable chairs with the threadbare cushions. The view out the window of the brick wall of the building next door was just fine to me. I didn't mind that the flip calendar was from the wrong month two years past. I had no problem at all with the stained carpet worn so thin in places it was beginning to show through to the rough planks of wood underneath.

This was what I expected from the life I had ruined. It was rather nice, life meeting one's expectations.

"He's going to laugh in our faces," Mason whispered to Rian and me.

Mason kept running his palms over his thick thighs. He'd put on the only suit he owned, which I supposed he only had in the first place for crashing weddings and plucking out a bridesmaid for the night. "There's no way he's going to extend our loan." He glanced at the frosted pane glass in the closed door. "Not with what we have to show for the last month."

"There were those days after Aurnia painted the alleyway," Rian said. It was to his credit that he cared about Dublin Ink enough not to put mushrooms in his tea that morning. He even managed to find a white button-down that wasn't covered in pencil stains. "That's got to count for something."

"Not when we nosedived after that," Mason said, breathing heavily at the tall cobwebbed ceilings. He turned to look at me. "How do you suppose we should explain that to him, Conor?"

I alone was in a t-shirt, the last of the ones I'd thrown in a duffle bag before leaving the apartment to Aurnia. I hadn't bothered to check for stains or tears. It was, like I said, my last one.

I kept my attention fixed on the empty rolling chair behind the desk and shrugged. "It's in a bad location. What more is there to say?"

Mason's fingers curled into fists. We had come close to blows on more than a few occasions recently. It would be very like us to finally explode at the bank. We were fighting, thrashing each other on the floor, within an hour of meeting each other at that tattoo competition.

"'What more is there to say?'" he hissed as Rian already began to raise his arms to keep us apart. "Did you really just say that? I swear to God, Conor, I—"

Mason was interrupted by my phone ringing. I hadn't been answering it lately. I didn't have any real desire to talk to anyone. Checking the caller ID was a chance to avoid a confrontation with Mason. Besides, my knuckles were too sore from the punching bag the other night to really want to bash in his cheekbone.

It was Diarmuid.

"We were talking," Mason growled. "Don't you fucking answer that when I'm—"

I raised a finger and took the call more to piss him off than for any other reason. I thought he was going to shatter the flimsy armrests of his chair as he cursed my name.

"Diarmuid, what's the craic?" I said and added, though Diarmuid hadn't asked, "Yeah, no, I'm not in the middle of anything."

Rian gave me a "did you really have to do that" look. I ignored him, too.

"I'm sure you were expecting a call from me," Diarmuid said, his voice far from happy, far from casual.

I was absolutely not expecting a call from him. As far as I knew I was to catch up with him at the end of each month to make sure things were on track with Aurnia. It was only the twelfth of November.

"Um, I—"

"Really I would have expected *you* to call *me* when something like this happens," Diarmuid said, "but I suppose you've got your hands full. So..." Diarmuid sighed. He sounded tired. Irritable.

"It's just that I thought things were going so well," he said. "When I came and visited, I really thought she'd gotten to the point where she was ready to leave this kind of shite behind her."

I glanced nervously at Mason and Rian, who quickly noticed the look on my face.

"What is it?" Mason mouthed.

I shook him away. I had no fucking clue. A sinking feeling in my stomach told me it wasn't good.

"Um, yeah," I said, clearing my throat, "I was just as surprised as you, Diarmuid. Things seemed to be on the right track."

Blurry images from several nights ago during the rainstorm flashed in my head. Deceit wasn't exactly a strong suit of mine. I wore my emotion right there on my sleeve. Just ask the long line of customers who'd been on the receiving end of my wrath. Just ask Aurnia.

Mason and Rian turned fully in their chairs to look at me, the beginnings of worry in their eyes. Could they see it in mine, too? I turned my gaze to my shoes.

"Well, I'm just glad she called you when they were processing her at the station," Diarmuid said.

I bit back a curse. *What have you done, Aurnia? What have you fucking done?*

It was easier to blame her than me. Never mind that I had driven her out.

Diarmuid continued, "I don't even want to imagine the number of seedy people she could have called instead. If she hadn't trusted you."

I squeezed my eyes shut, because I had to imagine them. The faces of the men in the hallway at her father's house all appeared behind my eyelids. Unfocused eyes. Pale faces. Sweaty brows. They were druggies and drunks and I'm sure they looked no different than I did to her that rainy night. Apparently they scared her less than me.

Rian nudged my shoe with his. I could just make out Mason whispering, "Is it Aurnia? Is something wrong with Aurnia?"

Even though I could barely hear him I wanted to shout at him to, "Shut up! Shut up! Shut up!" I wanted to squeeze his neck if that didn't do the trick. Guilt was already clawing at me like a wild animal.

"No, no," I said to Diarmuid. "You're right, it's a good thing she called me."

Rian's foot stopped prodding mine. Did he know that she hadn't called? Could he tell just from that that I was lying? Was it so obvious to him that Aurnia would never place her trust in me? Could never?

"It's obviously going to take some time to work out with the police and the store owner," Diarmuid said. "But they were able to catch the kids before anything was taken. Really a botched job, thankfully. Actually I'm a little surprised about that, too, given how smart I thought Aurnia was."

Fuck.

"And the place?" I asked.

"She didn't tell you?"

"Been giving her some space," I lied.

"You probably know best," Diarmuid said. "You two seem to have gotten close." I gritted my teeth as he continued, "It was a tattoo parlour on the other side of town. Almost the same name as yours, actually. Dublin Tattoo, I think it was. You should ask her about it. Would be a weird coincidence if it was one."

"Yeah, I'll make sure to ask her," I said softly.

"So she's there with you?" Diarmuid asked. "That's really why I wanted to call. Just to make sure she's there. And okay. You know, I've kind of taken a liking to her."

"Yeah, me too," I said, dragging a tired hand over my face.

What had I done? All I wanted was to keep her from that life. All I'd done was drive her right back to it. At least before she was in my apartment, at my parlour. She was under my watch.

But I'd chased her off. Where I couldn't see her. Where I couldn't keep her safe. What had I done?

"Well?" Diarmuid asked.

"What's that?" I said dumbly.

I had been elsewhere. In smoky drug dens. In filthy rooms with stained mattresses. Inside the minds of men. I shuddered and tried to focus as Diarmuid said, "Aurnia? She's with you?"

I glanced up at Mason and Rian, who were staring at me now with a mix of fear and anger. When they found out they would blame me. They should blame me. I blamed me.

"Yeah," I said, avoiding their eyes because I couldn't stand not to. "Yeah, she's right here with me. She's safe."

Saying those words make me want to throw up. I heard the shriek of a chair as Mason stood up, rage in his eyes. Rian's head fell into his open hands.

"Good, good," Diarmuid said. "I mean, that's all that really matters, isn't it?"

That was the one thing I had forgotten about when I yelled at Aurnia, when I drove her away. Diarmuid was right: it was the one thing that mattered. It was the one thing I failed to do.

"Yes," I said, though it came out as a shell-shocked croak.

"You're a good guy, Conor," Diarmuid said. "I could see she trusted you, that afternoon I was at the shop."

I dug my fingernails into my palm to keep myself from screaming. This was my reward for what I'd done: torture. Absolute torture.

"I don't imagine she trusts many people at this point in her life," Diarmuid added, twisting the knife in my gut.

"I've got to go," I mumbled.

"Right, right," Diarmuid said. "We'll talk more later about what this will do to her probation."

"Sure."

"You've given me some relief at least."

"Yep."

There was no relief for me, I knew that. I did not deserve any relief. I knew that, too.

I hung up the phone. When I glanced over at Rian and Mason, I saw anger. I saw fear.

"What did you do?" Rian asked, accusation in his strained voice.

I almost couldn't get the words out. It felt like there were fingers around my throat.

"Aurnia," I finally said, their eyes boring holes in me. "She's missing."

We left the office immediately. No one had to say a word further. The loan could wait. Dublin Ink could burn.

There was only Aurnia.

24

AURNIA

A part of me hoped that someone would see through the ruse.

I'd called him, after all, so it was stupid to wish that he would get caught, but hey, I never really claimed to be all that smart. As I dialled the number, I secretly hoped that someone might notice that it wasn't the one on the little piece of paper in front of me. As I spoke to him on the phone, I kept glancing at the officer spinning idly in his chair to see if maybe, just maybe he might notice that my voice didn't sound quite right. That I was tense. That I was uncomfortable. That I was lying.

It took a few hours for him to arrive at the station. In those hours, there on that cold, hard bench behind those cold, hard bars, I ran my palms over my thighs. I wouldn't mind all that much if he didn't show up.

But of course he finally arrived. I walked out to the front with the officer. I greeted him with the name that was not his as he grinned at me wildly.

Even then I held out for the slim chance that someone would recognise him. From a mug shot. From a person of interest list. From an altercation on some seedy city sidewalk. I signed my signature on the release papers slowly to give the officer at the front desk a few extra seconds. Just in case.

He lied through his teeth to the officer. "I'll give her a firm talking to, don't you worry. She'll not be doing anything like this ever again if I have anything to say about it. Boy, I *sure* was worried about this dear, dear little child.". How could anyone be buying this? Surely the officer wasn't going to let him just walk out the door with me. Sure he had tattoos, but they were clearly done with a ballpoint pen and a fifth of whiskey. Yes, he said the right name, but it was so obvious that it didn't fit him. It couldn't fit him. If I could see straight through him and his darting eyes, his stinking jacket, his fidgeting fingers, then why couldn't anyone else?

I dared to hope that as we were walking down the street outside the station toward his car, someone might run after us. "How'd you let this happen?" some sergeant would chastise the officer at the front desk. "Are you all lunatics?" he'd shout at the guys in the back. "This man is clearly not Conor Mac Haol!"

None of those silly hopes, those ridiculous wishes mattered now.

Because I'd called Nick.

I'd left with him.

There I was, sitting in his car with his hand on my thigh.

"You're a clever little one, ain't you, Aurnia?" Nick said.

The car shifted dangerously across lanes. He wasn't looking at the road: he was looking at me.

I forced myself to keep my eyes straight ahead. I didn't want to encourage him. A single glance was all it took to make him believe that I was his. In school we learned about this lady in Greek mythology with snake for hair whose gaze turned people to stone. Nick's gaze didn't turn you to stone. It just claimed your soul. I guess "fucking devil" would be a better name for Nick than Medusa.

And yet I had called him. There I was, not shoving aside his hand from my leg and leaping from the moving car.

"Did you like how I said I was so worried?" Nick said, tugging at the wheel just before we hit the chain-link fence of an abandoned warehouse. "I thought that asshole ate that right up. Like he was holding a goddamn spoon."

I remained silent.

"He fucking ate that right up."

I knew he was grinning. Grinning at the road in that dangerous part of town he thought was his. Grinning at the blanket of grey clouds he claimed as his own. Grinning at me. Finally back where I belonged. In his possession. He squeezed my thigh more tightly.

"Did you like how I grabbed your head and pulled it to my chest like that?" he asked. "Like I was just so overcome with emotion that you were safe and sound? I saw the way that prick looked at me when I did that. He really believed it. Someone should send me a goddamn Oscar, you know? My little baby Aurnia?"

Nick blew through a red light. I didn't turn my head to glance in either direction to see whether we were about to be hit; it wasn't worth the risk of catching Nick's eye. Death would be kinder anyway.

"Maybe you'd like that, eh?" Nick said. His tickling of my side felt more like the jab of a screwdriver over and over again. "Maybe you'd like to be with an Oscar winner. Maybe you wouldn't run off where I can't find you so often then, eh?"

"I really appreciate you picking me up," was all I said. "You can drop me off right here."

The car kept going. If the doors hadn't already been locked, I was sure that Nick would have locked them.

"Did you like when I said all that about being disappointed in you? In wishing that you hadn't done what you did? In feeling that you were slipping right through my fingers?"

Nick's hand was back on my thigh. His knuckles were white as he gripped me, the black of his tattoos all the blacker in contrast.

"Maybe you thought that part was especially convincing?" he said. "Well, let me tell you the secret to that part of the performance."

I sensed his head leaning toward mine just as clearly as if he had been a spider crawling over my bare shoulder. The car swerved on the deserted road, but neither of us seemed to care all that much if we crashed. Nick didn't believe it was possible; he was Superman. And me? I was simply unable to care anymore.

Nick's breath was hot against my ear. "The secret, little baby Aurnia, was that it wasn't a performance at all. I meant every single word I said to that fat pig. I meant it all the way down to the pit of my belly. I meant it from my fucking *heart*, do you hear me?"

"You're hurting me," I said, keeping my eyes forward, forward, forward.

"You've disappointed me. I don't like you away from me. I like when I can really grab ahold of you."

"You're hurting me," I repeated.

Nick just laughed and slapped my thigh. He swerved, barely avoiding a lamp post littered with missing children's posters.

"But all is forgiven, my sweet!" he shouted as he whipped the car roughly around a corner. "All is forgiven!"

His fingers at the back of my neck made my skin crawl as he squeezed me and shook me.

"You've found your way back to me and that's all that matters," he said, roughing up my hair. "And you won't do what you did, leaving me, ever, ever again, now will you?"

I shifted slightly away from Nick's possessive touch because I just couldn't stand it any longer. He laughed.

"Why did you call me, little baby Aurnia?" he asked, shoving me against the window.

Maybe he thought it was playful. I knew I'd have a bruise on my arm for weeks. The crack of my head against the glass was loud enough to block out his laughter for that blissful millisecond.

"I had no one else," I told him.

Nick clicked his tongue.

"No, no," he said, lighting a cigarette as he drove haphazardly with his knees. "No, I don't think that's why you called me at all."

I'd always hated my house. Always hated it. Always wanted to get away from it. As Nick and I drove past it, him without comment at all, I longed to pull into the drive. I longed for the dirty entryway with bodies littered across it like a war zone. I longed for my bed sheets that smelled like smoke and sweat. Because as least I knew it.

If we weren't going to my father's place, where were we going?

"Do you want me to tell you?" Nick asked.

"What?" I was distracted, resisting the urge to shift around in my seat and watch my dump of a house disappear in the rearview mirror.

Nick slapped my cheek, not softly. "Little dummy. Do you want me to tell you why you really called me?"

I shook my head to focus, because all I could think about was the infinite number of doors us passing by my house opened, all of them more terrible than the last.

I said, "I told you. I called you because I had no one else."

"No!" Nick shouted so loud and so violently that I jumped in my seat.

He ran his hand soothingly up and down my thigh and repeated in a softer voice as he shook his head, "No, no, no."

His hand moved to the side of my head and he petted my hair with clumsy hands that got caught painfully in my tangles. The speed with which he had a handful of my hair in his grip and used it to wrench my face toward his was frightening.

"You called me, because you know where you belong. You called me and had me pretend to be this 'Conor' of yours because you didn't want to call this 'Conor' of yours. You called me because you wanted *me* to come."

No one was watching where we were going. Why didn't we hit something? Why couldn't we just fucking hit something?

"Do you see?" Nick asked in a syrupy sweet voice that made me want to curl up into a little ball.

Before I could answer, Nick used the hair he held painfully in his fist to nod my head up and down. He smiled at me, revealing his yellowed teeth, his missing molar. He pushed me against the headrest and released me at last. I gasped like I'd been under water the whole time.

"Good," Nick said, returning his hand to my thigh like we were just two lovers out for a Sunday drive in the neighbourhood. "Good, little baby Aurnia."

I dared to look over at him in the driver's seat as he drove on, as he whistled an out-of-tune little song, as he put out his cigarette on the dash of his car.

From his profile you could almost call Nick handsome. A strong jaw. A sharp nose. High cheekbones. From his profile you couldn't see his eyes, black and sharklike. You couldn't see the disrepair of his teeth. You couldn't see how his lips were chapped and peeling in their perpetual grin.

I hated him. But I had said the same of Conor. Nick was violent toward me, but hadn't Conor also grabbed at me? Hadn't he also left bruises on my wrist? Nick was moody, mean. Conor was maybe even worse.

I'd thought that no one could look on Nick and think that he was Conor. But maybe I'd been wrong. Maybe my attraction to Conor, that flare of chemistry that had been sparked that very first moment, maybe it blinded me. Because Nick, too, from this angle was alluring.

Was Nick right then?

I didn't call Conor because I was mad at him. Because he had hurt me. Because I wanted him to feel the kind of pain and rejection that I had felt that rainy night.

Maybe I called Nick because the two were no different from one another. It wasn't that I had no one left: it was that I had two of the same.

Nick said I belonged with him. I thought I belonged with Conor. But what was the fucking difference?

I was right about one thing though: there was no one else. There was Conor. There was Nick. One had sent me away. One had picked me up. That was it. All there was to tell.

"Where are we going?" I asked, my voice sounding strange even to my own ears—dull and far away.

Nick's voice on the other hand was perky, almost happy, though I knew that was not an emotion he was capable of, if he was capable of any at all. "To a little welcome home party. I want to show you that I'm your family, Aurnia. Do you hear me? I'll always be here. No matter where you go, what you do to hurt me. I'll always come after you."

He turned the corner and pulled into a parking spot in front of a clothing department store, one nicer than any I'd ever been to. That wasn't saying much given luxury to me meant the Goodwill's full price section.

"A party?" I asked dully.

Nick shrugged as he switched off the ignition. "A party, a stakeout, toma*y*to, toma*h*to."

He shifted in his seat to assess me. He yanked my shirt down to reveal the top of my bra and then tugged down my lower lip.

"Pout," he said with a wink. "Pout for papa."

I stared at him, feeling numb inside. He clapped his hands and began to get out of the car.

"You know, it's funny," he said as he ducked his head briefly back inside to where I sat frozen stiff. "I knew a Conor once."

25

CONOR

*I*t was safe to say that I wasn't sleeping.

Not that I particularly tried. Every moment that Aurnia was missing was a moment when I should be out looking for her. That meant day. That meant night.

The bags under my eyes deepened as the days and nights went on. I hadn't seen them for myself; I didn't have time for mirrors. Not that I would have been brave enough to face one even if I had. It was Mason who told me this. Occasionally it was the women he brought back to the loft above Dublin Ink. Though when we hadn't found Aurnia after a week, they stopped appearing in the kitchen each morning. Rian, when he finally started talking to me again, told me this as well.

I was sure my hair was greasy. Strands no longer fell over my stinging eyes after several days. I didn't need to corral it back before putting on my motorcycle helmet. I couldn't remember if I bothered changing shirts. Though I was sure whatever I was wearing stunk like shit. I felt like I had a fever all those days I spent looking for Aurnia with no luck at all. My skin was clammy. I was covered in sweat like I'd just awoken from a terrible dream in a gasping start. Except it was constant. And my dream was a nightmare. My nightmare, a reality.

My fingers shook and it only got worse as I continued not to sleep, continued not to eat. It was whiskey that sustained me. Whiskey that gave me my only reprieves in those early hours of the morning where I passed out on the couch only to toss and turn. Whiskey kept me sane.

Or at least, kept me from going insane.

After leaving the bank, Rian silent and brooding, Mason trying to be positive, hopeful, the three of us had stopped on the busy sidewalk.

"Alright," Rian said pointedly to Mason. "I'll check her old school."

I didn't know her old school. I didn't even know if she was in school or not.

Mason said, "Right, and I'll go by that park she likes on the east side."

I'd never heard Aurnia talk about a park. The only park I knew she'd been to was the one by her father's house with the dead grass and rusted merry-go-round where I'd forced her onto my motorcycle.

The two of them rattled off a dozen places each they could think of where Aurnia might be before turning to me. I scratched the back of my neck awkwardly.

"I've got a place to look," was all I said.

I drove to her father's house and knocked on the door.

"Aurnia's not here," her father said.

"You told me that last time."

He showed me to her bedroom. He stood in the doorway as I stepped inside. I stared at the empty bed where she slept. It sagged horribly in the middle. It was lumpy and I was sure if I kicked at it with my toe a cloud of dust, or worse, would emerge. She'd grown so used to an uncomfortable bed that she couldn't get comfortable on mine. The reveal of why she slept on the floor in my apartment stabbed at my heart.

I glanced around the room for what I told myself were clues about where she would have gone. I wanted to see a piece of her. I needed something to grab ahold of. I realised I knew so little about Aurnia despite the grenade she'd thrown on my life. I hadn't allowed myself to know more.

And now she was...

"Gone," Aurnia's father said, slurring his words as he gripped the doorframe to keep from falling. "See?"

I left the filthy, horrible house with a heaviness in my chest. I sat on my motorcycle across the street for over an hour as my phone kept buzzing.

Checked the art museum Rian texted.

Checked that pizza place she loves Mason texted.

Checked the skate park where she said she had her first kiss Rian said.

Checked the bakery she swore had the best soda bread Mason said.

More and more kept coming. Checked here. Checked there. Checked places I'd never heard of. Checked places that were completely foreign to me. Each text was painting a different part of Aurnia's secret life. Each text was more painful than the last because I saw how little I knew. Because I felt how much I wanted to know.

When I returned to Dublin Ink, I found Mason and Rian huddled together over some sketches Aurnia had left in the parlour. I stood there at the door, numb and feeling hopeless, as I watched them. What would I see in the drawings? Nothing. I would see nothing. Mason and Rian could remember this conversation or that, could point to something she said the other day, the other week. I could do none of that.

I knew Aurnia liked Lucky Charms.

I knew Aurnia had a little freckle at the dimple of her lower back.

I knew Aurnia made me want to do things to her that I never could.

What help would that be in finding her?

"Where all did you check?" Mason asked when he noticed me at last. "We've been texting you all day."

That's when I went for the whiskey.

I drove drunk that night. Just followed the night down empty streets, swerving and squinting for any sign of her. It was futile, I knew. It was better than sitting in Dublin Ink. It was better than doing nothing, or worse, accepting the truth: I knew exactly where Aurnia was. As far away as fucking possible. That's where I'd driven her. That's where I'd ensured that she would go.

I'm not sure which night it was that I returned to Aurnia's father's house again, the best shot I had at stumbling upon her before she was gone forever. I was in enough of a drunken, guilt-ridden fog that I probably lurked outside in the shadows for nights on end before finally stumbling toward the door. This time I stood a chance in hell of convincing them that I was Aurnia's JLO. The moment her name came slurred and desperate from my lips the jig was up.

Without a pretend badge to protect me, it wasn't much of a fight: one against a dozen. I returned to Dublin Ink bloody and barely conscious. Rian found me in the morning and I'm pretty sure it was the first time in days that he spoke to me as he held a frozen bag of peas against my swollen eye.

"You're not telling us everything."

It was a chance for me to come clean. To be honest with my friend. To let him in.

I just took the bag from his hand and crawled up to the

guest bedroom in Mason's loft. Rian went back to not talking to me.

I'd broken something between us. I wasn't entirely sure that it had ever been whole in the first place. Our friendship had started on a lie. Why the hell wouldn't it end on one?

Mason had to cover for me with Diarmuid, who began to call with more regularity. "Nasty cold," I heard him saying as I came back one morning from hours on my motorcycle driving Dublin streets looking for Aurnia.

Mason eyed me mistrustfully as I went straight to the liquor cabinet in the kitchen. "Can't even say a fucking word," he said to Diarmuid. Loud so that I could hear it.

I lived in a constant state of misery those weeks. Physically. Emotionally. Psychologically. I grew more and more distant with Mason and Rian. My drives out on the motorcycle went longer and longer.

If I was drinking, I'd blink to find myself in some suburb an hour away. Outside some nice home. I'd rub my red-rimmed eyes, my black eye still sore and throbbing, and watch as a blurry family sat down to dinner. Maybe I ended up in those parts of town because that's where I wanted to find Aurnia. In front of a plate of Sunday roast. Her hand in her father's for grace. Candlelight soft on her cheeks.

I'd return to see Mason and Rian alone in the kitchen, chatting quietly over some takeout boxes. They'd look up at me, but I never joined them. I went to my drafting desk. To my whiskey. To my bad choices.

This was because of me.

This was because I kept her at arm's length. A violent, mean arm's length.

This was because in trying not to let her too close, I pushed her too far away.

These thoughts rolled over and over again in my mind till I

couldn't stand it any longer. That was when I returned to my motorcycle. It was in this hopeless cycle.

After Aurnia went missing, whenever Mason saw me, he would say, "We'll find her, Conor. We'll find her."

I wasn't not sure when he stopped saying that.

Or when I stopped hearing it.

It probably didn't matter: I didn't think I ever really believed it.

26

AURNIA

"You want me to go in there?" I asked. "You want me to go in there alone?"

"Alone?" Nick said. "Little baby Aurnia, do you call a kite alone just because the tail trails behind a little?"

Nick, as it so happened, was himself, high as a fucking kite.

"What does that mean?" I asked.

The lantern on the dirty warehouse floor cast ominous shadows of our hunched shoulders onto the high walls of mostly broken windows. Nick's hand came like a ghost out of the dark. He grabbed my chin. I could smell the reek of his breath.

"It means," he said, black eyes flashing in the lantern light. "That I'll be right behind you."

I tugged my chin away and said, "But I'll be alone until you do. You're sending me in there knowing what they could do to me."

Nick had finally revealed his plan to me about his next big robbery the night before it was to take place. Nick wanted to expand his territory and to do that he needed to take over a rival drug den. I knew the place he was talking about. Everyone did. It made my father's house look like a church basement during a sobriety meeting. On the outside it looked much the same as the trashy dump my father and I called home. But it was the inside that scared me...and it was the inside which was exactly where Nick intended to send me.

"I mean, how long can it take to wag your tail a little?" Nick was saying. "To bat your eyelashes a little? To show a little something, something? Get them distracted and I'll be right in there."

I glared at him over the lantern.

"And if they get a little too distracted?" I asked.

Nick shrugged and in the distorted shadows he looked like a vulture.

"You're clever enough, little baby Aurnia," he said. "You got away from me easily enough if I remember correctly."

His fingertips began to trail up the inner seam of my black jeans. I pushed myself away from the lantern.

"Where are you going?" Nick called after me.

It wasn't like there was far to go. Not a lot of nice places in an abandoned warehouse on the outskirts of town. I went to the cot Nick had stolen from a shitty hostel while I acted as the getaway driver. I'd almost laughed when the owner came out onto the sidewalk shaking his arm at us as I sped away. I'd almost convinced myself that Nick wasn't all that bad as he hooted and hollered and thumped his palms against the dashboard.

"Atta girl, Aurnia!" he shouted. "Atta girl!"

This was the life I was intended for, right? Life on the other side of the tracks. Life on the run. Life going job to job. Life that was rough, hard, real. Whatever I'd been doing at Dublin Ink wasn't me. Wasn't my life. It was just play pretend. It was just fantasy.

Nick was real. Nick was there. Or at least, that's what I was halfway to convincing myself was true.

I shoved aside the clothes Nick had bought me. I'd been stupid enough to think just for a second that he did it as a kindness to me. That the dresses were a gift. I should have known better, of course. His comments were always, "maybe a little shorter" or "that does nothing for your tits, love" or "you've got the hips of a little boy in that one". I knew what he had intended the dresses for. They weren't for me. They were for the men that inhabited the rival drug den. For their filthy eyes. For their dirty minds. For their grubby fingers—but only for a second, he'd said. Just a second or two, he'd promised.

I sat with a sigh on the edge of the cot. How pathetic was I? So eager to find some sort of family anywhere that I'd allow myself to think that Nick could care about me.

Nick, who made me fear barring my bedroom door because I knew it would be worse if he had to force his way in, because I knew he *liked* to force his way in. Nick, who stared at me over my father's shoulder with those black, possessive eyes like my father didn't exist. Nick, who I always knew saw me as a toy and who forced me to go limp because it was less fun for him that way.

Nick, who I feared. Nick, who my father feared. Nick, who frightened everyone but himself.

When I left Conor at Dublin Ink, I swore I'd not need anyone. I'd give up these delusions of family, of safety, of someone to protect me.

There was Mia and Lee and Jack. For a moment I believed. I relearned my lesson quickly enough after that. They were just using me. So I used them. Took them to a different tattoo parlour. Pulled the alarm while they weren't looking. I told myself again: I do not need anyone. I do not need a family.

Then there was Nick. Again those stupid hopes. I'd look for family anywhere. I'd *fall* for family with anyone.

In that moment, I hated myself.

I pulled the notebook from beneath my cot and began drawing in the faint light that came from Nick's lantern across the dirty warehouse floor. There was something therapeutic about the scratch of my pencil on the cheap paper. There always had been. It was perhaps the sole place on earth where I could escape: my art. And yet as I drew, another place slipped into my head.

I found myself drawing the ugly floral print couch. Its torn armrests. It's sweeping back. Its row of dingy tassels between the scratched-up legs. I lost myself in the petals of the dated fabric, drew each one with care. I sketched out Rian's tattoo chair. Added the little stool he often spent hours just idly spinning round and round upon. Then there was the big window over-looking the street. The heavy drapes. I could practically see Mason's worn fingertips on them where he'd pull them back again and again to check out a passing girl. I added one of several old oriental rugs, each more dusty and falling apart than the last. The broken neon sign above the stairs was easy enough to draw, the letters of 'Dublin Ink' fluid and sweeping.

I smiled down at the drawing. I'd never done much like that and the dimensions were off, the furniture appearing more like cardboard cut-outs than real couches and chairs and desks. My smile fell. Was I doing it again? Was I play pretending house? Was I moving Mason and Rian's arms and legs this way and that like paper dolls?

I crumpled up the page and shoved it with the rest beneath the cot. I needed to draw something different. Something that made me feel independent. Strong. I wanted to believe that I didn't need what I knew I needed. I needed a lie. A lie I could believe.

As I began to sketch again it was a pair of hands, big and strong and tattooed, that appeared on my lap. I remembered how they felt on my skin. Throwing me out of Dublin Ink. Dragging me out of my father's house. Holding me tight on his motorcycle. I remembered how they looked holding his own pencil. How they looked pouring milk for my cereal. How they looked shaking on either side of my head as Conor roared over the rain.

I was so preoccupied tracing over the lines I'd drawn till my fingertips were stained slate that I didn't notice Nick coming toward me. My only warning was his body briefly blocking the light from the lantern behind him. When I looked up, there he was.

"Not thinking of being difficult, are we?" he asked, rocking forward with his hands behind his back.

His voice had that fake sugary effect he put on when he was asking something as if there wasn't only one single acceptable answer. I quickly put the notebook beneath the cot and laid out, fluffing the limp pillow beneath my head.

"I'm just tired," I said.

I closed my eyes, half believing like a child that that was the way to make the monsters disappear. It was stupid to have ever called Nick. Stupid to have ever put myself back within his clutches. Stupid to allow him close enough to trail his fingers along the dip in my side the way he was in that very moment.

"I'm counting on you, little baby Aurnia," he said.

I could tell from his voice how close he had lowered his face. I didn't dare open my eyes.

"The plan only works with you," he whispered, his breath hot on my cheek. "Very bad things will happen to me if you don't do what I've told you to do. Do you understand? I've got people waiting. People...expecting."

Nick's fingers played at the hem of my sweatshirt.

"I understand," I said, eyes still squeezed shut as I tried not to shiver. "I go into that...that place. I go into that place alone. That's what you want me to do."

The cot creaked as Nick sank down on the edge. He sighed as his hand moved to the side of my neck. His fingers were clammy. He smeared his sweat across my skin as he circled his thumb along my jugular.

"These people," he said softly, "they're not like me."

I panicked when Nick's fingers began to tighten. My eyes shot open. Nick's gaze was boring into me.

"They're not gentle like me," he said as he tightened his grip even further.

I began to cough.

"They're not *sweet* like me," Nick cooed in my ear as I shoved my palms against him.

"Nick," I gasped. "Nick, stop."

My feet scuffed along the rough material of the cot. I was forced to stare into Nick's vicious eyes as he glared down at me and squeezed even harder.

"They're not like me," he said. "*They're* violent people."

He released me and I gasped in air, folding in on myself. I shuddered when Nick began making soothing circles on my back with the same fingers he'd just used to choke me.

"One more time then," he said. "Say it one more time for Daddy, little baby Aurnia."

"I'll do it," I said.

"You'll do what?"

"I'll go in. Just like you said."

Nick pressed a kiss to my temple. I could smell the alcohol that stained his breath.

"Good girl," he whispered.

Nick grabbed the notebook from beneath my cot before he left. I sighed in relief that I'd balled up the Dublin Ink drawing.

He leafed through it as he made his way back toward the lantern. I watched him use his lighter to set it on fire. He left it burning there on the floor when he disappeared into the dark. People to meet. Violence to enact. Other girls to fuck. Lucky for me, Nick didn't mix business and pleasure. At least, not yet.

His footsteps rattled on the metal stairs on their way out the abandoned warehouse and soon I was alone in the silence, alone in the dark. My heart was still racing. My breath still ragged. I knew this to be true: Nick had only left me alone because he believed that I wouldn't leave myself.

If he had had any suspicion at all, he would have stayed. Fuck, I wouldn't have put it past him to chain me to the old radiator in the corner. But he was certain I would sit there. On the cot. Like a good dog. He was certain the next day I would get up when he told me. Put on the slutty clothes like he told me. Smear red lipstick messily across my lips to make them all think I was drunk, that I was easy enough to take advantage of. Just. Like. He. Told. Me. Nick knew I would go into that place the next day.

But Nick didn't know that I had someone who told me I would never go back to a place like that. Who told me I was wrong when I said I lived in a place like that. Who risked his life to take me out of a place like that.

I wasn't sure just how different Conor was from Nick. I wasn't naïve, even if I was sometimes blinded by hope. But there was this glaring difference, something, at least, to hold onto: Nick would send me in. Conor would drag me out.

For now, that was enough.

I packed up my things as quietly as possible, afraid even then that it was all a trap. That Nick was waiting for me to do just this. That he was lurking in the shadows downstairs.

He didn't know. He didn't know about Conor.

I sneaked down the stairs and I repeated those words again

and again, step by step. *He didn't know. He didn't know about Conor. He didn't know. He didn't know I had Conor.*

Outside of the warehouse, the night swallowed me whole.

Nick was gone.

Because he didn't know.

27

CONOR

The broken neon sign cast my shadow on the wall behind me. If I would have turned around, I would have seen the shape of a monster. Wide, stooped shoulders. A head bent at the neck. Large. Imposing. Ominous in the night. I did not turn around. I would not turn around.

I was at my drawing desk and the wastebasket was filling up once more. Discarded sketches. Failures. One after the next. Things were getting back to normal. Mason had started bringing women back over. Slowly, but surely. Rian forgot he wasn't talking to me every once in a while when he got distracted by a new idea and started babbling.

Then there was me. Back to a hole I could not fill. There, trying to fill it.

Aurnia already felt like a brief fever. The kind that wakes you up in the middle of the night. Twisted in your sheets. Breathing hard. Soaked from head to toe. Gone in the morning.

We'd exhausted places to look. Exhausted people to ask. I'd drunk enough whiskey to fuck up my liver three lifetimes over. I'd blown what little cash I had left on gas. There was nothing more to do. I'd tell Diarmuid in the morning. Maybe he'd be able to find her. I guessed not.

Aurnia didn't want to be found. And she didn't want to be found by me.

The tip of the pencil snapped suddenly. I hadn't realised I was pushing so hard against the page. I looked down to find the start of a face: a supple cheek, a curtain of hair tucked behind an ear, the outer edges of soft lips taking form. I tore the page from the pad with a weary sigh. The paper disintegrated like ashes in my fist. I sprinkled them over the wastebasket like it was an open grave.

I was staring at another blank page when the little bell at the front door announced a visitor.

"We're closed," I grumbled, not bothering to look up.

The roughness of my voice, hoarse from hours of screaming, should have been more than enough to scare even the bravest soul away. It was with surprise that I heard a small, sweet little voice say, "Sign says 'Open'."

I looked up to find her there. Right fucking there. Standing in the doorway of Dublin Ink. Closing the door timidly behind her back as she stared warily in my direction. Was I seeing a ghost? Her skin did look paler. The purple beneath her lower lash line a little deeper. The hollows of her cheekbones a little blacker.

I'd spent so much time over the last two weeks trying to find Aurnia that I never paused to consider what exactly I would do when I did, *if* I did. I was unprepared. Her presence was an uppercut to the jaw out of nowhere. I was reeling. I had no clue what the fuck I was going to do.

A car passed on the street outside and its headlights briefly illuminated the interior of the tattoo parlour. I raised a hand against the glare of the light. I blinked and half expected Aurnia to be gone. My eyes adjusted once more to the dim light.

She was still there. Little fingers fidgeting with the loose hems of her too thin jacket. Teeth sinking into her lower lip. Eyes hesitant beneath dark eyelashes.

My heart beat faster as I stood. Slowly. Uncertainly. Was I going to yell at her? Was I going to scream at her and shake her and slap her sweet little face for doing something so stupid? For making me medicate with liquor to keep my sanity? For driving me to the brink? For nearly killing me?

I swallowed and my throat felt tight, painfully tight. Was I going to advance upon her? The shadow on the wall behind me growing larger and larger? Was I going to pick her up by those hips she hid under those baggy jackets and position her against the wall by the stairs? Rip her pants? Claw at her hair? Fuck her till she did the same? Fuck her till she dug her nails into my cheek? Fuck her till cursed my name?

As she looked at me and as I looked at her, I didn't know what I was going to do. The next five minutes of my life were as black to me as the slick asphalt outside. I was an animal. All instinct. All fight or flight. Whatever I did I would have no control over, I was sure of that. Whatever I did it would not be my decision to do. Whatever I did, I would not be able to stop.

"Conor," Aurnia whispered.

My name on her lips. Was I going to put my finger to them? Silence them forever so they couldn't hurt me anymore. So they couldn't hurt her. Was I going to bloody them? With my knuckles? With my teeth? With my cock?

"Conor," Aurnia whispered once more and I was not in control.

I was not in control.

I was not in control.

"Conor," Aurnia whispered a final time and I was moving toward her.

My feet were fast. Her words faster, "Conor, listen, I'm sorry that I—"

I was upon her. My hands were on her neck. Her eyes were on mine, big and wide. I was moving. She was being dragged along with me.

"Conor," she said. She begged.

There was no one to come for her. No one to stop me. Whatever I was going to do was going to happen. The sidewalks empty. The street barren. The phone silent. The night cold. I was moving. She was coming with me. There was nothing she could do to stop me. And there was nothing I could do to stop me either.

It took no time at all for me to drag her across the room. It was now two shadows on the wall behind me. One big. One small. One predator. One prey. One attacker. One victim.

Aurnia cowered, but that did not stop me. Nothing could stop me. Not me. Not the police. Not God himself. Aurnia yelped and turned her face away and flinched at the cold, but I did not stop.

"Take it," I commanded. "Put your hand around it."

I forced Aurnia's quivering fingers around it. Her hair had fallen over her face, over her dark-lined eyes. She glanced down at the tattoo gun she held loosely at her shaking chest.

"Like this," I said quickly. "You want to hold it like this."

I manoeuvred her fingers which no longer fought against me. Hers were ice, mine felt like fire. The calluses of my palms scraped against the smoothness of her flesh; I could hear it over my desperate pants. Aurnia was watching me now. I could sense her eyes on me behind that curtain of black silk.

I did not meet her gaze. My fingers moved fast over hers. The rising and falling over her chest was returning to normal, but mine was quickening. A calm washed over her, but I felt nothing but panic.

"How does that feel?" I asked in a hushed, frantic whisper.

Aurnia just nodded. Hunched over her small frame, I began, in that same hushed, frantic whisper, to explain the different elements of the gun. How it worked. The amount of pressure needed. Different models. Different inks. What to do if your hand cramped on a particularly long project. I was all over the place. I wasn't even sure I was making any sense at times. I spoke so quickly. So softly. Could she even make out a single word I was uttering like my last confession?

Whether she could or not, Aurnia listened. The whole time she kept her eyes on me. When I moved her hand here or there, she relented. She said not a word herself. She just watched me. She just watched me and listened.

The more I explained to her, the more I felt I needed to explain. The faster I spoke, the faster I felt I needed to speak. A terror was washing over me now that Aurnia was back with me. How was it that I was more frightened with her here than when she was gone?

When I'd told her all I could about the tattoo gun itself, I took it from her fingers. I took it gently. With a gentleness I didn't even know I was still capable of. My own fingers shook as I took her hand in mine. She followed me without question as I guided her around the shop. I whispered to her over the pages of our design book. I nudged her closer like it was a pool she could see to the depths of if only she could step a little closer. I moved to stand behind her. My arms encompassed her small frame as I reached around to flip the large glossy page. Her hair was against my nose. I breathed her in as I spoke fast, faster.

I was desperate that she understand this style and that. Abstract. Watercolour. American. Black and white, like mine. I explained histories and trends and evolutions. I darted from one to the next. No coherence. No direction. Just more. More. All that mattered was that I gave her more. That I gave her *all*.

With her back against my chest, I felt her heartbeat. The steadier hers became the more mine seemed to beat out of control. She let me guide her by the shoulders to the supply closet where I talked in the shadows about inks. About needles. About stencils. I pulled out half the contents of the closet. Tossed it onto the floor. Didn't bother to pick a goddamn thing up.

I was sweating through my shirt. My heart was erratic. My chest fluttered. My palms were slick on the small of Aurnia's back. I didn't feel like this even on my most challenging sessions at the boxing gym. On those nights where I attacked the bag in my garage with all my self-loathing, even then, I didn't feel like *this*.

I don't know how long this went on, my crazed explanations, my deranged teaching. We went from the supply closet to the chairs, from the chairs to the cabinet of bandages and ointments, from the cabinet to my drawing desk. All I know is that Aurnia put up no fight. I was the only one with flailing fists. With exhausted muscles. With a heart on the verge of giving out. Her little feet followed after me without protest. She moulded to my touch like wet clay. I kept my hands on her the whole time and she only leaned further and further into me. Her eyes, for the whole time, were on me.

At the drawing desk, I showed her how to sketch some basic designs. The page quickly became filled with anything and everything: flowers and tribal designs, coy fish and Chinese symbols, geometric shapes and foxes with jewels for eyes. Drawings overlapped drawings. The whole time I whispered into Aurnia's ear. The whole time she listened.

"Here," I said breathlessly as I bent to retrieve a new drawing pad and pencils from the bottom drawer. Standing was a fit of strength like none before. I opened Aurnia's arms, the arms of a pretty little doll, and put them all against her chest. I folded her arms back across my gifts like I didn't trust them not to fall straight to the floor. I whispered quickly, "Here, here. Please. *Please.*"

At last I met Aurnia's eyes as she gazed up at me in the pale light of the pink neon. There was no quiver in her voice when she spoke. No panic. No terror. She was steady as a rock. Calm as the moon hidden behind the shifting fog.

"Thank you."

I collapsed against her, my forehead against hers. I shook my head slightly.

"Don't say that," I said, my voice ragged from speaking for so long. It had been years, years since I had said so much. "Don't say that."

Aurnia was there. The cool of her forehead like a damp rag against my feverish brow. She was there and I understood the panic I felt. I'd felt what it was like to lose her. I'd felt the pain. The guilt. And I knew. I knew I couldn't go through that again. I wouldn't survive. Aurnia had returned and she had raised the stakes impossibly.

"Please," I begged, grasping at her body as I pulled her to me in desperation, "don't thank me."

"Then what?" Aurnia whispered, the notebooks and pencils, her little wrists caught between us. "Then what, Conor?"

It was the one thing I wanted. The one thing I needed.

"*Stay.*"

28

AURNIA

I'd always thought that the thing about not being able to breathe when someone hugged you too tightly was bullshite. Like real, utter *bullshite*. It was some hyperbole someone somewhere once wrote that people kept reusing for some stupid reason. It was the stuff of television and movies. It was some line for bratty kids to say when they ran away from perfectly nice homes where their only problem was that their parents loved them too much and returned with two police officers shaking their heads and wagging their fingers on the front steps.

I didn't believe you could be hugged that tightly. Bullshite. Bullshite. *Bullshite.*

That was before Mason and Rian came in the next morning to find me emptying the waste bins in the living room. I had to admit that maybe wasn't complete bullshite.

Even hours later it still felt like I was trying to refill my crushed lungs with air. Every time I managed to smooth down the hair that Mason ruffled with his tattooed knuckles, he would be back by me, drawing me into his side, crushing me with an arm around my shoulders, and ruffling it all back up again.

"I'm just so happy to see you," he'd say as I squirmed and tried to push him away (this was mostly for show, because the truth was, I rather liked it).

Throughout the day I'd find Rian smiling at me. I'd be putting down tea on the coffee table or running the vacuum over the rugs and I'd look up to find his chin in his hands, elbows propping him up on his drawing desk. I'd always assume that he was gone somewhere. But every time I shifted a little to the right or a little to the left, his dreamy eyes would follow. Like they say about the *Mona Lisa*. I'd laugh and when Rian still said nothing I'd just go back to my work and let him grin stupidly at me, happy that he was happy, the weirdo.

Neither of them asked where I had been, why I had gone. For that I was thankful. I was just welcomed back without interrogation, without requiring an explanation. I knew if I wanted to talk, they'd listen. It seemed that I was what mattered to them, not my circumstances.

Conor greeted me with a polite, quiet, "Good morning, Aurnia," when he came in. I brought him tea and lingered a little by his workstation to see if he would ask me to stay.

All he said was, "Thank you, Aurnia."

He sat with the three of us at lunch, though he was quiet. I kept glancing over at him, finding him already looking at me, but his eyes would flick away before our gazes could really lock. When he went to the sink, I thought this was the moment. He was going to talk to me now. We were going to talk about *us* now. When I tried to slip my hands next to his in the warm, soapy water he said, "I'd like you to take the time to work on some of your drawings, Aurnia."

I bristled a little. Conor was being polite. I didn't want polite. I wanted tear-my-panties-off rude, I wanted plunge-his-tongue-into-me crude, I wanted dirty talk and foul-mouthed kisses and vulgar threats of all the bad, *bad* things he was going to do to me.

I went into the main room of the parlour. Maybe he was just waiting till Mason and Rian were gone. I glanced over my shoulder. Conor was looking back at me with fire in his eyes.

It was later in the afternoon when I was sitting with Mason and Rian, who had each just finished up with clients. Conor had just returned from some errands and had disappeared into the back of the townhouse. Mason, Rian, and I were discussing over tea different ways that we could bring business to the shop.

"You know," I said, drumming my fingers against the coffee table, "we could just lean into the bad-tempered owner vibe. Make it our 'thing'. Some places get big reputations for having grumpy folks. Bartenders. Bouncers. Artists of all types really. So why not a tattoo artist?"

Mason and Rian gave each other doubtful looks.

"I don't know, Aurnia," Mason said with a shrug. "Conor kind of eats those guys for breakfast."

"We could tame him a little," I said, thinking of the night before.

Conor's fingers on mine. His hand at the small of my back. His words like liquid heat in my ear.

Mason and Rian just laughed.

"I'm pretty sure that's what the gladiators said about the lions," Rian said.

"Yeah," Mason added, "right before they were eaten."

They were wrong, but I was in too much of a good mood to contradict them. Conor showed me last night he could be different. He'd show Mason and Rian, too. We'd turn Dublin Ink around. Nobody would get eaten unless they were so inclined.

"Aurnia."

Conor had used my name many times that day and each

had sounded the same: soft, gentle, reserved. This time, though, without even having turned around to look at him, this time I knew it was different. I hoped that Mason and Rian hadn't seen colour rush to my cheeks as I quickly stood and turned around.

Conor was leaning against the wall that separated the kitchen from the living room. His arms were crossed over his broad chest. I could see the lines of his muscles through his t-shirt. A strand of hair had fallen across one eye and he tucked it behind one ear as he looked across the room at me.

"Can I have you...for a second?"

I think I nodded. I might have been too nervous to do even that. My footsteps felt wooden as I moved toward Conor. He was still there against the wall. Watching me get closer and closer. This was what I had been waiting for. For Conor to take me aside. For him to tell me that he regretted pushing me away. That he was sick of fighting against this. Against us. For him to draw me into his arms. To kiss me. And...*more.*

If I wasn't blushing before, I definitely was then. As I moved closer and closer, I tried not to let myself think about it, but I couldn't help it. Would he start off gentle? Tilt my chin back with his thumb. Brush his fingers down my neck. Sweep my hair from my shoulder. Make his way from my clavicle to my lips, finally my lips, with sweet, gentle pecks.

Would he nip at my lips? Maybe enough that I hissed in pleasurable pain? Then cover my hiss with a deep kiss. Would he tease me? Oh God, would he tease me? Kiss down my breasts first, pushing aside my bra, swirl his tongue around my nipples before sucking them into his mouth. To lick down my stomach until he reached my slick heat. A soft kiss on my clit. Brush one side of my lips and then the other before I couldn't stand it any longer and ground into him.

This was it. Conor was going to finally let me in. Let me in close. Conor was going to fuck me. Arms around my narrow shoulders. Hands clutching at my hips. Heat claiming heat. Closer. Closer.

Conor's eyes were warm as I stopped just before him. I shivered when his fingers intertwined with mine. He led me farther down the dark hallway toward the back. He was taking me away. He was bringing me with him. This was it.

He was going to find a quiet room. A quiet room for just the two of us. He was going to take me inside. The door would click quietly shut behind us. Would he lock the door? Would my toes curl at the very sound of it? Would I even be able to hear it over the thudding, thudding, thudding of my heart?

Would he flick on the light? To see me. To trace his eyes over my nakedness. To claim me before he even laid a single finger upon the throbbing vein in my inner thigh.

Or would he leave the light off? Would he want to find me with his hands out before him like a blind man? Would he desire to learn my curves with the rough calluses of his thumbs, with the sweat-slick lines of his open palms? Would he want the darkness to heighten his hearing so that he was surrounded by my breathing? My breathing which grew faster, rougher, more desperate under his mouth and hips? My breathing turned to panting? Would he want to turn on the lights only once I was laid breathless? Body glistening? Limbs boneless? Eyes dazed like I was on drugs as I stared up at him?

Conor's fingers tightened on mine as we came to the door of the small storeroom at the back. Inside I knew there was only room for a few tall shelves and a flimsy round table in the centre. Ah, of course. He'd take me against the shelves. Rough and desperate. Punishment for how crazy I'd made him. He'd pound into me till ink fell and splattered all over the floor. All over us. Or did he have the table in mind? Testing its strength against his? Did he want us to fall together? To lay in its ruins? To lay in our ruins?

I thought my heart would beat right out of my chest as Conor reached for the handle to the storeroom door. It was all going exactly as I imagined. His calling of my name. His leading me where Rian and Mason couldn't see us. His finding an empty room. His pushing the door open...

Conor stepped inside just like I thought he would. His arm extended and my arm extended and in the dark, he glanced back at me over his shoulder. There was something on his lips you wouldn't call a smile unless you knew Conor Mac Haol. It was the faintest lifting of the corners. It was the tiniest softening of the tenseness of his strong jaw. It was the smallest hint of happiness.

I finally had what I wanted: Conor wanting me. Conor taking me. Conor making me his. This was it.

His arm extended and my arm extended and then he was tugging me toward him. I went without complaint. Without protest. Would he prefer that I struggled? Would he prefer that I tugged back against his grip? Like I had the first time we met? Like I had on the motorcycle? Like I had every other time? Would he like it better if I provided even the smallest bit of resistance?

Well, it didn't fucking matter. Because there was no struggle in me. No resistance. No fight.

I wanted this. I wanted all of this. I came like a lamb to the slaughter and fuck how I wanted it. Heat was already pooling between my thighs as I stepped inside. I could feel the brush of my threadbare cotton t-shirt against my nipples and knew they were already hard. There was already a low moan at the back of my throat as Conor brushed against me on his way to close the door behind us.

I could already imagine what it would be like to be together in a room with him. His musk would smell stronger. He would feel even bigger than he already was. Anywhere I moved I would be within his grasp. I would be trapped. He would be my prison. Inescapable. And that was all I fucking wanted.

I winced against the sudden flood of light. It wasn't like I was unprepared for light. It was just that when I imagined it, I imagined something softer. This was the glare of an office building. Not like the brush of warm sunlight.

Maybe if my eyes had been able to adjust just a little bit faster, I might have stood a chance. I blinked and winced against the overhanging bulb and the stack of papers and pens on the flimsy table came into focus slowly. Too slowly.

"What the—"

I was interrupted by a sound. I turned around to find the door closed just like I had imagined, just like I had hoped. Only one problem: Conor was on the other fucking side of it.

I ran to yank at the knob, but not before I heard a lock click into place.

"Hey!" I shouted. "What the fuck?"

"Get to work," was all Conor said from the other side of the door.

"Get to..." I mumbled as I turned around and went to curiously glance over the materials gathered on the table.

There was my art portfolio. There were pamphlets on how to fill out applications. There was a stack of applications. To goddamn art school.

"Are you fucking kidding me?" I shouted, darting back to the door.

"Be thorough with your answers. I'll be checking."

"You'll be letting me out of here is what you'll be doing," I shouted.

There was no response after that.

"Conor?" I shouted.

I pressed my ear to the woodgrain of the door. I heard nothing.

"Conor?" I yelled a little louder. "Hello? Conor?"

I pounded on the door, but no one came. Art school applications? That wasn't how the afternoon was supposed to go. If I was supposed to gain entrance to anything, it was Conor. His heart. His body. All of him. Not fucking art school. I pounded on the door harder.

Oh, the irony. I thought I was gaining a lover. Instead I got a father. And he'd just sent me to my fucking room to finish my homework.

29

CONOR

*T*he pounding at the door hadn't yet stopped. Something told me it wasn't going to.

That was fine by me. I almost always had a pounding in my head anyway. If Aurnia thought she was going to annoy me into letting her out of the storeroom, then she was mistaken. She might be stubborn, but she was no match for me.

Besides, I had this one thing on my side: I knew I was right. I knew this was what was best for her. I knew that *this* was her only way out of the shite life she'd been dealt. I knew her way out couldn't be *me*.

So I put a door between us. That way I knew she was safe. She was under my protection. But she couldn't get to me. If she would just stop pounding that door and fill out the goddamn application, then she'd find herself in a place where I couldn't get to her. It was for the best. For her. For me.

She could keep pounding on the door. Tire herself out with those little fists. Throw her shoulder at the heavy wood till her skin bruised and swelled. Kick and fight till sweat beaded down her delicate neck, dripped between her slick breasts, moistened the little hollow of her Cupid's bow...

I shook my head to drive out the image and refocused on the bills in front of me. Aurnia needed to do what she needed to do. And I, well, I needed to do the same. Dublin Ink was my future even if it was about as bright as the deck lights of the Titanic. Aurnia was not my future. Could not be my future.

The numbers, more red than black, blurred in front of my vision. I couldn't focus. Couldn't think. Not when my mind kept painting her inside that little storeroom. Red cheeks. Panting. Eyes fiery. Irate. Chest bouncing as she flung herself at the door again.

I rubbed at my eyes, but with them closed the image became clearer: Aurnia atop me. Her cheeks red as her hair fell over her fiery eyes. Her panting as she flung her head back, exposing that neck, those trailing beads of sweat. Her tits bouncing as she rolled her hips on my cock again. Her little fists pounding at my chest because she was close…so fucking close…so fucking close. But she couldn't quite get there. So I grabbed her hips. Not caring that I was rough. Too rough. I rolled her over so she was beneath me and she was irate because she thought she was in control. But she was never in control. I thrust into her and she—

"That's not accomplishing a goddamn thing," I shouted toward the storeroom angrily.

This stopped the pounding for a second or two. Rian and Mason looked up from their work in the direction of the long, dark hallway toward the back. Time hung suspended.

The pounding resumed. I growled in frustration and tried once more to focus on the bills. These were real things. The thing with Aurnia was fantasy. It was an impossibility. It was madness.

The bills… Real money. Real debt. Real fucking life. *This* was what I needed to be paying attention. Not that little thief who kept on stealing and stealing and stealing from me.

A whisper between Rian and Mason caught my attention.

My eyes snapped toward them. They both stopped and lowered their heads.

"What?" I grumbled.

The two eejits shook their heads.

"What?" I repeated.

"Did you look at the ideas that Aurnia came up with for the shop?" Mason asked.

That was a diversion. Whatever they'd been saying, they didn't want to tell me. A diversion and a clumsy one at that. It was, after all, Mason. I saw through it all, but the pounding at the door was drawing me back into the tight, hot space with Aurnia so I allowed it. I used it as a diversion myself.

"I don't have time for that," I said, pushing farther away the stack of loose-leaf notes they'd left on my drafting desk.

"But you have time for that?" Mason asked, nodding his head toward the storeroom.

There was a grin on his lips. I noticed that Rian, who couldn't focus to save his life, was diligently clicking numbers from invoices into a calculator. I tightened my grip on my pencil till my nail beds went bright red.

"What the fuck does that mean?" I asked. "Aurnia is working on an art school application."

"Is that what they're calling it these days?" Rian muttered under his breath.

"What did you say?" I said angrily.

Rian shrugged, not daring to look over at me. "I said you should take a look at those ideas. I think the kid's got a talent for this kind of stuff."

"She's not a kid," I said quickly before I could catch myself. "I mean, she's young enough that— Shut the hell up and get back to work, alright?"

I snatched up the stack of Aurnia's ideas just to have something to hold onto. I felt my cheeks reddening. It didn't make it any better to know that both Mason and Rian were probably holding in laughter.

"It's not a sex thing," I told them irritably after a moment.

Mason held up his hands innocently, barely containing a grin. "Nobody said it was."

The pounding on the storeroom door continued. It was soon joined by pounding in my temples. I rubbed at them, elbows against the desk.

Aurnia's ideas were there in front of me. Ideas for a future here at Dublin Ink. Ideas for projects with the boys, projects with me. Ideas that would require long hours together. Long hours where the light faded. Long hours where the brain grew tired, the body hungry. Long hours where temptation increased and resistance fell away like the second hand on the clock. Long hours where mistakes were made...

"There's nothing here," I said, throwing the ideas hastily into the bin next to my workstation.

What I meant was that there was nothing here for Aurnia.

"Aurnia stays in the storeroom till she's finished," I said, pointing a finger at Mason and Rian.

"You're the boss," Rian said.

I thought that was the end of it.

Until Mason added, "You're the daddy."

My stool went clattering backwards as I stood angrily. "Enough," I said. "I've had enough."

Rian and Mason both laughed.

Mason said casually, "Oh, come on, Conor. We're joking around. We know you and Aurnia aren't up to any weird BDSM stuff, alright? We know you two aren't getting off on this little light bondage bit. It's just kind of funny, okay?"

The way that Rian and Mason were both looking at me

made me realise with horror that I'd made a misstep. I should have laughed along with the joke. Or at the very least I should have just rolled my eyes at the eejits and continued with my work. Shouting at them like this, I saw too late, was the worst thing I could have done.

Because the only one who couldn't see it was a joke was the one person who knew it wasn't a joke. Me.

To Mason and Rian it was ridiculous, the idea that any of us could be thinking anything but innocent thoughts toward the vulnerable seventeen-year-old girl placed in our care. But that was exactly what I had just been thinking.

Filthy things. Twisted things. Greedy, desperate, *hungry* things.

Mason and Rian could joke because they didn't want Aurnia like I did. They didn't need Aurnia like I did. They weren't fighting with everything they had not to take Aurnia the way I was. Every minute. Of every hour. Of every goddamn day.

I forced a scoff, the closest I got to laughter, and said, "Just don't tell Diarmuid."

Mason and Rian both chuckled, but I thought I caught a hint of something held back. Had they sensed something? A tension a little too tight in me? A flash of fear in my eyes? Had I just planted the idea?

They'd be more watchful now. Any interaction with Aurnia would be assessed more closely. Mason and Rian were my closest friends, but I couldn't let them know that there was something between the kid and me. I chastised myself. That wasn't the way to think. The way to think was this: there *wasn't* anything between the kid and me.

God, what was fucking wrong with me.

"I need some peace," I said, gathering up the bills and heading toward the stairs.

I didn't dare meet their eyes. I passed them quickly. I moved up the stairs even more quickly. The pounding on the door followed me.

The rhythm made me think of Aurnia's hips against my groin.

The protests of the door sounded like her groans.

And I could see her eyes. On me.

30

AURNIA

onor only let me out of the storeroom hours later when I told him that the application was finished. While the application was technically all filled out, it was a lie. I hadn't yet decided on which piece of art to send in as a representation of my work.

I'd flipped through my portfolio from front to back time and time again without coming to a decision. It was when my eyes had started to burn and my brain got foggy that I picked one at random, attached it to the application, and called it quits. Good enough. Fine. It'll do, it'll do. I didn't really care anyway. Art school wasn't for me. The only thing that was for me was getting out of the storeroom.

The slim application sat on the counter as Mason hurried out the door after a quick check of his breath. It sat there as Rian wandered out into the night, fingers drawing in the air as he disappeared without a trace of a goodbye. It had sat there on the counter, ready to be mailed away, as Conor got up stiffly from his drawing desk where he had been as immobile as a gargoyle for hours.

"Coming?" he'd asked, hesitating at the door.

It was easy enough to pretend that I was still pissed at him for locking me in the storeroom. He didn't have any suspicions at all when I flipped him the bird and told him I'd rather get groped on the bus by a hobo than get on his motorcycle with him. I think he even laughed. Though it was probably just the creaking of the old door.

The second the door closed and Conor's motorcycle roared to life, the folder with my application was no longer there, sitting on the counter. It was in my fidgety fingers. It was on the coffee table in front of the floral print couch. It was spread out in front of me as my toes tapped impatiently on the old musty rug.

Why did I care so suddenly? Why was I now so sure that I could do better? That I could show the board something better from me? Why did I want to showcase something *more*?

When I awoke that morning, art school was a place for rich kids with cashmere scarves and home theatres. It was wide lawns with old stone buildings and manicured gardens and very high walls, very closed gates. It wasn't a place for me. I was never going to impress a stodgy old group of men on some board. I was never going to have my art seen by a professor, unless they happened to get lost and find themselves in the wrong part of town where my graffiti was scrawled across abandoned buildings with crumbling brick and broken windows.

Art was an escape from the present; I wasn't sure you could call that a future.

The minutes and the hours were passing and I was still there, working on my application. Trying to make it better. Anguishing over what piece of art to show. It was strange: caring so abruptly over something I'd never even thought to care about. Art school had never been a possibility before, but in that pink neon glow it seemed to be like it was the only possibility.

I'd never had anything to lose before and suddenly I had everything.

I had art school. I had Mason and Rian. I had Dublin Ink. I had Conor.

The little bell above the front door rang.

Of course I assumed that it was Conor who came back for me. That he was back to apologise in that gruff voice of his.

"Look," I said, not looking up, "you can say you're sorry by helping me. I know I said I didn't care. But I do. I do care and—"

"Warms the heart," a voice not belonging to Conor said.

I whipped around to find Nick locking the door of Dublin Ink behind his back. He placed his hand to his chest and said, "Bless your sweet little heart, baby Aurnia."

There was only so far to scurry back away from Nick. I used up all that space in the span of mere seconds. My back was scraping against the exposed bricks on the far side of the parlour and still my feet were scrambling for more room. There was none. I knew that. Nick knew that.

He was sporting a nasty black eye and a fresh cut with rough stitches at the corner of his mouth. That didn't stop him from smiling wickedly at me before slowly eyeing the living room. I watched him, terrified, as he tapped in disapproval the broken "Dublin Ink" neon sign, as he dragged a finger along the couch to tsk at the dust, as he rifled through a tray of tattoo needles with a curious quirk of his eyebrow. The whole time he got closer. The whole time I could not get farther away.

"Nice place," Nick mumbled.

"How did you find me?" I asked, my voice cracking.

Nick's hands were behind his back. He was studying the room like he was in a museum. His attention wasn't on me. I wasn't even sure that he had heard me.

"Didn't your father ever teach you to clean your room?"

From his back pocket emerged the drawing of Dublin Ink. It fluttered halfway to the floor between us.

My stomach dropped: this was my fault. Whatever was going to happen, it was already my fault.

"Look, Nick," I started, voice still faltering, "I'm sorry about bailing on you, but—"

"Shh, shh, shh," Nick said, putting a finger to his lips. "I'm reading, love."

He had gotten to the front of the couch, to the coffee table, to my application spread out as if just for him. The neon light fell on his coat. I could see the tatters, the tears. The reprisal for Nick's failure had been swift, had been violent. I could only imagine what vengeance he intended to take out on me. My eyes darted toward the old rotary phone, but it was within arm's reach of Nick on the little side table covered in doilies. I wouldn't get two numbers in before he had his fingers around my throat. There was the door, but I'd have to outrun Nick to get to it, and I knew he was fast as a striking snake.

"Hmm," Nick said, tapping his chin with bound fingers. He read from my application, "'I guess I'd like to pursue art so that I can help people the way art has helped me. It's like art has given me a gift and, I don't know, maybe it's just right to give it back.'"

Nick raised his eyes toward me. They were shadowed beneath his cut forehead. But I could still see how they flashed. Even swollen and bruised, there was danger in them.

"I'd say you could sharpen the writing, baby Aurnia," he said, teasing me. "But the sentiment is sweet, nonetheless. And you know what?"

"What do you want, Nick?"

I was too afraid to ask the question I truly wanted the answer to: what are you going to do to me?

Nick approached slowly. I remained petrified as stone. I kept telling myself to make my move, to take my chances now...now...

now... But each tiny opening passed and I just stood there, shaking against the wall. Really the only thing that moved was my eyes. And that was to check the big windows outside the shop. Hoping against hope that someone was there. Someone big. Someone with broad shoulders. Someone who would crash through the glass before letting anyone touch a hair on my head.

I was looking at the terribly empty window, that blank expanse, when Nick's knuckle caressed my cheek. His breath reeked of cheap whiskey, hot and foul. I struggled not to turn my gaze to him. I fought against it with everything I had. But he had a devil's power, and I found my eyes moving.

I was surprised to find his eyes soft. I flinched when he lifted his hand. My eyes squeezed closed. But he only cupped my cheek.

He whispered, "I agree."

When I opened my eyes, Nick's attention was on my lips. He dragged his thumb across them and sighed contentedly. I was surprised when he looked over his shoulder, looked high into the corner of the room. And smiled.

"Yes, I do believe your little art is a gift, baby Aurnia. A beautiful, lovely gift indeed."

Of all the things Nick could have done, nothing would have been as frightening as what he did next. He could have threatened me. Threatened to do what those men he'd angered because of me had done to him. Threatened to do worse. Far worse. He could have grabbed me by the throat right then and there. Hoisted me high against the wall. Squeezed as my feet kicked and black dots played at the corners of my vision. He could have taken me with him. There were ways to keep me in that godforsaken warehouse. Ways to force me into that house. Ways to make me do what he had wanted me to do. All those ways alone were enough to make me sick with terror.

That terror was small compared to what I felt when Nick suddenly just...walked away. He'd barely touched me, nothing more than a brush against my lips. He'd barely even spoken to me. It was like I didn't exist as he crossed toward the cash register and idly opened the bottom drawer. It was a fear deeper than the fear of physical violence I felt as he thumbed, almost in a bored fashion, through the stack of bills. Deeper than very real threats against my safety. Deeper than the fear that arose in my chest when I imagined the very worst he could do to me.

Nick walked toward the front door after pocketing the cash. My knees gave out. I slid to the floor shivering, my fingertips suddenly ice cold.

Nick turned back and blew me a kiss. "Thanks, love."

It did more to petrify me than the flash of a knife or the tearing of my t-shirt.

If Nick hadn't come for me, what had he come for?

31

CONOR

I knew something was wrong the moment I stepped inside Dublin Ink the next morning.

Otherwise Mason would have been upstairs still with Miss Last Night instead of pacing back and forth with a bottle of whiskey. Otherwise Rian would have been facing the wall with his hands behind his back studying a beam of sunlight instead of waiting by the front door.

Otherwise Aurnia would have been there. Her eyes on me. Her gaze sending me into ecstasy. Into turmoil.

"Now whatever you do," Mason said, confirming immediately my suspicions, "don't freak out."

The bottle of whiskey was shoved into my hands as Rian rubbed at my shoulders, saying, "Remember that violence is not the answer."

"What's going on?" I demanded.

The two of them were herding me like sheepdogs. I glared and tried to shoo them away as I went toward the back. They blocked my every path. I was big, but Mason was, too. And Rian was crafty. I could take them, or at least I'd tried in the past. But I first needed to know if it was worth it.

"It's not a big deal," Rian said in this soft, soothing voice that was only serving to piss me off. "I mean, it's just money, right?"

"What do you mean 'it's just money'?" I asked, trying to dart past Mason who blocked me with another offering of whiskey. "Where is Aurnia?"

"We can solve things with words," Mason said. "Right, Conor?"

I swatted away the bottle.

Mason shoved it back. "Maybe a shot would help before we tell you."

"Tell me what? What the fuck is going on?"

"Nothing that requires the ripping off of heads or yanking away of limbs, eh, buddy?" Rian said.

I'd backed him up toward the counter. When he moved to block the cash register, I knew exactly what had happened. I pushed him aside and opened the bottom drawer: empty. Completely empty.

"Look," Mason said with a hand on my shoulder that I wanted to bite off, "she's still young. Still making dumb mistakes."

Rian added, "We'll just talk to her, Conor. We don't need to go flying off the handle."

I looked from one to the other. There was fear in their eyes. Fear of what I would do. Fear of what I was capable of.

I looked from one to the other and then said flatly, "Aurnia didn't do this."

It was more than obvious that this was the last thing in the world that either of them expected to hear.

Mason pointed at the empty cash register drawer like the only problem was that I hadn't seen it. Rian's head just tilted quizzically to the side as he regarded me silently.

"Conor, it's empty," Mason said. "Everything we've earned, scrimped and saved for...it's not there."

"I can see that," I said.

Mason shifted from foot to foot as his hand, still pointing at the register, fell slightly. Rian did not move at all except to narrow his eyes almost imperceptivity.

"Conor," Mason said slowly, "the money is *not here*."

"Stop treating me like an imbecile," I snapped. "I know it's empty. And I know it's Aurnia who didn't take it."

Mason's hand dropped. He looked at Rian, who was eyeing me like I'd caught some strange disease. Mason blinked between Rian and me.

"But I don't understand," he said. "It had to have been her. It certainly wasn't me or you or Rian."

"It wasn't Aurnia," I said, setting my feet wide like I was in for a fight.

Mason laughed a sort of confused, bewildered laugh. He threw his hands up.

"What is up with you, man?" he asked loudly. "Two days ago you would have suspected the kid of stealing our air and now, with no other alternative available, you say that it couldn't be her."

"It couldn't," I said gruffly, crossing my arms over my chest.

"You've got to be kidding me! Rian?" Mason said, turning to our friend in desperation. "A little help here?"

"It is peculiar," was all Rian said with his eyes still on me.

"Thanks," Mason scoffed. "As helpful as always." He grabbed my shoulders, levelled his gaze with mine. "Look, I don't know if you hit your head on your bike without us knowing or what, but Aurnia was the only one who could have taken that money."

His plea was impassioned. My tone was emotionless as I said simply, "No."

Mason's eyes darted between mine for a moment and then he roared. He gripped his hair and stared up at the ceiling.

"Why?" he moaned. "Why did I ever go into business with these two? What did I do to earn such punishment? I could be with Tina right now. Or wait—was it Tiffany?"

Rian stepped in front of Mason's meltdown, his finger against his chin. He moved very close. He studied me quietly before saying, "Why the change of heart?"

"What?" I asked, leaning my head back from his.

He just leaned in closer.

"Why are you suddenly so certain of Aurnia's innocence when not so long ago you didn't want her in sight, when not so long ago you were practically ready to drag her off to the gallows, when not so long ago you kept a near constant eye on her because of your belief that she would do exactly what she is now being accused of with fairly damning evidence?" Rian squinted. "Why, my friend?"

It was a fair question. It was not a question I wanted to answer. I couldn't say it was because I'd seen her asleep on the floor of my apartment. Seen her thin legs in the moonlight, her hands tucked beneath her cheek like a child. Seen the innocence of her lips, of her eyelids quivering in a child's dream.

I couldn't say that it was because I'd developed a bond with her that night she rode on my motorcycle. That I'd felt her struggle against me. Felt her heart pound against mine and her thighs move against mine. I couldn't say that I knew her because of it, understood her because of it.

I couldn't say that it was because I'd wanted to kiss her when she returned to the shop. That I'd wanted to press her up against the wall. That I'd wanted to give myself over to her. That I'd wanted, in return, for her to give herself over to me.

Because I wasn't supposed to have seen her sleeping. Wasn't supposed to have held her against me as I drove her away from her home. Wasn't supposed to have yearned for a child to relent to me, to give her all to me, to leave herself bare beneath my hungry eyes.

It seemed there was no way to explain the closeness I'd developed with Aurnia without all the rest: the desire, the lust, the obsession.

Rian had called my attention toward Aurnia a "near constant eye", but he didn't know that it was the eye of a monster who watched the little girl who'd stumbled into the wrong tattoo parlour. I watched Aurnia because I wanted her. If there was a "near constant eye", it was the "near constant eye" of a predator. The "near constant eye" of—

"The camera," I said suddenly after a silence that was too long, too suspicious. "The camera!"

We'd been so used to not having one at Dublin Ink that the moment I put it up to deter Aurnia from stealing anything further, I, and apparently Mason and Rian too, had promptly forgotten about it. But it had been there the whole time. With any luck it had been recording.

Mason and Rian stood stooped over behind me as I booted up the old computer at the back of the parlour. It was too slow to do much of anything on, which was why we wrote out receipts and such. The old piece of shite seemed to take extra time to bring up the app that came with the security camera. Neither Mason nor Rian believed that it could have been anyone but Aurnia. I alone believed it had to have been anyone but her.

It was a rather reckless belief. But it was unwavering. It left the question: if not Aurnia, then who?

We weren't exactly diligent with locking the front door. Anyone off the street could have wandered in if one of us left the living room unguarded for any amount of time. I began to fast forward through the footage looking for a stranger to come walking through the unlocked door at the front of the house. I wasn't at all ready to see someone I knew. Someone from a long time ago. Someone who I hoped never to see again.

Nick coming inside Dublin Ink was the worst kind of invasion I could imagine. But it only got worse from there. Mason and Rian both sucked in their breaths when Aurnia fled to the wall from him. I didn't have any air left in my lungs to gasp at.

I watched in horror as he walked his fingers over my things. It made my skin fucking crawl. Still it was nothing compared to the disgust I felt when he spoke to Aurnia. When he grinned at her like he knew her. My disgust turned to blood-boiling rage when I saw how frightened she was.

She knew Nick as well. That was the only reason for her to have such terror on her face. The sight of a rabid dog is frightening. But not nearly as much as the mark of his teeth on your leg and the knowledge of the disease spreading through your veins.

It didn't matter to me that he stole from the cash register. He could take all the money in the world for all I cared. What I cared about was Aurnia sliding to the floor. She alone, huddled and afraid, was all I had eyes for.

"Who was that?" Mason asked.

I couldn't remember a time I heard fear in Mason's voice before. But it was there now.

"Who the fuck was that?" Rian repeated, his own voice shaking.

But those were the wrong questions. The right question was this and this alone: where was Aurnia?

32

AURNIA

O'Connell Street in the centre of Dublin town was busy. More than enough people. With more than enough money. But no one stopped. No one cared.

"Portrait?" I offered a woman who, when she passed, clutched her purse a little more tightly to her chest. I called after her, "Portrait? Just five euros! It'll only take me a minute or two!"

The throng of people on the sidewalk pushed me this way and that. I struggled to keep the stack of blank papers beneath my arm and the straps of my backpack, filled with charcoal pencils from Conor, on my shoulders. I was elbowed one way only to stumble into the path of someone who stepped on my toes and sent me tripping into a back or a side. Though I apologised, all I received were angry glares, impatient remarks, and shoves away. The sidewalk only seemed to grow busier. And me smaller.

"Five euros for a portrait," I shouted to the sky. I was being swallowed whole by the uncaring masses. "Five euros and I'll draw you anything!"

"Draw my cock," a businessman in an ill-fitting suit growled before shouldering past me.

I retreated to the relative safety of the brick wall of the General Post Office, an imposing building with a six-columned Greek-style portico at the front. I pressed myself tight against it and held the papers tight against my chest. Dark, mistrustful gazes darted toward me from the corners of pinched eyes. Women sidestepped me. Men purposefully got close enough that their arm could brush against my chest. I came to the busiest street in Dublin because I needed people. Well, this was fucking people.

I was trying to do what I had always done for my whole life: figure things out on my own. Make my own way. Deal with my own shit. It was my fault that Nick had come to Dublin Ink. My fault he had stolen from the cash register. My fault that I did nothing at all but stare and shiver as he walked straight out the door. I was going to fix things. On my own. My own way. Alone.

I'd heard of people selling their art on the streets. Portraits on boardwalks. Cartoons in tourist traps. Even little love poems written hastily in leaf-splattered canals. I'd arrived early that morning with my supplies and thought it might be alright. I'd get some cash. I'd replace it in the register before the boys arrived. No one would know. No harm would be done. Things could continue as they had been. As I wanted them to continue.

Mason with his dirty stories of his nightly conquests. Him roughing up my hair even after I'd just smoothed it back down. Rian with his distant gazes, his perplexing questions, his sudden ideas that made his eyes bright and his breath quicken. And Conor. Conor with his door cracked open. Conor with his invitation held just out of reach past my straining fingertips. Conor with mysteries I was on the verge of discovering. Conor with…just Conor.

Dublin Ink had become the closest thing to home I'd ever known. What had I done with it? Let someone come in and take from it. Make it unsafe. Threaten it.

I hadn't slept all night. Pacing back and forth across the floor of the tattoo parlour, I had chewed at my lips till they bled, cracked my knuckles till they were swollen and painful, tugged at my hair till it came loose in my quivering fingers.

I wanted so terribly to stay at Dublin Ink. For Mason and Rian to finally trust me. For Conor to finally relent to me, to finally let me *in*. This mess with Nick had jeopardised it all. I couldn't help but feel that I was doomed. That any time I tried to escape I was going to get dragged back in. It made my stomach tight with knots, my palms sweaty, my eyes prick with childish tears.

"Portrait!" I shouted out of desperation as I plunged back into the madness of the crowded O'Connell Street sidewalk. My voice broke when I shouted again, "Please! Will someone please take a portrait!"

All around me was black. Black trench coats. Black brief-cases. Black luggage. Black handbags and coats and hats pulled low. I spun round and round in the midst of it and felt lost. Felt hopeless.

"Hello?" I shouted, my voice already going hoarse. "Hello?!"

Why didn't anyone care? How couldn't they see that my world, the little world that I'd built for myself and came to love, was falling apart? Why wouldn't anyone stop? Why wouldn't anyone even look at me?

"Portrait! Portrait any fucking body?!"

My father's house was cruel. It was dangerous. Strange men wandered free and untethered. My nights were restless. My ears always pricked for the telltale grating of a turning doorknob. But these streets with their indifference and apathy were not any kinder. Eyes faced forward, clear of my head, clear of my watering eyes. Hands moved away from me, not toward me. Feet quickened, not slowed. I was in no real danger on that sidewalk. But it was also true that I was never going to get help either.

This made the warmth of Dublin Ink even more alluring and my betrayal (my inaction *was* a betrayal) even more terrible. I'd had something. I'd finally *had* it. And now I was going to lose it.

"Please!" I cried as I got jostled about, feet stumbling across one another. "Please! *Anyone!*"

A man in a particular hurry hit me with his shoulder from behind. As I tripped forward, my sheets of paper fell from beneath my arm. The cruel wind coming off the Liffey caught the heavy paper and sent it flying in all directions like scared doves. I tried lunging for a sheet here, a sheet there. Each seemed to be carried just out of reach or blocked just at the right moment by a passing pedestrian. My knees collided roughly with the uncaring concrete and I scrambled between the impersonal click of heels. I stretched for a sheet that was flipping end over end on the ground, a boot came down heavily on my fingers. I yanked my hand back with a cry and clutched it to my chest as I began to sob. The crowds parted around me despite not a single soul seeming to realise I was there. I remained down there, the cold biting through my knees, crawling up my legs like floodwaters in an icy river.

"Portraits," I moaned even though my papers were gone, only flashes of them visible between quick-moving legs. "Anyone..."

My chin fell to my chest and I squeezed my eyes shut. What was left for me? I couldn't go back to Dublin Ink. I'd most certainly lost my place in that family. If I'd been in that family at all. Was it back to my father's house? To wedging chairs beneath doorknobs? To sneaking in through windows? To the smell of burning metal at midnight?

Was it back to Lee and Jack and Mia? To petty crime? To whatever came after petty crime? To prison?

Was it back to Nick? A cot in an abandoned warehouse? A

pawn in his games? A pretty head of hair to drag his dirty fingers through?

I wanted to curl up right there on the sidewalk. Collapse onto my side. Draw my legs up into my stomach. Wrap my arms around my knees. Sleep. Wake up somewhere warm. Somewhere safe. Wake up in Dublin Ink. But I knew that was a dream. If I slept, it would not be there where I awoke.

"Portraits," I mumbled.

"I'll take one."

The voice took me by surprise. I raised my head. In front of me was held out one of the papers that had gotten away from me. Maybe it was even the one that I'd gotten my fingers stomped on for. It was crumbled. Muddy footprints marred the smooth cream surface. The bottom third was wet from some puddle. Some gutter. But it was one of mine. And it was being held out to me.

I dragged my hand beneath my running nose and followed the paper to the hand that held it. Tattoos in black and white. A line of little starlings across a long pointer finger. A compass on the back of the palm. A snake wrapped around the wrist. The tattered edges of the leather jacket were as comforting as the fringe of a beloved childhood blanket. My eyes continued up the smooth, buttery leather to the faded collar. Tattoos peeked above it like flowers from a sidewalk crack. The eye of a beautiful woman. The tip of a fern. The hilt of a sword.

Along the strong jaw, beard tight and dark. Past the sharp cheekbones. Above the purple bags, signs of a lack of sleep, of nightmares when sleep finally did come. At last his eyes. Green in a sea of black. Looking down at me. A swirl of hesitancy and kindness, anger and tiredness, lust and helplessness.

Conor lowered himself to the sidewalk. He knelt just in front of me. Indifferent to the huffs of angry people who now had to go around a massive boulder. It was like they weren't even there.

It was only him and me. And the dirty, crumpled paper he extended toward me.

"How much are you selling them for?" he asked.

"What?" I croaked.

"The portraits," he said softly, sweetly. It seemed he wanted to reach out to me. It seemed he wanted to draw me in close to me and never let go. But he stayed where he was. He did not touch me as he said, "How much for a portrait, Aurnia?"

His tone was patient, but insistent. I sniffled and answered, "Five euros."

"I'll pay $759.39," he said.

I started to cry. So he knew. He knew the cash was gone. All that hard work, gone. The chance to save the business, gone.

"Conor," I sobbed, "Conor, I'm sorry. I should have done something. I should have tried to stop him. I let you down. I let our family down."

I gulped. I hadn't meant to say that. I hadn't meant to admit how much Dublin Ink had come to mean to me. My cheeks reddened as I ducked my face. I was a stupid little child.

Conor cleared his throat. I wanted to die.

"I don't know much about families," he said gruffly. "But I know they're not perfect. I know it doesn't require the people in it to be strong all the time for the family to be... For the family to be strong."

I was surprised when a hand came to rest on mine. It wasn't warm, his hand. It was rather cold actually. But when his fingers slipped beneath mine, when he closed his hand around mine, when he squeezed me gently, I couldn't really remember what the big deal was about warm hands anyway.

"Come on," Conor whispered.

He helped me to my feet and the city rushed around us once more. People passing with their own cares. People hurrying about without a second glance at us. People who wouldn't stop. No matter what.

But Conor was there. My hand was in his. He had forgiven me. Or understood me. Or pitied me. Or loved me.

"How'd you find me?" I asked.

Conor nodded toward the bus station outside Gresham Hotel just a half block away.

"I thought you might run."

"You told me to stay," I said.

Conor nodded at me.

All he said in his deep grumble was, "I did."

33

CONOR

I was happy to make tea. Happy to shuffle around my dingy kitchen. To drown out the voices in my head with the sound of water running into the tea kettle. To riffle through the assortment of teabags thrown in a dusty drawer along with old takeout menus, unused packets of sweet and sour sauce, rubber bands and a spare bolt or two. Happy to find a cup that wasn't dirty or chipped. Happy to search the dark ends of my cabinets for a saucer, which I was sure I didn't have. To stab into a shrivelled lemon. To feel the citrus acid on the cuts along my knuckles not yet fully healed. I was happy to keep myself busy.

Because otherwise I saw her again. On her knees. On the street. Crying. And it broke my heart all over again.

When I finally turned around with two piping cups of chamomile with thin slices of lemon, I found Aurnia setting up one of my old sketchbooks on an easel I'd forgotten I'd even had. A remnant from art school. Stashed away in my closet. Had she gone through my things to find it? What else had she found? My heart rate quickened and I realised how terrified I was of that: of her seeing. Of her seeing me.

"You don't have to do that," I said as I set the cups down on the flimsy kitchen table.

I gestured toward the chair where the cup of tea was waiting. Aurnia shook her head. She, in turn, pointed at a chair herself, one situated across from where she stood. Its proximity to her frightened me. It reminded me of a chair for an execution. If I sat in it, I knew I would be crossing a line just like all those doomed men before me. Death for them. Wrongness for me. I'd been toying with that line for so long and there it was. Just in front of me.

"Come have tea," I told Aurnia.

I should have known that the stubborn little thing wouldn't be so easy to persuade. My little thief didn't give up at the sight of a lock. She just put a pick between her lips and grinned.

"You paid for a portrait," she said. "You're going to get a portrait."

I pulled out the chair at the table for her as if that would make any difference in hell.

She still did not move from behind the easel.

"I don't want a portrait," I told her.

This was true. I didn't. I didn't want Aurnia's eyes on me. Focused. Intent. Unwavering. I didn't want to have to sit there and watch her tongue move at the corner of her sweet lips as she worked. I feared I didn't have the restraint to keep myself in place. I could grip the sides of the chair. But the plastic would bend easily beneath my white-knuckle grip. There were no straps to hold me in place. At least the men on their execution chair were given that luxury. To be held down. To be kept from that thing they so desired: life. Aurnia. *Life.*

But it was more than that. More than the physical pain of keeping myself from her when we were so close. I didn't want a portrait, because I didn't want to see how she saw me. I could barely stand the sight of my own reflection in the mirror through my eyes. My reflection through her eyes would be unbearable.

"I won't take your money otherwise," Aurnia said.

There was no wavering in her voice. Her feet were set like she meant business. They were too close, I could have told her. Too close to really stand a chance if I were to really put up a fight.

"It's already given," I told her, nodding once more at the chair at the table.

"Conor."

It was a cheap shot. Saying my name like that.

"Aurnia," I said, one last gasping attempt at freedom. "You don't have to do this. You should sleep. Rest. You look exhausted."

"Sit," was all she said.

I left the teas on the table. I went to her as if there were two guards at my side. I sat without protest even though I knew what was coming. Even though I knew there was no turning back from this point.

Aurnia pressed the tip of her pencil against her bottom lip as she studied me. My fingers were already at the sides of the chair. The plastic already threatening to bend. Promising to break.

The day had gotten dark early. Clouds hung low outside my window. Soon the street lamps would blink on one by one down the street. For now there was dusk inside my small living room. Aurnia appeared to me like a figure through a fog. I could trace the sharpness of her shoulders in her thin black turtleneck. Her legs were like shadows against the wall, slim and willowy. Her hair was the darkest of them all. It fell across the side of her face like midnight, shielded her one eye like a velvet mask, shifted as she tilted her head slightly to the side like the rolling of waves beneath a starless sky.

Aurnia was oh so close and yet there was so much still hidden to me. This was for the best. This darkness. This mystery. We shouldn't get closer. We shouldn't unearth one another. We shouldn't turn on the lights.

And yet there was Aurnia with a pencil in her slender fingers. Was there anything more dangerous than a pencil? Than what it could see? Than what it could create?

"I don't think this is a good idea," I said, shifting uncomfortably beneath her gaze.

She was so young. So goddamn young. Not yet eighteen. You wouldn't know it from her eyes. From the way she looked at me. There was nothing childlike in her studying of me. She was a woman. And I quivered beneath her gaze.

"Something isn't right," Aurnia answered.

I snorted. Something? Was she fucking kidding me? Nothing was goddamn "right" about this. About any of this. She was seventeen. I was thirty-one. It wasn't right that she was alone with me in my apartment. It wasn't right that she was about to draw me. It wasn't right all the doors I feared this would open between us. I wasn't sure I had a single fucking "right" thought about my little thief since the very moment I found her in Dublin Ink.

I jerked back when Aurnia stepped toward me. She noticed this and hesitated.

"What's wrong?" she asked, pencil held loosely at her side between two fingers like a cigarette.

"Everything," I said, my voice hollow. "Everything, Aurnia."

She thought a moment. Her eyes on me. "I don't think so."

"I know so."

"Because you're older?" she asked.

"Because I know," I said. I did not say, *Because I've been here before. I've been where you are before.*

Aurnia considered this, but then took another step forward. "I can't see you."

"Turn on a light."

"That's not what I mean."

I knew what she meant. Not that I wanted to. But I did.

Aurnia stood before me now. Her navel right in front of my nose. The waistband of her jeans longed to be slipped into. Just a finger or two. Skimmed along the front to the protrusion of her hip bone. I imagined tugging the thin material of her turtle-neck up. Her pale skin in the dim light. I looked up at her.

"I don't think it's wrong that I draw you," she said. "I don't think it's wrong that I see you."

Her fingers reached forward and I pushed them back. She looked down at me stubbornly. When she tried again, I pushed them back once more.

"Go back to your easel or we're done," I told her.

Her fingers came toward me again. I gripped them in my hand. How easy it would be to wrench them back. How quick it would be to snap them at the joint, to break the fine, delicate bones. How little resistance her wrist would give if I were to simply thrust her palm back.

I should have. I fucking should have. She wouldn't want to draw me then. She wouldn't want to see me after that. I should have shown her exactly who I was. It would have been the kind thing to do. Talk about fucking right. That would have been the right thing to do.

But I didn't. Of course I fucking didn't. Because I was selfish. Because I was greedy. Because no matter how much I shouldn't have wanted her, I did. I wanted her. So I kept her fingers whole. I spared her bones. I gave her no pain.

"No, Aurnia," was the extent of my resistance.

Weak. Pathetic. Pitiful. I fucking hated myself and yet it was all I could manage. I barely heard my voice, it was barely a sound. Aurnia might not have heard me at all. She certainly acted like she hadn't.

Her finger pushed against mine and I let her go. This time I did not stop her as she pressed forward. I watched her lick her lips as her fingertips brushed against the hem of my dark grey t-shirt.

She gripped a little bit of it, a child standing at a parent's bedside after a nightmare with a blanket in her hand, and her eyes went to mine.

"You're hiding," she said.

Not the words of a child to a parent. Quite the opposite really.

Up that close—way too fucking close—I could see that her eyes were still puffy from her tears. Red lines still streaked out from the grey irises. Some of her lower eyelashes were stuck together. Everything about Aurnia's appearance said child, child, *child*. And yet the intensity of her gaze was everything but.

She looked at me like she'd known me longer than her young years made possible. She claimed me like our bodies had already become one beneath sweat-damp sheets. She seemed to see straight through me, so how could she say I was hiding? How could I possibly be hiding when there was nowhere to fucking hide?

"Aurnia," I whispered, my only protest as she began to lift slowly the hem of my shirt.

Her only response was to whisper back, "You're hiding."

The room was warm. I still shivered as the skin just above my groin was laid bare. Aurnia's fingertips brushed against the muscles of my abdomen as she tugged my shirt higher. Her every touch was a stone dropped into a still pool: I feared the ripples would never cease.

"Aurnia," I said again. When I looked up at her again, her eyes were no longer on mine.

They were fixed on her task. She lifted my shirt with a concentration like I was made of glass. Like any wrong movement would shatter me. Like I needed to be handled with the utmost care. The greatest of gentleness. I knew this for certain: it wasn't me who would break.

The scar tissue over my wounds was far too thick to ever again fall apart. I'd protected myself in so many walls that I was certain I was impenetrable. There was no fear for my heart; it was already in pieces.

It was Aurnia who needed protecting. It was she who was fragile. It was she who would break. My fingers brushed against the thin skin of her wrists. My eyes trailed along her arms, delicate bone connecting to delicate bone. Her clavicle, visible through the worn material of her shirt, looked so fragile.

I was a beast compared to her. A monstrous creature. It would take nothing at all to split her in two. To destroy her. To leave her broken beyond repair.

I tightened my grip around Aurnia's wrist, my fingers easily circling the narrow bones. I said nothing. I just held her. Until her eyes returned to mine. This was my last defence. Her last warning. It took everything inside of me to hold her still. Everything inside of me to hold myself back.

Her name came once more to my lips in the dark.

I felt her fluttering heartbeat against my thumb. She did not look away. She hardly blinked. I thought she might have seen the light. I thought this last hesitation might have been what she needed to come to her senses. *Run*, I shouted at her in my head. *Run!*

But when the stillness was broken it was not by Aurnia pulling away, not by Aurnia running. Instead she did what I never would have expected: she leaned down and used her free hand to encircle my wrist which had been hanging limp at my side. Her eyes did not leave mine as she lifted my heavy arm above my head. Her eyes did not leave mine as she lifted the hand I had gripped in mine right after it. I did not stop her. I did not let go.

With my arms above my head, Aurnia let go of my wrist and pulled hers from my grip. I kept my hands where they were. How easy it was, how simple it was, to damn us both.

The well-worn material of my shirt was soft as she lifted it over my head. Her movements were slow, gentle. I only noticed just the slightest quiver in her fingers as she helped my shirt over my wide shoulders. Her face disappeared from view only for a moment and when she returned to sight, she was looking down at the shirt she held.

I watched her brush her thumb against the material, her eyes intent. When she lifted her eyes to my naked chest it was in much the same way as before: slow, gentle, with only the slightest of quivers.

"I better get to work," Aurnia whispered, her eyes darting to mine only for an instant.

She went toward her easel. Her hands still worked in my shirt, wringing it like an old rag. She was nervous. I was certain I was even more so.

We were wearing down whatever there was keeping us from one another. What was to happen when we were finally to come face to face? How could one think of that and not be frightened? To see so clearly what you wanted. And know all the time that one *should* not want it.

We were better in the dark.

But it was too late.

For light, damning light, was coming.

34

AURNIA

The sight of Conor shirtless and awaiting just before me was almost more than I could bear.

I had been bold. Perhaps too bold.

Who was I kidding? I was far too bold. Far, far too bold. But I hadn't been able to stop myself. There was something I wanted and I was going to get it. It seemed Conor hadn't been able to stop himself either.

I had seen the struggle in his darkened eyes. I had felt the quivering restraint in his muscles. The muscles of his lower abdomen. The muscles along the length of his arms. The fingers that wrapped like a vice around my wrist. I had felt it. I had seen it. His desire to stop me. His need to stop me. His absolute certainty that it was the right thing, the only right thing: to stop me.

I had also seen a helplessness in him. A weakness in those bulging muscles. A fading of the light in his eyes. Because there was something inside of him that was stronger than his restraint, stronger than his resolve, stronger than any idea of right and wrong. I had seen that, too: desire, lust, a longing to just let go, to just give in.

To me.

To me.

To *me.*

So there I was. Trying to keep my knees from buckling no more than six feet away from him. Struggling not to let my breath escape my chapped lips in desperate little gasps. Fighting with everything I had to keep the pencil gripped between my fingers from shaking. I had told Conor that he was hiding, but was I not doing just the same? I used the shadows of the room to mask my fear, the cover of the broken and bent blinds to conceal the unsteadiness of my feet, the distance, short as it may be, between us to hide the raggedness of my every breath.

I'd forced Conor out into the open, but I could not do the same to myself. I couldn't let him see how much he affected me by simply sitting there, watching me. I couldn't let him know that this moment, in the dark, alone with him, a pencil in hand, ready to claim him on paper, felt like a defining moment in my life. I couldn't reveal that I wanted more than him just on paper.

I wanted him on my body. I wanted him tattooed on my inner thighs, on my waist, on the hollow between my throat and my shoulder. I wanted him on my heart, on my soul. I wanted him everywhere.

It had been a battle to get him on paper. If Conor knew I expected this to only be the start, he would send the easel crashing through the window. He would drag me by scruff of my neck to the room. He would lock me in and I was certain I would never see him again. Diarmuid would be the one to release me. He would find me a new place to serve my proba-tion. Dublin Ink would be boarded up. Conor gone like the wind.

And so I hid. I swallowed every unsteady breath till my lungs burned. I dug the pencil into the thick paper set up on the easel to keep myself from pitching forward, from fainting, from waking up from this beautiful dream.

At first, I focused simply on the sound of the pencil scraping against the page. Any glance toward Conor sent my body into a flush and made me lightheaded so I grounded myself with stroke, stroke, steady stroke. Graphite on pulp, pencil on paper. Occasionally a car would pass on the street outside, its tires crunching, its headlights casting into the room. But otherwise it was silent. Otherwise it was nearly dark, just the fading light of the sun beneath low, heavy clouds.

When the street lamps finally flickered on, sending bars of light across us through the cracked blinds, it was practically blinding. When Conor finally spoke, his words were nearly deafening.

"Now I can see you, too."

I kept my eyes on the page, busying myself with the pencil, hardly aware of what I was doing. All I knew was that I could not look up in that moment. To see his eyes on me would be to show him everything. To look at him right then would be to look at him for the very last time.

My entire body was tense with electricity. I thought that if I moved my feet even just a little on the carpet, it would shock both of us. It made my hand cramp, my jaw tighten to the point of pain. I wondered if I was visibly shaking.

"Can you close your eyes for a minute?" I asked Conor, my voice almost hoarse.

"Why?" he asked.

Because if you see into me, you'll see how I need you. I couldn't say this, of course. But this was the truth.

"It's easier to see the shape of your eyes with them closed," I lied.

I paused a moment to straighten the pad of paper on the easel. I dragged a hand through my hair and found it sticky with sweat. Maybe this was a bad idea. Maybe I wasn't ready. But maybe I would never be ready.

I practiced a few deep breaths, trying to still keep them as silent as possible even as my chest wrenched. And then, like plunging into an icy pool, I lifted my gaze to Conor.

He sat on the chair with his eyes softly closed. The light from between the blinds cast bars across his naked chest, across the contours of his sharp cheekbone, across his precariously closed eyelids.

This was the first time I had been allowed to admire him without restriction. Before it had always been out of the corner of my eye, a glance here, a glance there. Adding up the glimpses to try to create a full picture. Before he always caught me looking. Always scowling. Always pushing me away. Always making sure I got no more of him.

My eyes moved over his face. My pencil moved almost as if on its own as I studied the way his hair fell from his bun. A quick, determined stroke for his sharp nose. Sketching in his beard was like little pricks of rain before a downpour. I could almost feel them against my skin, could almost feel them rough against my fingertips.

I gripped the pencil a little tighter when I moved on to Conor's chest. His broad shoulders threatened not to fit onto the page. I felt I was overdrawing the muscles of his arms, but they really were that big. He was that strong. I blushed—thankful his eyes were closed—as I outlined his well-defined pecs, as I continued on to count out his abs as they trailed down and disappeared beneath the waistline of his jeans. Where the hair of his beard looked like barbs, the hair above his groin looked like down: soft as grasses in the wind. My pencil etched each and every one down, down, down.

"Can I open my eyes?" Conor asked, startling me.

"No," I said too quickly, as the warmth that had been flooding my body left like a spooked animal.

"Please don't," I repeated, eyes watchful on his. "Not yet."

There were still his tattoos to draw. They were the reason I wanted him to remove his shirt. They were what I wanted to see: a glimpse, I was sure, into his locked-up soul. My pencil hung suspended above the page as I followed from one to the other. All in the same black and white style, they covered completely both his arms. A complete mosaic. His neck was consumed. The art dripped across his shoulders, swept down his sides, covered his lower stomach.

But it wasn't the painted skin that drew my utmost attention, it was the one patch of skin that was not. On the very centre of his chest, above a rising phoenix, was a blank space that served like a black hole for my eyes. Everything raged around it, but that one place alone was all I could see, all I could focus on.

As if reading my mind, Conor spoke into the silence. "I haven't seemed able to find the right one. For the empty spot."

His voice seemed far away. Full of...something painful.

I remained silent and the steady scratch of my pencil as I drew out the tattoos he did have. Conor kept his eyes closed, but I saw his hands, curled into tight balls at his side, relax. I noticed his breathing deepen as if before he had been holding all the air he could muster inside his lungs. The set of his lips relaxed, the tenseness of his jaw eased.

"What have you tried?" I asked after several quiet minutes with just the noise of pencil on paper.

Conor laughed sadly.

"What haven't I tried is a better question."

"Well then," I said, tilting my head to study if I'd gotten his rising phoenix right, "what haven't you tried?"

Despite the fact that Conor had suggested the question, he

seemed surprised by it. He opened his eyes and looked at me as I drew. I glanced at him briefly.

"Well?" I prodded.

Conor shook his head.

"I don't know," he admitted. "What's left after everything?"

I frowned as I blurred the lines of one of the phoenix's wings.

"Surely you haven't tried *everything*."

I was smiling, but when I saw the distress on Conor's face, I stopped. Conor was looking down at his fingers which he had laid in his lap. The fingers which had drawn beautiful art for all over his body. Beautiful art for everywhere save one central spot. Did he think the problem lay with them? Did he blame them for not creating the perfect final piece? Or did the issue lie elsewhere? Perhaps in the very place he intended to fill?

"You want something perfect," I said softly, watching him as my pencil stalled.

"No," he said, again shaking his head, brows furrowed in perplexity. "No, I don't know if perfect is the right word. I... I..."

Silence descended on the room like a wave. Not a car passed outside. The neighbours above and below, if they were home, were completely still. My pencil might as well have been an opposing magnet to the page; I could get it no nearer than it was.

A diagonal of light from the blinds fell perfectly across Conor's beautiful face as he leaned forward, elbows on his knees, dragging his hands through his hair. He sighed. When he lifted his eyes to me, they caught the light. I watched as his pupils disappeared in a sea of green.

"I don't know how to explain it," he said, his voice little more than a whisper. "It's like I don't have it in me. I feel empty. Like I pulled all these from my very soul and there's nothing left."

I watched as he ran his fingertips over his biceps, along his chest, trailing down past the empty space to his phoenix on his lower abdomen.

"I don't know, I just feel like I'm grasping at air when I try to draw," he said. "Like I keep reaching and reaching, but there's nothing more. It's all gone. It's... I'm a pit. I've dug and dug and I've hit rock bottom. And there's...there's just nothing left."

The silence felt deafening. More than deafening. It felt oppressive. A force against my chest. I could hear the pain in Conor's words. The desperation even. He'd never let me see this side of him. I almost wished he hadn't. For in that moment I felt small and helpless. How could I ever try to fill such a void?

Conor cleared his throat suddenly and sat back, the light from the blinds falling from his face.

"Anyway," he said in that gruff voice I was so used to, "it's just tattoos, right?"

I stirred myself and put the pencil to the paper if only just to make some noise.

I nodded, but I didn't agree. It wasn't just tattoos. Especially not for Conor, who had centred his life around tattoos. It was more. I knew it meant the world to him, this void, this emptiness. I could see it meant more to him than just ink and flesh.

I realised I was drawing only once I was halfway done. That happened sometimes with my art. It dragged me under. It had its way with me. Sometimes the most I could do was just hang on and gasp for air when it finally let me up.

I saw the piece come to life on the paper and my breath quickened. I certainly didn't have all the answers. Hell, I didn't have even half of them. I didn't understand where this sadness in Conor came from. I didn't know what made him feel this emptiness, this hopelessness. I didn't know how to heal him. How to help him.

But I believed I knew how to love him. If he would only let me.

Before I knew what I was doing, I dropped my pencil, it clattering to the floor and rolling somewhere. My fingers went to the hem of my turtleneck, pulling, pulling up, an extra tug to get it over my chin until it was off, my hair falling back down in a mess around my flushed cheeks.

I let go of it, too, the material crumpling to the floor as I lifted my gaze to Conor. His eyes were wide, like always, a mix of fear and fire.

"W-what are you doing?" His voice came out in a breath, gasping and raspy.

I answered by reaching down to undo my jean button with shaking fingers. His gaze followed my hands as the button popped, as I dragged the zipper down. The look on his face was like a starving man. His chest shook as he sucked in heavy breaths.

"Aurnia, wait..."

His words said *wait* but his eyes said *keep going*. His knuckles white on the arms of the chair told me he was holding himself back by the last thread of his willpower.

He wanted me. He wanted me, bad. Any hesitation I had disappeared to dust.

One push was all it took to force my jeans down off my hips, to send them crumpling around my ankles. One step had me freed from the pool of material. One shuddering inhale as I watched him watching me.

"Aurnia," he hissed, "y-you have to stop."

"No," I said, my fingers no longer shaking as I unclasped my bra, "you let me see you. Now you get to see *me*."

I let the straps slide off my shoulders, let the cups fall off my breasts. My nipples hardened as he stared at me, half naked, his gaze like hands on my skin, spray-painting goosebumps all over me. He and I took a matching shuddering breath.

I stepped toward him, drawn to him like a magnet. I needed his hands on me. His mouth on me like a brush on canvas.

He stumbled to his feet, kicking back the chair with an awful scrap. "Stop. Please, Aurnia."

I didn't stop. Because he and I both knew that he didn't really want me to. The painful looking bulge in his pants told the truth.

I slid my hands over myself, over my swollen breasts, my aching nipples, following my need down my stomach toward the centre of it, just under the waistband of my panties.

"I need you," I admitted. "Right here."

He let out a groan. "Jesus, Aurnia." His voice sounded torn and ragged. "You're only seventeen."

"Almost eighteen."

"You're *seventeen*."

I shrugged. "That's legal in Ireland."

"I'm thirty-one."

"So?"

Conor squeezed his eyes shut and mumbled something like a prayer.

"I promise you I feel like a woman," I dipped my finger into my pussy lips, finding them already wet, "am soaking wet like a woman."

His eyes snapped open.

I swallowed hard, pushed down my panties and stood up straight. "I'm not a virgin."

He froze, his every muscle tense. "Aurnia, we can't—"

"We can." I stalked toward him. I had him now. Conor was mine. He was still fighting it. But it was futile. I knew it. He knew it.

"*I* can't." He stumbled back, kicking out the chair, his movements now wild and jerky as I advanced.

I felt powerful. Like I was, for once, the predator. And he was my prey. It was only a matter of steps before he gave in. Before he was mine.

"You don't have to do anything," I promised, "you just let me do it."

"But they'll... Diarmuid will—"

"—doesn't have to know."

His back slammed into the bedroom door with a rattle. I couldn't help the triumphant smile as I closed the distance between us. He had nowhere else to go. Nowhere left to run.

He'd have to face me. Face himself and what he wanted, what he needed.

What we both needed.

What we've both wanted from the very fucking start.

I leaned in and pressed my breasts against his firm body, pushed my aching core against his bulge, letting out a low moan. *This is how we fit, Conor. Can't you see how well we fit?*

"Damn you," he hissed, his hands coming up to grab my shoulders. He didn't push me away. But he didn't pull me closer.

"Stop fighting me," I whispered into his mouth before I melded my lips to his.

For a moment, he didn't move. For a moment, he kept fighting. Fighting me. Fighting himself.

Why the hell were we so wrong? In a lifetime of wrongs this was the only thing that felt right.

My heart started to sink, the edges of my confidence blurring from the sting of rejection. His fight was too great. Or perhaps his need for me was too weak.

Then he moved, suddenly, like he was bursting out of a prison. His hands crushed me to his body, lifting me off my toes. His head tilting so he could lock us in further, his tongue meeting mine in a wild dance.

It was a violent unleashing, a whirlwind released from a bottle. We were hands and groans and clashing tongues and grinding hips. His hands slid around to my ass and he picked me up by the backs of my thighs like I weighed nothing, wrapping my thighs around his waist, spilling groans into each other's mouths as my pussy and his cock pressed together.

I heard him fumble for the door handle, the shudder of the door in its frame before it released and swung open. He stumbled us into the room like he was drunk. Swaying at the foot of the bed before he dropped me onto it. I landed with a bounce and a yelp.

He was like an avenging angel towering over me, his chest heaving, his wide shoulders like dark wings. My broken tattooed angel. I reached for him, arching my back as my nipples begged to be rubbed raw by the smattering of hair on his chest.

"Don't move," he said.

"But—"

"Don't. Move."

I lay there, trembling. Silently begging for him not to leave me here like this. I would die. I would burst at the seams of me, my need, my desperation too big to contain.

He kneeled at the foot of the bed. I lifted my head and yelped as he grabbed my ankles and tugged me down the mattress until my ass was hanging off the edge. He placed my knees over his shoulders. I felt so exposed, a shudder running up my spine.

I let out a gasp as I felt his breath on my inner thighs, as he traced the edges of my aching core and gently parted my lips.

"Fuck," he breathed, "you are...art."

Before I could respond, he lay his tongue flat on my centre and licked long and firm.

He painted me with his tongue over and over. Swirls over my clit. Long strokes from ass to tip. Firm dabs into my entrance.

All words left my mind. All sound except the rush of the

blood in my ears. My vision was nothing but the splashes of colour behind my closed lids.

What the hell was this?

I'd been licked out before but...now I realised the difference between an amateur and an artist.

His finger joined his tongue, teasing around my entrance, pushing through my lips. I bucked my hips up to him. More. *More.*

He chuckled, the vibrations rumbling through my core. "Greedy girl."

He pushed his finger in, slowly. I was so wet he slid right in. So needy my body just pulled him in.

He let out a hiss. "You're so fucking wet."

It wasn't enough. Where the ache had been was now filled with him, but the ache just seemed to grow, to expand.

I moaned, my fingers curling into the sheets, my hips bucking of their own accord. "Another," I begged.

"Are you s—"

"*Another.*"

He pulled out and I felt a second finger at my entrance. He eased them both in. This time I clenched around him, revelling in the sensation of being parted, of being filled.

"Yes," I hissed, giving him permission before he asked for it. Begging him.

He began to slide his fingers in and out of my pussy. At the same time, his tongue flicked left to right on my clit.

Sensation ricocheted around my body as my muscles tightened, as my mind went spiralling out of control. I grabbed his head, threading my fingers through his hair now damp with sweat.

I lifted my head to look at him. He looked like a god staring at me over my mound, his face and fingers buried in my pussy. I tugged at his head, a silent demand.

He lifted an eyebrow even as his fingers and tongue stilled. A question. Or perhaps he wanted to torture me. To make me say it. To make me beg.

"Please." My voice was a pathetic whimper.

He didn't move. That cursed eyebrow stayed lifted.

I let out a growl. "Please. Fuck me."

There was a long pause. I felt, rather than saw, him swallow. "You want to be fucked, little girl?"

"Hard."

"Yeah?"

"Yes." I grabbed for him, tried to pull him up over me. But he wouldn't budge.

"Not like that, baby," he said. "Not yet."

Before I could yell in frustration, he began to move again. This time there was an edge to the way his tongue lapped at me, sucked at me. A hardness to the way his fingers thrust into me.

It was going to be my undoing.

"Oh God," I cried out. I could barely think as he fucked me with his fingers, as he angled them in a way that hit that sensitive spot inside me, over and over, unrelentless pounding, demanding my release, the tension growing like a sun about to explode. His thrusts increasing in pace until the bed was shaking, until every nerve in my body was on fire, until a scream uncoiled inside me.

An orgasm roared through me. Like being slammed by a wave. I was crushed under it, unable to breathe for one long glorious moment.

When I fell back to earth, I was afraid my broken tattooed angel would be gone.

When I blinked, I found him not between my legs, but by my side. He was sitting up against the bedhead and had pulled me alongside him, my head on his bare chest.

He was still in his jeans, his bulge still straining against his zipper.

I reached for it. He grabbed my hand, laced his fingers with mine and pressed them to his stomach.

I tried to tug my hand away but he wouldn't let me.

"No."

"Why not?"

He was silent. I glanced up to find him worrying his bottom lip with his teeth, his gaze cast to the wall.

His only reply was a squeeze of my hand and a kiss on my head. "Go to sleep."

"But you're still—"

"Sleep, Aurnia."

35

CONOR

I stood there in the doorway, watching Aurnia asleep in my bed. Her cheek cushioned by my pillow instead of bruised against the cold wooden floorboards. Her toes wrapped tight by my comforter instead of frozen and exposed. Her lips exhaling even breaths that rippled softly the well-worn sheets instead of catching splinters on the floor.

She was safe. Protected. Guarded.

Except from *me*.

Even with eyes squeezed shut I could not help replaying the way she came undone for me last night. The way her body rippled around my fingers as she came hard, as her juices coated my tongue. What had I done?

Fuck. God only knows, I had fought against it. This. Her. I fought. I'd still lost.

Even now I wrestled with the demons inside me. Tried to reason with the voices inside my head that called me names. Monster. Pervert. User.

That's why I'd only made it about her. Made it about *her* pleasure. Only hers. Why I'd not let her touch me, to bring me to my own release. Somehow, it felt...justified. Barely. I had given her it all, had taken nothing.

You think that makes it okay, asshole?

Who was I kidding? The devil had already reserved a spot in hell for me.

Better not keep him waiting.

There was a pent-up fury in me that had not been—*would not* be—released on Aurnia. I had to find some way of unleashing it. I knew just the target.

When I was quite certain that Aurnia would not wake at the creak of the front door of the flat, I slipped out with nothing more than my leather jacket and the keys to my motorcycle. A bat would have been smart to bring along. There was an old pocketknife in the top drawer of my dresser that probably would have come in handy. Hell, even just grabbing a dumbbell from the garage where my punching bag hung would have only taken seconds.

But I didn't have the time. Couldn't spare a minute. Couldn't spare a second.

My rage had been caged ever since seeing Nick on the security camera footage at Dublin Ink. Finding Aurnia had been more important. Making sure she was safe. Making sure he hadn't found her. Making sure he hadn't...

My rage was now free and it was sinking its teeth into me. I only had so long before I was its victim.

The night was bitterly cold. The wind chapped my knuckles to the point of cracking. But I didn't care; I knew it was just the start. The street lamps lining the abandoned streets grew farther and farther apart. Glass crunched beneath my tires as the darkness increased. There would be no stars that night. Only a swirling mist. Only the headlamp of my motorcycle trying to cut through it as I shook. As I pressed the bike faster. As I tore through the night like a madman.

Aurnia's house appeared out of the fog almost before I realised it. I had meant to stop a block or so away to watch, but I was right upon it. I wasn't thinking straight. My thoughts were consumed by images of Nick's dirty fingers on Aurnia's neck. To see any trace of him left on her was enough to send my wheels spinning.

It wasn't good, my distraction. It was going to get me killed. Death seemed like a trivial thing compared to the thought of Nick being anywhere near my little thief. I might be racing to my death, but I wouldn't be going alone. Hell would welcome two goddamn monsters that night.

I wasn't certain that Nick would be there, at the house, but I had my suspicions. The connection between Aurnia and Nick almost positively had to be linked back to that godforsaken shitehole. His lurking, wicked presence there explained Aurnia hiding out at Dublin Ink. Her crawling in through her bedroom window. Her willingness to leave with me when I'd shown her nothing but violence and anger. I was not a good man. But I was not Nick. I was not my old friend. The lesser of two evils, I supposed. I would be that, at least, to Aurnia: the mad dog that rid her of the mad wolf.

It didn't really matter to me if Nick was there or not. If he wasn't, I would search elsewhere. I knew enough of the seedy underbelly of Dublin to know where to look, to know who to ask. I would find him eventually. If it took all night, if it took all my nights, I would find him. I would end this.

But it seemed that whatever god was up there above the mists wanted a show that night, because I wasn't in the shadows outside Aurnia's house for more than thirty minutes when the devil himself walked out the front door.

To see him on the blurry, unfocused security footage was one thing. But to see him there. In real life. Not more than a hundred feet away. That was something else.

To make out the tattoos on his fingers. To count the frays along the black hoodie he flipped over his shaved head. To hear his shoelace tap against the frozen sidewalk with every casual, easy step toward his car. He was the past come to life. I thought I'd put him behind me. Nothing more than a bad memory, a distant nightmare, a fading storm.

But he had found me through a weakness I never intended to have: Aurnia.

It was simple enough to follow his beat-up old car, even with it having only one working tail light. It was either that it was late enough not to suspect himself of being followed or he was high enough not to care. But whatever the reason, I was completely unsuspected behind him on my motorcycle. Or at least that's what I thought.

Nick climbed the rickety staircase of the abandoned warehouse with a whistle on his lips. I thought that meant he didn't know I was there in the consuming darkness, toes silent on the metal grating. He turned on a kerosene lamp in the centre of the damp, mouldy warehouse floor and set about laying out a blanket on the dirty floor. I waited in the shadow of the stairwell as he took a big swallow from a cheap bottle of whiskey.

I wanted to take him by surprise as he slept, to strike fear the way he had in Aurnia. The way he had in me, for having to watch. But I was not to take him by surprise. Because before he even spoke, I recognised the song he was so casually whistling. It was the song that was playing that night. It was our song, hers and mine.

He gave my blood just enough time to run cold before saying, "Are you just going to skulk there all night?"

His voice echoed up to the unseen heights where broken windows let in the harsh cold. It didn't matter, though; it could have been a hundred degrees inside with furnaces ablaze and I still would have shivered.

How long had he known I was there? Had I made a sound on the stairs? Did he catch sight of me in his rear-view mirror? Was it outside the house where he first noticed me, waiting? Or had he simply always known that I would eventually be there? Was this simply inevitable? He and I? Fist against fist. Hate against hate. Blood against blood.

I stepped out from the shadows. Nick extended the bottle of whiskey toward me, but I kicked it roughly from his hand. It shattered on the concrete floor just out of the range of the flickering lamp. Black eyes flashed up at me. A familiar grin, beaming.

"I thought we could keep the mess to the blanket, Conor," he said with obvious enjoyment. "You see, I'm really hoping to get my security deposit back and all."

My fist was raised and it was colliding with his cheek before I knew what I was doing. Nick laughed as he rolled on the tattered blanket, clutching at his most likely cracked eye socket.

"I have missed our deep, intellectually stimulating conversations, my friend." He peered up at me with one eye, crinkled at the edge with amusement.

My boot made contact with his ribs. He groaned as he curled up in on himself. I stared down at him in a wild fury that only grew worse as he began to shake with pained laughter.

"Reunions always are so interesting, aren't they?" he gasped, chuckling between each struggling word. "See what's become of people. See where they've ended up. See *who* they've ended up *with*."

A bloodcurdling roar came from the back of my throat. I fell upon Nick. I pushed away the forearms he used to protect his face and unleashed a series of brutal punches, letting them land wherever they may. The result when I finally stopped was a heart that raced almost out of control, pain that radiated up my arms, and spit on my chin. As for Nick, his face was a bloody mess.

I pushed myself with ragged breath to my feet and spit on Nick before wiping my mouth. All I really accomplished was getting the tang of copper on my tongue. I staggered from foot to foot as I pointed a shaking finger down at Nick.

"If you go anywhere near Aurnia ever again, I'll kill you," I said, voice tight because I couldn't breathe. I couldn't fucking breathe.

I began to stumble away, afraid that any moment I was going to pass out. The dark hollow of the stairwell seemed to move position every time I blinked. I put my arms out in front of me, hoping that I'd run into a wall before I fell down a metal staircase. In all of this Nick's voice came like a ghost.

"You never gave me a chance to explain, Conor my boy."

I tried to ignore him. Nothing he could say would justify getting anywhere near that child.

"Aren't you the least bit curious?" Nick taunted, humour sinking back into his voice like a goddamn cancer. "Even the teeniest tiniest bit curious?"

"God knows what depraved plans you had for Aurnia," I shouted back.

Nick laughed.

Laughed and then said, "Not Aurnia...*Shannon*."

I tripped on something on the floor, or maybe it was my own feet that betrayed me. Either way I collapsed to my knees. Hard. I felt the cold concrete beneath my palms as I panted in the dark. Before I could protect myself, Nick's foot was connecting with my own ribs. I heard a crack and gasped in pain as I rolled over onto my back.

Nick stood over me, one side of his face just caught by the flickering flame of the lamp. It was his turn to spit on me. Blood splattered onto my cheek. I was so focused on cradling my cracked rib that I didn't even move to wipe it away.

"I don't want to hear her name," I gasped. "Not from your mouth. Not from anyone's mouth."

The light filled Nick's smile with a blackness the colour of tar. As I blinked up at him through the pain, it seemed to drip from his chin like chicken grease. He smiled even more when he caught me grimacing up at him.

"'Don't say her name?'" he repeated, leaning over me slightly. "But Conor, you loved her."

I tried to sweep Nick's feet from under him. All I managed to get was the sensation of a knife to my side. Nick's ricocheting laughter made my skin crawl.

"That night was over so quickly," he continued, circling round me like a buzzard with his hands clutched behind his stooped back. "There was the ambulance and then there was the Garda and when I was released from the hospital you were already gone."

"You ratted me out," I hissed. "You betrayed me. You destroyed my life."

Nick clicked his tongue as he wagged his finger at me.

"No, no, no," he said, shaking his head. "I only destroyed the false life you were trying to live. I only made you see that it was never to be your life. I destroyed nothing that was real. No, Conor. I did you a *service* that night. As a *friend*."

Nick slipped from the arc of light from the lantern as he continued to circle around me. I thought maybe the pain was making me stupid. I didn't understand. I couldn't understand.

"Shannon was trying to make you someone you weren't," Nick said, his voice slithering to me from the concealing darkness. "She got ideas of art school into your head. Of improving your lot. Of making something of yourself. Lies, Conor. *Lies.*"

"What are you talking about?" I gasped. "What the *fuck* are you talking about?"

"We grew up together, Conor," Nick said, still hidden from me as I craned my neck. "I knew you better than anyone. We were going to rule our little underworld together. We were trash, but we were to be kings of the trash. We weren't meant for shining green lawns and fancy dinner parties and stylish apartments. No, no. We were the lowest of the low. We had nothing. But it was *ours*. It was *our* nothing."

Nick was smiling at me as he emerged from the shadows. Our eyes held as he took slow, meditative steps around me.

"I wanted more," I said.

Nick's face twisted in anger. "That's *her* talking! You wanted what I wanted. You wanted to be who you were born to be. You wanted to be what you were always meant to be."

I could hear Shannon's voice in the art room during those late nights when the school was long empty, the hallways dark. Her long red hair spread across her balled-up cream cardigan. My fingers trailing down the freckles of her sweat-slick stomach. "You can be whoever you want to be, Conor," she'd tell me. "You have the talent to go anywhere. To do anything. To *be* anyone." She had been twenty-eight. Me, eighteen. But what was age, when there was the whole world there before you.

Nick calmed himself as best he could, dragging a shaking hand across his face. His voice still shook. "It was clear I was losing you. Don't think I didn't know about the art school applications. I went through your trash. Don't think I didn't know you were accepted. I watched the night you opened the letter with her. I watched her give your cock a celebratory ride."

With a bellowing roar, I lunged at Nick's legs. He easily shoved me away. I hit the concrete floor hard. I could do nothing but gasp for breath.

"What was I saying before being so rudely interrupted? Ah,

yes. It was clear I was losing you and it was clear that there was only one way to save you. To tarnish your new little life, I had to tarnish the woman who had given it to you."

I shook my head as I watched Nick in horror.

"She was such a lightweight, you know?" he said, concealing a giggle behind wretchedly tattooed fingers. "Such a goodie two-shoes, your sweet Ms Calleary. Didn't know cocaine from powdered sugar, now did she? Not like us. She didn't know the real world like us."

I saw in my mind the light from beneath that bedroom door, my hand pushing it open. I saw her beneath him, hair spread out on the pillow like it had been for me, eyes black as she stared at me without recognition.

"You're not human," I said.

Nick only laughed.

"Of course not!" he shouted, throwing his hands up into the air and casting wild shadows on the broken windows behind him, on the shards of night. "I'm a dog, Conor. A *dog*." He pointed a finger at me. Wagged it. "But so are you. So are *you*."

I tried to shake my head, but wasn't he right? Shannon had given me the hope of something more. Because of her I was getting out of that shite hole. Because of her I had gotten into art school. Because of her I had a chance to rise above. But given the first chance to show who I was, what did I do?

I beat Nick to within an inch of his life like an animal. I ignored Shannon's tearful pleas and crashed my motorcycle driving away. Shattered my leg. Shattered my life. He was right to label me a dog. A rabid fucking dog.

Nick was close to me again. Bent over me. Smiling. Fucking smiling.

"You might not believe this, Conor," he said in a soft voice. In a voice that was almost gentle. "But I will always be your friend. When you lose your way, I will always be there to remind you who you are. Who you truly are."

I winced as Nick patted my cheek. It only got worse when he cupped his hand. When his thumb brushed across my cheekbone.

"No, no," he said as I tried to pull away with a whimper of pain at my cracked rib. "Please, don't thank me."

I spit up in Nick's face and it contorted in fury for only the fraction of a second.

"You look tired, Conor," he said. "That little Aurnia must be keeping you up. I can get her to stop, you know?"

I grabbed for Nick's collar, but he swatted my hand away easily.

"Sleep," he cooed. "Sleep, sleep, *sleep.*"

I just caught the sight of his lifted boot. Then there was nothing. Absolutely nothing.

Then again, when was there really anything more?

36

AURNIA

I should have known it was one step forward, five massive fucking steps back.

I should have known when I woke up the next morning to find the bed empty of him.

I knew I'd slept alone, the pillow next to me undented, the sheets untousled. He'd convinced me to use the bed at long last but, of course, he wasn't going to sleep beside me, no matter how much I might have wanted it. No matter how much I suspected he wanted it, too. It was just another one of his stupid rules for us. His "right" and "wrong" bullshite, the "allowed" and "not allowed" algorithm, the logic so complicated I wasn't sure even he truly understood it.

I should have known after last night—after I came apart all over him—he'd pull away, yet again. Like I said, one step forward, five massive fucking steps back.

He was not anywhere else in his apartment, my calls out for him coming back empty. That left very few places in his small and sparse life to sleep.

I ate a bowl of stale cereal alone and tried to comfort myself. He must have driven his bike over to Dublin Ink after I was asleep. There was the floral monstrosity of a couch in the parlour that was comfy enough. Or the rooms upstairs if he got lucky and Miss Last Night was rather quiet during playtime with Mason.

But he wasn't at Dublin Ink when I arrived.

Maybe he'd gone out for breakfast; a meal after he'd made a meal of me last night. I smiled to myself at the memory, hiding my cheeks when Mason clomped downstairs. Or perhaps he was out buying flowers for me. I'd never been bought flowers before.

With every passing hour with no sign of Conor, my heart began to sink. We'd made a connection the night before. There was an intimacy to being peeled apart by someone's hands, a vulnerability. He'd given that to me. He'd relented.

After work, I took the bus back to his apartment. I found it still empty, the lights all off, everything on the drying rack where I had left it. I checked the sink for another dish, checked the trashcan for added trash just to see if he'd been here during the day at all.

"Conor?" I spoke into his message bank after his phone rang out. "Where are you?"

I waited, praying he'd pick up with a rushed, *"Sorry, I'm here."*

But seconds ticked past and the messaging service was a silent void.

"Just let me know you're okay. Okay?"

I hung up, feeling more and more like a woman who had missed all the signals.

Had I been wrong? Had last night been a dream? A childish fantasy?

I wanted to think that it was possible for me, at nearly eighteen, to make a real connection with Conor, at thirty-one. But all night the doorknob did not turn. All night I remained alone on his bed. Awake. Listening for his key in the lock.

I knew he wanted me, but...what if that was all? What if his attraction was just a desire for something he couldn't have? Maybe I had made our connection up. Imagined the intensity of his gaze. The way he seemed to hold his breath when I was near.

I awoke from a sleepless night with my fingers already in my wet sex to sheets messed only by me. His absence just seemed to deepen the ache.

Had Conor just been palming me off, giving me a pity release after he'd found me so upset? After I'd thrown myself at him, practically forced myself onto him? What if his absence was him trying to tell me that he didn't want me? What if he just couldn't find the words to say that he wasn't interested in anything more?

Could I have read everything so wrong? The sensation of our thighs together on his motorcycle as he rode me away to safety. The way his tongue had claimed me as he held me against the bed. The pain in his eyes as he watched me cry on the sidewalk in that sea of black.

Neither Mason nor Rian were particularly worried when Conor failed to appear that day. And the next. And the next.

"It's certainly not the first time he's done this," Mason said.

"It certainly won't be the last," Rian added.

They both laughed. I couldn't muster the energy to do the same. If they became worried about anything, it was me.

"What's his name?" Mason asked one rainy afternoon, coming to join me at the big front window.

I jolted. "What?"

Mason slung his arm over my shoulders and I saw a flash of concern. I felt it, too: my body was held tight as a bow. I was sure I had knots in the back of my neck the size of golf balls.

Mason looked at me like a ticking time bomb; I certainly felt like one. Mason forced one of those smiles that seemed to usually come so easy to him and nodded across the street.

"There must be a new boy at the tobacco store," he said, struggling to keep his smile up as he watched me. "Or why else would you be standing here all day?"

He left the door open for me with his kind tone, with his soft gaze, with the slightly worried brush of his fingers on my shoulder. He could sense something was wrong, something was off. I knew he wanted to help.

I couldn't tell him the truth. I couldn't.

I shrugged and forced a laugh. "Is it really so obvious?"

It was a lie. Another lie. The guilt wormed in deeper as Mason hesitated, then patted me on the back with a small smile.

I stirred back to life after that, trying as best as I could to appear normal. I did my assigned tasks. I chatted with Mason and Rian in the kitchen. I asked them questions, showed them art. Pretended everything was fine. Just fine. But I knew: there was no boy. Of course there was no boy. There was only a man.

A week later I woke up eighteen. I imagined the day a million times over before that morning. A creak of the mattress when dawn was just a pale line over the smoking chimneys. The comforter sliding slowly down my arm. Fingers working beneath a t-shirt that was his, fingers brushing against a waist that was his, smoothing against a stomach that was his, caressing breasts that were his, his, *his*. A whisper, hot and desperate and lustful in my ear, "Happy birthday, Aurnia."

If the bed creaked it was only because I dragged myself out of it with a heaviness in my bones. If I was wearing his t-shirt it was only because I'd lost the energy to do laundry over the days since he'd left. If my nipples peaked and hardened, it was only because I touched myself in the long, hot shower imagining his voice in my ear. Happy fucking birthday to me.

Dublin Ink was much the same as it always was. I had expected as much. It wasn't like Mason or Rian knew it was my birthday. I was sure it was on some piece of paperwork in some file folder in some messy cabinet in the tattoo parlour. But Mason didn't "do" paperwork and Rian simply didn't have the focus for it. My birthday would pass like any other day. I thought it was going to be like a doorway opening. Conor could finally see me as an adult. He could take me without shame or guilt. I could step up to him on equal footing and demand what I wanted, what my body wanted.

It was nothing like that at all. All doors remained closed. All keys thrown away.

At least my work at the shop distracted me from thinking of my birthday and, consequently, thinking of Conor. At the end of the day, the closest thing I got to a gift was Mason asking if I could run to the supply store across town before closing up. It was half an hour away on bus and that meant at least an hour of not being in Conor's apartment. An hour of not being in his apartment without *him*.

My headphones were still blaring The Untouchables at full volume when I unlocked the front door of the darkened parlour with two bags of supplies slung over my shoulders. Better to drown myself in badass rock music than my own miserable self-pity. The plan was to drop the bags off in the storeroom, grab a bottle of Moscato from Mason's Miss Last Night stash, and hunt around for where Rian hid (misplaced?) his mushrooms. It wasn't really a party of one when booze and drugs were involved, now was it?

The sudden chorus of "Surprise!" and the blinding flash of light sent the bags spilling from my arms. With a bellowing war cry, I held up my pepper spray as I blinked rapidly and tried to orient myself to the attack. I flinched when a big arm came around my shoulders. I was tugged into a tall, warm side.

I went to jam my elbow into the nearest ribs, but a burst of laughter stopped me. I looked up at Mason, who grinned down at me before rubbing his knuckles against the top of my head.

"Happy birthday, crazy girl," he said, tugging the pepper spray from my shaking hands.

He tossed it to Rian, who sniffed it before tossing it over his shoulder with a shrug. He walked over and came to the other side of me.

"We kind of thought you might like to celebrate your birthday," he said. "But if you'd like to fight all of these people instead, that might be fun, too."

"Um, I brought cupcakes, if that factors into your decision," said a man stepping forward with a tray of delicately frosted baked goods. I stared at him and my mouth fell open when I realised who it was.

"You're—you're Declan Gallagher," I stuttered.

A winning smile I'd seen a hundred times from the ring on the TV filled the man's face. He inched forward as if still wary that I might attack him and held up the tray.

"Red velvet," he said. "Homemade."

"Bullshite," Mason coughed into his arm as I took one, still stupidly staring.

Declan Fucking Gallagher glared up at Mason.

"Well, they are!" he argued. "They were made in my home, weren't they?"

"By your *chef*."

I looked between the two of them, still dumbstruck as I took a bite.

"That's not the point," Declan said.

"Sure it is."

Declan's famous temper came to play as he angrily threw up his arms, nearly sending one of the cupcakes rolling.

"What do you want me to say then?" he growled. "Chef-made?"

Mason considered this with a tilt of his head to the left and the right and then said, "Yeah, sure. I'm good with that."

Declan turned to me and his red cheeks softened as he said, "Chef-made, my dear. Happy birthday."

I grinned and said through a mouthful of frosting, "They're delicious."

"He'll let his chef know," Mason joked.

Another man stepped forward from the small little crowd that Mason and Rian had wrangled up for me, and I would have fallen over if it hadn't been for the two of them on either side of me.

"Holy shite!" I gasped.

"Now, if you promise not to attack me," he said, "in return I might just be convinced to play you a birthday song."

My fingers wouldn't stop shaking as I fumbled around for my headphones which I'd yanked from my ears in my sudden fright.

"I—I—I was just— Here."

I held out the headphones and the leader of my favourite band in the world, Danny O'Donoghue, stepped forward, leaned his head in toward me, and put my earbud (my fucking earbud!) against his ear. I screeched when he began singing aloud to the song. He winked at me when the song came to an end, handing back the earbud.

"No pepper spray then?"

I laughed (giggled really, giggled like a silly little girl) and blushed as I said, "No pepper spray."

Danny held up his pinkie. I squealed again when mine wrapped around his.

"Promise?" he said.

I nodded enthusiastically. "Promise."

My face must have gone a million shades of red when Danny then kissed my cheek and wished me a happy birthday. From there Mason and Rian guided me through their group of friends, introducing me to each in turn. I met the gloomy Darren, who handed over a metalwork heart like the one I'd painted on the side of the shop, without comment, despite how kind the gift was. I met the "gang from The Jar": Noah and Aubrey and Candice, each bubblier and louder and more excited than the next. I met more people than I could remember the names of.

And I was happy and I was grateful. It wasn't until we had nearly made our way through everyone as the music played and the drinks poured that I realised that I was still hopeful for just one more. Just one more.

I'd shaken all the hands, accepted all the little gifts, received all the warm birthday wishes, and there was still a little sadness in me, because *he* wasn't there. Everyone else was there. Everyone I didn't know, but wished to soon was there. A whole little family was there.

But he wasn't.

Conor wasn't.

For the rest of the night, I smiled, but falsely. I laughed, but only because I forced myself to. I had fun, but the kind of fun that I had to convince myself I was having. No matter how many people, all there for me, I was surrounded by, I still craned my neck to spy the front door between them.

Danny played for me and Declan let me pose with my fist against his cheek and Mason and Rian never stopped making me feel special, but I couldn't shake the feeling that the thing that I'd really wanted for my birthday, the one true thing I'd wanted, I hadn't gotten. I hadn't and I wouldn't.

I shouldn't have felt that way. I knew that. It was the most anyone had ever done for me for my birthday. It was the very definition of kindness. Of thoughtfulness. Of caring. I'd always wanted a family and that's what Mason and Rian had given me for my birthday. It should have been enough. It should have been everything.

But Conor wasn't there. So a part of me, a bigger part of me than I probably wanted to admit, wasn't there either.

37

CONOR

I half expected my key not to work.

I wouldn't have really blamed them for changing the locks. For barring me from ever coming back. For barring me from ever causing more harm. If I was in Mason or Rian's place, I probably would have done the same. Hell, that's what I thought I was doing, too: protecting Aurnia.

My relationship with Mason and Rian had never been what you could call "smooth". From the very first day the three of us all came to know each other we were fighting. Arguments, disagreements, and physical scuffles were normal to the three of us, despite the name we used of "friends". But I wasn't sure I'd ever known them to be as mad at me as they were when they were trying to get me to come back for Aurnia's birthday.

That was a different kind of anger, and I knew it. Because while we could all hurt each other, it was unacceptable to hurt *her*. We were all big, strong men. All adults with our fair share of scars. All capable of picking ourselves back up.

But Aurnia? Despite turning eighteen, she was still a child. Still fragile. Still worth preserving in her beautiful innocence.

For the last week, I'd rarely had more than a few moments

of painful sobriety, but their voicemails and text messages were still sharp in my memory. Mason called me a prick. A fucker. A selfish asshole who deserved to have his balls go through a meat grinder and his cock through a vegetable peeler.

Rian's messages hurt more though. Of the two, he seemed more aware of what was going on between Aurnia and me. All he had to say was this: "She'll be looking for you. She'll be looking for you, and you know it, Conor."

As the day grew closer and the messages more frequent, angrier, I just couldn't. I couldn't put down the bottle. I couldn't stop myself from unzipping the plastic baggie tucked into my back pocket. I couldn't slow down my motorcycle. I couldn't keep the miles between her and me from increasing and increasing and increasing.

Maybe I stayed away because I knew I was in a bad way. Because I thought I would only ruin things for her, showing up the way I was for her birthday. Maybe I was doing it *for* her. Staying away because I knew I couldn't *stay away*. Keeping my distance because I knew it'd be a matter of time before I pushed myself into her and claimed her when I saw her next. Because I'd proven, with my tongue on her clit and my fingers against her g-spot, I had no willpower when it came to her.

Or maybe I was just a selfish asshole who deserved to have his balls go through a meat grinder and his cock through a vegetable peeler.

I don't know what it was that finally made my handlebars shift toward the exit sign two weeks later. It wasn't like I'd resolved anything. My mind was still a fucking mess. My body was still broken. The past still hung over my shoulder. Its weight still made every breath a struggle, every step a mile. And I was still too old for her.

Mason and Rian had stopped trying to call after Aurnia's

birthday. I received no more texts. No more voicemails. So it wasn't them who finally changed my mind.

The only explanation I could give was this: I was tired. I was so goddamn fucking tired. And I wanted peace. I wanted rest. I wanted to give up. I wanted to give in. I wanted Aurnia.

The drive back to Dublin was long. The last ten miles through the sleeping city even longer. When I found the apartment empty, I went to the only other place I was certain I would find her. The lights in the shop were out save one single bulb in one single lamp. I breathed in deeply outside the door. The key was in my fingers. All that was left to do was try it. Had I been shut out? Had I been cut off? Had any of them had any sense at all?

I prayed one last time the prayer that I had repeated across every mile: please, please let the door be locked. Let her be gone. Let her be out my reach. Out of my ravenous, all-consuming reach.

The key went easily into the lock. It twisted without resistance. I heard the click like a bullet entering the chamber of a gun. A loaded gun. That was me. A fucking loaded gun.

The door swung inward and she turned around at the sound of the little bell. She was in the shadows. As was I.

I expected her to be frightened. To be alarmed. An intrusion in the middle of the night. A pair of looming shoulders in the dark. A ghost having returned too late. But despite the unexpectedness of my arrival, Aurnia didn't seem at all frightened. At all alarmed. At all even surprised.

She stood the farthest distance across the living room from me, a broom in her hands. The soft light from the lamp did not reach her so I could make nothing out on her face. All I could see was that she stood steady. All I could see was that she breathed evenly, slowly. All I could see was that she was a woman. A *woman*.

The door fell closed behind me. I locked it once more. Behind my back. Without looking. Without looking away from her.

I hadn't planned what I was to do, what I was to say. I always intended for the door to be impenetrable, the locks changed. I imagined the shattering of glass. The splintering of wood. The wail of an alarm. I had no apology on my lips. No forgiveness sought in my heart. No soothing words, no tender caresses, no sensation of falling to my knees.

I stood there frozen. Mute. Not knowing what to do. Not knowing how to explain, to beg for forgiveness. Not knowing whether the space in her heart that I occupied was lost. My little thief gone.

It was Aurnia who moved first. It wasn't to raise a weapon. It wasn't to raise a call for help. It wasn't to run away. To dash out of the room toward the back exit. To pick up the phone for Mason. For Rian. For Diarmuid. It was to step, slowly but unwaveringly, toward *me*. Even when I saw her coming toward me, her footsteps the only sound, even then I could do nothing but watch. Wait.

Aurnia passed by the single lamp with its single bulb and I caught sight of her face, if only for a moment. She was eighteen. Eighteen at last. But she was so much more. She was a child who had been abandoned and grown strong. She was a victim of abuse who had finally learned to throw a punch. She was a little thief who finally decided to take what she wanted, what she truly wanted. Her face caught the light, but just as quickly descended back into darkness. She moved smoothly. Surely. I sucked in a breath as she came to stop before me.

Aurnia said nothing as her eyes trailed over me. It felt like just yesterday that she was drawing me in my apartment. But how different was her gaze.

Before I could see her nerves. The flutter of her chest. The rapidness of her strokes on the page. The flicker of her eyes, afraid to look at me for too long. There was none of that there before me now. Aurnia studied the bruising round my eye from Nick's heel without flinching. No colour flooded her cheek as she stared up at me.

I knew my eye was still ugly. The purples deep, the blacks deeper. The cuts were probably still caked with blood. My lack of sleep, lack of nutrition certainly didn't help. The alcohol, the drugs. Even if Nick had never touched me, I would look rough. Look hurt. Look near death.

Aurnia took all this in, took all of me in, and did not turn away. Her eyes saw the messiness of my hair, saw the looseness of my jacket, saw the cuts and bruises on my knuckles, and neither of us moved. I was sure she could smell the alcohol on my breath. I was sure she noticed how my fingers didn't stay quite so still at my sides, a lingering effect of the drugs. I was sure she took in every beaten and battered part of me.

And yet her gaze was steady. Her eyes met mine without judgement. Without anger. With nothing but a single intent: to see me. To see me clearly.

"Are you back?" she asked.

Was it my imagination or was the childishness from her voice gone? Was it that I wished her to sound like an adult? Or did she really sound like an adult? Her voice deeper. Firmer. The confidence from standing on the same footing as someone else. Was she different? Or was it just that my defences were worn down? My morals abandoned? My conviction stamped out with my eye?

"I missed your birthday," was what I said in return.

Aurnia, for the first time, ducked her eyes.

In a soft voice that nearly sent me running back out the door she said, "I know."

"I didn't get you a gift," I said.

She lifted her eyes to mine. Said nothing.

I licked my lips. I squeezed my fingers to keep them from shaking. I exhaled as evenly as I could. "But I want to."

Aurnia hesitated for a moment. "You want to…"

"Give you a gift," I quickly said, nearly stumbling over my words.

I wanted to draw her hands into mine. I wanted to hold them tight against my chest. I wanted to beg her forgiveness for ever leaving, for ever laying my hands on her, for ever taking her out of her father's house, for ever letting her *be* in her father's house, for wanting her, for needing her, for hating her and loving her and wanting to give her everything and fearing I never could, *knowing* I never could.

"Name something," I said when Aurnia remained silent. "Name anything."

I said those words even as I knew they were impossible. I believed those words even as I was certain I could do no such thing as give her anything. I couldn't even give her my presence on her fucking birthday. How in God's name was I supposed to give her anything? With no money. With no certainty for the future. With whiskey on my breath, cocaine in my veins.

It should have been a miracle that Aurnia said anything at all. Instead of shoving me aside, stalking past me, and storming out that door.

She looked up at me and asked for something I could give her. Perhaps the one thing I was certain I couldn't fuck up.

"Are you sure?" I asked.

Aurnia nodded. "I want a tattoo."

I tried to bargain for something else. Something less permanent. Something without my fingerprints forever on her skin. Aurnia stopped me with her small hand on mine.

"I'll have a tattoo or I'll have nothing."

I should have offered nothing. But she was close and her

eyes were sweet and I wanted to give her the fucking world even if I knew tomorrow, I would destroy it.

"What kind of tattoo?" I asked.

Aurnia didn't pause to think, to consider. She was as stupid as I was. As reckless, as dangerous. But she was a child. What fucking excuse did I have?

"I want you to draw something," Aurnia answered. "I want you to draw something for me."

"What do you want me to draw?" I asked.

In my mind, I was begging for direction. I was lost. I wanted Aurnia to show me the way. I needed Aurnia to show me the way. But Aurnia said nothing. Her eyes said nothing. Her breath, steady and even, said nothing.

"This is your first tattoo, Aurnia," I insisted in a panic. "This is forever. You need to tell me."

Aurnia slipped her fingers into mine. Without a word she led me to my tattoo chair. She climbed up onto it as I watched. She looked like a child using a stool to get to the kitchen counter. But when she turned to look at me, her hair darker even than the black leather, she looked like a woman waiting for me to join her in bed. Eyes hooded. Breath catching. Lips wet.

"Will you at least tell me where you want it?" I asked.

I could do nothing to stop Aurnia as she unbuttoned her jeans and slipped them off. The moment I caught sight of her pale skin in the pink neon...the moment I saw the hem of her simple black underwear...the moment I saw that she knew I was watching her...the moment I saw that she *liked* that I was watching her...I was helpless. Utterly helpless.

Aurnia smoothed her hand from the very top of her inner thigh down along her leg toward her knee.

"Here," was all she said.

"Aurnia—"

"*Here.*"

Like I said, I was helpless. I moved without further objection toward my drawing table. With no more than one last glance toward her, I clicked on my lamp. And began.

For what felt like a very long time there was only the scratch of my pencil against the paper and the occasional brush of flesh against leather as Aurnia shifted her bare legs on the tattooing chair. Did she fidget from nerves? Was it fear that kept her from keeping still as I worked? Was she moving so that she did not feel locked into her decision? I was almost certain this was the reason.

So I drew slowly. More slowly than I needed to. I wanted to give her time to change her mind. About the tattoo. About us.

I could only stretch out the drawing for so long. Once the image came to my mind it was like falling. Once I saw it coming to life on the page, all I could do was draw faster. Once I pictured what it would look like on Aurnia's thigh I had to have it. The need was as much physical as mental. I could feel it in my chest. In my fucking heart.

"What do you think?" I asked at last, turning the drawing for her to see, adjusting the lamp so that the light fell upon it.

It was in my style: black and white. A black dragon twisting around a swirl of falling white lotus flowers. As I watched Aurnia's eyes move across it, a part of me hoped she didn't like it. There was too much of me in it. All of me, even. One day she would regret having me there, on her inner thigh, down her leg. One day she would wish me gone, as I most certainly would be. But there I would be. Permanent. Forever. Me.

I was not to be spared. Aurnia's eyes lifted from the page. Lifted and met mine.

"Yes."

38

AURNIA

*N*othing could have prepared me for that first pain. That first plunging of the needle into my skin. Into my body. That insertion. That violation. That bliss.

My whole body was held tense as Conor raised the tattoo gun, not looking at me as he arranged the cord, checked the flow of the ink, referred once more to his drawing beside him. Every muscle inside of me seemed ready to burst. All inside of me was strain, tightness. I was coiled like a snake about to strike. Frozen like a deer on an icy highway.

There was the hum of the gun. The flash of pink neon on the tip of the needle. Ink in my body. Forever. Forever.

My eyes were fixed on the ceiling as I gripped the edge of the chair with quivering fingers, but instead of more pain there was a hand. Callused, but warm. Not soft, but gentle.

"Aurnia," Conor whispered in the quiet of the parlour, "you need to relax."

I kept my chin high as I counted the tin squares on the high living room ceiling.

"I am relaxed," I said through a clenched jaw.

Conor's hand glided over the length of my thigh. My tensed muscle twitched under his touch.

I gritted my teeth and insisted, more like the child I wanted to put behind me than the adult I wanted to be, "I'm relaxed."

"Okay...okay."

Conor's words stopped there as did the buzz of the gun, but his hand on my thigh did not. He brushed the tips of his fingers back and forth along the tensely held muscle.

"You can keep going," I told him, pouting.

I was embarrassed that he had to baby me. I wanted to show him that I was strong. That pain did not scare me. That *his* pain did not scare me. Instead he had been forced to stop tattooing. Forced to tend to me like I had a scraped knee after falling from my bicycle. Forced to soothe and hush like I was crying and couldn't stop. That alone was what made me want to cry.

Me, being a child. Conor, an adult.

"I'm just getting the image in my mind," Conor said, a kindness which made me want to scream.

I fixed my attention on him. But like Conor said, he was not looking at me (although he was still brushing his fingers up, down, up, down), but instead looking at the drawing of the dragon and the lotus.

As usual, a few strands of hair had fallen from his bun. Ripped out by the wind while on his motorcycle, I guessed. While on his way to *me*. Or pulled free when he dragged his fingers through his hair just before stepping inside. Thinking of *me*. Deciding, debating, changing his mind, and changing it again about *me*. Or pushed from behind his ear by the pencil he rested there as he considered before a blank page what to draw for me, what to draw for my body. His whole focus on *me*.

"Good," Conor suddenly whispered, his hand coming to rest on the place where my tattoo would soon be. "That's it."

Without realising it, my body had relaxed. The muscles in my thighs had released their tightness. I had sunk into the chair instead of straining out of it like I was held down by bindings around my ankles and wrists. My limbs felt heavy, my fingertips and toes warm and tingly. My hands came to lie flat beside me, palms facing upward like I was praying for blessings. My head came to rest against the chair. I melted against the leather. I exhaled unevenly just once and then it was like I could breathe again. In and out, in and out. My heart rate slowed. I was certain that Conor sensed all of this, felt all of this through the heat of his palm.

Without another word between us, the hum of the gun began once more and Conor bent back over my exposed thigh. This time I did not look back up at the ceiling. Instead I watched Conor.

The gun rattled against me and the needle darted in and out of me and there was a violence in it that frightened me, but Conor steadied me. His calmness became my calmness. I watched his lungs expand and constrict through the thinness of his shirt on his back and I matched my breathing with his.

Every few moments his face would turn to the drawing on the cart beside him and I would look, too. I would try to see what he was seeing: the curve of the dragon's spine, the flick of the tongue, the delicate spindle of the lotus, its points finer than the needle he held in his hand.

Conor's eyes would return to my body and mine would return to his. He was claiming me, with his needle, with his gun, with his art, but I was claiming him, too. I was drawing him on my heart. The width of his shoulders as he bent over me. The shadow that fell over his eyes from his brow. The scars along his fingers which dabbed at my skin with a cloth. I had nothing to draw with but my eyes. Nothing to put him down on but my memory. Nothing to make sure he remained, like the ink would remain, but the sensation in my body.

So I tried to hold onto it. That warmth. That pain. That glow that came from having someone so committed to you and you alone. Why couldn't I ink that into my body? Why couldn't I keep that forever? That pleasure. That flooding sensation. That heat. That fucking *heat*.

"Aurnia?"

I blinked into awareness, a haze disappearing from my eyes. I found Conor closer to me, his rolling stool moved farther up my leg. His hand was on my hip. As if to steady me. As if to keep me still. As if to ground me. Conor's gun was off. He'd placed it atop the drawing on the cart beside him. The tattoo was halfway done, the part closest to my knee finished, the part closest to my heart not yet started. Conor's eyes were fixed on me. They glowed amber in the pink neon light. There was concern. There was concern and there was something else. Something more.

"Are you in pain?" he asked, his voice soft.

I stared at him like I did not understand.

"Aurnia," Conor pressed, even as his fingers pressed. I could feel his thumb below my hip bone. I could feel his fingertips at the swell of my ass. He was trying to get through to me. I shook my head because it was thick, cotton-stuffed, slow-moving as molasses.

"What?" I asked dumbly.

"Are you in pain?" Conor asked once more, patiently, slowly.

"No," I replied, shifting a little uncomfortably on the tattoo chair, the backs of my thighs sticking from the heat. "No, I don't think so."

Conor's eyes assessed mine. Then he assessed my body. I noticed then, too, that I was tensed once more. My hands were back around the sides of the chair, my fingernails digging into the leather on the underside. My breathing was back to being ragged, uneven, breaths held for too long, the air around me somehow thinner than it should have been. The muscles of my inner thighs were shaking uncontrollably. My back was again stiff as a board as if Conor had sent not ink into my flesh but high voltages of electricity, again and again and again.

I didn't understand what was happening to me. It wasn't fear that was making me react like this. Or at least I didn't think it was. I didn't feel pain. Or at least not pain like I usually felt pain. It wasn't the sting of torn skin or the dull ache of a bruise or the quick white heat of a cut from a too sharp kitchen knife.

The pain was an ache, a needing, between my legs. I tried to release the tension in my body, but it remained. Outside my control. Completely outside my control.

"Are you sure?" Conor asked, his eyes returning to mine before looking at the half-finished tattoo. "Because the skin here..."

He touched the pale skin where the white lotus was still to go. God, so close to the edge of my panties. A shiver went down my spine. Between my legs throbbed like a heartbeat.

"...the skin here can be very sensitive," he explained. "Many people find it painful... Especially for their first time... When they don't know what to expect..."

Conor looked at me and I saw it again. The way his gaze kept drawing to my inner thighs. The flush to his cheeks, the hitch in his breath. He was remembering. Remembering what it felt like to kiss that sensitive skin. How I arched my back against his tongue. How I came undone for him.

"We can stop," he said, pulling his hand from my hip, dragging it through his hair. Was his breath ragged, too? Was the air around us thin for him like it was thin for me? Was he having just as hard of a time getting anything, anything at all into his starved lungs as I was?

"We can stop and continue later," Conor said as I watched his chest, watched his lungs beneath the thin material that now clung to him, stuck to his body like my bare legs stuck to the leather chair. He continued more to himself than to me, "We should stop. We shouldn't go any further."

My hand was on his before he could put the tattoo gun away.

"Keep going. Please," I said. "I'm not in pain."

His eyes met mine and I could see he believed me. I could also see that it was the answer he was not hoping for but fearing. I could see that this was exactly what he hadn't wanted to hear. I could see that things would have been simpler for him, for me, for us, if I had just said, "It hurts." If I had just said, "It hurts and I want to stop." If I had just said, "Please stop."

I said the opposite. I begged the opposite.

"Please," I said, the word desperate on my tongue, "don't stop."

Conor ran his hand over his mouth.

"If I continue," he said, slowly and with hesitation, "if I continue, we'll see it to the end."

I did not look away as he watched me in the dim, pink-hazed light.

"Is that what you want?" he asked.

I sucked in what air I could and said, softly but firmly, "Yes, I want it."

There was that something else again in Conor's eyes. There was that something more. I only caught a passing glimpse of it as he picked back up the gun and again leaned over my bare thigh. I had hardly any time to stare at it, to puzzle at it, to try to piece it together. But it left a spot on my vision like the sun. A blackness. A strange void. I tried to cling to it before I blinked it away. Before it disappeared and I could no longer remember what it looked like at all. I tried to name it. To name it.

Relief?

Fear?

Lust?

I had little time to think more on it because it wasn't long before the steady hum of the tattoo gun and Conor's intense focus on me had once again dragged me under like a tide. Soon it was all I could think about: the pain/pleasure of the needle against my skin moving higher and higher, Conor's fingers sweeping along my flesh higher and higher, his eyes focused on nothing but my bare skin. Higher and higher.

All I could think of was that night he had me laid out naked and spread out before him. The way his hair tickled my inner thighs. The way his fingers coaxed out even more and more pleasure from me.

Maybe it was seconds after that or maybe it was hours after that, but at some point I wasn't even thinking at all.

I knew nothing but instinct and desperation. All I could do was try to hold on. Conor said if we continued we would see it to the end and he seemed intent on it now. He held the thigh he was tattooing firmly, even as the rest of me squirmed. My heel dug into the leather. My skin was slick with sweat so I could find no purchase, but still I tried.

My back kept arching against my will as Conor and his needle and his hands and his fucking breath continued up my thigh, twisting round to the very inner part where the last petal would stretch to its fine, delicate point. Any time I tried to force my back against the chair I found the leather wet, my shirt wet. Everywhere there was heat, the source coming from between my legs.

Everywhere there was unmoving, heavy air. The hum of the tattoo gun sounded like a fan, but there was not the relief of a fan. Outside it was cold, freezing, but inside the windows fogged and steamed and sweat hung heavy on my brow.

It didn't seem like it was only me burning up. Conor's shirt clung to each rib along his back. His hair was plastered against his forehead and his heavy breath rushed against the tops of my thighs as if it was trying to get under the edge of my soaked panties.

I clutched at the sides of the chair, but it did nothing to stop my back from arching, nipples hard against my thin shirt. I clutched at the chair, but it was really Conor alone, his fingers digging into my flesh, that kept me there. It was the vibration of his gun. The pain and pleasure of his needle. It was the unrelenting focus of his eyes. It was his fixedness to finish his work, to finish me.

It was going to kill me, to overcome me completely and utterly.

I didn't think that Conor could move any higher, could get any closer to my core. But he did. His knuckles brushed against my panties. An accident, I'm sure. Him being so close.

It didn't matter though. It felt like he'd meant it. I took it as if he meant it.

All the holding on I did proved useless. All the struggling to maintain control was for nothing.

The only thing I could hope for at that point was to keep myself silent.

I wasn't even to have that small mercy.

My body quivered as I came and there was nothing to stop the little gasp, the desperate whimper that escaped my wet lips. The waves of white pleasure that crashed over me hadn't completely finished and I was covering my hot cheeks and turning my face away from Conor.

I had never been more embarrassed. Never more horrified. To lose control in front of Conor. To fall apart from a single accidental brush. To react like an inexperienced teenager in the back seat of a parent's car. I wanted to curl up in on myself. I wanted to die.

His hand around my wrist did nothing to help. I felt tears

prick at my eyes behind my hot, sweaty fingers. I pressed down on my eyes tighter. Tried to hold the moisture back.

"Go away," I begged, my breath hot in that cocoon.

Conor let go of my hands. I heard the rolling stool creak.

He was leaving. He was embarrassed, too. He was embarrassed and he was leaving but at least I would be alone. Shite. He'd never let me see him again. This was the end.

If I wasn't crying before, I certainly was now. It'd ruined it. Ruined us. Not that there ever was an *us*.

I waited for the quickly retreating footsteps, but I didn't hear them. I almost peeked when a weight pressed onto the chair, but I kept my fingers tight. I was sure it was my bag. A sign to leave. The footsteps would come now. Any moment. The end would come. It had to.

My body tensed at the sudden sensation of Conor's fingers on both of my legs. My breath quickened behind my hands. My tears stopped. I waited. Conor kept his hands still as he said in a soft whisper, "Aurnia, there's nothing to be embarrassed about."

Avoiding my tattoo, he slid his fingers up my thighs, chasing after the goosebumps that he caused.

"There's nothing at all to be embarrassed about," he whispered as he hooked a finger under my panties and pulled them to the side.

His hot tongue between my legs made me whimper behind the cover of my hands. He licked me long and slow.

In a voice thick and deep, he murmured, "Look at me, Aurnia. Look at me."

It took a moment or two for me to relent. I was afraid that with the way I was breathing so heavily, gasping almost, if I kept my hands over my face for any longer, I would run out of air and pass out. So I parted my fingers, just enough to breathe. Just enough to spy Conor between the gaps.

What I saw was almost more than I could handle.

A man on his knees in front of me. A giant of a man. A man who could kill me with one hand. A man double my size. With arms larger than my legs. A man. My man. *My* Conor.

Conor with his tongue greedy against my pussy. Conor with his mouth wet from me. With his hair tickling my inner thighs. With his murmurs of pleasure buried inside of me.

Conor with his eyes opening. Finding mine. Black as the night.

"Fuck," his gravelly voice vibrated through my clit, "you taste so damn sweet."

My hands went to his head, his hair without being told. I wrapped my thighs around his shoulders despite the pain from my tattoo. I leaned my head back and moaned louder as his finger circled my entrance.

As he parted my lips to lick even deeper.

I almost lost control when he pushed a finger inside me—so easily, I was already so ready, so needy for it—even as his tongue worked circles around my clit. I was drowning in pleasure.

"More. Conor," I heard myself beg in a voice that sounded like a woman's. "Don't stop."

He gave me more. He curled his finger around and found that spot inside me. I came hard, a scream tearing from my lungs. My body bucked against the seat as electricity gripped me.

Conor held me for a long while as I softened, as all my bones turned to liquid. He mumbled with satisfaction against my slippery lips.

39

CONOR

J told myself I was lifting the sheets on Aurnia's sleeping form beside me in bed to check her fresh tattoo. I told myself that my eyes were trailing over her breasts beneath my oversized t-shirt simply on my way to her leg. That I peeled back the bandage at the inner most part of her thigh because I needed to make sure nothing was inflamed. That there were no signs of anything to worry about.

It was bullshite. All bullshite.

There was plenty to worry about. In fact, there was everything to worry about. Because I did all that for one reason and one reason alone: I wanted her. I wanted her gasping and shivering uncontrollably beneath my touch. I wanted my face between her legs, her taste on my tongue, the shimmer of her wetness on my lips.

The sound of the phone in the living room cut through my apartment. Shook my guilt to the fore. Stripped my dirty intentions bare. What if Aurnia woke up? What if she found me as I was? Rock hard. Yearning. On the fucking edge of doing something that I knew I shouldn't, that I shouldn't *ever* do.

I listened to Aurnia's breathing to see if she stirred. The

damned phone kept ringing. I pulled back the sheets to go and answer it. To face it. My guilt. It had to be Diarmuid. Calling about the girl he'd entrusted into my care. It had to be reality ringing. It had to be the cold, hard light of day intruding into the soft warmth of Aurnia's cheek against my bicep. It had to be faced, didn't it? I couldn't just run from it forever. Stay in bed with my little thief till the end of time. I couldn't...

The moment I moved to get out of bed, I felt fingertips brush against my cock, protected only by the thin material of my boxer shorts. Maybe Aurnia had just shifted in her sleep, hopefully dreaming nicer dreams than me.

But as those delicate little fingertips trailed up and down my throbbing shaft, my heart stopped and my chest clenched. I could no longer believe my little thief was asleep. Could no longer believe I was going to get up and answer that phone. Knew I never wanted to face reality ever again.

She'd caught me unaware. Caught me in a moment of weakness. That's the excuse I'd give for not batting her hand away.

That and I was just so tired. Tired of fighting. Tired of denying myself. Of denying her.

Aurnia's fingers were uncertain, almost trembling as she caressed me with a featherlight touch. It made me shiver despite the warmth of our bodies beneath the sheets. My desire was already driving me to grab her, to roll over atop her, to thrust deep inside of her, to command those delicate little fingertips to better use: on her nipples which were peaked through the thin material of my old t-shirt, on her sensitive clit as I fucked her hard.

As Aurnia touched me, her face, eyes still shut, remained peaceful and innocent. As lovely as an angel. The only evidence at all that she was fully aware of what she was doing, fully aware of the impact that she was having on me, on my body, was the slight quiver of her bottom lip, like it was already tingling from just imagining the things I could do to her. The pleasure I could give.

"Look at me," I whispered, voice already tense, tight.

Aurnia's fingertips grew bold as she slid them into my boxers and wrapped her little hand all the way around my cock. I tensed, holding back a groan I was sure would scare her. Her fingers hardly met as they looped around me and began to move. I thought I sensed a tremor go through her petite frame. Was it fear? Arousal?

Shame?

Shame like mine?

"I don't want to open my eyes," came her response a few quiet moments later after there had been nothing but our breaths growing heavier.

I wanted to grab her. I wanted to drag her out of the bed, prop her up against the edge, kick her bare feet apart, and take her from behind as her fingers curled in the bedsheets. I wanted to watch her body atop mine. Her hips rolling. My hands clutching at her breasts as if they were a lifeline. Her throat long as she threw her head back. I wanted to give her the pleasure of a woman. To fuck her like a woman. To tug the hair at the base of her neck like a woman. To make her teeth sink into the delicate sink at the base of my neck as she came, came over and over again like a woman.

Instead there, with sweet little lips and long doll-like eyelashes and a face shaped like a heart, was a child. Touching me tentatively, exploring me softly, slowly discovering what made my breath catch in my throat.

"Open your eyes, Aurnia," I told her.

Her pinkie caught the bead of pre-cum which had slipped from my cockhead. She paused. Unsure. Afraid even. Had she not known how dangerously close to the edge her little ministrations were already taking me? Had she not known that I wouldn't be able to endure this for much longer? Keeping myself still. Restraining myself. Holding back as she drove me off a fucking cliff with barely a touch.

Aurnia swirled my pre-cum across the head of my dick. I groaned and I was suddenly not sure of anything that Aurnia had or hadn't known.

"Open your eyes," I told her again, and this time it sounded like I was begging.

"I'm afraid to."

"Why?"

I was practically gasping now that Aurnia was running her little fist up and down my length. Her fingers slick. Her grip loose but tightening.

"Why?" I pressed.

Aurnia held her hand still at the base of my shaft. I trembled in her hold. Twitched with need. Would she scream if I pinned her hands over her head? Would she thrash if I tore at the t-shirt that was mine? Would she open her eyes when I shoved violently inside of her because I couldn't fucking take it any longer?

"Because I'm afraid that if I open my eyes, I'll see that it's not real," Aurnia whispered her hand still damnably still. "I'm afraid I'll see that you're not real. Not really here. With me."

Aurnia shuddered and I felt the tremors through my cock like an earthquake.

"Aurnia," I said, "open your eyes. I'm not a dream that will disappear. I'm not a dream at all. Please don't...goddammit, please don't make me that."

How could I be her world when I was sure that I was the one who was someday, somehow going to destroy it?

"I need this to be real."

"It is."

"Prove it."

I hesitated. "How—?"

"Fuck me."

I sucked in a breath.

What we did last night—what *I'd* done to her, pressing my face into her folds, licking and sucking the moans right out of her—had been wrong. But somehow, I could justify that I hadn't taken advantage of her. That I hadn't drawn my own pleasure from her young lithe body.

But to *fuck* her...to sink my hard, greedy cock into her innocent flesh, to take her, possess her, own her, to brand her with my jaded cynical hands like a tattoo she'd regret?

I almost said no. I almost pulled back. There on the precipice of my utter damnation.

If not for the rough swirl of her hand over my cock.

I let out a groan as her gravity pulled at me. "Are you sure this is what you want?"

Aurnia laughed a little. Nervously. Anxiously.

"Isn't that a question you should be asking yourself?" she said.

"I wanted you from the very moment I touched you," I said, too fucking honest for my own good. "All I want is you. I want your body, your voice, your heat beside me at night. I want your tits in my mouth in my bed and your toes against mine under the table at breakfast and the sound of your pencil beside mine at work. I want to fuck you and love you and destroy you, Aurnia. Absolutely destroy you. But—but that's the problem. I — You're too innocent to be destroyed. Too young. There's too much of life for you that doesn't yet have to be stolen."

"By you?" Aurnia whispered.

My finger brushed against her hipbone, just visible past the raised hem of my t-shirt.

With her eyes still closed, Aurnia said, "I've wanted you from the very moment you touched me. All I want is you. I want your strong arms around me to keep me safe. I want your words in my ear as you show me how to tattoo. I've want you to get jealous over me, to fight for me, to press me up against the wall when the shop is empty each night because I'm yours. Yours and no one else's. I want to belong in you, Conor. In your tattoo chair. In your bed. In your ecstasy as you call my name. I'm too young to be destroyed, but I already am. All I want... All I've wanted is for someone to heal me. For *you* to heal me."

It was the first time I'd moved since I felt Aurnia's fingers on my cock. It was the first time I'd *allowed* myself to move.

There was a reason I'd restrained myself in that way: I knew that the first move would be like the first shifting of an avalanche. There was no stopping it after that. There was no stopping *me* after that.

My hand moved to her neck and I clung to her like that alone could keep her there. Could keep her there with me. I tipped Aurnia's head up to mine with a thumb beneath her chin before I could stop myself, our lips crashing together.

Even still, I drew her closer. Clung to her as she clung onto me.

Because I needed her. Because I wanted her. I wanted to heal her as she healed me. Because I *wanted* to be her dream, even though I knew I never could be.

We gasped against each other, as Aurnia's hand squeezed around me. As her hard nipples brushed against my searing-hot chest. As her hot pussy pressed against my thigh as she slung her leg over my hip. It was the gasp of finally reaching air after being submerged too long. Held under too long. Crushed beneath the weight of a goddamn ocean for far, far too long.

I swept my arms around Aurnia and rolled her onto her back. Aurnia's chest rose and fell heavily. Sweat already made my t-shirt cling to the small of her back as she sucked in air. Her nipples were straining to be touched. When I brushed my finger between her legs, knees up, feet planted on the mattress, I found her soaking wet.

Any restraint I had left shattered.

I mounted Aurnia's narrow hips. Tore off her shirt. She shivered as I sucked and bit my way down to her nipples, small, pink and peaked. Fuck. I wanted more of her. Wanted all of her.

Consequences be damned.

I tore off her panties. Chased the goosebumps down the length of her legs. I ran my greedy palms all the way back up, carefully around her bandage, even as I pushed her thighs even wider open for me.

Holy shit.

She arched her back, rocking her glistening pussy toward me with a moan.

"Please."

I was going straight to hell.

She looked equal parts angel and devil laid out naked and needy for me. With her nipples strained and her inner thighs twitching.

I had to take a second to squeeze the base of my cock. To still myself. I was going to make her come. With me inside of her. But I had to control myself. I had to get control of myself. Or I was not going to last.

"Do it," Aurnia said, all innocence gone from her voice. "Conor, fuck me."

I lined myself up with her pussy, causing her to gasp.

"Yes."

I pressed slowly until I was just inside of her. Stopped. Stopped for her. Stopped for me. She was stunning in the pale grey light that filtered in through blinds. I wanted to devour her. I wanted all of her. But I didn't want to hurt her.

At least, not yet.

Aurnia's hands went around my back. They slid down to my

hips. Reached around for my ass. She pulled me toward her, into her with a strength that I had no idea she had.

I gasped and she gasped and I felt her clenching around me. I felt her wet heat. I felt *her*.

"Can you feel me?" Aurnia asked.

My forehead came to rest against hers. My brow was already slick with sweat as my stomach muscles spasmed.

"Yes," I practically groaned.

"I can feel you. We're both real," she said, hips moving slowly, as if against her will.

"Yes."

"Neither of us is going to disappear."

I leaned over her exposed body to scrape my teeth against her hard nipple.

"No."

I sucked at her throat as she shifted her hips, taking my cock in and out of her.

"We're here," she said, fingers tangling in my hair as we rocked harder together, faster together. "You're inside of me."

"And you're around me," I gasped between hungry licks at her breasts, wild like a dog, "you're everywhere."

We breathed heavily as I thrust into her, the sheets wet with our sweat, our bodies slick against one another's. I could feel my balls tightening, could feel that inescapable need for release coming like a goddamn freight train. When I looked up into Aurnia's face to see if she was close, I saw that amongst the strands of dark hair plastered to her wet forehead, her eyes were finally open.

It was too much for me. Too much and yet not enough.

I drove into her hard as I groaned around her name.

Instantly her eyes shut like I'd seen into a room I wasn't supposed to and the door slammed. Her head whipped back and her back arched into me. Her fingers grabbed painfully at whatever flesh of mine she could find as she came hard, clenching around me in waves. Her cries of release deep and hoarse like they were being squeezed out of her.

I fucked her till her body collapsed, till she was gasping and writhing, till she couldn't fucking take it any longer. I pulled out and came across her stomach. Hot and fast. Long streaks lashing her like rope.

I fell to the side of her, panting and out of breath. When I opened my eyes, I noticed Aurnia's fingers moving through the cum.

"What are you doing?" I asked.

She turned her head and grinned at me. "I thought you said never to waste good ink."

I kissed her like a stupid young idiot in love. Held her cheek. Smiled.

"And what are you drawing?"

Aurnia lifted her chin. Faintly, through the cum that was quickly transitioning from white to translucent against her peach-fuzz skin, I saw a sun. Aurnia laughed and sucked a wet finger into her mouth and I thought there couldn't be anything brighter in the whole goddamn world.

We cleaned up in the shower (and then cleaned up what we did in the shower). When we got to Dublin Ink after, Mason offered to show Aurnia a new tattoo style.

"I'm teaching Aurnia today," I interrupted him, resisting the urge to possessively put my arm around my little thief, *my* little thief.

She hid it well, but I saw. I saw the blush of her cheek. The little grin.

The happiness.

Goddamn me.

40

AURNIA

$\mathcal{I}$ didn't ask questions.

I didn't want to fucking ask questions.

I wanted to get pushed up against a wall and used when Rian and Mason ducked out to pick up takeout. Or to knock off all the ink bottles on the storage room shelves with our desperate limbs. Or to make the plaster fall from the ceiling as the gold metal-frame bed upstairs pounded against the wall.

As the little bell chimed fifteen minutes later, I wanted to swipe my lip gloss from the corner of his lips with my pinkie. To have his teeth nip at me as he grinned down at me. To sink against the faded wallpaper as I stared dreamily at the darkened chandelier and felt my heart pounding out of my chest.

I wanted to meet his eyes from across the parlour when Rian and Mason were bent over their work. I wanted to play that dangerous little game of ours where we saw who dared to look the longest. Who risked getting caught. I wanted to see the fire in his eyes and know that they were only reflected in my own. I wanted to laugh and hide my blush and make up some excuse to leave the room when Rian or Mason looked up.

I wanted the pent-up energy, the suffocated sexual desire,

the unquenchable lust that comes from holding oneself back that Conor unleashed on me the second we got back to the apartment. I wanted the head banging against the wall. I wanted to sting of tugged hair, the bruises from fucking on the kitchen floor, the scalding hot of sex in the shower. Conor keeping himself from coming so it wouldn't be over. So we didn't have to go to work. So he could keep me naked and in his arms and tight around his cock.

That's why I didn't ask why it was so important that we keep our relationship a secret. Why Rian or Mason couldn't know. Why on the streets we couldn't stop at a light pole and kiss like other couples. Why at the store our hands couldn't touch on the shopping cart. Why if we went to the park, it was to fuck in the dark behind a tree, not lay out in the open on a blanket, lips red from too much wine, hands a little too familiar on each other's body for public.

I didn't ask, because I wanted Conor whispering in my ear each night as we fell asleep. Whispering about art, about tattoos, whispering about his dreams for the shop. I didn't ask, because I was in those dreams.

"When you get your first client." "When you develop your own tattoo style." "When you have people coming from all over the city just for you. Just for the work you do." I wanted the excitement in his voice, the quiver of his heart against my back as he held me tight, the thrill as he nestled his nose against my hair.

I didn't ask, because I wanted, oh, fuck, how I wanted these three little words: "I want you."

Mason was "giving a tour" to a potential client, a *female* client. Rian was so absorbed in a sketch that he hadn't even flinched when the door upstairs slammed shut amongst giggling and thumping. I was at one of the drafting desks when I felt Conor against me. His erection obvious against my ass. His need intoxicating as he tucked my hair behind my ear and whispered hotly, "I want you."

We both looked over at Rian, brow furrowed, pencil moving with almost desperation.

"What about him?" I asked.

"Can you be quiet?"

I turned to face him. Conor's arms caged me against the desk. I looked up into his lustful eyes.

"As a mouse," I said.

Conor's fingers intertwined with mine. The only sound as we went to the supply room at the back of the shop was the creaking of the old floorboards. My heart leaped as Conor inched the door closed behind us.

There was never much light in Conor's bedroom, but there was always something. A few rays of sunlight that managed to sneak through the clouds. The orange glow of a street lamp. The passing glare of yellow headlamps. But in the supply closet it was complete darkness.

Conor's hand on my shoulder took me by complete surprise. When he walked me back till my shoulders collided with the tall metal racks, there was nothing I could do but relent. When he spun me around so I was facing away from him, I was as useless as a raggedy doll.

"Arms up," he commanded in the dark.

My sweatshirt went easily over my head. I heard it flung somewhere that might as well have been over the edge of the universe. I shivered as Conor's hands reached around my front. He groped at the button of my jeans and a second later I was kicking out of my boots, kicking out of my pants. It was a new vulnerability. Being naked in the dark. Conor had hardly even touched me and heat was already flooding my pussy. When he pressed me against the rack, the cold bit at my skin, the metal hard against my nipples. A second later Conor's body was against mine and it was nothing but pure raging heat.

"Hold on," he whispered, nipping at my earlobe.

How did he know my body so well? How could he find me as if the lights were on?

I fumbled for the metal posts. My fingers curled around the icy shafts.

I could feel him stroking himself just behind me. Could feel his rough knuckles against my ass. Feel the tremble of his chest against the shivers that ran down my spine.

"Are you holding on?"

I nodded even though he couldn't possibly have seen.

"Words, Aurnia."

"Yes."

"Yes, what?"

I swallowed. "Yes, sir."

"I'm going to fuck you. Hard."

I bit back a moan. We were supposed to be quiet. I could be quiet. I could be—oh, God, how I wanted to moan. How I wanted to lean my head back into the crook of Conor's neck and bite my lip as I growled his name. How I wanted to bang my fists against those metal racks till Mason and Rian came running down at the noise.

"Fuck, you're so wet," Conor said, his cock at the dripping lips of my pussy. "You want to be fucked hard, dirty girl."

I whimpered and tightened my grip on the icy rods. Conor's hands were like brands on my hips. As he thrust deep and hard into me, I released one of my hands to cover my mouth. I would have screamed otherwise. I would have screamed, "More, more, fucking *more*."

Conor stopped.

"You gotta hold on, baby," he said, his voice like a whip, a whip I wanted *harder*.

I sank my teeth into my bottom lip before grabbing once more, this time with a trembling hand to the cold, hard metal.

Conor slapped my ass and bit my shoulder as I tried not to gasp.

"Good girl."

Conor fucked me. Just like he said he would: harder than he'd ever fucked me before. His cock reached places I didn't even know existed inside of me. I was being split apart, torn in two, ravaged, and I couldn't utter even a single peep. The cold of the rack was like ice cubes run along my hard and aching nipples, and I wanted to groan as I arched my back and savoured the sensation. All I could do was clamp down on my bottom lip till it hurt. Everything would be fine if I could just cover my mouth to muffle my groans of pleasure and need, but if I let go Conor would stop. That was the one thing I didn't want: for him to fucking stop.

So it was torture. Blissful, perfect, mind-blowing torture. With his hands on my hips, Conor thrust into me so hard and so fast that if I weren't so goddamn preoccupied with being quiet, I would have come right then and there.

As if sensing how close I was, Conor suddenly turned on another gear. I thought he was giving me all he had, but it was like the revving of his motorcycle engine when it was already whining and protesting on the highway. As I struggled to hold on, something fell from the rack, landing noisily on the floor beside us.

I expected Conor to stop, but he just fucked me harder. My toes nearly left the ground. My breasts were swinging wildly. I couldn't fucking think. More things fell and still Conor kept going, thrusting into me like it was the last time he would ever fuck a woman. No, like it was the last time he would ever fuck *me*.

It was noisy. Noisier even more so because I was without my sense of sight.

"I thought we were supposed to be quiet," I gasped. If I had more control of my body, I might have tried to stop him, to slow him. But I was completely at Conor's mercy.

Conor's response came with a smile against my ear, "I never said *I* was to be quiet."

His mouth swallowed mine as I craned my neck around. I groaned madly into him as he groped at my sweat-slick tits. He bit my lip and I hissed in pain before grinding my ass harder against his groin. Soon we were nothing more than animals crashing about the in the dark. Conor's arm caught me under the knee and hoisted my leg to plunge deeper inside of me. My toes knocked over bottles of ink, stacks of paper, God knows what else.

I came with my teeth clamping down on Conor's arm. Was the sticky heat sweat or blood? I didn't know. I didn't care. I was consumed by waves of pleasure that left me sagging weakly against Conor. He held me, softly, sweetly, carding his fingers through my damp hair.

"What about you?" I asked, reaching around for his still erect cock.

Conor gently tugged my hand away in the dark.

"I can't come without screaming your name," he said between kisses against my temples. "And I want nothing more than to scream your name."

We left the storage room with excuses about reorganizing gone wrong, but Rian was still absorbed in his sketching and the ceiling was still very much shaking from upstairs.

Later that night, in a cracked garage, I rode Conor with the handlebars of his motorcycle digging into my back and he hid the roar of his scream, the roar of my name behind the revving engine.

And so I didn't ask why we had to be a secret. Why Conor sometimes felt distant after we had sex. Why he looked away almost guiltily if I wandered unannounced into the kitchen with nothing on but his boxers. Why promises of the future only came in the dark, in the dead of the night, in the hidden intimacy of his bed.

Because I had Conor screaming my name. I had him reaching for me, loving me. I had him at last.

Or maybe I didn't ask because I didn't want to know the answer. Ignorance is bliss, they say. Well, if I had anything it was fucking bliss. The best fucking bliss of my life.

I guess I should have known better.

41

CONOR

I woke up that morning like I had most mornings: to a raging erection and a deepening well of guilt and shame. Waking Aurnia up with my palm circling her nipples beneath my threadbare t-shirt, watching her lick her lips as she awoke in sweet pleasure, tugging down her panties before drawing myself into her helped. God, it fucking helped.

Aurnia and her body and her sweet little voice chattering over cereal at the kitchen table only kept the guilt away for so long. I was taking what was not mine to take. What should not be taken. I wasn't sure I could stop. I was goddamn sure I didn't want to stop.

Also much like other mornings, I woke up with the phone ringing. Being with Aurnia had disconnected me from everything except her. Her waist and how it drew in and quivered just before she was about to come. How her toes curled as I fucked her on the bathroom counter. Her smile as she rolled over to kiss me and mutter into my mouth, "Good morning."

My goddamn cell phone had nothing at all to do with her. So it had gone ignored. Voice messages piling up. Texts stacking up in the dozens.

Just like most mornings, I was going to ignore the phone ringing out in the living room. But something told me this morning was not like most mornings.

I moved slowly to keep from waking Aurnia, at least not until I could return. Return between her legs. To my fingers pushing aside her panties. To my tongue swirling around her clit.

I palmed at my erection as I padded across the cold floors to my phone. When I saw the name on the caller ID, all thoughts of fucking Aurnia fell from my mind. My cock softened like it goddamn should have. Like I wasn't a predator. Like I would dare do anything to the child sleeping in my room.

"Diarmuid," I said into the phone in a low voice that I was certain sounded every bit as suspicious as it goddamn should. "Diarmuid, hey, it's early, isn't it?"

"It's past fucking ten," came the sharp reply. "You need to tell me what's going on."

I glanced at the clock on the microwave. 10:18 a.m.

We had stayed late at Dublin Ink the night before. Mason had stayed at Miss Last Night's flat. We had the place to ourselves. I checked on Aurnia's tattoo and well, one thing led to another. She'd returned the favour of that first night I'd tattooed her.

How long had she sucked me? How long had my fingers twisted in her hair? How long had I laid there, spent, as I watched Aurnia's tongue swirl in the cum splattered across my stomach, her eyes fixed seductively on mine?

Time didn't seem to exist with her. I didn't remember a dawn. But then again, I wasn't sure I saw anything but her. Not as we left the shop. Not as I drove us home on the motorcycle, her hands around my waist. Not even as I closed my eyes beside her in bed, her cheek on my bare chest.

"Conor?" Diarmuid shouted. "Did you hear me?"

I glanced at the closed door of the bedroom and moved farther away.

"Yeah, yeah," I said, cupping my hand over the bottom of the cell phone. "It's past ten. Is that a crime?"

"No," Diarmuid said sharply. "But I suspect something else is."

His words made my chest clench painfully.

"What do you mean?" I said slowly.

"I just came from Aurnia's house," he said, and my stomach dropped. "You know, an adult doing his job. An adult trying to make sure a child is safe. An adult doing what he's supposed to do. In the eyes of the law. In the eyes of what is just and right. You know?"

"Diarmuid—"

"And do you know what I was told at the door of the godforsaken place, Conor?" Diarmuid asked. "Because Mason didn't know. And Rian didn't know. But I have an inkling that maybe you know. Do you know, Conor? Do you know what I was told?"

Diarmuid was yelling now. I could hear the anger in his voice. It was an anger I knew all too well. It was an anger I had for myself. An anger I beat myself down with. An anger that consumed me.

Until that night. Beautiful, horrible, incredible, disgusting, can't happen again with a girl way too young for me, must happen again and again and again that night and every night since.

"Look, Diarmuid," I said, dragging a hand over my face. "Look, I should have told you."

"Told me what?"

A chance to tell the truth. A chance to tell the whole truth. A chance to get Aurnia free from my clutches. A chance to remove her as a temptation. A chance to make things right after letting them go so, so, *so* wrong.

Of course I didn't take it.

"She's been staying at my place," was all I said, all I admitted to.

"Conor."

"Diarmuid—"

"Conor!"

"Diarmuid, would you just listen?" I said, raising my voice before remembering Aurnia was asleep in the next room. "Diarmuid," I half whispered, "would you just stop shouting for a minute and *listen* to me?"

"Listen to *you*?" Diarmuid hissed angrily. "Conor, do you know how many codes you've violated? Fuck, do you know how many codes you've pinned against the wall and fucked? Absolutely *fucked*? She's a goddamn minor!"

"She's eighteen," I said.

That was the wrong fucking thing to say.

"Jesus fucking Christ," Diarmuid yelled.

"Diarmuid, I'm sorry," I said, "but when I went there to her house...fuck, that *dump*... When I went there and saw..."

Diarmuid sighed heavily. What I was telling him was nothing new. In his position, I'm sure he saw what I saw on a near daily basis. Maybe even worse. Probably even worse.

I continued anyway. Because it was Aurnia. Because it was *Aurnia*.

"When I saw the people that lurked around that house," I said, bile already rising in my throat at the thought of it, at the thought of *them*. "When I saw her have to climb through her goddamn bedroom window..." My voice was rising again. I was going to wake her if I wasn't careful. But the only way I could make Diarmuid understand was if I kept talking about it. Why was I always in this fucking position? "Diarmuid," I tried to whisper, "Diarmuid, when I saw her in there...so small...so alone...so...so helpless..."

My fists were shaking. I regretted not taking the call down to the garage. There was something to hit down there. There was no one to wake up with my yelling down there.

Diarmuid was quiet for a moment and then all he said was, "I know...believe me, I know."

I rested my forehead against the wall as I tried to even out my ragged breathing. I uncurled my fist. Finger by goddamn finger. But it didn't matter. They kept curling back up no matter what I did. Nails digging into my palms.

"So you understand?" I asked, struggling to keep my voice steady. "You understand why I—"

I stopped because I'd done more than just take a helpless girl into my home. I did more than shelter her. Feed her.

I'd done far more than that. I couldn't tell Diarmuid. *That* he could never understand.

"Yes," Diarmuid said, sadness in his voice until he quickly amended, "I mean, no. Goddammit, Conor, no. I mean yes. Of course, yes. But no. No. We can't— I mean, you can't."

"What was I supposed to fucking do, Diarmuid?" I shot back angrily, again too loud, again far too loud.

I glanced back at the bedroom door. It was still. It was quiet. Thank fucking God.

"I don't know, Conor," Diarmuid responded with just as much frustration. "You could have called me. Her JLO. The person with resources. The person who could get her help. The person who could put her somewhere safe. I mean, fuck, Conor, you brought a minor into your house!"

"I know full well what good the government is to kids like Aurnia. I know exactly what you could have done, or not done, if I'd have called you."

"And that's the reason?"

Diarmuid's question caught me off guard.

"What?" I asked.

Diarmuid hesitated a moment. Silent a moment.

"Conor, these kids...when you want to help them...and... when you see them and you see yourself in them...it's just...I know...I know *boundaries* can get blurred."

I don't know if I was madder that Diarmuid had the gall to imply what he was implying. Or that he was right. Dead fucking right.

"What you're suggesting is wrong," I said, vehemence in every word. Vehemence at Diarmuid. Vehemence at myself.

"I know," Diarmuid said, sounding more tired than anything. "I mean, yeah, I know."

"I thought you knew me better."

"I thought I knew myself better," Diarmuid said so quietly that I almost didn't hear him.

"What?"

"Nothing," Diarmuid replied quickly. "Nothing. Look, forget it, alright? It's just something that...happens sometimes. And I have to ask. Because, like you said, it's wrong."

"So wrong," I said, letting my head fall into my palm.

"Of course it's wrong," Diarmuid said quietly.

The two of us were silent for a few moments, I guess each of us lost in thought. I turned to look once more toward the bedroom door. My shoulders came to rest against the wall and I slid slowly to the floor. Tired. Guilt-ridden. Confused. I pinched my fingers at my temple. Head hanging. Chin against chest. Defeated. Fucking defeated.

"Diarmuid?"

He took longer than I would have thought to reply. "Yeah? Yeah, I'm here."

I sucked in a long breath. I couldn't stop the exhale from shaking.

"I just... I just want you to know this..." I began, the words quickly stalling.

The night before flashed in my mind. Everything I'd wanted. At last getting everything I'd wanted. Aurnia's eyes on mine. Her body beneath mine. Her heart against mine. I remembered the softness of her skin, the quiver of her lip, the way she gasped.

"You still there?" Diarmuid asked.

I rubbed my eyes. "I'm here."

My gaze was once again on that door. Aurnia just behind it. As I thought of her, asleep in that bed, in my bed, I knew this: I wanted her. Fuck, how I needed her.

The only thing I wanted more than her was a life for her. A chance for her. A future for her.

"All I wanted to say was that I would never do anything to hurt Aurnia. I... I care about her. I want nothing but the best for her. I won't let her make the same mistakes I made. You should know that."

"Conor—"

"Look, this should tell you all you need to know," I said, staring at the door. The closed door. "She doesn't deserve the life I have. So I can't. I can't."

Diarmuid was silent for a moment. "I know we haven't been super close for a while. There's been a sort of, I don't know, distance. But...but if you want to talk—"

"I don't," I said. Too rude. Too brutish. Too cruel. But it was all I could manage. I'd watched my world fall apart one too many times. I'd lost the ability to handle it with good fucking manners.

"I've got to get to Dublin Ink," I told Diarmuid and then hung up without waiting for an answer.

I would have flung the phone across the room if I knew it wouldn't wake up Aurnia. I would have pummelled my fist into the drywall again and again and again if I could have done it without screaming my lungs out. I would have stormed out, but

I was fairly certain that the door would have rattled so hard it would have brought the whole shitty building down.

I wanted Aurnia to hold onto her dreams for as long as she could. Just because mine were over didn't mean hers had to be too.

So I stayed there on the floor. Silent. Absolutely silent. Gripping my wrists to keep myself still as I shook. Shivered like a little boy.

Afraid.

And alone.

And *alone*.

42

AURNIA

I couldn't hear much. With my ear pressed against the frigid woodgrain of the door, Conor's words were mostly muffled, mostly distant. I closed my eyes and strained to hear, but it sounded like the inside of seashells: a murmur and nothing more.

When I thought I would hear nothing more, nothing distinct, nothing remotely clear, I heard these words as if they were being whispered straight into my ear, as if Conor was right there beside me, as if his hair, fallen as always from his bun:

She doesn't deserve the life I have. So I can't. I can't.

I don't know if Conor's voice returned to a murmur or if he said more after that because all I could hear was the blood rushing in my ears.

I didn't deserve the life Conor had? I didn't deserve what? Friends that loved me? That cared about me? That would do anything for me? I didn't deserve a business? Something I built from the ground up? Something that gave me purpose? Something I could look at and call "mine"? I didn't deserve a life of art? Of doing what I was passionate about? Of making a living off something I was good at? What? What didn't I deserve?

And why not? *Why not?*

If it hadn't been for the creaking of the old wooden floor-boards in the apartment, I probably would have been standing there, frozen and stunned and red-faced, when Conor inched open the door and slipped back inside the bedroom. I had just enough time to tip-toe hurriedly to the bed, duck beneath the covers, and bury my burning cheek against the pillow before the door handle turned. I squeezed my eyes shut just as light from the hallway stretched over my face. In that moment, caught in the yellow light, I was certain that Conor would be able to see that I'd heard him. I was certain he would take one look at me and know that I knew. I was certain he would sigh and then brush my arm as he whispered softly, "Aurnia, let me explain."

The light from the hallway came and went and the two of us were plunged back into darkness as Conor shut the door once more. The floorboards moaned beneath his weight. I was too stick-straight. I needed to relax. I needed my muscles to unclench, to sink, to melt into the mattress. But it was impossible. Impossible. Because all I kept hearing was, "She doesn't deserve the life I have". And all I kept thinking was, "Why? *Why?*"

Conor's hand came first to the mattress, pressing down. I was faced away from him, but I was sure he could see the strain of my spine. I was sure I looked not like a human girl, but a moulded statue, my muscles hard as stone.

But maybe Conor couldn't see me in the dark of the early grey dawn. Because the mattress creaked and just like the night before, Conor lay himself down beside me. Just like the night before his fingertips came softly to my side. Tentative once more. Hesitant as always. I tried to breathe evenly as he kept them there for several long minutes like he was testing the waters of some dark lake. I tried to breathe evenly. The hitch as I

fought back a wave of hurt. I wanted nothing more than for
Conor to notice. To see me. To *see* me.

After those several long minutes with his fingertips there on
my side, he moved in closer, just like the night before. Like
nothing was wrong. Like he hadn't said what he'd just said. Like
he didn't feel what he truly felt. What he'd kept hidden from
me. What he'd intended to go on keeping hidden from me.

My heart raced as Conor's chest pressed against my back.
How could he not feel that? Why wasn't he concerned that in
my sleep I was running? Sprinting? Trying to escape something?
Why didn't he want to know what I was running from? Why
didn't he hold me tight with those big, strong hands on my
shoulder and shake me gently awake and whisper in my ear,
"Aurnia, Aurnia, there's nothing to run from. I'm here, I'm here."

Just like the night before, Conor's arm wrapped around me.
At first, he seemed to be holding his arm up. His skin barely
skimming mine. The hairs along his arm just barely brushing
against mine. Just like the night before he seemed to be fighting
with himself.

Conor held himself there, suspended, and then, like the
night before, stopped fighting. He melted against me. Whereas
the night before I felt cocooned, felt safe, felt protected, that
morning, after overhearing him, I felt trapped.

Tears pricked at my eyes. In my mind, I begged Conor to
notice how it took everything inside of me not to squirm. Not to
push him away. Not to try to free myself. Silently, as the first hot
tear wetted my half of the pillow, I pleaded with him to see. To
understand. To comfort.

I urged the tear to spread to his cheek. To draw a trail across
the worn linen to the tip of his tongue. I wanted him to taste salt
and know it wasn't from the heat of our bodies. To know it
wasn't from pleasure, but from my pain.

I felt like I was gasping as I tried to hold back more tears and yet Conor's breathing behind me only seemed to soften, to slow, to even out. He was falling asleep, I realised with a sort of panicked horror. I knew how difficult Conor had found sleep recently. Anyone could see it in the dark bags beneath his eyes. In the red streaks around his green irises. In the quick snap of his temper.

With my body pressed against his, sleep came to him like a child. There I was upset because of his words and there he was, resting at last because of my warmth.

So that was what I was to him. Not someone to bring alongside his life. Not someone to join Dublin Ink. Not someone to share his friends with. Not someone to create art with. But a sleeping pill. A healing tonic. A prescription for a good night's sleep.

Conor was using me. Just like my father had used me. Just like Nick had used me. I was and I would always be the little thief that was serving out her sentence. Paying her dues. Rectifying her crime.

All this time Conor had such guilt and reservation about being with me because he didn't really want to be with me. He wanted to be with my body. The body of a seventeen-year-old. The body of a seventeen-year-old at last turned eighteen, thank fucking God.

I had stolen from Conor and I would never be forgiven. I would never be deserving in his eyes. I would always be the trash that he repurposed before eventually throwing out.

I was being used.

I shuddered against Conor, but of course he did not feel it. Did not feel me. I was as dead to him as the pillow beneath his cheek.

As the tears ran hot and fast now, I remembered the anger in Conor's eyes that very first day. That very first moment he laid eyes on me. That very first moment he laid hands on me. It was a startling fury. A brutal anger. A rage that his massive body seemed even incapable of containing.

Conor was a man who life itself stole from. I didn't yet know what was stolen. He would, of course, not let me know that. Why would you open yourself to someone you were simply using? You don't tell your secrets to your pencil, your kitchen knife, your fucking bus pass. I didn't know what, but life, or someone in it, stole something from Conor.

I'd come along. Hand in the cash register. Taking. Taking. Taking. I hadn't realised it in that moment, but I had committed a cardinal sin in Conor's eyes. There was never any chance of forgiveness, even after the bruises around my wrists faded. There was no chance of redemption no matter how many people I brought into Dublin Ink. No matter how many drawings I made that he liked with a simple nod. No matter how far I spread my legs on the tattoo chair.

I had been a fool. Turning one year older hadn't changed that. It had just made me a socially acceptable fool to fuck. To gain pleasure from. To use before discarding.

I cried, feeling more like a stupid child than I had in years. Years. Conor slept, his breath warm against my ear.

Maybe he'd notice the stain of my tears in a few hours. But I had a feeling he wouldn't.

Or simply couldn't.

43

CONOR

I didn't have much time.

Aurnia was due back into the shop in less than twenty minutes. Mason was upstairs with Miss Last Night. He could be up there for hours, but since he'd gone up with only half a bottle of champagne and a rather sad-looking banana, I knew it wouldn't be.

Rian was in the corner. Bent over at the waist. Hands clasped behind his back. It was a moth that he was watching. A fluttering, dying moth in the shadows. Normally when he was like this, I would leave him be. Interrupting him usually resulted in his being hopelessly lost, hopelessly useless the rest of the day or his just scowling and walking out. To go where, only God knows. While normally I would not do what I was about to do, as I said before, I didn't have much time.

"Um, Rian?" I began as I went around the couch toward him. "Rian, hello?"

It wasn't entirely surprising that just calling out his name didn't work. Wherever he was I knew it was much too far for him to hear me. The next step was to touch his shoulder. Risky, but necessary. In this case.

"Rian?" I repeated, a little louder this time, punctuated with a light rap of his upper arm.

Hmm. No response. Rian just continued to tilt his head to one side and then the other. His eyes fixed on the little grey thing flopping pathetically in the dusty corner. With a quick, silent prayer toward the ceiling, I continued to the last resort.

Grabbing Rian's shoulders, I forcibly turned him toward me and practically shouted his name, "Rian!"

Rian swatted me away and blinked like I'd awoken him from a deep sleep. He wriggled his finger in his ear and grumbled, "God, you don't have to yell all the bloody time, Conor. I'm right fucking here."

"I need a favour."

"Do we have a jar?"

I watched in frustration as Rian shouldered past me and wandered toward the kitchen. I followed and kept him from opening one of the cabinets with my hand against the door.

"Rian?" I said, trying to catch his still distracted eye. "Rian, a favour."

He dismissed me with a wave of his hand as he turned around in a circle. "Yeah, yeah, whatever you want."

I blocked his path from the kitchen. "I need you to talk to the admission board at the Limerick Art School."

Rian huffed impatiently. "Unless they have a jar, I don't see what exactly I have to talk to them about. Now, if you don't mind."

He nodded for me to move aside.

I sucked in a deep breath before adding, "For Aurnia."

The mention of Aurnia's name brought more clarity to Rian's eyes than anything I had tried before that. His lips moved as he repeated what I'd said: art school...Limerick...Aurnia. A frown tugged together his eyebrows. His fingers fidgeted at his chin.

Finally he said, "Tea?"

I glanced at the clock on the microwave. Aurnia would be here soon. Or Mason and Miss Last Night. Or, given my goddamn luck, a customer. Still, I relented with a nod.

"Sure."

A few minutes later, Rian's spoon swirled round and round his cup despite using neither sugar nor milk.

"I don't understand," he said at last.

"I want her to have a chance to interview. It's late in the process and a recommendation from an alumnus like you would go a long way in getting her ahead of the queue."

Rian shook his head. His eyes were sharp as he looked over at me on the couch.

"No, no," he said. "I understand that. What I don't understand is... Conor, there are art schools in Dublin."

I reached for the whiskey to add to my cup and I sighed. "I know."

"So?"

I added a little too much whiskey. I added a little too much more.

"So what?" I looked up and gave Rian a cool gaze.

Confusion flickered across his face. "So why have her go all the way out to Limerick? Why make her find a new place? Why make her find a new job? Why separate her from Dublin Ink?"

I supposed that I should have expected these kinds of questions. It probably wasn't a very good idea for me to be, at least as Rian was concerned, irrationally irritable at hearing them. But I couldn't help it. Maybe because I knew I couldn't stop them. Maybe because I had no good answer.

"The school in Limerick is the best," I grumbled as I tried to keep my foot from bouncing.

Rian tapped his finger against the edge of his cup before returning it to its saucer.

"Yes, it's a decent art school," he said. "You and I both have a lot to owe to it."

I gave nothing more than a grunt of agreement. Rian seemed to accept it.

"But still," he said, leaning forward with those cutting blue eyes fixed on me, "a lot of people in Dublin would disagree. I can't imagine that given the choice between uprooting her life and not uprooting her life, Aurnia would care much about squabbles in rankings and whatnot."

Rian hesitated and then added, "Can you?"

I stood up. Stood up too quickly. The porcelain rattled and tea spilled and dripped off the side of the coffee table onto the rug. Rian seemed more surprised by my reaction than I expected. Not good. Really not good.

I couldn't reel myself in as I said too angrily, far too angrily, "It's not uprooting her life. It's starting a life. It's *building* a life. Uprooting? Uprooting? What roots has she dug in this place? Hmm? Tell me. What roots has Dublin Ink, a failing tattoo shop in the wrong part of town given her? What roots have we given her? A druggie who stares at moths all day, a womanizer who lives in his dead mother's townhouse, a bitter old man who's more likely to die on his motorcycle than find success in this fucking world? What roots can grow here, Rian? What roots can grow in soil that is parched and dead and covered with goddamn salt? Uprooting. Uprooting my ass."

I was not only being an asshole. I was being stupid. So fucking stupid. Lines gathered on Rian's face and I saw it. I saw what I hoped I would never see: suspicion. *Suspicion.*

To cover my ass, I sank back down to the couch and grabbed my cup of tea. It sloshed over the edge messily, but still I took a sip from it. It burned my lip and the whiskey stung, but I sipped it like I was a gentleman. I cleared my throat and tried to speak as calmly as I could as Rian stared and stared at me, his new hopeless moth in the dusty shadows.

"I'd really appreciate it if you just talk to them," I said, gripping my knees till they hurt. "As a favour to me."

Rian was still looking at me. Still suspicious. What he was piecing together, I wasn't sure. Looks from Aurnia. Looks from me. Brushes in the hallway. Whispered conversations behind closed doors. What was so fucking great was that he was probably imagining something far more than there was. More than I'd allowed there to be.

Rian's voice was hesitant. "Why don't you talk to them? You went there, too."

I pounded my fist on the table. "Because—"

I almost didn't stop myself in time. I almost blurted out the secret that I'd managed to keep from Rian from the start. From the start and for all these years. The secret that our relationship was based on. The lie that he called the start of our friendship.

"Because," I repeated, dragging my fingers through my hair, "because we both know that you had a better track record there than me."

"But your art," Rian said, scooting to the edge of the couch. "But Conor, surely your art speaks for itself."

I dug my fingers into my eye sockets. I was surprised when I heard Rian get up. Surprised when I opened my eyes to find him in the chair next to mine. His hand about to reach out to my knee. It was only my eyes on his hand that stopped him. He drew it back and sighed.

"Conor...I feel like you're not telling me something."

I snorted, because wasn't that the fucking understatement of the year. If Rian knew all that I wasn't telling him... Rian thought he knew me, but he didn't. Neither did Mason. Neither did anyone who was masochistic enough to call me "friend".

Rian touched my hand. I snatched my hand back like he'd placed a hot iron against my skin. Despite this, Rian persisted. He leaned forward even closer. His eyes were more focused than I could remember them being in a long, long time.

"Conor," he said, and I wanted to get away. Far away. "I want you to know that you can tell me. You can tell me anything."

It was funny before. Now it was fucking enraging. I wrenched my hand away from his and stood abruptly. My knee hit the coffee table and this time there was no chance for the little teacup. It fell and shattered and my only regret was that I didn't drink the precious whiskey.

"Don't say shite like that," I said, pointing at him with a shaking finger. "You don't know what you're saying."

"Conor—"

"I mean it, Rian." My eyes checked the big window for any sign of Aurnia. I paused to judge whether they'd heard me upstairs. In a hiss I said once more, "You don't know what you're saying."

Rian's hands were held upward like I was his goddamn priest or something. He looked up at me earnestly as he shook his head. "What do you mean? We're family."

I thought I was going to lose it. Upturn chairs. Smash bottles of ink against the floral wallpaper. Drag down the broken neon sign and hurl it onto the sidewalk. My heart was pounding painfully in my chest and my vision had grey at the edges. I managed to control my breathing enough to speak only four words.

"No, we are not."

I didn't stop to see Rian's reaction as I stormed toward the front door. I already knew what it would be: hurt, disappointment, confusion, fear, concern. It wasn't like it was the first time I'd been given that look. It certainly wouldn't be the last.

"Call the school," was all I said before the door slammed shut behind me.

I was on my motorcycle just as Aurnia turned the corner down the street. I was away, far away into the cold before Aurnia had even a chance of catching a glimpse of me.

A good morning overall. A good fucking morning.

44

AURNIA

*I*t was strange, hearing my name on someone else's tongue.

Every time I heard it, my name, I heard Conor. I heard his gruff tone. I heard that undercurrent of anger and guilt and desire. I heard the way he said it like a curse. Like a prayer. Like a secret. No matter who said my name at that point it was Conor who I heard.

Whenever I realised that it wasn't Conor, it was always the same strange sensation as when you wake up in a bed that isn't yours, dragged out of the warmth and startled as if by a freezing bucket of water.

Rian's hand on my shoulder made me jump.

"Hey, hey," he said, coming around to sit on the coffee table across from me on the couch, "I didn't mean to startle you. It's just that—"

"You've been calling my name?" I finished for him, smiling sheepishly and averting my eyes.

I was embarrassed for being frightened over something so silly. Still, I shifted in discomfort. Everything was fine. I was safe. Yet it took a while to shake off that strange sensation, that conviction that I wasn't where I was supposed to be. Not who I was supposed to be with.

"You okay?" Rian asked, lowering his face to try to catch my eye.

I forced myself to look at him and nodded. "Great."

"You kind of had that look that people say I get," he said, still studying me with a cautious eye.

"What's that?" I asked, dragging a hand that shook a little more than I'd expected through my hair.

Rian shrugged. "I don't know. A sort of a faraway look. Like I'm somewhere else." He chuckled. "I hadn't really known what in the hell they were talking about till I saw you just now."

All I could manage was a polite smile.

"Well, listen," Rian said, clearing his throat and adjusting himself on the edge of the coffee table. He put his hands on my knees and then immediately took them off. He cleared his throat once more. He clapped his hands together awkwardly. "I have some good news!"

I raised an eyebrow.

"Um, good news for you, that is," he added.

I frowned slightly. For apparently good news, Rian sure did seem hesitant to announce it. I watched his eyes go to the front door like he was hoping a client would waltz in out of blue.

He inclined his ear up toward Mason's room, almost eager for us to be interrupted by a creaking mattress and a metal frame pounding against the wall. I think if it hadn't been so quiet you could hear a pin drop, he would have feigned hearing the phone ring just to hop up and buy himself a few seconds of reprieve.

"Rian?" I asked, my suspicion growing by the minute.

"Well," he said, scratching at the back of his neck, "it's good news, is what it is."

"You've said that already. Good news for me."

"It is though," he insisted, leaning forward earnestly.

This did not make me feel any less wary. I matched his leaning forward by leaning backward.

"Shite, I'm already making a hash of things," Rian said, letting his head fall into his hands.

How do you make a hash of giving good news? If it really was good news there shouldn't have been any bad way to give it. Which meant...

"I got you an interview for art school," Rian blurted out.

His voice sounded happy, excited. It was certainly the voice of someone delivering good news. But Rian's head remained in his hands, his eyes fixed on the floor between his rapidly tapping feet.

Good news wasn't supposed to give you a pit in your stomach. It wasn't supposed to make you feel like the floor was dropping out beneath you. It wasn't supposed to give you the dread of...of...of bad fucking news.

"That's great," I said, though my voice was weak.

Rian's feet were tapping in time with my heart.

"Um," it was me who now had to clear my throat, "um, which school?"

Rian's arched back rose as he drew in a big breath. "A great one."

A lot of fucking "greats" going around. So why wasn't I feeling it? Why wasn't I feeling fucking great? Why was I actually feeling really *not* fucking great?

"Which one?" I asked once more.

Instead of answering me, Rian shook himself, sat up, smiled at me, and then joined me on the couch. He took up my hands into his, his eyes wide and earnest.

"Aurnia," he said, "this really is a great opportunity. An interview with the admission board is a leg up that most people never get when applying to art school. You'll get a chance to show them your art in person. To show them your passion. To show them who you are. Listen, really, this is going to be the best thing that ever happened to you. There's no way that they meet you and see your work and listen to your ideas and *don't* fall in love with you the way that we have. You take this interview and you'll get into one of the best art schools in the country. You have to take this chance. You have to go."

Nearly breathless, Rian glanced down at our interlocked hands and then awkwardly placed mine back over my lap.

"Sorry," he mumbled, "some people say I'm not great with this whole...interpersonal thing."

It wasn't the touching that was upsetting me. It wasn't Rian's confidence in me, either. Nor his kind words. He was a gentle spirit, if maybe a little hard to grab ahold of. It was not him who was making my palms go clammy and my eyes prick.

"You still haven't said which school," I said, my voice no more than a whisper.

Rian smiled at me weakly and replied, "I haven't, have I?"

I shook my head.

Rian hesitated and then said, "Look, I would have loved to get you an interview here in Dublin, but I really only have connections back in—"

"Limerick," I answered for him.

I had been waiting all this time for him to say it. But I had known. In my heart, I had always known. Rian was going on about his time at the school and the different programs and the energy of being surrounded by other aspiring artists.

"I'll have to move."

Rian just stared at me, unsure of what to say.

"I'll have to pack up all of my things and go."

"Aurnia—"

"I'll be gone from Dublin Ink. Gone from Dublin. I'll be gone."

Gone from Conor.

Rian tried to smile and mostly failed. He went to reach for my hands again, but then decided against it. Both our sets of hands remained limp in our laps.

"It's a great opportunity," was all Rian said into the silence.

I nodded as I stared without blinking.

"Thank you for thinking of me," I said numbly. "I mean, it was your idea, wasn't it?"

What did I expect? Like really, what did I expect? Did I expect Rian to turn on an old friend, a business partner, a guy he regarded as family for some wrong-side-of-the-tracks juvie brat? Did I expect him to stick up for me when he'd already done just as Conor had asked him to do: get rid of me, the plaything that had become dull, the fuck toy that had been fucked, the little kid who didn't know her place and had to go?

Did I expect him to grab my hands again and say, "I don't want you to go, Aurnia. You're a part of our family at Dublin Ink. Conor's an eejit. A fucking eejit."?

It was almost goddamn funny. Because I did.

It hurt like hell when Rian, with a tight jaw and pursed lips, lied through his teeth. "All my idea."

When was I going to learn? When was I going to stop thinking I could find family, find love? When was I going to stop thinking stupidly that maybe, just maybe this time someone wouldn't hurt me? When was I going to give up the dream that wasn't ever to be mine? When was I going to accept that I was all I had? When was I going to learn? When was I going to learn that it would be a whole hell of a lot less painful that way?

It took everything inside of me to maintain my composure, to smile, to lie straight through my teeth. "Thank you, Rian. It does sound like a great opportunity."

The bathroom wasn't far from the couch, but in that moment, it felt like a million miles away. I felt Rian's eyes on my back as I tried to not hurry my step, tried to hold back the tremor that threatened to run down my spine, tried to keep my nose from sniffling. The last thing I needed was for him to feel bad for me, to feel bad for doing as Conor asked, to feel bad for taking out the trash.

The bathroom wasn't far from the couch, but when I finally reached it and closed the door carefully and turned on the faucet to full blast and sank without a noise to the floor, I was gasping for air like I had just run every single one of those invisible million miles.

It was while I was in there that I heard the little bell at the front door of the shop. Faintly over my gasps for air, I heard Conor's voice speaking with Rian. Oh, so casually. Cheerfully even.

I don't know if it was rage that filled me. Or pain. Or hurt. Maybe they're not all that different from one another in the end. They all take hold of you. They all make your actions not your own. They all make you reckless, stupid, inclined toward self-fucking-imploding.

I pushed open the door of the bathroom so violently that the knob dented the wallpaper of the hallway.

"I need to talk to you," I said loudly, brazenly.

Both Rian and Conor craned their heads to see the commotion down the hall. I didn't have to explain who the hell I meant.

Conor stormed toward me. His hand grabbed my elbow. Hard. He hissed in my ear not to cause a scene. He was angry. Well, so the hell was I.

The back door of Dublin Ink slammed open just as violently as the bathroom door, but this time it wasn't me who had done it. I tripped down the stairs and Conor let me catch myself against the opposite brick wall of the alley.

"Tell me to my face," I said, not even giving him a chance to speak. I pushed myself back from the wall and whirled around to him. "Tell me to my fucking face that you're breaking up with me."

Conor dragged a hand through his hair. He looked exacerbated as he searched the deserted alley.

"I don't know what you're talking about, Aurnia," he said.

I advanced on him like he didn't have a foot and a hundred fifty pounds on me. I jabbed my finger against his chest.

"You can think I'm a child," I hissed. "But that doesn't mean you have to take me for a stupid one."

"Rian was just telling me—"

"Don't."

"You should seriously consider it, Aurnia."

I was shaking with anger. The anger was fine. The desire to hit Conor was a-okay with me. I had no problem wanting to punch him and kick him and fuck him. It was this creeping need to cry, to weep, to sob that scared me. That made me speak quickly, stumbling over my words.

"Tell me you want me gone and I'll go," I said. "But say it to my face. Like a man. Like a grown man who knows not to mess with a child's heart."

Conor avoided eye contact with me. Was it because he couldn't say it? Or was I already so gone from his life that he had better things to do? I hated *this*. I hated all of this.

"Say it," I said, voice breaking like a little kid. I hated that, too. I fucking hated it. "Say it and I'll go."

"Aurnia," Conor said, and my name didn't sound right on his lips. Like it was a sweet fruit that had soured. Gone bad. "Of course we all love having you here—"

"*We?*"

He swallowed. Looked down at his hands. "*I* love having you here. But you must think of your fu—"

"Don't say future," I said bitterly.

Conor's eyes darted only momentarily to mine. Too fast to catch much of anything. A train speeding by without stopping at the station where I stood alone.

"Just consider it," Conor said in the same tone of voice as the school counsellors who pushed pamphlets for chess club across the desk at me without looking once at the dark circles under my eyes. "I have to get back to work."

Conor turned his back on me and it was that first week all over again. Him dragging me out the back. Him shutting the door.

"Tell me!" I shouted, pounding my fist against the door. "Tell me and I'll go!" I shouted still even when there was no response. "If I'm a child, then tell me like a man!"

Like before, I listened with a pounding heart at the door. This time, I heard only silence.

So this was the end. The end of Dublin. The end of Dublin Ink. The end of Conor and me.

It was the kindest cruelty I'd ever known. I swore it hurt worse than an open-palm slap to the face. I cried because this wasn't a wound I could place a Band-Aid over. I couldn't dull the sting with some ointment or a pack of ice. I couldn't watch the scab form, the scar fade from pink to white. Whatever healing there was for me would be out of sight, impossible to see, to judge. The gaping wound was inside of me. Maybe it would sew itself back together with time or maybe I would just keep bleeding out till there was nothing left of me but that hole.

There was one comfort, though. It was a small one, but it was something. I would take the interview. I would go. I would not fall to my knees before Conor and beg. I would not wrap my arms around his leg. I would not even reveal that I fucking knew it was him.

If he'd had his fill of me and wanted me gone, I would go.

I'd always been an orphan, even with a father. I'd always been alone, even with Conor.

I would go.

45

CONOR

I don't know why I went with Aurnia to the bus stop. I shouldn't have.

I'd gotten exactly what I'd wanted. Or what I'd said I'd wanted. Thought I'd wanted.

After our fight, Aurnia had embraced the idea of Limerick. In the shop she was already talking about living on campus. About packing her bags. About how difficult it might be for her to come visit once the semester started. But that she would try. If she could. But she probably couldn't.

Her interactions with me were also exactly what I'd wanted. Cool. Professional. Brief. Her eyes hardly met mine in the parlour anymore. If I found her at the apartment, she was bent over a Limerick Art School pamphlet that she didn't look up from when I came in. An opportunity to move on from Dublin, from me had presented itself and she was taking it. And that was good. That was what I wanted. Right?

I couldn't ruin her life if she was far away. That's what she would soon be, far away. That's why she was walking to the bus stop that cloudy, heavy afternoon: for a chance to get far, far away.

So why didn't I just let her go? Say goodbye, good luck from the door of the shop? Wave from the big window till she was out of sight? Go back to my business, my literal business, and send her nothing but best wishes and nothing more? Why did I insist that she needed help with the little tattered backpack that couldn't have had much more inside it than her portfolio, a few folded clothes, and her toothbrush? Why did I offer her my jacket when the bus stop wasn't more than a block and a half away? Why did it sting when she refused it?

"You don't have to wait with me," Aurnia said as we stood under the makeshift bus stop, nothing more than a piece of corrugated metal on wooden posts littered with gang tags.

"Did you remember the CVs from the printer?" I asked as she checked the schedule on the faded, tattered pinned-up paper once more.

Aurnia's eyes flashed to me, more contact than she'd given me since Rian told her about the interview, and I was surprised at how much anger there was.

"Seriously," she said, focusing on the gum stuck to the metal roof of the bus stop. "You can go."

"I can throw out some practice interview questions while we wait. You know—"

"*We're* not waiting," Aurnia said, not looking over at me. "*I'm* waiting. I don't know what you're doing."

She'd braided her hair for the journey, but the wind had already tugged free several strands that lashed her pale cheeks. Why did I want to tuck them back behind her ear for her? Why did I want to block the wind for her? Hold her tight? Keep her warm? All I should have wanted was for the bus to come and Aurnia to get on it and for it to carry her far, far away. Far, far away from me. Away from ruin.

"If that's what you want," I said.

Aurnia snorted.

I stepped closer to ask her what the hell that was about when her phone rang. She slipped it from her back pocket. Her whipping hair concealed her eyes from me as she flinched and rejected the call. The phone was back in her back pocket without hesitation. Aurnia was leaning out from the stop, looking past me for the bus as if I were a ghost down the street.

"Who was that?" I asked.

"Nobody," was Aurnia's answer.

"It was saved as 'Don't Answer'."

Her hair had covered her eyes. Not the screen.

She shrugged. "Some asshole trying to sell something."

"Aurnia."

Aurnia yanked her hair back behind her ear as she turned to face me, chin jutting up defiantly.

"Conor, *go*," she said. "Just *go*. I'm not your problem anymore."

"You were never my—"

I stopped myself, dragging my hands in frustration through my hair. How was I supposed to tell her that *I* was the problem? I was a thirty-year-old fuck up that was going to weigh her down like stones lashed round her ankles. I was bad news and bad luck and bad timing all rolled up into one big fucking bad package. I was somehow, some way going to ruin her life before it even began. I was talking from goddamn experience. I knew. I *knew*.

"Aurnia," I said, exhaling unsteadily through my nose, "just tell me who that was and I'll go, okay?"

Aurnia laughed bitterly.

"Just tell me so that I can have peace of mind," I said.

"That's all you want, isn't it?" Aurnia asked, staring across the street, refusing to look over at me. "Peace of mind? All you want is to know that I'm not getting needles stabbed into me in some drug den? All you want is to know that I'm not starving on the street? All you want is to know that you gave me a fighting chance? So what? So you can sleep at night, Conor?"

I was getting angry. The way Aurnia's lips moved when she talked was drawing me to them like a moth to a flame. The way her chest was rising and falling with this pent-up anger I didn't understand was reminding me of that first night. Her on my tongue. Her around my cock.

"Give me your fucking phone," I growled.

I was done messing around. I was going to check that fucking phone. Check to make sure Aurnia was safe. And then I was going to go. To leave. To let her fucking go. Because if this went on any longer, there was no way I was ever going to be able to.

Aurnia did not respond. Did not move. When I reached for her phone there in that back pocket where my hands should have been, squeezing her ass, Aurnia jerked suddenly away. Her eyes were aflame as she hissed, "I'll scream."

Anger of my own rose in my chest. Was I angry that she was threatening me? Was I angry that this meant that the blocked call was from someone dangerous, someone deadly dangerous? Or was I angry because I knew I wasn't leaving? Angry because I knew I couldn't leave? Angry because I knew I didn't *want* to leave?

My face was in hers and our heavy breaths were warring against one another as I said, "You're going to give me that *fucking* phone, Aurnia."

We hadn't been this close in days. We'd been moving around like the other didn't exist. Like we were in a thick fog and couldn't even see who was right there beside us. Like we were already forgetting.

I missed this. The speckles of green in her eyes you could only see this close. The thickness of her eyelashes like a tangle of thicket. All thorns. No way out. The little bit of lip balm that glistened on her Cupid's bow like sweat despite the bitter cold and the cruel wind.

It always made me think of the last time we'd fucked. That time I'd tied her to my bed and worked her body till we were both spent, exhausted. The sheets soaked.

"I'm not a part of your life anymore," she whispered, lips curling as she noticed my anger melt into lust. "You don't get to do this anymore."

"Do what anymore?"

Aurnia stepped closer so that our bodies were tight against one another. I felt her thigh move to my groin. Just enough that it brushed my cock. Just enough that I knew that she knew: it was hard.

"That," Aurnia said, pulling away just as quickly as she had come close.

My fist collided with the post of the bus stop before I even realised what I was doing. My knuckles were bleeding and splintered and I didn't even feel them as I stalked down the sidewalk. I could have been leaving a red trail behind me for all I knew. All I knew was anger and desire. I wanted both of them. I wanted to *feel* both of them. No more numbness. No more cold. I wanted to fucking *burn*.

"Bus already go?" Mason asked as I stormed back inside Dublin Ink. "I don't think I saw it go—Conor, you alright, man?"

Rian startled when I grabbed the keys from the hook just beside his head.

"What the—dude, you're bleeding. What happened? Is Aur—"

The front door slamming shut behind me once more cut off that cursed name. I was vaguely aware of the two of them running out after me onto the sidewalk as I started my motorcycle with a vengeful kick. Teeth grinding. Jaw tense. Knuckles white. Maybe they shouted my name. I don't goddamn know. I couldn't hear anything over the roar.

A car screeched to a halt as I whipped into the street without looking. Their horn echoed off the nearby buildings, but I easily outran it. Maybe the driver rolled down his window to call me an asshole. Maybe I didn't give a fuck.

The city block raced by me and then I was jumping the curb and leaving a long black tire skid on the sidewalk and nearly sending myself over the handlebars as I stopped in front of the bus stop.

"Get on!" I shouted to Aurnia, who either wasn't afraid or was doing a damn good job hiding it.

I pointed a shaking finger to the sidewalk beside me when she said nothing, moved nothing.

"I'm taking you," I said over the churning, coughing engine. "Get. On. Now."

Aurnia moved. But it was only to cross her arms. Set her feet wide. And narrow her eyes at me.

"Get on the fucking bike, Aurnia. Right fucking now," I growled. "Or else."

She had the audacity to laugh. To keep her eyes fixed on mine. Flashing. To purse those lips I'd imagined again and again wet around my cockhead.

"Or else what?" Aurnia shouted over the motorcycle which sounded like a roaring river dividing us. "You'll drag me across the sidewalk in broad daylight? You'll twist your fingers in my hair and wrench back my neck? You'll pull out a pack of strip ties from your jacket and lash me to the handlebars? You'll send us both crashing into some guard rail when I fight you the whole fucking way?"

I glared at her and she glared at me.

"I'm taking the bus," she said.

"Last chance, Aurnia."

46

AURNIA

*H*e swung a leg over the motorcycle. I sucked in a breath.

It took about two and a half steps for me to realise that he was serious.

The way his motorcycle boots seemed to crack the asphalt beneath him. The way his thick, broad shoulders were stooped over like some monster. The way his eyes bore into mine, never once glancing around him. At open windows that might have snooping eyes. At either side of the street which might have cars and witnesses passing by. At the dark little alleyways where there was always a pair of eyes blinking wearily from the shadows. At Rian and Mason who were outside the shop, staring at us, and not moving.

Conor only looked at me and I knew in that moment that there was only me. No pedestrians with phones. No police. No one to stop him from doing exactly what he wanted with me. He would even ruin his friendships over me. Of this I was certain.

Whether it was to keep me safe or drive me to his apartment to fuck me or murder me in some cold, dirty river, it didn't matter. He was getting his way. And I was helpless to it, his desire, his want, his need.

It took about two and a half miles for me to realise that I'd made a mistake.

I thought I hadn't had a choice. I thought whatever happened I was going to end up on the back of that motorcycle. But I did have a choice: I could have fought.

I realised as the engine roared and the clouds whipped by and the streets widened beneath us that I should have. I should have fought. I should have kicked and screamed and made a scene. I should have clawed and scraped and bit. I should have made Conor drag me to his motorcycle by my hair as the asphalt stripped my skin. I should have made him bind my wrists and duct tape my thighs and stuff my mouth. I should have fought with everything I had.

Because a fighting's chance in hell was better than what I had now: no chance at all.

I loved him.

I loved Conor. I wanted to be with him and only him and never not him. I didn't want to go to Limerick. I wanted to stay. In Dublin. In Dublin Ink. In Conor's arms. I wanted him to turn the motorcycle around and take me back. Take us back.

It took almost no time at all for my body to sink against his. To melt against his. To join with his as surely as if his cock were inside of me, as if the rocking of the machine beneath us was him rocking me in his arms.

As if he were taking me, making me his, making us one. Our ribs interlocked like fingers. Our hearts beat in time with one another's. Our thighs quivered against one another's like lips hesitant and scared and wanting. My cheek found the hollow between his shoulder blades and it was as if the space was carved from the flesh of his body just for me, as if he'd been clay sculpted and moulded for me.

As my fingers held handfuls of Conor's leather jacket, so soft, so buttery, supple and smooth against my palms, I relaxed. I eased. I dropped my guard. At last my fingers slipped beneath the hem of his jacket, beneath the frayed edge of his thin, dark grey t-shirt. At last I splayed my fingers against Conor's stomach. At last I held onto him. As much of him as I could get. As much as I could take without ripping him apart.

The clouds turned from dark grey to black above us, sank low to threaten us, but Conor was warm against me. We were hurtling a million miles an hour, but I was safe. We didn't say a word to each other, but I could hear him. Even over the roar of the engine. Even over the whipping of the wind. Even over the cars screaming by in the opposite direction, their headlights in the early dusk blinding.

I don't know which first wet Conor's jacket: an errant raindrop or a hot tear that slipped from the tip of my chin.

Conor kept saying I was a child, a child, a child, but the truth is that I'd never really felt like much of a child. I'd been forced to grow up at a moment in my life where I wasn't even yet capable of recalling memories. Meaning there was no time where I could look back and see something little and innocent with chubby legs or hear unencumbered laughter without an edge or taste ice cream on a warm day at the park, because there simply was none. I'd just never been a child.

Yet in that moment there on the motorcycle, I felt what it might be like to be one. To be a child. If just for a little while.

Because, put simply: I didn't understand.

I didn't understand why Conor was driving me wildly into the gathering storms like the only option we had together was to drive off the edge of the world itself. I didn't understand why he couldn't open up to me, couldn't let me in. I didn't understand why we couldn't just *be*, him and me. Loving one another. Holding one another. Driving into the night if that was what he wanted, if that was what he wanted. I didn't understand why the end had come before the beginning. I just didn't understand.

Isn't that what being a child means? Looking around you and seeing nothing but question marks, mysteries, unsearched dark corners?

It took less than two and a half minutes for me to realise that something was wrong. That something was wrong and only going to get worse.

My body was so close to Conor's during the ride that I felt everything. I knew before he flicked on his turn signal that he was going to change legs from the twitch of muscles in his left or right side. I knew when he was going to shift to a high gear by this restlessness that permeated the whole length of his spine. I knew when to lean and which way from the slightest movement of his thighs. I knew when we were going to race around a too slow car (and they were all too slow, the cars we whipped by in the gathering darkness) just by the momentary calming of his heart, like he was steadying himself to dive off an impossible height.

I knew everything in Conor's body as if it were my own. So when the muscles along his left thigh tensed and didn't release, I knew something had changed. Lanes were shifted, cars passed, curves in the countryside twisted and turned and yet that muscle pressed so close against mine remained like a bow pulled back too tightly, wanting desperately to be released.

Rain began to strike us like whips at the speed we were going, which only increased even as the streets grew slick. Thunder rolled around us. The rain came harder, faster and Conor's left leg seemed to be petrified.

I blinked against the lashing rain and felt the muscles along Conor's body like I was performing an autopsy. They'd too gone hard, unmoving. Held tense like he was expecting a blow to the gut, a sucker punch from the lightning that illuminated the horizon.

The movement of the bike grew jerky as nightfall raced after our tail. I pulled my hands from the warmth of Conor's skin, the protection of his jacket and squeezed his arms. It was like he'd been injected with a paralysing poison. His arms were straight as boards, stiff as concrete.

I tried to shout his name, but the wind and the drumming of raindrops against our helmets stole my voice. I leaned in close and shouted again, but it was like trying to call to someone in a hurricane.

The shaking that started in Conor's left leg and moved through his body, moved through me the same way the reverberations of the engine beneath me did, gripped my heart like a vice.

Conor was not someone to be shaken. To be moved. To be tossed about like a fallen leaf. Conor was the strongest man I knew. A boulder. A monument.

From what I could tell this quivering, this trembling of his body as the motorcycle drifted and corrected only to drift again was entirely outside of his control.

That's when I realised that the true storm was coming. The rain and the lightning and the thunder was nothing.

I called Conor's name again as we hurtled on.

There was no response.

47

CONOR

I probably pushed it too far.

By the time I finally jerked the handlebars toward the muddy side of the road I was barely in control. My whole body shook. My vision was blurry and fading in and out. Flashes that had nothing to do with the lightning on the horizon blinded me like the passing headlights stabbing through the pouring rain. A fever consumed my flesh. Ate at my brain.

When I said that I would take everything from Aurnia, I never really thought that would mean her life. But I risked that, too. Out there on that black slick highway. I was so goddamn selfish that I pushed. And pushed. And pushed some fucking more.

I knew if I blacked out, even for just half a second, the bike would skid. The asphalt would tear. Aurnia would be thrown against the hard metal guardrails like a rag doll. Bones crushed. Lungs punctured. Life extinguished.

And yet I told myself a little farther. I could go a little farther. And if I made it a little farther, I could make it a little farther after that. I could string together a little farthers till we reached Limerick. Till I proved myself, the world, motherfucking Fate herself wrong: I was not bound to destroy Aurnia.

I could help her. I could be there for her. I could heal her like she'd hoped I would. I could do for Aurnia what was not done for me.

A little farther and I could get her to Limerick. A little farther and I could get her to that interview. A little farther and...

A growl of frustration began deep in my belly and rose to a rumbling roar as I finally ran out of a little farthers. I yelled because I was admitting defeat. Because this, *this* was the end.

I didn't fucking want the end.

I hadn't killed Aurnia out there on that long stretch of highway. But I might as fucking well have.

Aurnia was calling my name over the rain as I staggered off the bike, whole body shaking. She shouted for me as the bike tipped. Fell. Caught her leg underneath it. Took it down with her. No, no. It was *me. I* took her down with me. I turned back to the bike, my vision wavering in front of me. With a scream of rage and pain, I flipped the bike off her.

It hit the pavement with a horrible crunch. The handlebars lay in an unnatural position. The metal was scratched and crumpled. I probably wouldn't be able to ride the goddamn thing anymore. I made sure of that. I kicked the fecking thing till my bad leg gave out and I fell to the muddy gravel on the side of the road.

Aurnia hadn't moved from the spot where she had fallen. She had stopped calling my name. Cars splashed water across us from the highway as they sped by without a care. I gripped at the old wound that burned like I was being branded. I shivered as the rain fell harder. But there was no escaping the pain. No pills. No liquor. No drugs to cut the edge. Just me and my fucking agony. Just me and my fucking fate.

Aurnia crawled toward me, helmet cast aside, hair dripping wet. I held up a hand to her.

"Don't come any closer," I shouted over the downpour. "Just stay away."

But Aurnia kept coming.

When she reached me, I pushed myself back, dragging my leg like an invalid. I collapsed as the pain overwhelmed me. Rain splattered against my face as I clenched my eyes shut, grinding my teeth.

I almost relented when delicate fingertips brushed along the spasming muscle of my left leg. I almost let her press her cold palm like an icy compress against the fire. I almost allowed her to draw the back of her hand against my forehead. To feel me. To heal me.

But it wouldn't have been fair. Or right. Or anything close to love.

I grabbed Aurnia's wrist with the speed of a viper's strike and squeezed till she winced in pain, cried my name, and tried to pull away from me.

"There!" I shouted, pushing her hand away from me as I sat up. "That's what a reasonable person does, Aurnia. Feels pain. Tries to get away. That's what you should have been doing all this time. Getting away. Getting far, far away as you can...from me."

She remained drawn into herself there on the gravel, hand clutched to her chest. I forced myself to my feet. I stumbled for balance on my right leg, growled in agony as I had to catch myself with my left.

I fought off the nausea, the waves of sickening heat, the flashes of blinding white across my vision and stayed upright.

I sent a quick text. I slipped the phone in my pocket just as Aurnia looked up at me.

The rain fell around us like a curtain and she blinked away the drops that caught in her eyelashes. On Aurnia's face wasn't hurt. But anger.

"Why did you make me get on your stupid motorcycle?" she asked.

My face contorted in a nasty snarl.

"To show you," I said, spitting raindrops from my lips like some rabid dog. "To show you, my little thief. That I was right. That I was always going to be right."

"I was going," she said, glaring up at me from the ground. "I was seconds from taking the bus. From leaving Dublin. From getting out of your life. You didn't have to prove whatever insane, fucked up thing you believe about you. So why, I ask again, Conor, did you make me get on your stupid *fucking* motorcycle?"

I was sure the rain was sizzling as it contacted my hot brow. I was sure I was covered in steam. Literally fucking fuming.

"Because of just that, my dear," I said. "Because you still don't believe me. When I say I'll destroy your life. When I say I'm wrong for you. When I say I'll fuck you up and leave you empty. Because, my little thief, you still believe in *us*. You still nestle your cheek against my back as I drive you off the cliff. You still crawl to me through the mud and rain and stabbing rocks, when I practically kill you on the side of the highway. You still try to heal me as I cut your life to pieces. To fucking *pieces*, Aurnia!"

Aurnia was silent in her fury. Brows drawn. Lips frozen like marble. Eyes filled with the flames that seared my burning leg.

"Because you won't learn," I said, laughing bitterly as I threw up my arms. "Because you won't fucking *learn*."

I pointed down at her, half out of my mind in anger, half out of my mind in pain.

"Because you need to know the fucking truth," I said wildly. "You need to know what your future with me looks like. I can tell you exactly what it looks like, because I was you, Aurnia. I was the child smitten with the adult. I was the starry-eyed innocent who would do anything for my lover. I was the thing that needed to be protected and wasn't."

Aurnia still fixed her gaze up at me, but there was something different in her eyes. The anger flickered. Hesitated.

"If you stay with me, you won't go to art school," I shouted at her as the rain fell around us and the cars passed, indifferent as the rest of the fucking world. "I can tell you that much."

"You went to art school," Aurnia said in a low tone.

She was already second-guessing. Already seeing the real me behind the curtain. Already understanding. This was good.

"Oh, but I didn't, my love," I said cruelly.

"But—"

"I lied," I hissed. "I lied to you. I lied to Rian. I lived with Rian on campus and lied every single day. I called him my best friend and to this day I keep this lie like a locket around my throat."

Aurnia's voice quivered as she said, "I don't understand."

I smiled darkly. "I want you to, my little thief."

I told Aurnia about meeting Shannon. I could tell in her eyes as I described my feelings for my high school art teacher that she felt those same feelings about me: luckiness to have found me, conviction that she was made to be with me, deafness when I tried to tell her how wrong it was. It had all been the same with Shannon.

I told Aurnia about the hope Shannon gave me. A chance to get out of my shitty town. A chance to improve myself, make something of myself. A chance to escape violence and drugs and a dead fucking end in life. It was Shannon who got me into art school. Who helped me win that scholarship to pay for it. Who dreamed bigger dreams for us than I'd ever dared of dreaming myself. I told Aurnia how I mistook that hope for love.

I didn't give her a chance to protest that with us it was different. Because it wasn't. It couldn't be. I went straight into telling her about that night. That night we were supposed to leave for Limerick. That night I found instead of her waiting at the door, a note. That night I wandered through the halls of that party with the last of the innocence I would ever have in the world. That night I swung open that door to find her naked. Writhing. Moaning. To find Nick inside of her.

"Your Nick," I said.

Aurnia was too stunned to speak.

"Don't you see?" I asked, laughing bitterly. "Even the villain in our stories is the same."

I told her how I fought Nick. My leg threatened to collapse underneath me as I recalled how he stabbed it and then, when I was down, he broke it. We both ended up in the hospital that night. But only one of us ratted. Only one of us lost a scholarship, an admission spot, a chance to get out. Only one of us had a love ruined. A life ruined.

"I have nothing because of Shannon," I said, spitting out her name because it burned on my tongue even then. "She gave me everything only to rip it all away. And that's worse. That's always worse than never having anything at all."

I wondered if Aurnia could see that I had loved Shannon. That she had been the single pure, gentle ray of light in my dark world. And that love had callused over like all my other wounds.

"I don't want to do that to you," I said, shaking my head till it made me dizzy. "Do you see now? Do you understand now? I don't want to, but I will. I can't stop myself. I'll never be able to stop myself. *You* have to stop me, Aurnia. You have to save yourself. You have to get away!"

Aurnia pushed herself slowly to her feet. Her chin was against her chest. Her wet hair fallen over her face. She lifted her head and stared up at me.

And punched me in the face.

48

AURNIA

*I*t wasn't like I hadn't punched people before.

Growing up the way I did, bloodying your knuckles on someone's cheek for the first time was as much a rite of passage as those rich kids learning to ride their shiny new bikes. It was all pretty much the same, hitting someone. No matter who they were. It always hurt. A pack of frozen peas always made my knuckles feel a little better.

But there was something about my fist connecting with Conor's cheekbone in that freezing rain that was different. It was as if Conor was somehow harder. Made of marble. Made of stone. It was as if I knew that the cracks I heard along my knuckles as my punch connected would never heal. That the swelling would never go down. That the blood would always be there, frozen peas be damned.

I wasn't known as a particularly fair fighter. How could you be in the house I was raised in? You fight clean, you lose. So dirty it was. Dirty it had to be. Dirty was king.

I didn't wait for Conor to recover from the shock of being punched in the face by his "starry-eyed innocent". As he raised shaking fingers to that delicate skin just beneath the eye, as his wild eyes tried to focus. Tried to find me. Tried to figure out who in the hell I was and what in the hell just happened.

I didn't wait. I attacked. I launched at him. I gave him all I fucking had.

"You eejit!" I screamed, throbbing fist balled like the other at my side. "You goddamn, fucking gobshite, Conor!"

I shoved at his chest. He stumbled backwards and I advanced.

"You have everything that I've ever wanted. You have a career. Something you've built for yourself from the ground up. Something good. Something you made. You have your days filled with art and creativity and passion. Day in, day out you have the chance to draw the world you want to see. The world you desire. You have a fam—"

My voice choked on that word. It got caught in my throat. Something I didn't want to release. A hidden desire. Private and delicate and painful. To say it, to say *that*, above all else, was what I wanted. To see that I didn't have it. To come face to face with the cold, hard truth: I wanted something I would never have.

It hurt. It fucking hurt.

With eyes squeezed shut, I forced out the words I'd never said aloud, "I want nothing more than a family, Conor, and you have one."

When I opened my eyes, Conor's fingertips had fallen from his cheekbone. They still trembled, but now at his side. The muscle of his left leg spasmed. His skin was pale and his face glistened when a passing headlight illuminated it. He looked like any goddamn second he was going to pass out.

All I wanted was to go to him. To hold him. To throw his arm over my shoulder and take some of his weight. All I wanted to do was punch him in the fucking face again. And again after that.

I clutched at my dripping-wet hair as I screamed in frustration.

"You just don't see," I growled angrily. "Why don't you fucking *see*, Conor?"

Conor remained silent. This was, it seemed, the worst thing he could have done. I wanted him to yell back. I wanted him to grab me and shake me. I wanted him to punch me back. But he just stood there. Already resigned. Already gone.

"That tattoo," I said, pointing my finger at his stomach like I was holding a loaded gun, "that tattoo, that phoenix of yours? It's a *lie*. It's a *joke*."

I was growing desperate. Trying to provoke him to something. To anything. To me. He could wrap his fingers around my throat. He could drag me away. He could fuck me right there on the ground. Anything that brought him to me.

But he seemed every second to be slipping further and further away into the shadows. Soon I was sure that not even the whipping headlights would be able to reach him, be able to find him.

"You're not rising toward anything," I shouted at him, voice high-pitched. Panicked. That's what it was. Panicked.

"You're still there in the ashes, Conor," I shouted, wanting to hit him again. To make him feel something. Anything. Me. Fucking *me*! "You're not just there in the ashes. You love the ashes. You feel safe in the ashes. You never want to leave those lovely fucking ashes."

I hardly knew what I was saying. It was like stabbing in the dark. I was trying to hit something. To draw blood. To hear the noise of something hurt, but alive.

"Look at what you've done to keep yourself there," I screamed over the rain, arms waving crazily. "You shut down any idea that might bring business to Dublin Ink. You yell at customers and practically turn away money. You go over past due bills again and again like you're self-flagellating instead of doing literally anything to spread the word that the place even exists!"

I tugged at my hair again when there was still no response from Conor. The only change in him was the slow blooming of a bruise on his cheek. The slow swelling of his black eye.

"You keep Rian and Mason at arm's length. Never sharing everything. Always withholding. We didn't have to be a secret because you were scared they would judge you because of our age difference. We had to be a secret because family shares everything and how could you wallow in the ashes if you had a family? People who love you? People who care about you? People who would do anything for you? Goddammit, Conor! *Goddammit.*"

I ran at him and my fists railed against his chest, but he wasn't like stone. He was stone. I was trying to break through stone with nothing but flesh and anger.

"Why won't you go to a doctor if your leg brings you so much pain?" I asked, and it was like I was begging. "Why do you want to feel it so intensely after all these years? Why do you want to fear a storm cloud like a child? Like a fucking child?"

I was gasping for breath. Exhausted. Drained. I stumbled back and I knew why. It was useless. All my yelling. All my screaming. All my fighting. It was for nothing. Conor was never mine to have. He was never even there, there for the having. He was in a morgue in Limerick. More than a decade in the past. Frozen. Glassy-eyed. Heart not beating.

"That phoenix of yours died the day Shannon and Nick betrayed you, the day you had a chance to actually rise from something," I said with nothing but sadness now. All the anger slipped away with the rain down the drains. "That phoenix inked forever in your skin isn't a reminder, Conor. It's an obituary."

The cold seeped into my bones. For a long time we stood there, across from one another. Shivering. Blinking away droplets from our eyelashes. Not seeing the other.

A pair of headlights fell across us but didn't pass on. They grew brighter. Wider. Closer. In the yellow glare, Conor looked like a ghost. Skin almost translucent.

I heard a car door open behind me and feet moving fast on the gravel. Mason was there in front of me, holding me by the shoulders, searching my face with wide, frightened eyes, and shouting if I was alright.

"I'm fine," I told him flatly. "I need to get to Limerick before tomorrow though. And I need to get warm."

"Of course, of course," Mason said and pulled me against him as he hurried me to his car.

We both looked at the overturned motorcycle as we passed.

"Thank goodness you two weren't hurt," Mason said. If my lips weren't so cold and my heart so heavy, I might have fucking laughed.

Mason sat me in the passenger seat and fussed about me, not caring that he was still standing in the rain just outside the door. Cold tea in this thermos here. Blankets here and here and more in the back, if you need them. Heat on full blast. Hot water bottle on the floor mats.

"Is Conor alright?" Mason asked as he looked across the headlights' beams to the giant statue still standing there.

"He's not coming."

"Not coming?"

I watched through the rapidly swiping windshield wipers as Mason ran through the pouring rain. As Mason put his hand on Conor's shoulder. Said something. Tried to urge him toward the car.

Conor replied. It wasn't more than a few words, I thought.

But they nevertheless struck Mason like a whip. I watched Mason walk back slowly toward the car.

Then it was just as I predicted. The headlights moved away from Conor and left him in the dark where he could not be reached.

Could not be found.

49

CONOR

The cab driver asked if he should take me to the hospital. I told him no, just home. When he asked if I was sure, I repeated what I'd first said.

"Well, then, where's home?" he asked as his tires crunched along the gravel.

Somehow, I ended up on the sidewalk outside of Dublin Ink. The lights were all out. Even the pink glow of the neon sign that normally ran all night was missing. It had always been missing a letter two, always imperfect, but had it gone out completely and I just hadn't noticed? Had I replaced that soft, gentle light with another? Had that gone now, too?

I limped to the front door and unlocked it with trembling hands. I was too afraid to test the neon light. To flip the switch. To see whether it would come back. Or whether it was gone forever. Besides, the dark was fine with me. It was all I wanted. To sink into it. To be absorbed by it. To let it take me away where there was no pain.

I had just enough strength left to grab pills from the kitchen, whiskey from the bar cart, and a stack of drafting paper from my desk. After that there wasn't even enough in me left to slowly lower myself to the couch. I fell like the dead. I gritted my teeth and swallowed back the pain. All too much like the living.

Rain still pattered on the big front window. I tugged the threadbare old crochet blanket that lived on the back of the faded floral print couch over my shuddering body. Maybe I wasn't aware that it wouldn't do much. Maybe the fever that wracked my whole body made my thoughts jumbled, my reasoning warped. Maybe I wasn't aware that I needed to take off my soaked clothes. Change into dry ones. Turn up the heat. Put on the kettle. Or maybe I was thinking perfectly clearly. Maybe I just knew all that wouldn't make a damned difference.

I was bound to spend in the night in agony. In alternating waves of fiery heat and bone-chilling cold. In shivers that kept me from sleeping. In back-arching pain as that knife was plunged again and again into my thigh. Striking bone. Carving away at me.

The bottle of whiskey shook so much as I raised it to my numb lips that it ran down my cheek. I swiped at it with the back of my hand and left the rest pooled in the hollow of my throat to tremble with the rest of me. I choked on the pills. Leaned over the side of the couch as I coughed. Tried not to throw up. Sank back with an unsteady groan.

I hated that the pain of my eye where Aurnia hit me felt soothing compared to the rest of me. I hated that counting my heartbeat in its steady throbs lulled me like a child counting sheep. I hated that I clung to the puffiness of my eyelid like a pillow. Because soon the rain would stop or the pills or the whiskey would kick in and then that was the only pain I would feel, that little discomfort at my eye. It would be all I knew. All that I couldn't escape from.

What was worse? That, too, would soon be gone. A day or two. At most a week. I would feel fine. The bruising even, wouldn't last forever. And then I would have nothing. Nothing to escape from. Nothing to escape to.

I flipped through the drafting pages to find a blank one to sketch on. I needed that scraping of charcoal against pulp. I need to draw something that wasn't me. That wasn't Aurnia.

As I was flipping through, letting papers fall to the side of the couch from an open hand like a dying man's letter, I stumbled upon a smaller stack of pages forgotten in the mess.

It was Aurnia's application for art school. She'd wanted me to read it. She put it on my desk so I would remember. Had I purposefully hidden it so I wouldn't have to? Or had it just been lost because it was always meant to be lost? Because it was better off, in the end, lost from me?

The fever really must have been taking its toll, because I brushed my thumb over her sweeping cursive like it was her hair. The rest of the room spun like I was drunk or being tossed about at sea, but those messy, sprawling words of hers remained fixed in my vision. I read over them, muttering them aloud like a hesitant prayer.

To be honest, whoever is reading this at whatever school I'll probably not get into, it was really hard to decide which of my pieces of art to submit. (By the way, I am still kind of having a hard time calling what I do "art".)

I know that doesn't sound great considering this is an application for art fucking school, but I figure it's best to be honest upfront so I don't get there and get uncovered as a fraud on like the first day or something. I don't know what I'd call what I do. It's always on brick or asphalt, rough things, hard things. Not smooth, soft things like paper or canvas. It's never what I expected, whatever ends up on those rough things, those hard things. It just seems my heart takes off and I black out or something. When I wake up there something is that wasn't before, you know? I don't know, what would you call that?

Shoot, I think I've already messed this up. What was I supposed to be writing about?

SMILING FELT SO strange in that moment. But I couldn't stop myself. I heard Aurnia in her words. I saw her bright eyes. Her fast-moving lips. I saw their colour. Lips and cheeks competing for the brightest pink. Smiling made my swollen eye throb and it felt right: I fucking deserved it.

IT WAS hard to decide which of my pieces of "art" to pick.

You said to choose something that represented me. That said something about me. Something important to me. Or some bullshite like that. I probably shouldn't write bullshite on an application form. It doesn't matter. I'm only doing this so the monster of a man who's keeping me captive won't lock me in the supply closet again.

Joking. Just joking. Man, I'm bad at this.

NOW I KNEW it was the fucking drugs, the goddamn booze. Because she was there. Right there beside me.

I LOOKED through everything I had painted like a gazillion times and nothing felt right. I couldn't see myself in any of it. I knew I had painted it. It was mine.

It wasn't me.

.   .   .

I WANTED to reach out and take her hand. I wanted to tug my little thief onto the couch with me. Have her nestle tight and bring me her warmth. I wanted her little voice to tickle my throat.

ONE DAY I saw another artist's work. This brilliant artist. A real tortured soul type if you know what I mean. He showed me this phoenix that he did.

It was beautiful. Stunning really.

Also, and maybe this was because I loved him, because I had always loved him, this phoenix was also sad. Its wings were so bright and so wide and just looking at it you were sure that it could reach dazzling heights.

But above it was there was this nothingness. Not nothingness like the sky. Nothingness like a hole. Like an emptiness. A swallowing nothingness.

I COULD FEEL Aurnia's fingertips brushing along the wings of my phoenix.

I DON'T KNOW if it's within the rules to draw something special for the application. I guess I don't really care either. What I had to draw had to be drawn. It was like something that had to escape my soul before it was consumed.

Because I don't really care about your art school. I already have my things I care about.

So if you don't like this "art" then you can suck it.

AURNIA BURNED NEXT TO ME, defiant, angry and stubborn.

. . .

Anyway, I drew this sun because a phoenix can be rebirthed from the ashes, but if it doesn't have anything to rise toward it will always just stay there, in the ashes. I drew this sun, because his phoenix needed a sun. I drew this sun, because I wanted him to have it. And if that's not a good reason to use for selecting a piece for an art school application than you can suck it.

Wait, didn't I already say that?

I TUCKED the essay safely against the side of me, where she should have been, and looked upon the sun that Aurnia had drawn on the next page. My fingers trembled as I held it. My heart raced. But I was not cold.

I pressed the sun against my chest like its rays of coloured pencil could radiate through me. I closed my eyes.

It was raining in Dublin, but I had my sun.

It was raining in Dublin, but I knew what I needed to do.

It was raining in Dublin, but the rain could suck it.

I was going home.

50

AURNIA

*E*very answer up until now I'd answered with nothing but complete confidence.

What art style are you drawn to? What artists do you consider as influences on your work? What classes interest you at Limerick Art School? What do you consider your artistic strengths? Weaknesses?

My responses came as easily from my lips as if I'd been asked for my name, age, place of birth, and height. Even abstract questions like, *Tell me how you would define beauty*, I weaved my way through as naturally as water through stones in a creek.

In that leatherbound chair with its austere wooden arms, dark and highly polished, I felt assured. Sitting across from the dean of admissions in his tiny gold-rimmed glasses and narrowed eyes, I did not flinch or hesitate. Despite the grandness of the ornate frames housing great works of art, art I could only aspire to like I aspire to be the clouds themselves, despite the tall, moulded ceilings, despite the expansive windows overlooking a rainy lawn of manicured hedges and stone statues, I felt like I belonged. Or at least, like I could belong.

That morning in the motel I'd taken care to make sure I looked the part. Aspiring artist. Capable university student.

Hard worker. Diligent. Motivated. The searing hot shower I'd stood beneath for nearly an hour rinsed away Dublin from my skin. Dublin and all that it held. The soap I scrubbed over my knuckles till they stung washed away any last traces of ink from the shop, sweat from holding Conor too tightly, detergent from his sheets.

I combed my hair. Pulled it away from my face. Twisted it into a bun I'd only ever seen the rich girls at school wear. I refrained from smudging black eyeliner under my eyes. I wielded the mascara wand like it was a fine paintbrush. I applied a soft pink lipstick I'd picked up at a gas station along the way as Mason pumped gas. The clothes I'd brought for the interview I dried on the radiator overnight. The steam from the shower freed them of wrinkles, freed them of any remembrance of the night before. Of the highway in the rain. Of the man I left behind.

Of the man who left me behind.

The final result in the mirror was exactly what I wanted. I looked like a prospective student of the prestigious Limerick Art School. I looked like *this* was where I belonged. Not back there, but here. Forward. Always forward. I could almost believe it too. Staring there at a reflection I hardly recognised. I could almost believe this was me. This was where I was to find family. Where I was to find life.

The dean leaned back in his chair. He bridged his long liver-spotted fingers beneath his chin. He eyed me. The hair I'd arranged so perfectly. The mascara I'd brushed on. The inoffensive, neutral lipstick.

Then he asked, in his sharp voice, one last question.

It settled into the silence that I think he fully expected. My eyes darted nervously to his, but his gaze was steady, patient.

It was important, this one last question. I opened my mouth to say what I should have said. To answer the only answer there should have been. To ensure my place in this place.

But I found my mouth closing on its own. I stared at the rain as it streaked across the broad windowpanes.

The morning was grey and the low clouds moved quickly. The rain slashed at the glass and as I struggled for an answer its noise seemed to grow louder. I hadn't heard it before. When the questions were easy. When I was confident, assured. When this was where I wanted to be.

"I, um, I..." I began to mutter before again falling into silence.

I shifted uncomfortably in my chair. *Just say it*, my mind screamed at me. *Just say the words and it'll be over. You'll be in. You'll be gone. Gone from there. Gone from him. It's easy*, my mind screamed. *Just say it.*

"Dr Walsh," I began and once more stopped.

The words were easy enough. Why couldn't I get them out? Why did they feel like gravel on my tongue? Like I'd fallen back there on the side of the highway. Scuffed my knees. Torn the elbows of my jacket. Filled my mouth with rocks.

"Dr Walsh," I tried again and then laughed because it was stupid.

What is wrong with you? This is it, this is your chance!

Still, I stared again at the rain and the lawn beyond it. So manicured. So trim and taken care of. So perfect. Nothing like the graffiti-littered alleyways of Dublin. Nothing like the sidewalks with trash tumbling along on the wind like tumbleweeds. Nothing like the faces dirtied with grime, etched with hard times, eyes burning behind curling tendrils of cigarette smoke in the dark.

The Limerick Art School was a blank slate. But I wasn't. I'd been stained. Drawn upon. Inked with blood and sweat and tears. Tattooed by a man I couldn't just wipe away or erase. He was there on me. On my skin. The city of Dublin was in me. All over me. I was the furthest thing in the world from a blank slate. I was a tapestry. A brick wall of spray paint. A portfolio with torn edges and crumpled corners. I was who I was. And I wouldn't be torn away like a page from a notebook to reveal beneath it a clean one. I would be proud of the mess. Proud of me.

"Dr Walsh," I said. He leaned forward because, I was sure, he could hear the change in my voice. "I—"

The door suddenly swung open, crashed against the wall, shook the crystal chandelier overhead, threatened to knock those great pieces of art in their ornate gold frames from their pegs.

Conor's eyes on me were the same eyes as when he caught me that very first day with my hand in the cash register at Dublin Ink: fury and desire and something more. He grabbed me and wrenched me up from the chair much the way he handled me then, too. All violence and strength, restraint and conflict, a battle to fight, a war raging.

"Security!" Dr Walsh called. "Secur—"

"I know him," I said, holding out a palm to the terrified dean of admissions. He wasn't used to wild animals breaking into his office. "I know him."

I said the words, but were they truth? Did I know him? Did I know Conor Mac Haol? Could I ever?

"Aurnia," Conor gasped. His face was the same sickly pallor as it had been in the headlights in the night before. He burned with a fever that soaked his leather jacket just as much as the rain. He leaned heavily on his right leg as he held me, as he squeezed me harder. "Aurnia, I don't want you to go to school here."

"Conor, how did you get here?" I asked.

He smelled like motor oil. Like black slick highways. Like

bitter wind. Had he driven here? All the way here? In the night? Through the night?

"Aurnia, please," he said, eyes on fire just like his skin as he tried to cling to more and more of me. "I was wrong. I read your application and— I don't want to be in the ash. I don't want it on my tongue. I want you. I want you on my tongue."

"Excuse me, sir?" Dr Walsh asked in the shocked voice of the highly respectable.

A grin came to my lips. "Conor, I—"

"This place isn't where you belong," he interjected with his voice a desperate plea. "You belong in Dublin. At Dublin Ink. In my bed and in my arms and all around me. All around me like that morning. That morning, I want that morning. Again and again and again."

"Sir, this is a respected institution of high—"

"I'm done pushing you away, Aurnia," Conor said, pulling me to him. "I've been a fool. I want you close. I want you as close as I can get you. I want your glistening skin against mine—"

"This is extremely inappropriate!"

"Conor," I said, trying to not laugh, "just let me say one—"

"I want your breath against mine, your screamed name against mine as we come together."

"Sir!" the dean rose to his feet, chair scraping the floor to punctuate his indignation, "I will not tolerate—"

"I want to rise to you, Aurnia," Conor exhaled like they were his final words.

His breathing was rapid in the ensuing silence. His eyes flicked between mine like he was awaiting a life sentence. I cleared my throat, hid back a grin as best as I could.

"I was actually just about to answer Dr Walsh's question before you, um...well, before you joined us," I said. "He asked if I truly wanted to attend the Limerick Art School."

"And?" both Conor and Dr Walsh asked at the same time.

My two roads, forking.

I looked at Conor and smiled. "I was just about to say...fuck no."

Conor exhaled like he'd held his breath all the way from Dublin as he drew me into his chest, arms shaking but sure around me.

Dr Walsh, in a flat tone, said, "Get the hell out of my office."

51

CONOR

The campus was quiet. The hallways dark. The rooms empty. Chairs on desks. Blinds turned down. Easels stacked against the walls. With Aurnia's hand in mine, I paused to try a random door handle. It relented and I pushed the door in.

"Are we supposed to be here?" Aurnia whispered.

The academic building with its old wood floors and stained-glass windows intimidated her. It once intimidated me, too. But then I met my little thief.

"Absolutely not," I told her with a devilish grin before tugging her inside after me.

I closed the door. Drew the lock. I limped to the professor's desk at the front of the room. Aurnia watched, one arm across her stomach, clutching an elbow, as I opened the top drawer and collected everything atop the desk into it.

"This was the place where I once imagined my fresh start would take place," I explained, pausing to glance around the room.

There were still ghosts lingering. The ghost of a young artist taking diligent notes at his easel. The ghost of a boy with a woman, red hair, naked, in his mind to paint. The ghost of a student who has had dreams bigger than he should have. Those ghosts were still there, drifting like the low-hanging clouds outside as the rain fell. But they were fading to wisps. Fog to be cleared by morning light.

I grunted as I hoisted the duffle bag I'd brought up onto the desk. The painkillers I'd gotten from a late-night ER were wearing off. I had more, but I wanted to be present for this. Here. Here with her.

"For the longest time, I thought my new life—that stupid, stupid dream—had been ripped away from me. "

Aurnia was still behind me. She was watching. Listening.

I arranged the tattooing tools and ink along the edge of the desk, my fingers shaking around the tiny pots of yellow and orange and red. "And yet all these years later this is exactly where I am going to get just that: my fresh start, my new life, my stupid dream."

I slipped out of my leather jacket. It was nothing but cold and wet anyway. I tore the t-shirt over my shoulder. "It's not the way I expected it. Hell, it's nothing like the way I expected it. It's messier. Dirtier. Harder even. But it's here. It's been here, even when I hadn't wanted to see it. When I'd been too afraid to see it."

I turned to face Aurnia bare-chested. All my scars there for her to see. Her eyes met mine as I touched the empty spot on my chest. The place above the phoenix. The only untouched skin on my body. The hole that had been like a canyon over my heart.

"Come here," I told her.

She came to me and I took her hand in mine. I placed her delicate fingertips where mine had been. I wanted her to feel my heart.

"I want you to tattoo me," I said. "Here."

"Conor—" Aurnia tried to protest, but I held her hand in place.

"Right here," I insisted, splaying her hand over my skin. "Right here I want your sun."

"I can't," she said.

Aurnia looked up at me from beneath those long, dark eyelashes. There were no black smudges beneath her eyes like usual. She trembled, closed her eyes, leaned into my touch as I brushed my thumb across her eyelashes. When she opened her eyes, they were embers burning in coal: my little thief.

I took the tattoo gun from the desk and tried to place it in Aurnia's hand. She shook her head, panic in her eyes. I forced her fingers round the tool even as she tried to push it away.

"Conor," she whispered, her voice desperate.

I said nothing as I released the gun. It was hers to either hold onto. Or watch drop.

"I'm not fighting anymore," I told her, pressing a kiss to her forehead.

With the fever that still lingered, her skin felt cool. I kept my lips against her. Breathed in the scent of her shampoo. It was the cheap stuff they keep in tiny bottles in motels. But on her it could have been the most expensive perfume.

I inhaled deeply and then pulled away from her. Without a word, I lowered myself to the desk. My left leg shook like I was going to the electric chair. Like I was waiting for a lethal injection in the neck instead of a droplet of ink in the heart.

"Conor," Aurnia said as she stood over me like a nurse who could do nothing for her dying patient. Her eyes trailed over my chest, my arms, my neck. She shook her head. "I'm too inexperienced. I hardly know what I'm doing. All your other tattoos... Conor, they're beautiful. They're art. They're perfect. If I— I'll ruin it. I'll ruin you."

My only response was to reach up and switch on the gun. Its

hum competed with the patter of the rain against the windows. It relaxed me. Relaxed my body. I could almost imagine it was pouring outside. That my leg wasn't on fire. That I was at peace.

The pain Aurnia could bring me would be a relief. A gift. A mercy. I touched my finger to my sternum like I was showing her how to insert a knife between two ribs.

"Right here," I said.

"Didn't you hear me? Didn't you hear me at all?"

"Right here," I repeated.

"I can't do it," she said, her little fist shaking at her side. "I won't do it. I'll mess it up. I'll mess everything—"

I took her by surprise. Of course I did. I'd told her I wasn't going to fight anymore and then there was my hand around the back of her neck. There I was grabbing at her with that frightening speed: a snake against a baby bird. There I was catching those sensitive little hairs at the nape of her neck. There I was tugging her toward me.

There was nothing she could do as our lips collided. There was nothing I could do as the rattling gun slashed at my skin. I hissed in pain against Aurnia's mouth and she gasped in surprise against mine, but I held us together in place so that neither of us could retreat. Not from fear. Not from pain.

I kissed her with a fierceness that she fought against. Tooth and nail she fought. Fought with that same fire and stubbornness as the day I met her. Fought like I knew she could. Fought like I loved she could. Maybe we bloodied each other's lips. Maybe we chipped each other's teeth. Maybe we left the skin around our mouths bruised and swollen. Maybe we were always bound to.

But all I cared about in that moment was that Aurnia, in her own violent, rough, desperate way, was kissing me back. We would always fight. Always fuck. Always love with a wrongness that to us was the only thing right in this blackened world.

We kissed and bit and battled with our tongues till we were both gasping. I released my deadly grip on Aurnia's neck. We both looked at the cut along my chest. At the smeared ink.

"There's nothing perfect left," I told her, guiding the hand which still held the gun back in place. "There's nothing left to ruin, Aurnia. There's only something to make beautiful. To make *yours*."

Aurnia looked down at me once more. The fear, the apprehension in her eyes had been replaced with that fire I knew. That fire I loved. She drew the back of her hand across her mouth. Wiped away that pale pink lipstick that did not suit the freshly bitten wild raspberry stain of her natural lips.

She was the girl I found robbing my cash register that cloudy afternoon. I knew she'd be stealing from me day after day, night after night. I knew there would be nothing at all I could do about it. Nothing at all I wanted to do about it.

I wanted her to have my everything and more.

Aurnia steadied her hand. Her gaze was focused, determined as she lowered the gun to my chest. This time she didn't stop when I sucked in a breath at the first bite of the needle.

Good girl.

My girl.

52

AURNIA

J finished Conor's tattoo in soft yellow lamplight. Night had fallen early with the heavy cloud cover that remained throughout the day like a blanket. I wiped away the last little drop of blood and ink, sucked in a shaky breath as I stared down at the sun inked across Conor's inflamed skin: my very first tattoo. And Conor's last.

Conor winced as he raised himself up onto his elbows to look at the finished product.

I fidgeted with the ink bottle lids and wiped nervously at the desktop. "I'm sure there'll need to be adjustments...fixes here and there...the line of this sun ray looks a little thin and—"

"Something to rise to."

I looked over at Conor and found his eyes not on his new tattoo. But on me.

"It's not perfect," I whispered.

His fingers intertwined around my wrist, his thumb pressing against my heartbeat in the blue of my veins.

"I don't want perfect."

"It's a little amateurish," I admitted, biting my lip as I appraised the tattoo critically.

Conor squeezed my wrist. "It's perfect."

I raised an eyebrow as my eyes darted to his. He was grinning. More like a child than I'd ever seen him.

"But you just said—"

"Aurnia," he said, a strange lightness to his voice that I thought I could get used to hearing, "when are you going to learn to stop listening to me?"

I smiled and he brushed a thumb across my cheek.

"I want to be inside you," he said, eyes flicking between mine.

"But your tattoo."

"But yours," he said, drawing a finger across my inner thigh.

I took his hand in mine. Raised it to my lips to press a tender kiss to the back of it.

"I'm healed already," I told him.

He drew my hand to his lips. Kissed the back of my hand much the same.

"So am I."

In the soft glow of the lamp, Conor's eyes remained fixed on me as I slipped out of my black jean jacket. As I pulled my shirt over my head, shadows played across his face but they no longer reached his eyes. I watched his chest hitch as I wiggled my jeans from my hips. His fingers gripped the edge of the desk as I stepped slowly out of them. First one foot. And then the other. Like emerging from a pool at midnight.

The bones along his knuckles shone like ivory as I unhooked the clasp of my bra. He held his breath till I let the straps fall from my shoulders, the cups from my breasts. His eyes followed my panties as I drew them down the length of my legs. My hair fell over my eyes and when I tucked a strand behind an ear, he had his bottom lip between his teeth, his chest rising and falling unevenly.

I came to stand over him like he was a pew in some church. I wanted to kneel in front of him. To grasp his warm skin and be comforted by its warmth, its strength. I wanted to rest my forehead against him and whisper prayers in the dying light.

"Aurnia," Conor begged, drawing my eyes to his.

My fingers were sure as I unhooked the button of Conor's jeans. They did not quiver. Did not tremble. Conor's cock was already hard as I helped him slip off his pants. Already twitching. Already glistening with pre-cum.

Conor's hands at my waist helped me onto the desk. I shifted a leg over his hips. The desk was cold and hard against my knees, but I didn't care.

Our bodies and lips met. He hissed into my mouth as my breasts brushed against his fresh tattoo, but he didn't let me pull back. He gripped me harder, pulled me closer, his fingers digging into my back, into my hips.

There was no need for delicate touches. No time for languid kisses along the throat. We were both so ready. We'd been through the fire and we were ready to rise. His body to mine. Mine to his.

He kept hold of me as I guided his cock between my legs. I shuddered as I lowered myself onto him, my arms shaking as I gripped his wrists for support. My eyes fluttered shut as I savoured the sensation of him filling me, deeper, deeper, deeper. We let out twin groans, neither of us moving as I settled against him, ass against his groin. He was as far in me as he could go. I could take no more of him. And yet it never felt like enough. Never enough of him. Never close enough.

My eyelids lifted slowly, heavily, like I was just awakening from a deep sleep. Conor's own eyes were hazy, his pupils wide. He looked drunk. He looked high. Like he was seeing a mirage in the desert.

I wanted to prove to him once and for all that I was real. That I was *here*.

I first guided his hands toward my inner thighs as I remained stilled on top of him, as he remained stilled inside of me. I splayed his fingers wide so that he was claiming as much as he could of the tattoo he'd done that pink-hazed night at Dublin Ink. His eyes found mine, a question in the dark. I answered him by pressing his hand firmly against my skin. The tattoo was mostly healed but I could still feel a lingering ache as his fingertips dug into my skin.

His chest hitched when I skimmed the edge of his fresh tattoo. I sucked in a breath of my own and after exhaling shakily I placed my hands over the edges of the sun I'd just created. Conor's fingers tightened on my thigh and we hissed together. Our eyes met. Locked in pain. Locked in pleasure.

I wanted Conor to know that we were one. Through it all we were one. My pain was his, my pleasure his. And his mine. I wanted him to feel all of me, to hurt all of me, to send every single nerve throughout my body singing with white-hot bliss. I wanted to know I was real, I was here.

Keeping my hands against his chest, I began to ride him. I rose off him till his fingers squeezed the tender flesh of my inner thighs and then I sank deeply, smoothly, tightly back down onto him. We continued that rhythm together. Pain. Pleasure. Pain. Pleasure. It quickly became all the same. The more I pressed on the rays extending from the centre of Conor's chest, the faster I could fuck him. The harder. The more he burrowed his vice-like grip around my thigh, the more desperately I would come crashing back down onto his cock. Ass against his groin. Hips rocking. Both of us yearning for more. Always more.

Steam from our panting breaths crawled up the base of the tall windows in the art classroom. My knees on the desk were slipping, banging painfully, but I urged us on, my nails digging into his skin. The metal legs of the desk were scraping horribly on the wooden floors, but all I could hear were our grunts and groans, our desperate gasps for air as we barrelled closer and closer, faster and faster to our release.

My vision was nothing but starbursts of light and Conor's eyes on mine. My back arched, my tits straining into the hot, humid air. Everything in me was on fire as I came hard around him.

With a roar that almost frightened me, Conor slammed me down onto his cock with such beautiful violence. All I could hope to do was hold on as he came, too.

When he released me, his hands falling limply at his sides, I sank against him, chest against chest, and we just breathed together.

"It's not wrong if it's love."

His words came out of nowhere.

I stared up at him. His gaze up at the ceiling, a small smile at his lips.

"What?" I asked.

"There's going to be a lot of people with opinions. A lot of people who want to paint us, what we have, as something ugly. But...I love you."

Conor's hands found the small of my back. I felt the calluses. The scars. He breathed in deeply and I rose on his chest like a butterfly on the back of a mighty beast.

I hid my smile and tucked my head into his neck, breathing in the scent of the man who loved me.

It was as complicated and as simple as that.

53

CONOR

*T*he cemetery gate was rusted, the hinges ungreased for what seemed like years if not decades. A chain was wound through the bars. When Aurnia and I finally found someone with a key to unlock it, he looked at us suspiciously. He wanted to know what we wanted. We thought it was obvious. Apparently, it wasn't.

We had to wander for a while to find her. We didn't know exactly where she was. There was really no way to find out other than walking row by row. We were silent, Aurnia and I, her warm tiny hand in mine, as the nearby highway droned on. As the clouds drifted heavily overhead. As street lamps flickered on one by one, dusk again come too early.

"There," Aurnia said, tugging at my hand.

She stopped two steps away when she saw I wasn't moving with her, our arms extended, hands gripped exactly halfway between us.

How easy it would have been to just keep going. To pull Aurnia the other way. It wouldn't be hard. She wasn't strong enough to stop me. If I decided to run like I'd been running all these years. To pull her to the motorcycle parked outside the gate. To drive her home. To make love on the bed we shared. To hold her beneath the warmth of the sheets. To wake up to sunshine. To hope. To her.

Aurnia's gaze was soft in the amber light. Kind and patient. She didn't say a word, but her standing there was enough.

I needed to do this. I needed to face my past. Forgive myself. Let go.

I came to stand beside Aurnia with a pounding heart. Together we looked down at the simple, state-issued headstone carved with nothing more than a name and two dates. One for birth. One for death.

I sucked in a shaky breath. My lungs didn't seem to think it was enough. Like the air here was thin. Aurnia's fingers tightened around mine.

Shannon had overdosed in her sleep not long after we broke up. Her heart just stopped beating. She had died without knowing. Died without anyone knowing. It was childish of me to believe that maybe she was dreaming of family when it happened. Dreaming of me even.

I'd always wondered why she'd never reached out to me. Never tried to find me.

I'd just assumed that she didn't think I had been worth fighting for. That she hadn't loved me enough. Or never loved me at all.

The story wasn't new: naive girl gets caught up in something bad. Gets dragged under by a current she didn't know was so swift and violent. A tide unrelenting. Something lovely carelessly crushed. Like a violet underfoot.

When Aurnia and I learned of Shannon's passing, the news threatened to wreck me. But Aurnia held me, anchored me, when I tried to withdraw in on myself. Gently pulled the whiskey bottle from my fingers when I emptied it too fast.

Pulled me into her body, to ride her, crash into her, rather than to lose myself along a storm-drenched highway on my bike.

I said I should have known, but Aurnia reminded me that I'd had my own pain to swim against. I tried to say it was my fault, but she gently kissed my blame away. I tried to say that I could have stopped it, but she stripped me of my guilt as she stripped me of my clothes.

So I was there at Shannon's grave to forgive her. To forgive myself. To set us both free.

Ever since that night, Shannon had been the cage that I lived in. And Nick had twisted the key in the lock. I'd hated her. I'd loved her. I'd ruined my life because of her.

But I didn't want to sink anymore. I wanted to rise. To my sun. To Aurnia.

But the words wouldn't come. I told Aurnia this.

Staring down at the little grave marker, Aurnia sighed softly and said, "You know, I don't know whether my mother is alive or dead. When she left my life, she left it completely. No Christmas cards. No calls on my birthday. Nothing. If I were to find out that she was...gone... If I were to come to a place like this and find her. A horrible place. A lonely place. A place without any flowers in sight. I think I'd be feeling much the same as you are."

She turned her pretty little face to look up at me. I smiled sadly and laughed just a little.

"And how is that?"

"Sadness," she explained, keeping her gaze fixed on mine. "Sadness that someone I loved wasn't there for me to love. Sadness that someone I wanted to give my everything to was someone who didn't want it until it was too late. Sadness that I was right here. Always right here."

I turned to look down at Shannon. The concrete was

cracked around her. Rust was already moving in at the corners of her resting place.

Aurnia was silent beside me as I looked around at the rest of the grey cemetery. Treeless. Flowerless. Not even the overgrown vines on the rusted fence had any trace of colour. I looked at the cars whipping by on the highway. Tail lights red. Glaring. Angry. I thought of the red of Shannon's hair. I thought of strawberries. Of picnic blankets under clear skies. I thought of lips stained from red wine. I didn't think of anger.

Softly, slowly, I began, "Shannon, I'm sorry for the life we had stolen from us. Maybe you were the thief. Maybe it was me. Maybe it was Nick or the world or all of us. Or none of us. It's too big for me to understand. To ever know. But I just want to say that I know that for a time I loved you. And you loved me. For a long time I thought that was the greatest curse of my life. Our loving one another so terribly. But I was wrong."

I turned to look at Aurnia. Her eyes were still downturned. Her attention on the woman who came before her, on the reason that I was the way I was.

I smiled as I watched the wind sweeping dark hair from her pale cheek. "I learned that love makes you want to rise, to be better, to be happier. And that is never wrong."

The corners of Aurnia's lip rose in a soft, gentle smile. Her eyelids fluttered closed for a moment or two in the ensuing silence. I wondered what she was thinking. What she was saying as she lips mouthed something I couldn't hear. Something I wasn't meant to hear. A prayer maybe? I'd never known Aurnia to be religious. Was she saying something to Shannon? To herself? To me? I knew it would be another of those mysteries in the universe. Another of those things that I could never know. Never understand. Another of those things I wasn't meant to.

She seemed surprised when I leaned over and pressed a chaste kiss to her bare cheek.

"What was that for?" she asked.

I shook my head and smiled.

"Are you ready to go?" I asked her instead.

She nodded. "If you are."

"I'm ready."

We went together, still together, back down the line of the grave markers unattended by family or loved ones, lovers or friends. It was a sad place. But it was a place that I knew I would return to again. From time to time. To see Shannon. To speak to her. To maybe share things I couldn't quite yet. To maybe cry for her. For us.

But as Aurnia and I left the gates of the cemetery, I knew I had my present. And I had to live it. I had to move forward. And as I felt Aurnia's hands wrap around my waist on the back of my motorcycle I knew exactly who my present was. Who I had to live for. Who I was going to move forward with.

I had my sun.

I had my little thief.

My Aurnia.

54

AURNIA

The streets were empty. Dark. I was walking alone. I wasn't surprised to hear the echo of footsteps behind me.

The calls from Nick hadn't stopped. I guess he missed the memo that I'd gotten my happy ending. That the story was over. The villain had lost.

Conor hadn't ended him with fists or a knife. But that visit to Shannon's grave had been for the passing of two lives: hers and Nick's. Nick could no longer hurt Conor. There was nothing left to hurt him with. Conor was moving on with his life. Working toward happiness. And love. Building Dublin Ink. Building *us*. Opening up to Rian and Mason. Coming clean with Diarmuid. Whispering futures into my ear at night. Futures for the two of us. Bright futures. Futures together.

Nick was gone. Dead. Over.

That didn't stop me from seeing his missed calls on my phone at night. Hand cupped over the screen to hide the glow from Conor. At the grocery store one lane over from Conor, remembering we needed rice as excuse to see who had called. At the parlour, ducking into the supply closet, throwing my phone and the name that was there on it into a bucket of cleaning supplies when Conor slipped in seconds after me.

I should have known that there was only so much ignoring I could do until he came looking for me.

I tried to remain calm as I glanced as casually as I could over my shoulder. It could have been anyone. Another girl like me in the wrong place at the wrong time. Groceries on her arm. A duffle bag on her shoulder. Missed the train. Missed the train that would have let her walk home in the light. But as my eyes scanned the sidewalk behind me there was no girl like me. No nervous eyes like mine. No bags of groceries. No reassuring smile. Just shadows. And echoing footsteps.

I faced forward and considered quickening my step. If it was just someone who meant me no harm walking faster would do no harm. If it was someone who did mean me harm, walking faster might just set off the chase. I didn't want to do that.

It was difficult to keep my steps even. Another peek over my shoulder revealed nothing more. Was I just making it up in my head? The second set of footsteps? Was it just my own echoing on the frozen hard concrete? Stopping to find out was out of the question. I imagined doing just that. Stopping. Craning my ear for a sound. I'd be like a deer that sticks its head up to spy the danger instead of doing what it should have done to save its life: run.

When I turned the corner and the footsteps followed, keeping pace, I knew I was in danger. It wasn't my mind. It wasn't another nobody out a little too late. I was being followed. I was being stalked. This time I couldn't help it: I moved faster.

Clutching the straps of my backpack tighter, I quickened my step. I swore I heard laughter behind me. But I was breathing so heavily that I couldn't be sure. My eyes darted to the buildings around me, but the windows were darkened.

The stores around me were locked up tight. Even the

liquor stores and corner stores knew better than to stay open this late. There was not a soul around, at least none that I could see.

I darted down a laneway and sure enough, the footsteps followed. When I reached the looming brick wall of the dead end, there was nothing left to do but turn around slowly and face my stalker.

It took what felt like forever for Nick to finally emerge from the dark. In his black hoodie and black tattoos, he seemed more a part of it than the light. Like he had to tear himself away from the shadows.

"Little baby Aurnia," Nick said, smiling wildly as he spread out his hands. "You've been hurting my feelings."

I tried not to let my voice shake. "Leave me alone."

Nick stopped a few feet away from me. An eyebrow arched mockingly.

"Leave you alone?" he said. "Leave you alone now that I have you alone? No, no, I don't think so."

Nick clicked his tongue and shook his head.

"No, no, my sweet," he continued. "Now that it's just you and me, I think we're going to make up for some lost time."

His eyes shone in the dark like black marbles. The eyes of a shark just out of striking distance.

"Now that I have you all to myself, I think you're going to show me what a fun time looks like. Don't you think?"

He was revolting. Demented. I took a step back, but there was no more room. My heel scuffed against the brick. My jacket snagged on the wall.

Nick noticed. Smiled. Stepped closer.

"Now that you're all alone," he said, rubbing his hands together, "I think I'll make you a woman for Conor. Make you an empty, broken woman. Wear off a little of that glimmer. Dull that sweet little sparkle in those eyes. What do you say, baby?

Do you think he'll still want you then? Do you think you'll still go running off into the sunset then?"

My hands were flat against the wall behind me, pressing against the unrelenting bricks.

"Now that you're all alone—"

"No."

My voice cut through his as if it were a knife. Nick's head tilted to the side. "No?" He laughed. It didn't sound right. "What does 'no' mean?"

This time it was me who stepped closer. "It means no, I'm *not* alone."

From the doorways behind Nick came Mason and Rian. A baseball bat for one. A golf club for the other.

Behind them came more. Darren with an old chain from his shop. Noah with a near-empty whiskey bottle in his hand, no doubt grabbed from The Jar. Declan with his fists wrapped and murder in his eyes. Danny and Diarmuid with shining knuckles and set jaws.

Nick's head whipped back around to face me. His finger was shaking with fury as he hissed, "You bitch."

There was a noise and Conor landed softly beside me after jumping down from the wall. He rose to his full height, and I saw Nick's eyes rise like he was searching for the peak of a mountain in the fog. Conor took my hand in his. He said nothing, he just stood beside me. He would no longer fight *for* me, but *with* me.

I smiled sweetly at Nick as he squirmed for an escape like the rat that he truly was.

"A bitch with a family now," I told him. "A pretty bitchin' family, if you ask me."

I was never truly panicked with Nick following after me. It was the plan, after all. But it was wonderful to see *him* panicked. Eyes darting. Heart rate jumping.

"Shannon's dead," he blurted out, spitting the words at Conor. "Your old bitch. She's rotting in some grave."

"You can't hurt him anymore, Nick," I said, speaking for Conor. "You can't hurt him and you can't hurt me. We're beyond your control now. Past your mind games. Your cruel tricks. We're going to be together. And we're going to be happy."

Nick's face twisted in rage.

"She's a child, you sick fuck," he tried, the pathetic lashing out of a man who's lost.

"If we ever see you again it's all of us that you'll face," I said, voice cold. "You won't worm your way between us."

Nick sneered, "Because you're a family?"

"Yes." It was Conor who spoke this time.

I smiled up at him. His grim face was fixed on Nick's. But I didn't miss when he subtly squeezed my hand.

Nick made a show of shoving through the line of men behind him. I don't blame him. He had to save what face he could. He was muttering something as he rounded the corner of the alley, but none of us cared to figure out what. Nick wasn't going to be a problem anymore. He thrived on the weak. And together we weren't. We were strong.

We were family.

EPILOGUE

CONOR

*W*hen I brought Aurnia pancakes in bed that morning, she rolled her eyes.

"What?" I laughed, something that I was getting more and more used to. Something I was liking more and more. "It's a big day!"

"No," Aurnia insisted, hiding her face in the pillows. "It's not."

"Well, I can take these away then—"

"Don't you dare."

Because, of course, pancakes.

But the bouquet and balloons I had Mason and Rian arrange at the shop were "too much".

"It's not a big deal," Aurnia complained before popping one of the balloons with a tattoo gun and storming off.

Mason and Rian grinned over their glasses of champagne which was deemed "*way* too much".

"Do you think she's seen the banner yet?" Mason asked me.

He choked on his bubbly when her angry shout came from the storeroom. Rian grabbed the rest of the bottle and bolted upstairs as Aurnia came stalking back into the living room, dragging a torn banner behind her.

"What is *this*?" she demanded, stuffing it against my chest.

"You don't like it?" Mason asked, holding back a burst of laughter.

A glare from Aurnia had him clearing his throat. "Um, I wonder where Rian got off to with the champagne," he said before taking the stairs two at a time.

"Aurnia," I said, trying to brush her cheek as she shooed my hand away.

"Why is everyone acting like I've never done this before?" she grumbled as she sank miserably to the couch. "I've totally done this before."

I let the custom banner that read "Happy First Tattooing Day" fall to the carpeted floor and joined Aurnia. She scooted her knees away from mine when they brushed against one another's. Her toes were bouncing. She was yanking at her lip. Her eyes darted around the room from equipment to equipment.

I placed a hand on Aurnia's leg. I held it in place firmly as she tried to tug it away.

"You're going to do great," I said.

"I know," she countered petulantly. "That's what I've been trying to tell everyone. It's not a big deal. I've done a tattoo before. Hell, I've done *your* tattoo. Why is everyone making such a big deal?"

Calmly, I repeated, "You're going to do great."

With desperate, panicked eyes, Aurnia turned to look at me. Her voice was close to breaking as she said, "But what if I *don't*?"

I laughed and drew her against my chest. I hugged her till the little bell sounded at the front door. She pushed me away like an embarrassing dad in the drop-off lane.

"Samantha, hi, come in, come in," Aurnia said, all bravado and confidence. "I'm all ready for you."

It was hard not to hover. Hard not to pace back and forth behind her like a father awaiting the birth of his child. Hard not to double-check that everything was going alright every two seconds. I tried to busy myself as much as possible during the tattooing. Content myself with listening to the two girls chat. Sam was a friend Aurnia met at art school, at a great program here in Dublin.

I swept. I wiped down the kitchen counters twice. I organised the storeroom and then the teas and then the packets of soy and chilli sauces from the local takeout in the junk drawer.

At long last I heard Aurnia say, "Do you mind if my boss takes a look?"

I was ready when Aurnia peered around the corner.

"'Boss'?" I mouthed around a grin.

Aurnia stuck out her tongue, but I saw the happy glimmer in her eyes. "Do you want to see or not?"

The tattoo was perfect. A recreation of *Starry Night* on the girl's waist. Midnight swirls along the ribs. Ribbons of gold dipping beneath the low hem of her jeans. Samantha was twisting this way and that in the mirror. Aurnia was fussing with it here and there. I was just about to say that it was one of the best tattoos I'd ever seen, that I'd never been prouder, when the front door crashed open.

A woman strode in like a force of nature, her long brown and honey hair flaring behind her like she was in a commercial. She stopped, hand on hip, commanding the space like she owned it. She whipped off jet-black sunglasses, pursing large red lips as she scanned the room.

"Can I help you?" I asked.

"I'm looking for Mason Donovan," she said with a distinct accent.

I'd never known one Miss Last Night to be American. Europeans of all kinds, sure. He sampled Asian women like his dick was a set of chopsticks. I was sure he'd fucked Canadians and Mexicans and even a chick from Greenland. But I couldn't recall one single American.

I tried to handle the situation quietly, inviting Miss Last Night into the kitchen for a quick cup of tea. That usually worked for the scorned ones. The ones who thought they'd made a real connection. The ones who didn't understand why Mason never called. A quick cup of tea. A pat on the back. An agreement: yes, yes, he *is* a bastard.

The American was as immovable as a brick wall.

"I'm not looking for fucking tea," she growled at me, cat-like eyes flashing. "I'm looking for my fucking, and apparently fucking a lot, *husband*."

Well, fuck me.

Miss Last Night was a *Mrs*.

I didn't know Mason had Miss Last Nights who were American. And I certainly didn't know he had Miss Last Nights who he'd put a ring on, on the way out the door.

I guess every family has its secrets.

DEAR READER

Thank you so much for reading Dublin Ink. I hope you love Conor and Aurnia as much as I do.

I'm currently writing Mason's story, Dirty Ink, and I am having the best time putting him through hell, haha. I can't wait to share him and his mysterious wife with you!

Check out his full blurb on Goodreads and add Dirty Ink to your shelf!

In the meantime, read about Diarmuid in Irish Kiss, where it all began...

Irish Kiss

Saoirse

I wanted him since the day I met him. Bearded, tattooed and tall as an Irish giant. He was more than just handsome, he was drop-dead gorgeous. It didn't matter to him that my father was a criminal and my mother a whore. He was my best friend.

I could be anything I wanted.

Except *his*.

Because I'm too young and he's my Juvenile Liaison Officer.

Diarmuid

It's been years since I last saw her. No longer a girl, she has the body of a woman. When our eyes met again, I saw the only one who ever broke through my asshole mask. I saw my best friend. She could be anything she wanted.

Except *mine*.

Because she's only seventeen and I'm too old for her.

I'm so screwed.

Cause I'm so fucking in love with her.

Irish Kiss is a slow-burn, angsty, second chance, age-gap love story with a Happily Ever After, but damn, it is going to hurt along the way.

Out now

Did you enjoy Dublin Ink?

Please post a review!

Just one sentence. One word. An emoji!

It really helps other readers to decide whether my books are for them. And the number of reviews I get is super important.

Thank you!

xx Sienna

BOOKS BY SIENNA BLAKE

Dublin Ink

Dublin Ink

Dirty Ink ~ *coming soon*

Irish Kiss

Irish Kiss

Professor's Kiss

Fighter's Kiss

The Irish Lottery

My Brother's Girl

Player's Kiss

My Secret Irish Baby

Irish Billionaires

The Bet

The Fiancé

The Promise

Billionaires Down Under

(with Sarah Willows)

To Have & To Hoax

The Paw-fect Mix-up

Riding His Longboard

Maid For You

I Do (Hate You)

Man Toy (Newsletter Exclusive)

All Her Men

Three Irish Brothers

My Irish Kings

Royally Screwed

Cassidy Brothers

Dark Romeo Trilogy

Love Sprung From Hate (#1)

The Scent of Roses (#2)

Hanging in the Stars (#3)

Bound Duet

Bound by Lies (#1)

Bound Forever (#2)

A Good Wife

Beautiful Revenge

Mr. Blackwell's Bride

Paper Dolls

ABOUT SIENNA

Sienna Blake is a dirty girl, a wordspinner of smexy love stories, and an Amazon Top 20 & USA Today Bestselling Author.

She's an Australian living in Dublin, Ireland, where she enjoys reading, exploring this gorgeous country and adding to her personal harem of Irish hotties ;)

tiktok.com/@siennablakeauthor
facebook.com/siennablakebooks
instagram.com/siennablakeauthor

Printed in Great Britain
by Amazon

16850746R00233